do not ask the river her name

Praise for *Do Not Ask the River Her Name*

'Sheela Tomy shares the searing tale of Malayali nurses who are trapped amidst incessant wars and destruction, toiling in the distant, mythical lands of Israel and Palestine. Sheela blends ancient myths and contemporary realities with dexterity, guiding readers along the paths once tread by Jesus Christ himself. She weaves a saga through a meandering narrative. This is a must-read novel given the disquiet pervading the Middle East today.'

—M. MUKUNDAN, winner of the Sahitya Akademi Award, JCB Prize and Crossword Book Award; named Chevalier des Arts et des Lettres

'Jerusalem and the adjoining areas are beloved and holy to all the three Semitic religions. The religious powers have been battling it out for thousands of years—for domination over that piece of earth. Then, there is the resistance by the people—caught in between—who are fated to get injured, lose lives and become exiles. The stories of human suffering are never-ending, even if told and retold. Don't ask the river of sorrow her name.'

—BENYAMIN, author of *Jasmine Days*; winner of the JCB Prize

'In this novel by Sheela Tomy, exquisitely translated by Ministhy, the life struggles of the ones not having a foothold on earth and forced into an exodus, merge with those fated to be refugees in their own land of birth. At a time when the world is splintered based on caste and religion, this book upholds the politics of humanity, reinforcing the need for a new world order.'

—V.J. JAMES, scientist; author of *Anti-Clock*; winner of the Sahitya Akademi Award

'Perhaps no other novel is so right for our times, and for all of us who are under siege.'

—ARUNAVA SINHA, award-winning translator

do not ask the river her name

sheela tomy

Translated from the Malayalam by Ministhy S.

HARPERPERENNIAL

An Imprint of HarperCollins *Publishers*

First published in English in India by Harper Perennial 2024
An imprint of HarperCollins *Publishers*
4th Floor, Tower A, Building No. 10, Phase II, DLF Cyber City,
Gurugram, Haryana – 122002
www.harpercollins.co.in

2 4 6 8 10 9 7 5 3 1

Originally published in Malayalam as *Aa Nadiyodu Peru Chodikkaruthu*
by DC Books, Kottayam

P-ISBN: 978-93-6213-990-0
E-ISBN: 978-93-6213-677-0

Typeset in 11/14.7 Adobe Caslon Pro at
HarperCollins *Publishers* India

Printed and bound at
Nutech Print Services - India

This book is printed on FSC® certified paper
which ensures responsible forest management.

To those who have no place on their birth-soil

—SHEELA TOMY

To my friend, for encouraging me to take up this project and remaining a silent presence all through the river's flow

—MINISTHY S.

Don't ask the trees for their names,
Don't ask the valleys who their mother is.
From my forehead bursts the sword of light
And from my hand springs the water of the river.
All the hearts of the people are my identity
So take away my passport!

'Passport', Mahmoud Darwish

CONTENTS

THOSE WHOM WE MEET ON THE STORY-WAY

Menahem Family

1. David Menahem (Abba), retired professor of the Hebrew University, Jerusalem (In Hebrew, pronounced as *Daveed.*)
2. Esther Menahem (Eema)
3. Asher Menahem
4. Leah Menahem
5. Job Menahem (Grandfather) (In Hebrew, pronounced as *Iyob.*)
6. Miriam Menahem (Grandmother)
7. Elijah Dod

Manjottil, Padamala

8. Ruth Albert
9. Albert
10. Teresa
11. Catherine
12. Esthappan (Ruth's father)

13. Valiyammachi (Ruth's grandmother)
14. Lonappan (Albert's father)
15. Annie (Ruth's mother)
16. Kunjanamma (Albert's mother)
17. Mother Superior
18. Parapara Ammayi (Ping Pong Aunty)
19. Maluvettathy
20. Molly

Jerusalem

21. Sahal Al Fadi
22. Gazan Al Fadi
23. Sarah Al Fadi
24. The old man in Zaitun, Abu Murad
25. Suleiman
26. Shamir, pickup driver
27. Father Aloysious
28. Nina
29. Riya (Nina's daughter)
30. Kochuvelikalachan aka Father Kochuvelikkal
31. Jaisonachan aka Father Jaison
32. Jose Sir
33. The Ammachi from the pilgrimage group
34. Sister Matilda
35. Mariam (Mary) of Bethany
36. Sofia (Young girl)
37. Lilly Joseph

38. Women of Bab Hutta
39. The boy from Bab Hutta
40. Joshua
41. Joshua's Saba
42. Joshua's Eema
43. The old artist
44. The guard at the Rockefeller Museum
45. Dr Eilat Mazar
46. Binu Samuel
47. Holocaust survivor Naomi Bergman
48. Jacob Daniel Cohen
49. Rebecca (Jacob's Eema)
50. Abraham Dod aka Uncle Abraham (In Hebrew, pronounced as *Abram*.)
51. The old woman at Erez Crossing
52. The woman suicide attacker
53. Dr Yehoshua
54. Photographer Abu Assad
55. The coffee shop owner at Masada
56. The old man at the Wailing Wall
57. The child at the Chapel of the Holy Face (Chapel of Veronica)
58. The missionary sister dressed in sky-blue
59. The priest at the Jerome chapel
60. The man selling crucifixes
61. The priest at the parish
62. The helper at the parish

63. Policemen
64. Army officers

Dubai, Switzerland

65. The helper at the airport (Programme Director Aravind)
66. Freddie's driver
67. The Ethiopian receptionist
68. Shahjahan
69. Freddie
70. The Pathan taxi driver
71. Noor Jehan
72. Kanya
73. Kanya's customer
74. R.J. Shivakami
75. Shiny (Nina's mommy)
76. Sound Engineer Rafique
77. Kalyani
78. Dr Shahana
79. The stranger who calls live
80. Bedouin girl
81. The Arab in the desert
82. Agnes Chacko
83. Rachel Aunty
84. Devan
85. Sky Sweet aka Akasha Mithai

THE ONE WHO EXITED BEFORE THE STORY ENDED

Tuesday, 25 May 2021
Fearless Biblical Archaeologist Eilat Mazar Dies at 64

Dr Eilat Mazar, a pioneering archaeology professor at the Hebrew University of Jerusalem's Institute of Archaeology died today. She was 64. Dr Mazar, who unearthed King David's Palace in the City of David, leaves a lasting contribution to the understanding of the archaeology and history of ancient Israel and Jerusalem.

It was while arranging the magazines that the news caught my eye, leaving me stunned. The departure of a character from the novel I was working on! The excavations conducted by Dr Mazar's team in two places of David's City—above the Gihon Spring and in the lower slope of Temple Mount, at the Ophel Al-Aqsa esplanade—are already part of history.

Asher Menahem, did you hear about this sad news? Ruth and Leah are in search of you.

Also, this writer …

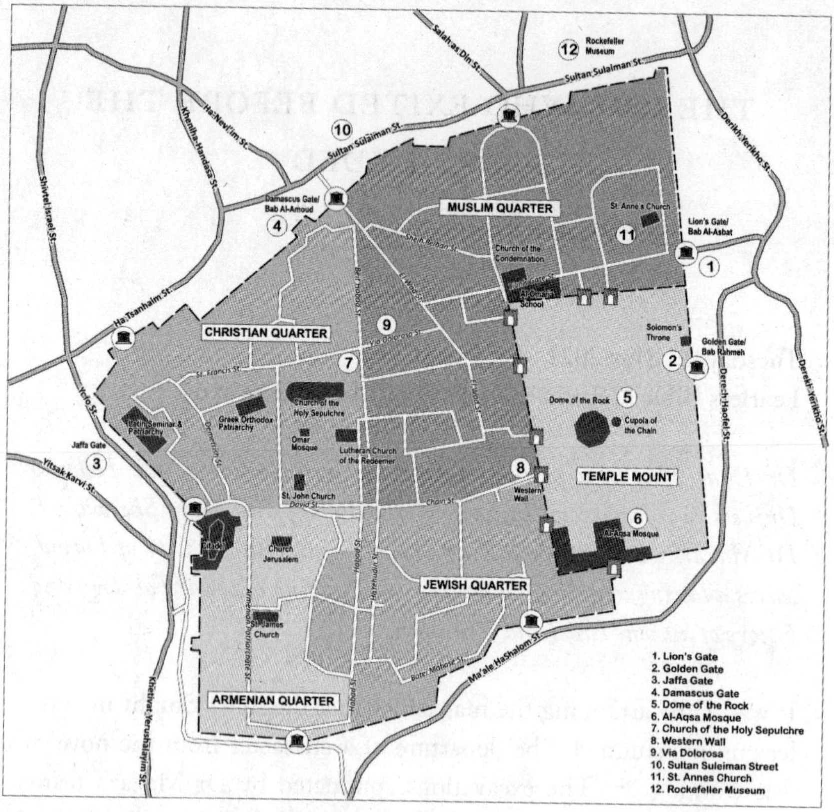

The Ancient City Map of Jerusalem

1

SAFA MARWAH

Then what? A woman soldier shouted:
Is that you again? Didn't I kill you?
I said: 'You killed me … and I forgot, like you, to die.'
('In Jerusalem', Mahmoud Darwish)

Monday, 10 May 2021

Far beyond, yellow sunrays fell obliquely on the Kidron valley, lazily spreading across the mountain slopes and the huge cemetery ensconced within white-stoned walls, where the ancestors had their final repose. The sorrow of the tree layers—almonds, oaks and cypresses—cast shadows, keeping guard over the eternal sleep of generations. For ages, they have been lying in wait for Yahweh, for his appearance at the summit of the Mount of Olives. Asher was waiting too, on top of the mountain, where death lay hidden in ambush.

Asher was now near the Lion's Gate of Temple Mount, on the slope of the main path which circuited the Old City. Ramadan was coming to an end. Beloved Sahal would arrive for the prayers in Masjid Al-Aqsa. But it was not known how he would gain an entry, since the whole Al-Aqsa complex was surrounded by the police. Asher felt as if Sahal was cycling through the crowd in the

Sultan Suleiman Street, manoeuvring through the twists and turns, whistling all the while. Just like the old days.

Asher scrolled down a Twitter handle depicting the horrifying scenes of the raid in Masjid Al-Aqsa complex. Smoke and dust billowed over the mosque and its surroundings. Exploding grenades, unending screams. People were running helter-skelter, racing towards the mosque and rushing outside, seeking refuge. Stones were being pelted all around. The shoter—the police—had chased a few protesters to the wall and were taking one into custody. Asher was shell-shocked. That face was familiar—he had seen it somewhere!

Caught in the clutches of anxiety, Asher read through the news updates, one by one. There was a report from the Hadassah Medical Centre about treating a Jewish girl who had a head injury. Also, pictures of injured police officers.

'Why are they targeting our Aqsa Mosque in the holy month of Ramadan?' someone called Javed raged in the Facebook page of 'Warrior of Light', bubbling and frothing with fury. 'I was praying inside the mosque. Suddenly, the sound of gunfire! They are starting a religious war.'

The sunlight was fading, but Asher's inner heat surged forth. He was exhausted after wandering about in search of Sahal through the day, enervated both in body and mind. But there was no question of withdrawing without finding Sahal's whereabouts. Sahal's poem was wailing from the depths of Asher's heart …

For aeons, emerging out of the Galilee,
Transfiguring into islands, oh my sorrows …
Would it not come,
The time, when these mounds of earth turn into volcanoes?
They looted and pillaged,
Those old, wine-hued twilights, dawns …
They stole forever,
The night-time lullabies of mamas
The fingertips of babas … the light … laughter …

An altercation broke out, distracting Asher from his thoughts. A youth was pelting stones at vehicles. A white car was chasing him to the edge of the footpath. He narrowly escaped being crushed! Out of nowhere, an infuriated gang of youngsters appeared—the keffiyeh, chequered black-and-white scarf, wrapped around their heads. Palestinian youth. They tore open a car's doors in an attempt to assault the old man inside the vehicle. The driver was Jewish. He had a kippah, skullcap, on his head. Asher stood devastated. A siren rang, as if sniffing an impending disaster. In a matter of moments, the police rushed towards the crowd. The youthful throng scattered, and fled from the spot. In all nooks and corners of the city, especially Temple Mount, there were cameras. And there were police officers stationed every hundred metres. Some of them in mufti.

A stone flew past Asher, and he flinched.

'Where is your mask? Why are you standing here? Go home! The lunatics are on the loose!' a policeman, running past him towards Lion's Gate, yelled. Watching him, Asher felt as if a burning torch was on the move.

'Lunatics,' Asher repeated, with self-loathing. He remembered a prophetic warning that the city wall would catch fire and all the eight doors would be devoured by flames. Asher, caught in the frenzy, shivered at the thought that Temple Mount would turn into a volcano, spewing venomous smoke.

The wait for Sahal seemed endless. Where was Asher supposed to check now? Or was it better to stop the search? Asher remembered once having entered the Safa Marwah Coffee Shop in the Muslim Quarters, accompanied by Sahal, to meet Suleiman. Even after months, he could recollect Suleiman's posture as the latter gazed at the fading evening light. He had a very discernible limp, and a peculiar gait, leaning towards the right. Asher could visualize, even now, how Suleiman posed a question about archaeology and Sahal looked at him in astonishment. Maybe Suleiman would be able to provide some helpful information. He could not recollect the street where the cafe was located since the complex comprised four hundred and one alleys.

Sahal's phone was still switched off. A shocking thought, like a sharp-edged stone, impaled Asher's heart. Was Sahal caught and taken into custody?

As he dithered due to the uncertainty of the situation, his phone rang. It was Leah, his sister. She was frantic with worry.

'Ahkh, Eema is heartbroken after seeing the news. Hamas's drone hovering over Ashkelon …'

'Akhot, tell Eema that all's well here. Ashkelon is so far away. I am in the flat,' Asher consoled her.

'Liar! You are at Lion's Gate. You have been caught live on video.'

'Really? Please don't tell Eema. Who posted it?'

'No idea. It's a WhatsApp forward. A car trying to run over someone.'

'Leah, Sahal is in danger. He is in some place nearby. I have to find him.' Asher fretted.

'Don't be stupid. This is not the time to find him. Get back home, Ahkh.'

Leah sounded hassled and grave.

Throwing caution to the wind, Asher crossed Lion's Gate. He made his way slowly through the narrow pathway of the Muslim Quarters. Safa Marwah Coffee Shop remained hidden from his view. Darkness was creeping into the alleys and the intersections were quiet. There were no street vendors, no visitors either. Most of the shops were shut. Asher presumed that the cafe must have closed too. A staccato of gunfire could be heard resounding from afar, blending in with the endlessly wailing sirens. An unbearable dread seized hold of him.

An old man, his beard snow-white, was watching the news in an abaya shop. When Asher peeped inside, the man got startled. Fear and uneasiness surfaced on his face; his eyes blinked incessantly.

'My child, why are you wandering around at this time? Are you searching for someone? If you are not in a hurry, sit down for a while.'

Accepting the invitation, under some unknown influence, Asher stepped inside.

'What's the matter, Baba? Anything bothering you?'

'They caught my boy! That scoundrel was pelting stones. Where shall I search for him? Can't go home without him. His mama would kill me.'

The old man sounded miserable and furious. Asher gazed wearily at the street.

'It was a mere stone that he threw, Baba.'

'Now, that's the issue. How many missiles will they fire tonight because of that single stone? How many Palestinians will lose their lives? Fools! Never step into a battle which you are not sure of winning, my child! Didn't you watch the news? All our leaders are taking different stances. Brutes!' the old man ranted.

Asher felt a sense of kinship with the man, as if he had known him for ages.

The police siren was drawing closer. Most of the lights on the street were snuffed out. They could see the arch of the gateway to the Al-Aqsa complex. The whole area was under strict police control. Unexpectedly, a name board caught Asher's eye. Right at the next corner, there was the shop, Safa Marwah! It was closed.

'Baba, do you know Suleiman of the cafe? I came searching for him.' Asher asked, filled with hope.

The old man looked at him sharply.

'Suleiman was shutting his shop. But he was late by thirty seconds and they arrested him. The value of time!' The old man scratched his head. Asher blanched in shock.

'They took him away just a little while ago,' the old man informed sadly.

'Why did they take him away?' Asher asked tremulously.

'A college student used to frequent the cafe. He was there earlier today. They interrogated Suleiman about his whereabouts. When he expressed his ignorance, they threw him to the ground, kicked him black and blue … Poor man, even after all that suffering, he never uttered a word.'

Asher sat dumbfounded. Did Sahal visit Suleiman today too? Where did they take Suleiman?

Sahal, where are you?

The old man got up and gently closed the abaya shop's door. Then he switched off the lights.

'Sometimes, it is our light that betrays us.' He sighed deeply.

Now there was only a small hurricane lamp inside the shop. Asher was seized with an inexplicable feeling that he was on a remote island, at some distant corner of the earth. A promontory, where only he and the old man existed. Outside, the sea was on fire.

Agitated and distressed, Asher searched 'Warrior of Light' for updates in his mobile yet again. They had posted some vignettes from Al-Aqsa. Someone, his face concealed under a red cap, was effortlessly moving through the crowds. As the camera zoomed on the face fleetingly, Asher saw the big mole on the right cheek. Sahal had slipped inside the mosque, escaping the police, even today!

'How do you know Suleiman?'

Asher was disconcerted by the old man's query.

'The visitor … he is my friend, Baba.'

After contemplating for a while, the old man retrieved a pocket diary from his desk drawer and extended it to Asher.

'This fell from Suleiman's pocket. I don't think it was accidental. When they pushed him, he must have hurled it afar.'

Asher stared at the diary. It was familiar, very much so!

'There are some pictures inside. You take a look, my child. I could not make any sense of those. Maybe you'll find something to help them …' The old man looked on eagerly as Asher hurriedly flicked through the pages, his heart drumming in panic.

There were a few pencil sketches of Masada, with the initials SAF scrawled beneath.

Sahal Al Fadi, what are you doing in Masada, right under the nose of Israeli police?

Some parts of the drawings were intentionally darkened and Asher could not guess what it meant.

'Baba, did Suleiman visit Masada often?' Asher asked.

'Likely that he did ... Suleiman sold shawarma to a shop in Masada.'

'What has that got to do with Sahal?' Asher felt bewildered. He remembered Ruth, his abba's metapelet, female caregiver. She was also a friend, a sister. Ruth had visited Masada to feature the palace of Herod and the ancient rock plateau in her vlog. Besides, she was very observant by nature. What if Ruth remembered something? Asher called Ruth.

'Yes, I remember a shawarma shop. It is there in my vlog. There is some connection between your soldier classmate and the cafe. Didn't you say so once?' Ruth became apprehensive.

A storm roiled inside Asher, one that had crossed the Dead Sea. The diary, filled with indecipherable motifs, mysterious as the Qumran Caves Scrolls, trembled in his hands. Suddenly his eyes filled with the image of a soldier curled up in a foetal position, next to the left wall of the Synagogue Church, in the heart of the old market at Nazareth. In his right hand, the soldier clutched a broken, drooping olive bough. It appeared as if someone had planted it in his hand.

'They who are slain with the sword are better than they who are slain with hunger.' Asher remembered what Abba quoted that day.

Here I am, Sahal, reaching out to you ... at an arm's distance.

The old man noticed the lad cutting the call and jumping up.

'Baba, I am leaving now.'

'Just a moment, child. Look at this page, the penultimate one.' The old man, taking the diary from Asher, hastily turned the pages.

Asher stared impatiently at the small letters spaced narrowly. 'Scholarship ready. Reach Amman by May 15.' How did the old man discover this? It was time for Sahal to join the University of Malaysia!

If you reach Amman, in an aeroplane taking off from Queen Alia Airport, Habibi, you shall fly.

Asher exulted, wishing to leap around in his joy. But how would he get Sahal to Amman, avoiding the eagle eye of the police? He imagined River Jordan getting flooded, and the surging waters washing away the check posts. Asher could hear the great rumbling of water at the borders.

A skiff, filled with heaps of oranges, was making its way through the water plants, across the river. At the helm, he stood … Sahal … the one who whistled to the tunes of thc iconoclastic Lebanese singer Marcel Khalife's songs … The one who dreamed of a land without walls or check posts …

'Baba, is someone travelling to Amman? I mean, shortly?'

'There is a consignment which is supposed to be sent there. But I have to get my blessed son out from the police station first. Ruffian!' The old man stroked his beard, looking embittered and sad.

With a sudden wave of inspiration, Asher queried, 'I have to visit Amman. Shall I take your consignment?'

'That will be of great help, my child. If the load does not reach in time, I will have to end up paying a fine.' The old man sighed with relief at Asher's offer.

He called up Shamir, the driver of his pickup van, and introduced Asher.

'We should leave early morning tomorrow. I shall inform you about the location later. Listen, I have some cargo too. I will give the details tomorrow.' Asher cut the call.

The old man was alert to the unsteadiness and keenness in the voice of the lanky youth in front of him. Also, the glitter in his eyes.

'Everyone has his own tisamat, destiny. Certain tasks have to be fulfilled, and after that, the return. May Allah be with you and your deeds. Ma'a salama.'

The old man, like an enlightened mendicant, hugged him warmly. Asher felt scorched, as if he had been embraced by a street on fire.

Only after moving forward in the darkness did it strike him that he had not sought the old man's name or number. Neither had he noticed the shop's name. The old man hadn't asked anything about him either. Not even if he was a Jew or a Muslim. Perhaps he felt there was no reason to do so. The one who came into the shop at such an odd time, who sat as a companion in the darkness for some time, was a human being. Just a human being. The mirror image of the Most Compassionate God.

As Asher turned to take a backward glance, he saw that the Muslim Quarters was dark. Just a glimmer of light, like a firefly, was visible through the glass window of the shop. That old man all alone in the great darkness. Asher remembered a mother squatting in front of a makeshift stove, making challah, the traditional bread. And the fragrance of olive oil …

Asher recollected the old man's words again.

'Sometimes, it is our light that betrays us.'

He switched his phone off. He had just a single goal now. 'Fast, fast,' the mind commanded the feet.

Asher moved as if he was fleeing from a great danger.

As he flicked through the *Times of Israel* the next day, during a long journey, he would come to know that his intuition had been right. He would be shattered on reading the front-page news. The old man who had spoken to him the previous night, the one whose name remained unknown, was lying on the ground, shot dead in cold blood, in front of the same shop. Now, Asher was able to read the name of the shop clearly.

Zaitun. Olive.

'Here lies the messenger of peace, shot dead.' The caption of the picture should have been scripted thus. But that was not what the newspaper screamed.

'The Palestinian who provided refuge to the Hamas terrorist in his abaya shop has been shot dead. The police informed that they had to shoot him when he tried to escape. The picture of the terrorist, who left the shop around nine at night, was caught by the nearby closed circuit camera. The traders announced that they shall be shutting down shops in the Muslim Quarters to protest against the police action.'

'The person who exited Zaitun yesterday at 9 p.m., the one who was offered refuge by the old man, is Asher Menahem ... Listen respected citizens ... Asher the Jew, born to Esther Menahem of the Ashkenazi Jewish descent and the Arab Jew David Menahem,' Asher wished to scream. 'That poor father called his son a scoundrel for pelting stones at the police! Is he an accomplice of Hamas? Where did Mossad, known for its precision and thoroughness, err?'

His eyes brimmed over with tears at the memory of the old man. 'To which god should I pray for that man?'

Asher remembered Sahal. His poem seemed to resonate with the times:

A river shall flow through this city,
The afternoon sun shall die by diving in it.
Our forebears, whom they took away,
Shall sprout anew, as figs and olives.
Hey, come to this riverside,
To melt into Oud music,
That cannot be vanquished by grenades or tanks.

On the night when the old man at Zaitun was killed, those hours which seemingly spanned aeons, Asher's sojourn was through a series of profound events. Ruth Albert, the vlogger, who had wandered many times in the past three years through the Old City pathways—spread across the Muslim Quarters, Christian Quarters, Jewish Quarters and Armenian Quarters—could not, however, capture Asher's journey.

The world media was inundated with news from Jerusalem again.

The smouldering Jerusalem became incendiary all of a sudden. Protests are common enough in the city, against the controls in Sheikh Jarrah, or the forcible evictions. But nobody could guess that the remonstrations on that Monday, when a Zionist march was planned through the Muslim Quarters, could lead to a war. If "Jerusalem Day", which commemorates Israel's annexation of East Jerusalem, is a day of celebration for some, the defeated lot views it as a bitter memory—when their homeland, olive hills and houses were plundered. The skirmish between the police, the Palestinian protesters and the ultra-right-wing Jews, eventually set the city on fire.

2

NAZARETH

Have you ever stood under the burning sun, without even the shade of a tree branch, your body melting in the sweltering heat? Have you ever hunkered down in a crazily swaying boat, your hand on your heart that is beating two hundred and fifty times a minute? Seeing a mad, raving predator running towards you, have you stood speechless with horror, with no place to flee? Have you ever sunk to the depths of indifference, realizing the cruel truth that not a sliver of chance exists for escape? Have you, at least once?

(The prelude to Ruth Albert's vlog 'Nazareth')

Some wondered why Nazareth needed such an introduction—nothing justified this preface. Yet, within a couple of months after she started the channel, Ruth had around one lakh followers. It was something which astounded even the godfather of Nazareth, Asher himself. Ruth simply captured the scenes of the Holy Land. There was a lightness of spirit, as if she was relishing a trip with her friends. That was all. Ruth's slender, lissom figure, her long, loose hair, the effervescent naughtiness and the sparkling nose ring—these merged into something captivating.

The comment box was flooded with suggestions and recommendations, that she should do more homework and provide more authentic information. Ruth would respond that she had just one holiday in a week and that the entire recording and editing had to be undertaken on that day. Besides, all these gimmickries were conducted with a smartphone! Most messages under her posts on her vlog Nazareth were filled with affection for the woman who brought before one's eyes the blessed paths imprinted with the Lord's footprints and the Holy Land, unlikely to be visited by most viewers. For her followers, Ruth was younger sister, older sister, daughter. There were even those who asked the forty-year-old lady whether she was married to which she would reply with just a smiley.

Pesaha, Passover: Maundy Thursday, 1 April 2021

The day which commemorates the Last Supper. The holy day of the special unleavened bread. A starkly different post appeared on Ruth's vlog Nazareth that day. A beautiful place of worship built of white limestone. To the north, ancient stone steps descended listlessly towards the valley. Ruth was climbing up to reach the churchyard. A golden coloured rooster could be seen on the minaret.

'Friends, these are the Maccabee steps. The ancient path which existed, winding down from the city on top of the mountain, right to the Kidron valley. The same path which Jesus took after the Last Supper, as he walked to the garden of Gethsemane in Mount of Olives. The very same path through which he was dragged like a criminal.'

The camera now moved to focus on Mount of Olives. Then slowly, it edged back to the statue in the churchyard. The inscription on the sculpture became slowly visible:

'*Woman, I know him not.*'

'Once, a woman told a man seated next to a fire kindled in this same courtyard: "You were also with Jesus the Galilean." He swore that he did not know the man. The cock crowed at that moment. Then the Lord's words resuscitated in his memory: "Peter, before the cock crows, you will deny me three times." Peter started weeping bitterly. Let him cry. Come, let us go inside.'

Ruth stepped into the church, leaving behind the statues of the Roman soldier and the woman. There was a shaft, resembling a well, cut through white limestone, deep into the subterranean region.

'Now I am stepping into the dungeon where they kept our Lord incarcerated. In the Roman days, these caverns were used as storehouses, or for collecting water. They must have pushed him down through that hole, tied up in chains.'

Ruth was immersed in deep thought for a moment.

'Look, this must be my fourth or fifth visit to this dungeon. The first time I stepped down, I heard the clanging of chains ... As if someone had pushed me down a pit, thousands of years ago! In a matter of seconds, the dungeon of Caiaphas expanded in front of me; then it contracted. Pitch darkness, humidity, cold. I thought that I would suffocate and lose consciousness. At that time, I read what was inscribed on the white rock that you see over here.

'"Akhot, have you learned Aramaic too?" Asher, who had accompanied me, wondered aloud. What had I spoken? The same language that our Lord spoke in the olden times! The moments when I transfigured into the "Daughter of Jerusalem", who lived two thousand years before ... An experience transcending the senses ... I was enduring a thousand ancient agonies ... Like the apostles at Mount Tabor, I prayed that the hour never ended. I heard that poignant voice; perhaps, I alone.

'"*You believe that I was crucified due to your sins. Your faith has healed you. Do you know, entangled in chains, blood dripping from my wounds, I crouched in this dungeon one full night. I could not stretch my limbs or even stand up straight. Spiders and cockroaches ran freely over my body. Rats nibbled at my toes. Ah ... the hours when everyone denied me! In the Hours of Suffering in the Garden of Gethsemane, my disciples were a stone's throw away, although they were asleep. Even when I fell, while carrying the Cross, there were many with me ... my mother, the women of Jerusalem, Simon of Cyrene, Veronica … But I was all alone in this prison, knowing that nobody would arrive to help … A mere human being … Even before I was lowered into this pit, I heard my friend Peter denounce me. Do you know what is the greatest pain in the world? To be rejected by those whom you love deeply. No Cross would weigh so heavy. No flagellation would hurt so much. Listen, you must have experienced at least once, moments of rejection, days of abandonment. And God is the human being who sinks into those depths, forgives, absolves and emerges ashore."'*

Ruth was standing on the side of the cave, without disturbing other visitors. Her voice broke. As the viewers wondered why she was becoming atypically emotional, Ruth continued, 'I saw that lonely man, that cast-off in many around me. I saw those who suffered due to the actions of others. I saw those who were crucified. There are some who carried the Cross for me, accepted death for me. A few, ordinary people.'

Thousands were watching the Pesaha live from the church commemorating St Peter's triple denial of Jesus, the Church of St Peter in Gallicantu.

Suddenly there was a shout amidst the gentle ripples of sound … 'Catch her!'

It created a horrendous echo in the narrow cavern. The shocked face turning to take a backward glance … The feet started hurrying away, disappearing among the pilgrims … In a matter of moments the live broadcast stopped.

Nazareth's comment box was flooded that day.

One message went thus: '*The Lord resurrected from the tomb in Golgotha. And you, Ruth Albert, from the Al Ain desert.*' *(Bhargavi Kutty)*

Ruth had reached Nazareth, Asher's home, three years ago along with the pilgrimage group of Father Aloysious.

3

ZION TRAVELLER

Three years and six months ago …

Wednesday, 20 September 2017

Discarding the bundle of sorrows in the city of Dubai, Ruth boarded the morning flight at five o'clock and landed at Amman. As she made her way through the Queen Alia International Airport, she tried to reassure herself that the passage across the sea of fears was over. At the emigration counter, Father Aloysious had to wait around for a long time, with the passports of the travel group members.

'Ruth's passport was slightly tricky. Lucky, we managed.' Waving the papers held in his raised hands, Aloysiousachan laughed like the skies. Leaving behind the olive groves, the terraced farmlands and the alluring sea of purple flowers, crossing the flock of pigeons rising in the air beyond the pines, the blue and white deluxe coach of the Jordan tourist company moved onwards. Ruth of Padamala did not exist any more. Another Ruth, part of an unknown group of émigrés, was undertaking an exodus from one enigmatic land to another.

The first stop was at Mount Nebo. While they stood on the summit, Father Aloysious pointed afar. The Promised Land seemed nebulous. Far away, in the hazy mist, were the Judaean mountains. All those who had fallen, under the tortures unleashed by the Pharaoh, facing the trials in the desert, were wandering without salvation, in the winds of the mountain folds. The Prophet, who embraced death, without ever setting foot on Canaan, walked amidst them.

'No journey shall ever be complete. Even the heroes retreat, before reaching the destination. Time alone shall continue untrammelled.' Aloysiousachan was speaking.

Ruth was oblivious to everything around. Before her eyes, there was neither Moses nor Joshua. Only an unending stillness.

'Zion traveller, crossing over,
Let not the waves terrify thee.
Standing steadfast in the ark,
Is the One who commands the wind and sea.'

The pilgrims were singing and clapping in tune. Smiles and radiance wreathed their faces. Their hearts were filled with prayers. For Ruth, though, there was only the biting chill of uncertainty. In front of her, there was a gaping abyss. Even Father had no idea about the place she was journeying to. It was a Jewish family, that was the only fact known to them. Apparently, Sister Matilda had taken care of the rest.

'Do not be scared, my dear. The Lord walks ahead of you.' Aloysiousachan consoled Ruth, noticing her slouching in her seat. She tried to smile. There were two groups of people in the world. Those who were able to be happy, and those who were incessantly besieged by woes. Valiyammachi, her grandmother, belonged to the joyous lot. She would tell Ruth, 'Do not cry, come what may!' How would Valiyammachi know the innumerable cruelties the world held in store for Ruth!

The bus trundled down the hill towards the Jordan border. Desiccated earth, similar to bleak, greying lives. Intermittently, there was a smattering of a few masara, goat farms. There were patches of thorny plants speckling the desert. The highway, stretching endlessly forward, was engraved with the ragged, scorched footprints of millions of refugees. Monstrous trucks were on the move, teeming with mysteries. Unlit villages, small towns. In between, tiny hills of hope, wind, a pleasant nip in the air. The lonesome trees on the mountain slope were swiftly fleeing past. Ruth felt dizzy.

She was falling from the steps! A fall, as if a whole mountain had collapsed on her. Ignorant of her state, the rest of the pilgrims continued to travel. Struggling to rise, Ruth was now stumbling forward. Even as she gazed, the desert swallowed the hills. A hurricane lashed around demonically, tossing the sands sky-high. Her feet were plunging into the sand … deeper, deeper. Hunkering down, face close to the chest, she tried to defend herself from the dust storm. 'Hey Ruth, you are being buried under a mound of sand!' She awoke from her reverie with a jolt.

'What happened, Ruth?' Nina hugged her close. They had become acquainted only a few weeks ago. Yet, Nina was like a younger sister. 'Don't worry. You will have a wonderful time there.' Nina spoke soothing words.

'Ruth, you?' She ignored the derisive question emerging from her own mind.

'Hakuna matata … that means no worries!' Mimicking the prancing Simba in her tablet, Riya jumped into Ruth's lap. She hugged the child close. It was Nina who had said that the desert nights were remarkably beautiful. But the Dubai desert night hadn't been like that at all. She had encountered a wilderness, unseen by others, a few weeks before. A horrifying desolation, unknown to the rest.

'Here, we have reached the Jordan border. Now we're going to cross the King Hussein Bridge. It is also called the Allenby Bridge. Afterwards, it is "No Man's Land". Neither Israel nor Jordan has any authority over the area.' Aloysiousachan stood up in the front end of the bus and announced loudly.

There was a formidable, grim-looking bridge just ahead. A flag was fluttering in the breeze. Red, white, black, green …

'See, the flag on this side is of Jordan. The Israeli flag is at the other end. Can you see the blue Star of David against the white background? Countless tears have fallen on this spot. Those who yearned to cross this bridge and died during the wait … those who were murdered … those without documents … those who could never enter their birthland. We cannot gauge the agony of someone who finds the land beneath his feet disappearing.'

Aloysiousachan's words were not permeating Ruth's consciousness. Here was another woman, banished from her land. A wooden bridge, forever forbidden, ahead of her. It terrified her with its groans and upheavals. Its name was life.

Huge iron barricades could be seen on the border. There were four armed soldiers in military uniform. Was the colour black or deep blue? Ruth wondered, observing their impassive expressions and statue-like bearings. X-ray scanning, checks; every formality, as per routine.

'The black boots of a cold-eyed soldier would crush me at any moment! He would tear apart my passport and papers. Place manacles around my wrists. Ruth, you are a criminal who can be caught any moment … Dear Lord, why do you fill me with such dread?' Panic seized her. Ruth repeated her Valiyammachi's psalm. *'For he will command his angels concerning you to guard you in all your ways. On their hands they will bear you up, so that you will not dash your foot against a stone.'*

After the formal scrutiny, a sense of relief settled in. Ruth felt an overwhelming affection for the soldier—the one with the icy cold demeanour—who examined her documents, eventually returning them to her. She remembered the young man who had saved her from isolation in the vast desert. At that moment, courage emerged unknowingly.

Some people are like that, even their memory fills us with life force. They are not great men or women; very ordinary folk. Perhaps, even thieves.

After the procedures were over, they boarded another coach. An all-white Israeli bus. The Jordan bus, which had taken them till the border, was disallowed entry into Israel. The coach moved towards Jerusalem. Ruth left behind the city of Dubai at the Jordan border; the city which had thrown her life into chaos! Father Aloysious enthusiastically launched into a historical narrative.

'We are now traversing through lands which embody prosperity. A land condemned to be under the yoke of foreign rule from ancient times. A land which was conquered by the Jews, centuries before the birth of Christ. Two regions: Israel and Judaea. In AD first century, after the siege of Jerusalem by the Romans, when they took over the city and its temple, the Jews were treated as slaves. The Jewish people scattered all over the world. They reached even our homeland. In many places when they emigrated, the Jews were loathed. Their plight was really pathetic. We know about the Holocaust in the twentieth century. Hitler killed almost sixty lakh Jews. In those days, the conscience of the world was with the Jews. The Zionist movement, which took root in the latter half of the nineteenth century, kindled the flame of a dream—establishing a homeland for the Jews. During the colonial rule, after many political manoeuvrings, interventions and declarations, the people who were dispersed across the world started returning to the Promised Land. It was in 1948 that Israel officially became a country, with the blessings of the United Nations. "Aliyah", the immigration to Israel, became more intense afterwards.

'Soon, the Holy Land witnessed another injustice. "Nakba" or the mass exodus. There was forcible displacement and dispossession of the people who had been living in these lands for centuries. Almost seven lakh Palestinians became refugees during that time. Listen, in the story of the exodus from Egypt, there were supposedly six lakh men. However, more than that number lost their homeland during the Nakba. The blatant stories of injustice became never-ending afterwards. Many fled to Jordan and Lebanon. Those who could not escape anywhere, became the living dead in refugee camps; the victims of a never-ending war. Unimaginable, horrendous sufferings turned some of them into terrorists. The selfish agendas and the infighting in the Arab League, once expected to help the Palestinians, turned the situation worse. Even after the Oslo Accords, the terms not fully acceptable to Palestine, there were violations from both sides. After all attempts at negotiating peace, the occupied land still yields news of wars and uprisings. And Hamas continues to provoke and invite self-destruction. Today, Palestine is the largest humanitarian crisis of the world.'

Kochuvelikalachan rushed in, to throw down the gauntlet in the arena of Aloysiousachan's enthusiasm. 'Listen, we don't want to listen to history! Those who read the Scriptures know that the Jews have been chosen by God as his special people. Those who raise a sword against them, whether Arab, non-Arab, believer or atheist, shall perish like Sodom and Gomorrah. Read Amos 1:7 … "*So, I will send a fire upon the wall of Gaza, and it will consume her citadels.*"' Kochuvelikalachan intoned the words in a sing-song manner.

'Calm down, Kochuvelikalachan! Excavating quotations from every cranny and nook—are you trying to justify savagery? Will any father let his sons fight among themselves? If God created man, the One who crafted the Jew and the Arab remains the same! Is there a God who supports Jews exclusively? Utter nonsense! "God's chosen people" is likely a myth conjured by someone to render hope to those enduring tribulations and slavery from ancient times. King Solomon was an unparalleled poet, wasn't he? There must have been excellent storytellers in those times too.' It was Jaisonachan, a young priest, who objected thus.

Even as Kochuvelikalachan readied to battle yet again, an elder leader of the pilgrim group, Jose Sir, hastily intervened.

'Listen, on that particular matter, we will decide a course of action after returning to our village. I am feeling very thirsty! Can we procure some manna from the heavens? And a goblet of wine?

Did you bring us all the way to the Land of Canaan intending to starve us?'

A wave of laughter rippled through the bus.

Till then, Ruth had never mulled over the thought that historical occurrences possessed the power to turn life upside down. Neither did she consider the conversations around her to be of any significance to her life; fate decreed otherwise.

4

ROSH HASHANAH

The bus moved towards Ein Karem. Only after entrusting Ruth to Sister Matilda's care could Father Aloysious rest a bit. He had taken over such a heavy responsibility a fortnight ago. After the tour schedule had been finalized, an unexpected message had reached him from Nina. Out of the blue, Ruth had to be included in the group. After that, it had been a frantic rush to get Ruth's documents in place. It was only after crossing the Israeli border that Father felt a sense of relief. He would have been clueless about the next step if a possible obstruction had reared its head at the border. An eternal belief, that everything would turn out all right, was his sole guidance.

'If the Lord had tried to sabotage the rescue plan of a helpless girl, rest assured, I would have squabbled with Him.' Father guffawed.

The bus transformed into a psalm. Like the aloes the Lord had planted, like the cedar trees beside the waters …

How beautiful are your tents, Jacob
your dwelling places, Israel!
Like valleys they spread out,
like gardens beside a river …

Now they were ascending the Ein Karem mountains. A green-swathed slope, covered with a carpet of flowers, lying south-west of the historic city. Moving past the cedars and fences of bougainvillea, the bus grunted to a halt in front of a convent belonging to Franciscan nuns. The passengers stretched themselves.

Father Aloysious raised his voice. 'Hey everybody, please don't disembark. Let us not delay over here. This beautiful hill where we stand now is the birthplace of John the Baptist. The place where Virgin Mary visited Elizabeth. Ein Karem literally means "Spring of the Vineyard". We will return to step into this spring. Now let us baptize Ruth in the waters of Ein Karem.'

Father Aloysious reached Ruth's side.

'Nazareth is your ultimate destination. It is one hundred and fifty kilometres from this place. Our route is different. Now you are left with yourself and the Lord.'

Nina hugged Ruth tightly, as if afraid of never meeting her again. As Ruth lowered her head and started to step down from the front door, a white-haired old woman, counting the rosary beads, planted a sound kiss on her cheek. Jose Sir blessed her, his hand over Ruth's head: 'Praise be to Jesus.' She respectfully folded her hands in response and followed Aloysiousachan. Some pilgrims waved goodbye. Ruth did not give a backward glance. All the sounds started to cease, only the words of the desert resounded ... *'The axe is already laid at the root of the trees; therefore every tree that does not bear good fruit is cut down and thrown into the fire.' ... 'Every valley shall be exalted, and every mountain and hill brought low; the crooked places shall be made straight, and the rough places smooth.'*

Sister Matilda was waiting for them when Ruth alighted from the bus. Her face was brimming with serenity. Ruth remembered Mother Superior of Amala Bhawan and the paths to the nursing school. Asher had already reached the convent. Sister Matilda had called him while he was returning after meeting Dr Eilat Mazar at the Hebrew University campus in Mount Scopus. 'Metapelet shall arrive soon.'

Everything happened rapidly. In the Church of the Visitation at the hilltop, Sister Matilda handed over Ruth's care to Asher. As she followed the young man down the white stone steps, Ruth did not notice the bougainvillea which blossomed forth on either side. Neither did she see the valley beneath, lush with date palm trees resembling umbrellas. The green line of olive trees and the wind whistling through the fig trees escaped her attention. She was on another journey, unaware of the destination, accompanying a stranger.

The car moved through the Sharon Valley, leaving behind strange villages and crowded cities. Except for a smile, while handing over a cup of Karak tea during a stopover at a junction, Asher had not spoken a word. The radio in the car, possibly an FM channel, was chattering continually. The silence of the banished woman sank in that babble. Ruth remembered another young man. He had come searching for the woman who sat in the shadow of death and darkness. *'I will go before thee, and make the crooked places straight …'*

After a heavy silence that stretched for two hours, they arrived at Nazareth. It was the Jewish New Year. Rosh Hashanah, in the month of Tishrei. Their entry was into a flood of light, into the illuminating radiance of the festival. Lighted candles and ornate lamps were omnipresent.

The creature that walked in was a bundle of nerves, albeit with hands and legs. Hesitantly, as Ruth crossed over the doorway, what struck her eyes was the wooden plaque: 'Shalom.'

'Hey, Ruth! Why did it take you so long? I have been waiting for you …' She could hear Shalom whispering.

A huge fig tree stood in the west yard. This would be referred to by Ruth as 'Mariam's fig tree' in the future. Beyond, were wistful-looking apple trees. A young woman with blue eyes ran towards them, dressed in a pale rose frock. A pristine white scarf covered her head. So beautiful! Shalom's angel! Ruth felt extremely abashed about her own dishevelled form and her crumpled six-yard sari.

She was akin to a poor moth that had descended into a flame and hurriedly fluttered to a side without singeing its wings.

'Shalom! Shanah Tovah.' The angel shook Ruth's hand warmly. 'I am Leah.'

An aged couple seated on the carpet with their legs stretched, repeated the same words. 'Shalom! Shanah Tovah.' That particular 'Shanah Tovah' was just the beginning of a mountain of Hebrew surprises in Ruth's path.

The old man stared at her, after removing his dark-framed glasses. The long beard and the tranquil face accorded him the look of a monk.

'Hey, Happy New Year.' Leah winked at the woman who stood dazed in the wonder of 'Shanah Tovah'. Then she introduced everybody to Ruth, in crystal-clear English.

'The lady in the yellow frock is my Eema. She is into big time worship! When the Messiah arrives, He shall enquire first of all, "Where is my beloved, my own Esther Menahem?"' Leah laughed.

Suddenly, thinking about something, her forehead furrowed. 'Do you understand English?'

'Of course.' It was an 'of course' which stepped in tremulously.

Lean continued. 'This cute gentleman is my Abba. A bizarre creature who subsists on books! But now, he cannot read. Suffice to say, it was his own fault!'

Leah giggled, enjoying her own joke. Ruth observed that her laughter was attractive. The young woman possessed a very charming nature.

'The one who brought you here, is my ahkh. He digs out secrets. Not trustworthy, keep him away.'

When Eema snapped at her, Leah's translucent English gabbling ceased suddenly. Ruth guessed that it might have been a rebuke. Asher had departed from the scene by then. A deluge of neighbours and guests came in—many introductions, queries, hustle-bustle.

A place of worship with massive arches was situated opposite Shalom. Its front yard was crowded with men clad in long robes and skullcaps. There were men with long beards dancing in groups. A few were blowing into hornpipes shaped like a ram's horn. Ruth would learn later that the instrument was called 'shofar'. She was like a young child trapped in the middle of a bustling market, with nary a touch or shove, silently speaking and grimly smiling, never seeming to stand or sit.

Meanwhile, Leah did not forget to offer her honey-cakes and apples dipped in honey.

Slowly, before Ruth's eyes, the synagogue replete with musical instruments, transfigured into an intimidating forty-storeyed monument. She saw a young woman running exhaustedly through the twisted corridor of the nineteenth floor. Ruth also watched her racing down four hundred and two steps, panting and perspiring. The blowers of the hornpipes were still celebrating boisterously. Father Aloysious and the soldiers at the border had long turned into riddles. It was then that Ruth recollected never having seen the white-haired old woman, who sat in the front of the coach, in the pilgrim group. Where had the rosary-counting Ammachi sprung from at that moment?

5

METAPELET

It was the beginning of winter in Nazareth. Dewdrops dangled from the olive branches and apple trees at dawn. Pigeons cooed from their hideaways. A few other birds screeched interminably. Ruth remembered Padamala. Seated on a boulder in the backyard, Ruth would converse with Shalom with its sloping bell-metalled roof. At times the conversation would be wordless; other times in soft whispers.

'Hey Shalom! I too have a nest across the sea, on another hilltop. My Alby, Kathu and Teesa live there. We have mists there too, and the same pleasant chill. Shalom, there are many fruit trees and plants that you do not know of. There is ginger, spreading across one and a half acres, and pepper vines embracing the murukku, the Indian coral tree. There are four or five jackfruit trees—Thenvarikka variety—that yield honey-sweet fruits. Then we have the common property of the village—naattumavu—the native mango tree.' Shalom would listen with much alacrity.

When one lives in a mysterious land, in an unfamiliar home, for a long time, one morphs into another being. Days become filled with anxieties, misgivings and uncertainties. Strange language, new rituals, the niggling apprehension that one's actions might go against the householder's traditions. The stress of not being able to discern what was 'kosher', legally acceptable, and 'ashur', what wasn't …

A teeny-weeny bit of spoken English, taught at Amala Bhawan, was all that Ruth knew. She would jot down the new Hebrew words that came her way. Since the discussions at Shalom ran at the speed of the Shatabdi Express, at the beginning it was difficult for her to comprehend much. Later, after Asher introduced her to a Hebrew teaching website, a nervous Ruth would find her Hebrew vocabulary expanding.

Abba was a diabetic. Sometimes he was troubled by asthma too. Ruth's job was to take care of him. Both food and medicines had to be administered at the appropriate time. She had to update the family physician regularly. The colostomy bag—now an irreplaceable part of Abba's body and life after his cancer surgery—had to be cleaned at regular intervals. On certain days, when Abba felt uncomfortable, he had to be helped with his morning routine. Ruth had to accompany him on the walks through the pathways amidst the olive groves. His favourite songs had to be played for him. Abba was blind. Nobody had expected his world to grow dark all of a sudden.

The university professor, who beat cancer and returned to life, the one with a strict disciplined lifestyle and diet, had suddenly lost his eyesight! If someone were to ask him the reason, Abba would shake with laughter. 'The nerves going to the retina stopped working! Just because I relish my baklawa and kunafa, should they have been so cruel? Rascals!' Abba, who used to relish sweets secretly, away from Eema's sight, had never expected such a retaliation. The diabetes worsened and turned into retinopathy. Eema would peevishly allege that Asher was the main culprit. Whenever Asher—who worked in the Rockefeller Museum at Jerusalem—came home on Shabbat days, he would bring along baklawa or kunafa for Abba. This would happen without Eema's knowledge.

She would grumble that after Asher started his research work in archaeology, he had changed completely, displayed less affection towards her, and would hardly ever call home! Leah would mocking say, 'Well, by the looks of it, he is on the verge of discovering both Noah's ark and the hidden treasure of Solomon's temple.'

There was one task which Ruth enjoyed the most at Shalom. She would wait eagerly for it. After aruchat boker, the morning meal, she had to read aloud English newspapers and books to Abba. It was during these reading sessions at Shalom that many classics came searching for her. For Ruth, it was like regaining the letters lost during her long struggle for survival. After the reading was over, the professor of yore would start his classes—about literature, society.

'See, Abba still thinks he is teaching at Hebrew University. Leave that poor Ruth alone, Prof. David!' Leah teased.

'I yearned to study literature. But I hardly got books to read back then.' Ruth's smile hid the darkness of her childhood.

'Oh please, as if one can fall in love with literature at forty!' Leah was sceptical.

After slurping on his Karak chai, Abba corrected his daughter. 'Leah, there are no age constraints for studying or writing. Talent and interest are all one needs. Daniel Defoe wrote his first book at the age of fifty-nine. Paulo Coelho ...'

'Enough, enough! I concede defeat,' Leah chirped. 'Listen Ruth, the founding father of Hebrew University, Albert Einstein, happens to be the grandfather of Professor David Menahem.'

Abba burst into laughter at her impishness.

'Einstein was a European Jew. He believed in loving humanity. The great scientist was not of the same mind as the Zionists. Incidentally, I hail from Iraq. In my childhood ... it is a long story ...' Abba's eyes searched for Ruth. Though images appeared obscure, he could see everything; he knew everything too. Ruth was not aware that Abba's mind was filled with rabid streets and burning structures. Neither was she cognizant of the small boy who still remained within Abba, eyes widened in horror as he stared at the road from the first storey of a Baghdad apartment.

'It has started again! From the Shalom broadcasting station, here is Radio Jockey David Menahem …' Gently nudging her father, Leah slipped away.

The disgruntled look of a child, stopped on the verge of narrating his tale, appeared on Abba's face. Whenever he started recollecting his memoirs, it was always the same situation. The onlookers would disappear without a trace, in the blink of an eye. Even Eema did not have the time to listen. Abba wouldn't stop, once he began his outpourings.

Ruth would laugh to herself: 'See, Ruth, they have appointed you for listening to RJ Abba. A time is imminent when servants would be hired to listen to lonely souls.'

Leah was preparing to go to university in the USA for her postgraduate studies. There were examinations and associated complexities. Asher was harried, carrying out his job and research work. 'There should be such busy people on earth. Otherwise how would a metapelet get hired? Let the poor earn his or her daily bread.' Ruth would gratefully pay her obeisance to the stressed lives of the hassled folk. She would pray that the rich were graced with the lack of time always.

In Shalom, there was a small local kingdom directly under Eema's rule—the kitchen. Ruth was often caught red-handed for violating norms. Even after taking extreme care, errors would creep in somehow. Ruth would remind herself daily that she shouldn't do anything to upset Eema. By the time she gently closed the door on that rumination, she would be trapped! It was ashur, forbidden, to deposit milk, meat and fish in the same sink. There were separate washbasins for each food type. Ruth would unwittingly wash Abba's milk cup in the non-vegetarian sink. Or she would slice lettuce for making a salad with the knife meant for gutting fish. Out of the blue, Eema would appear in the arena! 'Hey, again you did it, my girl!' That was Eema's superpower. Any time, she could apparate anywhere! For Eema, violating laws was akin to death. Even Asher was petrified of her but Leah was different. If Eema beckoned from one direction, the smart girl would scamper in the opposite way!

'Man does not exist for law. Law exists for man.' Ruth would argue with herself. 'What goes into someone's mouth does not defile them, only what comes out ... ' Ruth would mutter. Inadvertently, the sound would escalate.

'Mova?' Eema would raise her eyebrows.

'Ah, my stupid memory!' Ruth would grin with embarrassment.

A single egg, vegetable salad, cheese, a piece of kuboos, fruits sliced into curd which hadn't soured. Then hummus, made by blending chickpeas, ground sesame seeds and olive oil. Or else labneh, made from yoghurt cheese. Or moutabel, prepared by boiling and mashing eggplants. Ruth had already acquired an expertise in understanding Abba's likes and dislikes and could cook his favourite dishes. Eema would heartily congratulate her on that ability.

Ruth would gratefully remember her Parapara ammayi, aka 'Ping Pong' aunty, restless and always scurrying around doing a thousand chores, back in her village. Ruth was taught the basic lessons of cooking by her. Yet Ruth would avoid introducing Kerala dishes in Eema's province. What if she dishonoured some law? Besides, Abba was discomfited with the spicy masala smells. Ruth quickly became acquainted with Jewish recipes and with Shalom.

For Ruth, who had moved out of home in her childhood, the residence at Shalom was like just another change of nests. In no time at all, Ruth, relinquishing her snowballing anxieties, transformed to become an elder sister to Asher and Leah.

Ruth had another companion in Nazareth. In the night-time, when the songs ceased in the synagogue, someone would descend the hill slope, her arms swaying languorously in the moonlight. Scribbling something on the scroll with her ink-dipped quill, she would sit at her usual place. On a low tree bough. 'Ruth, you have become half Jewess, in your build and food,' the woman would chuckle. She was

Mariam of Bethany, an enchantress, who controlled a panic-stricken metapelet's tongue and thought. The refuge of her soul.

'Don't say anything which is displeasing to Eema, my dear. It is not easy to free those who are entangled in rules,' Mariam would remind her. 'A fool's chatter is like a burden on a journey, but delight is found in the speech of the intelligent,' she would continue.

'Who are you, Mariam? My keeper?' Ruth would be playful.

'If the Lord does not keep watch over the city, it is meaningless for the keeper to be alert.'

'What is it that you are always writing?' Ruth would ask.

Mariam would reveal what she had written with a budding smile.

'The history of exiles over the last two thousand years.'

Mariam would walk into the moonlight with a sombre look in her eyes. Ruth would gaze after her for a while. As she watched, Mariam would turn into the moonlight. At that time, a poem would come floating from an unknown place.

Do not ask the river her name
Never ask the water-creatures,
The land from where they hail …

And Ruth would remember, for the hundred and first time, about loneliness, which was redolent of death. She would slowly crawl her way to Padamala. Like a sliver of a scream, she would snuggle into the small space between Alby, Teesa and Kathu. Indulging in a game of trapeze between time and nations … until she opened her eyes at dawn, hearing the cooing of Shalom's pigeons.

6

MARIAM OF BETHANY AND RUTH ESTHAPPAN

There are certain invisible bridges which inadvertently come into existence and pull together some human beings. Like the bridge which brought Agnes Chacko, from the tranquillity of the Alps, to Galilee. Agnes was the daughter of Ruth's maternal aunt. Periodically, when her voice crossed the frontiers of the continents and reached Nazareth, it evoked the fragrance of Wayanadu's Kaima rice farmlands, ripe and golden. It brought to mind a young girl, walking across the farm ridges that extended to the forest. Later, searching for Agy Chechi or Agnes Chacko, Ruth would make a solitary trip through snow. However, before that event transpired, Nazareth had much in store for her.

There are certain other bridges, invoked between human beings and souls. Like the bridge that brought Mariam of Bethany to Ruth. She had seen Mariam for the first time in the cave of a mountain slope, located west of Shalom. There was an abandoned house with crumbling walls—a gigantic oak tree in front of it. The place served as Ruth's peaceful sanctuary during sweltering afternoons. Sometimes, a small girl of four or five, and her puppy, would give her company. Sofia was a child from the neighbourhood and sang beautifully. The child had an artificial limb. Once, as Ruth was waiting for Sofia, she saw a young woman climbing down the hills. She approached Ruth, weaving her way through the olive trees. The folds of her lengthy, yellow robe fluttered in the breeze. A sea-blue headscarf; a pensive, beautiful face. The young woman had a wheatish complexion, and a look of utter self-possession.

'I am Mariam. Sister of Lazarus of Bethany.'

She was smiling. That smile, flitting between open and opaque, seemed strangely familiar.

'Which Lazarus?' Ruth asked in wonder. She yearned to get away but Mariam forcibly stopped her.

'Please don't leave, be seated.' It was a request. Mariam's hand was exceptionally cold. The scents of frankincense and aloe wafted from her body. A few peacocks were flapping towards the lush verdure of the oak tree.

'Where do you stay?' Ruth enquired.

'Does it matter?' Mariam winked in reply. Then she leaned against the oak trunk, and started reading aloud from the book which she was holding close to her heart.

'Do you know the ordinances of the heavens? Who gives the ibis wisdom, or the rooster understanding?'

Ruth looked to the skies. The sky was overcast above the river. The peacocks were roosting on the oak tree.

'What is an ibis?' Ruth asked.

Mariam laughed delightedly and planted a kiss on both her cheeks.

'Don't you know? The bird with the premonition of time when the waters start swelling in the Nile.' Mariam's voice sounded like that of a peacock's cry.

Ruth frantically ran down the slope. 'Hey Ruth, I am your ibis. Your third eye,' Mariam called after her.

It was their first encounter. That evening, when Ruth was sitting under the fig tree, the woman from Bethany was sighted again. The same languorous walk …

'Why are you glaring at me? Saw you huddling under the fig tree,' Mariam's eyes twinkled with mischief, 'just like Nathaniel.'

Seated on the stone perch in the kitchen, Mariam spoke again. 'Listen, seated in the kitchen foyer of our Bethany home, someone used to tell me lots of stories! Whenever He returned after His countless trips across the lands, there was only one listener. Martha was never free from her chores. Overwhelmed by His narrations, I used to bite into the corner of my tichel. I have preserved it till today.' Mariam showed Ruth the hole in the left corner of her headscarf.

'Do you believe now? Blessed is the woman who has not seen, yet has believed. The vineyard of love belongs to her.' Mariam vanished amongst the grape vines, with an unfathomable look in her eyes and that same unworldly smile.

Later, Ruth would meet Mariam of Bethany again, at different times and different places. Once, feigning indifference, with her arm dipped in the water, Mariam sat in the front seat, while Ruth was enjoying a boating trip on the Galilee Lake. Another time, Mariam was sitting cross-legged on the sands, next to the huge doorway of the sea wall on the Mediterranean shore. During a bus journey to Tiberias, Mariam was standing all alone, on a desolate bus stop on Highway 90. In the St Anne's Cathedral, Mariam was snoozing away, leaning against the statute of Anne. Another time, in the Abbey of the Dormition, Mariam was kneeling in front of the sleeping Virgin Mary. Then, in the Stella Maris Monastery, located on the slopes of Mount Carmel, in the cave where the Prophet Elijiah hid, Mariam was playing a string instrument. A few curious onlookers surrounded her.

Soon, Mariam became a regular visitor at Shalom. Usually she arrived humming the same song: 'Rivers that end in tears.' Ruth had revealed all these mesmerizing ploys of Mariam only to Lilly Joseph. 'Become totally insane, eh? A Jewess who speaks Malayalam?' Lilly would burst into hearty laughter. This 'heartily laughing' Lilly was Ruth's friend. She had met Lilly three days before Mariam entered her life. Their meeting took place in the Church of the Annunciation at Nazareth.

'Havera, never share some matters with anybody, not even a friend. There are certain bridges … only two people can cross those, to reach the other. The rest of the world cannot see them.' Mariam would advise Ruth one day. The pigeons would be cooing atop Shalom's terrace then. And Ruth would reminisce about her childhood days.

Sometimes pigeons assumed the colour and sound of childhood. But Ruth never wished to return to that phase of her life. What was there to remember and rejoice about? A small hut with a woven-grass roof; mud and thatch fences separating the lands. Two fences apart, Maluvettathy's house; and the television which played movies on Sundays. The interesting fact was that fences continued to chase her, even in Nazareth. This was another village like Padamala. Instead of mangoes and jackfruits, there were olives, grapes and figs. In place of copra mills, there were olive presses.

On a future day, in her vlog about the Garden of Gethsemane, Ruth would elucidate further. *'In Hebrew, the word "Gethsemane" means "olive press". Jesus sweated blood while praying in the garden where an olive press probably stood, in the Mount of Olives. On those stone steps, meadows, wooden benches, in the Basilica of Agony, at the courtyard, in front of Christ's thorn jujube trees, one can sit forever, gazing at Temple Mount far across. One can look at the golden gate, which shall never open. One can visualize the teeming visitors of ancient times, as they jostled their way through the gate, thousands of years ago. Heart pounding, we can follow the wounded revolutionary leader wearing a crown of jujube thorns, who drags himself forward, denounced by all, mocked and decried …'*

WHAT ELSE REMAINED in the bundle of memories? A funeral procession, which passed through the middle ridge of the farmlands. The whole village had lamented during the rites at the church. Amma had passed away even before Ruth had any recollection of her. Appan never bothered about a second marriage. It was Valiyammachi who had brought them up. She was a hunchback, with gold piercings on her elongated earlobes. Ostensibly, Ruth's late mother, Aniyamma, had the special gift of identifying birds through their chirps! Flocks of birds belonging to various species, including parrots, used to frequent their house at Padamala. But they were not seen any more after Amma's death.

Another beloved face of Ruth's childhood belonged to a visitor who crossed over tea plantations to reach her side. Agy Chechi, the daughter of her mother's elder sister. Disembarking from the bus in front of a small tea shop, manoeuvring through Palchuram—the milky mountain road full of hairpin curves—crossing many formidable ravines, jumping across the springs scattered on rocky boulders, the girls would walk together. Agy Chechi had the voice of the forest stream, and the scent of fresh green tea leaves. She went away to Delhi after her nursing studies. When she returned, there was a man called Devan with her. Then Agy Chechi went off to the Gulf and forgot all about Padamala. After the passage of much time, it was Dubai city, that had gifted Agy Chechi back to Ruth.

Yet another home loomed in Ruth's memory. By the riverside, the house of a distant uncle named Kunjacko. The place was tumultuous, with four hundred activities happening all at once! At the tender age of ten, Ruth was sent off by Valiyammachi to this house, to help the owner's wife. Sheltered under the wings of compassion belonging to Parapara ammayi, 'Ping Pong' aunty, who ran about doing a thousand chores, sweaty and dishevelled, Ruth had completed her schooling without knowing the pangs of hunger. She finished her pre-degree education and become an efficient cook by working in the kitchen. When Valiyammachi became sick, and her seat at Maluvettathy's Sunday movie sessions remained unoccupied, Ruth was forced to return to Padamala.

The Mother Superior at Amala Bhawan had dropped in to visit Valiyammachi one day. Her heart was touched on seeing the smart young girl who was providing care to her grandmother. Suddenly, there was an unexpected twist in the tale. Ruth Esthappan's name was included in the list of needy nursing students applying for foreign funds and sponsorships.

'How long will you act as my caregiver? Go and find your way.' Valiyammachi had pushed Ruth to accept the Mother's offer. 'Little girl, after you return, try to straighten out the spine of this hunchback woman!'

Ruth had left Valiyammachi behind. The visage of her grandmother, with her beaming smile and dangling earrings, would stay forever in Ruth's memory.

Valiyammachi passed away soon afterwards, into the heaven of hunchbacks. A paradise belonging to those who overcame every affliction with hearty laughter! After finishing her nursing studies, Ruth had walked back into a desolation, dark and decrepit. Her itinerant father, Esthappan, had long forgotten the path to his home. But wonder of wonders! When Molly of Kurukkanmula arrived with the promise of a job for Ruth in Riyadh, without muttering any objection, her Appan had mortgaged his one-acre property and provided the funds. The property was eventually, tragically, lost. That is another story.

In Ruth's recollections about her father, his moist eyes, as she waited with Molly for the boat at the ferry, stood out starkly. That was a long time ago ... a very, very long time ago. It had been her first Gulf journey which never achieved its goal.

On a twilight eve, as she sat huddled up, disturbed and upset, clutching onto the swollen and teary memories, Abba had gently coaxed it all out of Ruth. The parrots circling over the synagogue occasionally peered at the duo.

'Don't lock up the sufferings inside your mind. Bat, you should share it with someone. What cannot be spoken, try to write down on a piece of paper. Then you should mince the page to small pieces and scatter the scraps in the winds. Let the innards cool down. That is how one survives …'

Abba's sightless eyes were glittering.

Holding firmly on to that sagacious advice, Ruth prised away from her heart the image of another Ruth standing aghast on the fourth storey of a tall building. Also, the picture of two young girls, sobbing incessantly in front of the monstrous iron gate of Riyadh's Labour Court. (Two girls, two embodiments of utter fear …) And the piteous woman who sat exhausted beneath a date palm tree in Deira …

'The one who unravels everything within shall attain redemption from himself. A person who has redeemed himself thus shall wipe away the tears of another.'

Abba was speaking, watching without seeing, as the sun disappeared amidst the cypress trees. Sofia's grandfather, with the child on his shoulders, was climbing down the hills that moment. A military vehicle clanked its way through a narrow lane. Clouds of dust shrouded Shalom.

7

SHRINE OF THE BOOK

Asher hurried through a lane, cutting across an impoverished area of western Jerusalem, and then joined the busy crowd on Salah al-Din Road. Striding past the foreign exchange shops and food courts, shrugging aside the curious glances darting his way from the aged folk seated indolently on the benches on the cobblestone yards abutting the cafes, Asher walked forward. He was remembering Sahal's words while negotiating his way through the pungent aromas of coffee and spices.

'Habibi, this city smells of gunpowder.'

Sahal, these streets smell differently at different times. Sometimes, the fragrance of Oud. Other times, of saffron. Occasionally, the coffee scent of the evenings we spent together. And then again, at certain times, an unknown smell.

Sahal, dearest, when the siren for Shabbat rings out on Fridays, when the call of the muezzin rises five times a day, when the bells of the churches chime hymns at every nook and cranny, when everybody hails the place as 'the Holy City', I can still see the fury on your face.

'This is not a city of peace, Habibi. It is a city of explosions, made of splinters! The hearts of the residents are also splintered into a hundred fragments.'

Yet, regardless of whether one is a Jew, Christian or Muslim, how much everyone loves this city! The bitter outrage of having been robbed of everything one loved, everything that one possessed, isn't that the fire raging in your words, Habibi?

If only Sahal came cycling, with that flashing look in his eyes, just like the olden days, making his way through the crowd thronging Sultan Suleiman Street!

Sahal, beloved, you who reside in the memory of a day when the flesh was scorched, you who love to read stories about children flying like birds, over a country without check posts, where are you?

Walking across Salah al-Din Road and reaching Herod's Gate, Asher then turned to the familiar Sultan Suleiman Street, while ruminating on the Crusades. Every stone in the city was inscribed with stories: how the Jews fought shoulder to shoulder with the Muslims in the losing battle against the Christians, who wished to reclaim the Holy Land. And how, after two centuries, Sultan Salah al-Din, aka Saladin of Egypt, defeated the Crusaders and proclaimed that the Jews could return to their homeland. The legends spoke of how the Sultan had been compassionate enough to send his royal physician to help his enemy, the wounded King Richard. He had spared the lives of his Christian captives too.

Asher could see the heraldic eagle, soaring from the Sultan's headgear, and circling over the grey buildings of Bab Hutta Street. It landed on the Egyptian flag. Could he hear the trumpets of war? He became cautious and his stride quickened. Bab Hutta was in the Muslim Quarters, to the north of Temple Mount. In Arabic, 'Bab Hutta' meant 'Gate of Forgiveness'. There were other names to that area too: the street of whores, the street of the penurious ... As Asher threaded his way through the narrow gullies of Bab Hutta, the image of the Sultan vanished from his mind. He was now focused only on the paths leading to Sahal.

HOPE, an organization of which Sahal was a member, had taken up the cause of education of the poor children of the street. The kids would flock, travelling great distances, just to attend Sahal's English lessons. The children must have grown tired of waiting for their mu'darris.

There was a house in the neighbourhood that Sahal used to frequent. It had termite-ridden doors. Though he was befuddled for a while, from among the hundred sad-faced houses, one seemed to hail Asher. Once, the police had caught Sahal from there. Asher stood indecisively before the shut door. A little boy, clad in a soiled long robe and clutching a tattered book, opened the door. Fixing his gaze on Asher, he called out: 'Mama.' A woman with tired eyes peered out. Catching a glimpse of Asher, she glared at him and pulling the child inside, hastily shut the door. Casting a wary look around, Asher called softly … 'Sahal.' There was no reply.

A puppy whined from somewhere.

A woman who was passing by, paused, and her forehead wrinkled. Standing by the window, she called out in a loud voice, 'Um Ali.' Ali's mother, possibly the woman who shut the door on Asher's face, did not respond. After a few moments, Asher retreated, frustration building inside him. The woman standing near the window was muttering to herself.

Weaving his way through the vigorous street peddlers, with his eyes darting cautiously everywhere, Asher moved forward. He saw the eagle circling overhead once again. A group of old men playing backgammon, their chairs on the cobbled street, stared at him curiously. An old lady, standing on the terrace of a sand-coloured building, was calling someone. 'You better stop playing and come inside, or else, stay hungry tonight.' The woman's rasping voice petered out in the raucous street. From amongst the boardgame players, one man responded.

Asher recollected Sahal revealing that the majority of residents of the ancient city were starving. Their secret was wrapped up in charming grandeur. The menorah lampstand, rosary and crucifix, pictures of the saints, Roman statues, textiles … whatever the item for sale, there were many who went home without earning any money.

There was a long queue in front of a man selling coupons for buying bread. Some charitable organization was behind it. Maybe, members of HOPE. What if they could provide information about Sahal? Little Ali, whom he had seen earlier, was among the crowd of children. Or perhaps, it was someone like him. Always, everywhere, poverty had just one face. A police vehicle came screeching that way. In an instant, the children and the charity workers scattered in different directions. The poverty line, that had stretched on endlessly, was obliterated in moments!

The men in blue, who emerged from the police vehicle, rushed inside a perfume shop. There were raised voices, followed by a fracas. Were they attempting to evict the shopkeeper? Asher noticed the young man who was trying to drag the owner, an old man his father's age. Perchance, the shop's documents were outdated. They must not have been renewed. Disturbed, Asher watched the young man enforcing the law. His face was not cheerful and the expression was that of indulging in a forbidden act. Asher noticed the young policeman surreptitiously wiping his eyes. Was the perpetrator of injustice crying?

Nearby, holding a red thread, a woman was heckling an Indian priest. Quickly casting a backward glance at Asher, she brushed past him, probably to check whether he was a tourist. The Jewess was selling the 'thread of fortune' for a few shekels. 'This thread shall bring you good fortune and prosperity. Buy it, please!' She was pleading with the man for the umpteenth time. Would the history of this woman, selling good omens, get recorded somewhere? Which genealogy did she spring from? Who were her forebears? 'Who can count Jacob's descendants, as numerous as dust? Who can count a fourth of Israel's people?' Asher started pondering. The extremely intricate human lives and the mishmash of alleys of the Old City sew together the disjointed seams of Jerusalem: The Holy Land that was split into two—east and west, Israel and Palestine.

Starting his car, parked by the Damascus Gate, Asher drove to the Israel National Museum. He noticed again the eagle in the sky. Once again, the puppy's whine echoed in his ears. The cry was more mournful than before.

There were acquaintances at the museum who might know about Sahal's whereabouts.

'How long shall we climb down these steps?' Asher could still hear Sahal's anguished voice as he gazed at the white dome and descended the flight of steps to the vast courtyard. He could still see Sahal standing by the black basalt walls of the Shrine of the Book.

'The colours, black and white, symbolize the war of the sons of light against the sons of darkness.' A tourist guide was expositing to the visitors. Sahal had turned back, incensed. Asher could see it all happening, as if in the present.

'There are no sons of darkness! They are pushing the nation's sons into darkness. The heirs to this earth and water.'

Sahal's voice had been quivering with emotion.

'The symbols of establishment are transgressions into another's rights!' Harshly, severely, furiously, the words had flown … Asher could hear them clearly even now.

Standing inside the cavernous corridor of the Shrine of the Book, in front of the glass casements holding the clay jars with the Dead Sea Scrolls and the ink-stained quills, Sahal was laughing vehemently. 'Hey archaeologist, these are two thousand years old, are they?' Sahal's question that had resounded in the cave, and the sharp-edged mockery therein, was still vibrant in Asher's memory.

Sahal dearest, where are you? I am fatigued searching for you. Exceedingly tired.

What's engraved in stone shall never disappear. Certain loves too.

A delay was caused on the road: a procession by Palestinian youth, declaring their support for Gaza. Some drivers were raining abuses on them.

'Go and carry out your protests at Gaza. Why are you blocking our way, damn it!'

An infuriated young man retaliated, 'You are annihilating us as a civilization. Driving us away from all sides, to control entire Jerusalem! And now you are snarling because of a mere half an hour's delay?'

The grand gentleman became furious too.

'You brat, this is our piece of earth! We Jews, owners of the land, are fighting for our property. It is our generosity that we allow those like you, treacherously strapping bombs onto bodies and trying to cause explosions, inside!'

The war of words would have escalated into something far worse. Luckily, the police arrived on the scene. They propelled the protesters to a side and opened up the traffic.

'This is the land of the robbed. And that of the robbers ...' Asher muttered to himself.

Abba's call came when Asher's car reached the museum campus. It was to check whether he had traced Sahal yet. Abba had always been against the brutal methods adopted by the ultra-orthodox Zionists. He also objected to Hamas's impulsive acts. The compassion which Abba showed to the Palestinians marked him out as an odd man, even among friends. Abba argued that many Jews held anti-Zionist views, albeit secretively. But nobody dared to express them openly. No wonder that Abba dedicated his life to the organization Denying to Be Foes established by the holocaust survivor Naomi Bergman; the blazing torch was handed over to Asher.

Sahal dearest, Abba is tormented by your absence.

At the Shrine of the Book, the news which met Asher was about the arrest of a young man who had smashed the glass case storing the jars with the Qumran Caves Scrolls.

Habibi, let that not be you!

8

THE LEARNING PLACES OF ORPHANS

The saddest and most silent shrines of the world—
Learning places of orphans.
Listen, can you hear
The mutterings of the termite-eaten books?
Resembling shattered homes,
The broken line of alphabets.
On the empty seats, multiplication tables, riddled with holes
The attendance register, with undeleted names
Of dead children.
Its binding unhinged ...

(Sahal Al Fadi)

It was Abba who told Ruth about Sahal. The young man who carried in his heart a day with the odour of burning flesh!

A boy with a sad face and blinking eyes—that was Sahal Al Fadi. He once admitted to the UN volunteers at the Jalazone refugee camp, that his only dream was a country without walls or check posts. It was not bread or toys that Sahal requested from them. Instead, he asked for books. Stories. Of children who flew like birds, in nations without wire fences and barricades. Stories of children who never had to cower in front of a soldier's gun barrel.

They were three siblings. Sarah was younger to Sahal. The youngest, Gazan, would gambol around like an inquisitive lamb on the mountainside. The three leaves on a bough, bending towards the earth as the final wind gusted … *three tiny leaves …*

Today, Sahal yearned to leave West Bank, forgetting Mount Zion's dream of freedom. Life, at the end of a gun's barrel, had become unbearable. He was interested in researching on drones. Now, Sahal was waiting, having applied for a scholarship at the University of Malaysia. Of course, Sarah's life had to be settled before he joined. His baba, Abu Sahal, used to speak about his son becoming a world-famous athlete or engineer one day. Sahal's photograph would grace the *Palestine Telegraph*. Baba did not know then that Sahal was destined to be the cover story of the world's media, owing to mysterious, excruciating circumstances.

In the future, Sahal's memoirs would be published in a series on Al Jazeera's website. Later, it would turn into a book titled *Howdy Death, Hello Freedom.*

'If we remain mute, these rocks shall scream.'

I am Sahal Al Fadi. Someone, who dreams of the return of those old dawns when we raced fearlessly to gather ripe figs. Someone, who dreams of a time when one can travel to the ends of the world, crossing villages and cities, never facing a soldier's interrogation.

I love books. Growing up, stories made me cheerful. Because, the children in those stories were so different from us. They never stood in queues for hours on end, waiting for a scrap of bread. They never quenched their thirst from murky streams riven with wastes. They never lay cold and dead inside stinky cubicles. They had never seen camps. They had never run for their lives through a burning city. They never stood dumbstruck seeing their baba and mama lying burnt to cinders inside a scorched home. They had never heard of a lullaby choked by smoke. Never.

They do not know these wounded little human beings … with hearts as heavy as the earth …

It was difficult for me to believe that a world as beautiful as the one in stories existed outside the camp, outside the country, across the river … I had never seen such a world. Storytellers seemed to be the greatest fibbers! But I loved their lies a lot. Listen, the world has still not understood our stories. I swear that the entire Babel of languages of the world, the six thousand and more, cannot encompass those! We are a farrago of novels, essays, poems and tears.

You, who have never seen wars, having never raced across borders horror-struck, with your home on your back, can never comprehend our lives. We are the truth that you, free people, are loath to write about. You might be remembering the enemy army assemble on the Sinai border and the preparations of graves, expecting a huge loss of Jewish lives. You might be remembering how Egypt, Syria, Iraq and Jordan fought for us and lost the battle. But what was defeated, and gets defeated daily, is peace, amity and us … None, but us.

Nobody could conjecture that our lives were going to be turned upside down that day. Except those who planned the war. I can scarcely bring myself to recollect those moments. Yet, I will make an attempt. I was eight years old when the city was attacked. Unexpectedly, one afternoon, missiles rained on West Bank. We were at school then. There was a roar of planes in the skies. The relentless sirens were warning about the danger. Shutting the windows and doors, we huddled with our elders inside the building, shell-shocked by the unremitting gunfire, hugging one another tightly … In the wake of a horrendous explosion, the school building shook. People started screaming. I remembered my baba and mama. I prayed, 'Allah, keep them safe.' Before the prayer could fly through the door, the reverberations of another ear-splitting explosion began … One part of the school building collapsed. Shrieks and laments reached the skies. Terror-struck children scattered in all directions. Even after the sounds died off, the smoke and dust kept billowing around.

I discovered Sarah, cowered in one corner of the classroom. Her right leg was seriously burnt and it was difficult for her to walk. Clutching her hand, I dragged her along through the tendrils of smoke. We could find Gazan only after a long search. He was struggling to pull out his friend Salim—his body totally charred—from beneath the benches. There was no fear in his eyes, just a frozen look. He did not want to leave Salim behind. Gazan was toiling with his mu'darris Abu Kalam, retrieving the bodies of living and dead children from the ruins. Sobbing, the teacher embraced Gazan. 'Go home quickly, my child,' he cried. We somehow managed to get outside. The gory sight of human remains, perhaps belonging to our friends, was everywhere. One limb here, a crushed head there … a tiny hand still touching a book … another leg … a little body lying on its face, kissing the earth … Was the way home to the left, or right? We stood stunned at the junction where a pool of blood was visible.

The streets we loved, the beloved square with the fruit shop, bakery, bicycle shop—everything had vanished from sight. The pathways where we used to play were piled with rubble. We saw cattle burnt to cinders in their sheds and toppled roofs. Under an iron pillar, a blood-soaked old woman was raising her hand desperately. We three small humans tried to help her with all our combined strength. The heartless iron pillar did not budge. The old lady groaned and slowly, her eyes closed. She was murmuring something at the final moment. Sarah started screaming for Mama. She could not walk any more; neither could she endure the sights any longer.

The huge fig tree in front of our house recognized us. The branches beckoned us warmly. We three small humans limped towards the tree. We did not know then that never-to-be-forgotten sights were awaiting us inside.

By the vessel of knafeh, which Mama had prepared for Sarah's birthday, her beloved white kitten was lying dead, scalded and swollen. On the porcelain plates, the chicken bones of the musakhan dish were blackened with soot.

Nearby, amidst the broken and burnt furniture, like another charred log, lay Baba! I forcibly shut Sarah's eyes. Leaning against the half-collapsed kitchen wall, were the remains of what looked like a burnt flambeau. It was not easy to recognize our mama. She must have been cooking when it happened.

We were shattered. Three small humans ... little hearts heavy as the earth ... our tender feet reddened with blood ...

For weeks, the city reeked of burnt flesh. Sarah lay shivering with fever in the refugee camp. In a few days, Gazan found new friends and started playing and smiling again. Sarah did not play or smile. Even after her wounds healed, she refused to attend school. Most days, she avoided food. Gazan felt famished all the time. He insisted on eating Mama's knafeh and hareesa. If we stood in a queue for three hours, some bread pieces were granted as rations. Those were hardly sufficient! I would give my portion to Gazan and go hungry. I became used to starving. Every day, I grew thinner.

On certain nights, I would dream of Baba, who would hoist me on his shoulders, and climb down the hills to pluck the olives. As usual, Baba would be chatting with Mama about the city news. My mama would gently wipe away the knafeh threads dangling from my mouth. I would taste her knafeh again and my hunger pangs would be assuaged. I would kiss Mama's fingers and find myself enveloped by her scent even after I awoke. The fragrance of butter and olive oil. Every night I prayed to dream about Baba and Mama.

It was Sarah's state which troubled me the most. Wouldn't she ever become the old Sarah again? I also worried about Gazan. Why wasn't he enquiring about Baba and Mama? Why wasn't he remembering them? Did that wretched day wipe away every beautiful memory of childhood in the blink of an eye? Still, it was a stroke of luck that Gazan was not hovering at the edge of insanity, seemingly half-alive, like Sarah.

On that blazing afternoon, as I stood hugging Sarah and Gazan close to my heart, I was no longer an eight-year-old; I had stepped into the age of eighty. Even after the passage of years, when I remember that day, the odour of burnt flesh suffocates me. The skies were filled with vultures those days. Circling around ceaselessly, they still haunt my sleep.

Tell me, has such a helpless, terrifying moment occurred even once in your life? Else, how will you understand us? How will you recognize our wounds?

The elders consoled: The hands of Allah the Compassionate shall aid the destitute and the orphans. They asked us to beseech Rabb for his benevolence. We trusted their word and performed the salat, praying five times a day. We were three wounded small humans, with feet red with blood and hearts heavy as the earth … How were we to know that more catastrophes, that would uproot all hopes, were waiting ahead ?

I wonder often, even as I write, about how that eight-year-old child survived those days.

9

AUSCHWITZ AND THE PILOT OF MITSUBISHI

Seven springs, the waters streaming across boundaries and time periods, embraced one another ecstatically at Tabgha, in the north-western shore of the Sea of Galilee. Seven springs, seven hundred thousand human wounds, flowing as a unified river into the Lake of Gennesaret.

The lake was serene.

Some lives are similar. Unexpectedly they become one, though the mountains they originated from are different. Though the forest paths they left behind are not the same.

'It is already inscribed in the Lord's sociology book, that at *a* particular time, *this* person shall be a succour to *that* person.' It was a woman, whom she met out of the blue, at the Basilica of the Annunciation at Nazareth, who revealed that to Ruth. When they saw each other for the first time, a group of migratory birds were descending from the skies to perch on the church's spire. Ruth felt that she was standing in the courtyard of an ancient Nazareth home, listening to the sounds arising from Joseph's carpentry shop, just across the fence. Beneath an apple tree, a foal flicked its ears and smiled at her.

'Why are you stopping me? I am promoting tourism!' A spirited young woman was fearlessly challenging the cops who stopped her video-shoot. 'Who is this? The Virgin listening to the Annunciation?' The firebrand chortled at Ruth's wondering look.

'Do you work in the media?' Ruth asked.

The woman winked in reply.

'You are new, right? Don't ask the Indians in Israel about their jobs. Most are caregivers. This is just a hobby. There are lots of vloggers over here. Just like me, Lilly Joseph.'

The firebrand lady had returned that day, taking hold of her new friend's adoring heart. During Lilly's future travels, Ruth would accompany her; except for a solitary journey in May, in a distant future.

Lilly's workplace was at Ashkelon. She was a companion to the Auschwitz survivor Naomi Bergman. Ruth was familiar with that name. Abba had been effusive about his days working with Naomi at her organization, Denying to be Foes. Lilly had a 'sharing room' in Jerusalem. A house like a tree caught in a storm! On holidays, almost ten or eleven metapelets congregated there. They arrived from kibbutzes, small towns and cities. Then the fun would unfurl. Dances, music, naughtiness … They would weep while sharing stories. Sometimes they would laugh boisterously and roll around helplessly. The women would enthusiastically prepare their favourite dishes. Red rice, sambhar, fish curry made with tamarind …

Lilly insisted that Ruth join the bird's nest. That entailed an investment of seventy-five shekels. Ruth's visa duration was for four years and three months. She had to shoulder a plethora of responsibilities. Alby's medical care, the children's studies, debts, more debts … She did not have even five shekels to spare. When Ruth laid out excuses, Lilly scolded her. 'The burden of the whole world is not resting on your shoulders, is it? Give some priority to your own needs! Or you will regret it in your dotage, *Lord, I never lived my life!*'

Ruth joined the bird's nest only due to Lilly's stubbornness. It was then that she was exposed to the dark sides of a metapelet's life.

In most homes, the old patient was all alone. Typically, the children lived far away. Even if the kin and kith were around, they would drop in only rarely. Many caregivers hardly got a holiday; and getting to sleep was a luxury. Some kept watch over Alzheimer's patients, while others were looking after men and women suffering from dementia. There were metapelets who had patients who were bedridden. They could not leave the bedside even for an hour.

Most turned into female versions of Kumbhakarna on reaching the bird's nest. They could be seen sleeping for countless hours! Watching these slumbering women was similar to observing an ancient cemetery. Ruth would be reminded of corpses lying amongst the cypress trees, in open vaults ... The women's feet were frozen due to the cold wind blowing from an unearthly world and their lips evoked memories of enigmatic paintings ...

If the patient passed away under her care, the metapelet's job would be at stake. Then, each would need a sanctuary. A bird's nest.

'I suffered quite a lot before meeting Naomi,' Lilly confessed. 'Not every house is a Shalom. Not all towns are Nazareth either. The first woman I looked after was a regular Bhadrakali! She would lose her temper and hurl the nearest object at me. By the time I swept clean the shattered bits, the next atrocity would begin. Once she choked me with her tichel. I managed to escape somehow or that would have been my end! Couldn't catch a wink when she was awake. And that old ghost would never sleep day or night! She would go berserk on seeing me on the phone. Oh, I can hand over a long list of Hebrew expletives, if you like!'

Lilly Joseph slowly retraced her path through that tough phase of life, when every atom of her body had screamed, 'Get away!'

'The woman would spit the soup right at my face. In her eyes, I was some sort of vermin ... The despicable heathen in the Old Testament. Ah, those days of survival! The daughter was worse than the mother. Whenever that haughty woman traipsed in, it was like a hell within another hell! Lord, she would run her fingers on the television, on the handle of the almirah, fridge and check for flecks of dust! Then she would holler, "Is this how you maintain a patient's room? Are you being paid for this sluggishness?"

'The agency somehow got me out of that hell. Then I shifted to a house of kindness, a Beit Avot,' Lilly said.

It was the twenty-seventh day of the month of Nisan. The Holocaust Remembrance Day. Yom HaShoah. In the blare of sirens, the streets came to a standstill. Motorists stopped their cars in the middle of the road. Villages and cities paused, turned inert and silent.

Cattle car trains, packed with condemned deportees, rushed suffocatingly through the hills. The gusts of smoke from the gas chambers rose like a mountain and spread beyond countries and time. The helpless humans, festering with lice and fleas, struck with typhus and dysentery, curled up in the concentration camps, turned their bleary eyes to the skies.

Hearts filled with prayers for the forebears who had sacrificed their lives, enduring excruciating agonies. On that day, as they assembled in the club, Lilly had met the dignified old woman, who had opened her heart before the audience. Naomi Bergman was eighty years old. She had escaped from the burning embers of Auschwitz.

As Lilly listened in wonder to Naomi, she did not know then that her escape from the 'abode of the damned' was being unfurled.

'Shalom le' kulam. When I see you seated here, listening to my story, I recollect my own childhood. My family name is Bergman. It means, 'from the mountains'. But I come from the erupting volcanoes. One night, they corralled us from the summit of the snow-clad mountains. Savta was narrating stories as usual, as we sat around her, just like today. She was exhorting us not to lose heart, come what may, through that story. The intruders barged in and took Savta and Saba away. We heard three or four gunshots soon afterwards. The elders started sobbing, trying to muffle their sounds. Even then, we kids were waiting for the rest of the story. We never saw Savta and Saba again. I remember everything as if it happened yesterday.

The Nazis were using the psychology of unspeakable terror, to devastate individuals and groups, both physically and emotionally. My memories begin with those days, where we hid from the armed forces, which could rush in any moment. The chilling days in Poland, when we could not venture out into playgrounds, parks or restaurants. And one day they came to take us along. My younger brother Adon and I were playing cops and robbers then. We were allowed ten minutes to gather our things. As we raced to the bogie of the cattle car train, chock-full of other livestock like us, Adon assumed that it was part of the game. How were we to guess that suffocating hours were awaiting us, without food, water or even sufficient air to breathe? After a while, the bogey turned into a mass of human screams. Both adults and children were shrieking in horror. Adon wept, asking me to end the game. We children, oblivious of the worldly games.

Ah, it happened afterwards. They pushed us out at some station. And then, we were driven to a place with a white-coated doctor, who by pointing his forefinger, towards left or right, decided the boundaries of life and death … We children, innocent of the worldly games …

The doctor pointed the thin eight-year-old girl to the group of the living. Adon screamed then, his hands stretched out towards me … how shall I ever forget his final look, and my Eema's tears? How will I narrate about morphing into another of the vermin, among the sick and infested … of struggling to survive on scraps of bread? The times when I stared curiously at the curls of black smoke rising from the gas chambers, unaware of what was happening … Days when I waited for Eema, Baba and Adon to come searching for me … The moments when my heart broke as the man with bloodshot eyes revealed that most mothers and those who could not work had been dumped inside the gas chambers! I was a train in those days. A train of lamentations. A train which rushed forward breathlessly. Not just me, thousands … We children, unaware of the worldly games …

Finally, with the help of a volunteer, I was shifted to a military hospital, half-dead. In a real-life train, a move to a Swiss camp. I waited for a long time, hoping, trusting, praying that my loved ones were safe in another camp … For their sake, all the while, my eyes watched this beautiful universe. For their sake, all the while, I carried on with life. For their sake, all the while, I loved humanity. Still I am glad that Auschwitz could not take away my soul …

The audience dispersed after the meeting. Lilly did not return. With hesitant steps, she inched forward to Naomi's side … straight into her heart …Today, it all seemed like a dream. Lilly became Naomi Bergman's metapelet. 'Assisting an Auschwitz survivor implies taking care of someone who had accepted all the sorrows and helplessness of the world. It means being the companion of a woman who had crossed over the Red Sea of Fears.' Those were Lilly's words.

Naomi Bergman vehemently opposed the unspeakable brutalities of occupying territories forcibly, the viciousness of snatching babies from the breasts of mothers and shattering families. She established the NGO Denying to Be Foes, so that Jews and Palestinians could unitedly struggle, adopting the path of non-violence, against all the manoeuvrings of warmongers. Lilly was happy in Naomi's home. She would vouch proudly, enthusiastically, that a sea of courage would surge within anybody who conversed with the great woman.

Time passed.

One afternoon, unexpectedly, Ruth would end up meeting somebody. As he stepped inside Lilly's bird-nest, the earth quaking in his wake, the image of a school on a hill slope clustered with rubber trees, appeared in Ruth's mind. 'What do you want to become in life?' Baby Sir asked the question, wiping away the sums scribbled with white chalk on the blackboard. 'Pilot!' he had shouted, first among all, at the topmost pitch. Now he was standing in front of Ruth. The same Binu Samuel Keerikkadan!

'Ruth, the scrawny keelback! Tell me, how did you land up here?' Binu took her hand lovingly.

'Live and let live, boss! Hey Pilot, what are you doing here?' Ruth retorted.

'I am taking care of a pilot's father nowadays. He is in America. And I am in the pilot seat of his car!' Binu guffawed. 'My Appan's business failed and we were overwhelmed with debts. Had to survive, right? Made my way here.'

Binu Keerikkadan was the caregiver of a retired military officer. The old man was fond of him. In Ramat Gan, Tel Aviv, in a two-storey house, the world consisting of Binu and himself had become the man's army and brigade. For the last three years, Binu had been his companion, providing loving care to the man, indulging him by saluting him and playing chess with him. The son had flown in just one time to see his father in the whole period. Now, after a stint of hospitalization, the old man was in a shikum, rehabilitation centre. So, Binu had decided to travel a bit.

'Don't share my gospel with your villagers! My father has been bragging about my super successful business here. The family pride has to be protected always.' Binu stroked his balding head.

Ruth felt that the naughty adolescent of the schooldays was standing in front of her even now.

'Binu, isn't it a good job, giving companionship to the lonely?'

Binu grinned yet again.

'Good to say! Try falling from the heights. Then you will know …'

From that day, in the route map of Ruth's Israel days, Binu Samuel and his Outlander would have their special place. Her journey, after that, had been to centuries past. Ruth Esthappan, as a girl, had never dreamed that she would be wandering through a mysterious, historical country, along with a classmate, in the vehicle of an Israeli army officer. How could the indigent girl ever imagine that at the age of forty, both she and Binu would end up doing the same job in such a country!

'Let us grill St Peter's Fish now! Lilly, I have got some snapping tilapia!' Binu announced cheerfully.

He entered the kitchen. There wasn't any change in him. No full stops or commas! Rushing into the kitchen of a home exclusively used by women! Ruth did not smell the fish cooking. The whole atmosphere was redolent of wild chempakam flowers.

Ruth's heart was brimming over like the Lake of Galilee when she returned to Nazareth that day. That night, in her dreams, Mariam of Bethany made an appearance.

'These words are faithful and true, Ruth. *Why then have you broken down its walls, so that all who pass along the way pluck its fruit?* Ruth, you better build fences around your heart.'

Ruth smiled mysteriously.

'Hey beloved, that was what the Lord told you once!'

Mariam flushed on hearing that.

'Once Jesus came home with a catch of tilapia, caught from the Lake Gennesaret.'

'And then?' Ruth wondered aloud.

'When Martha baked the barley bread, the Rabbi grilled the fish perfectly … in olive oil!'

Ruth giggled, listening to Mariam's words.

'As if the Lord had no other job!'

'Ruth, the Gospel written by men has been intentionally silent about Jesus in the kitchen,' Mariam insisted stubbornly.

'Oh, the Gospel of Martha Mary!' Ruth mocked.

Mariam emerged from the dream, and wandered away, humming a song.

It was Lilly who persuaded Ruth to change from her starched saris to the kurti-and-jeans ensemble. And it was Lilly, yet again, who pushed Ruth's boat into the Lake of Fearlessness akin to Gennesaret and encouraged her to start a vlog. However, it was Asher who baptized her vlog, which started without much publicity, as 'Nazareth'. It was he who taught Ruth the basics of shooting videos and editing them. Slowly, the grapevines of Nazareth started crawling over Padamala. Alby, Teesa and Kathu began waiting for the episodes of Nazareth. The bramble fence of Ruth's heart, much prone to sharp thorns of sorrows, started blossoming anew. Ruth's days underwent a sea change, like the bougainvillea flowers of Ein Karim.

Noah's ark was bobbing on the Mediterranean Sea. The voyagers included Abba, Eema, Asher, Leah, Sofia, Lilly, Binu, a few sleepy metapelets, and Mariam of Bethany. Captain Ruth Albert spread open the wind map.

A few cities of sand stood sentinel, holding the winds of a thousand years within.

10

THE BALCONY ON THE FOURTH FLOOR

Ruth could never forget her travels with Leah. Once they went to Tel Aviv, the 'Spring Hill'. Leah would playfully knock down the kippah of a passer-by. Then she would apologize and pick it up for him. Sometimes, she would hold the hand of a flustered old woman standing at a zebra crossing, and help her across the road. At times, she would build sandcastles on the seashore. Once, she winked at a young Israeli soldier, armed to the teeth. What a girl!

The Tel Aviv journey was part of an enquiry. A Notzri family—family of Christians—once lived in the house, now dilapidated, lying to the west of Shalom. A young woman, Annie, who was an ornithologist and journalist, had lived there. She was the unique voice of the online media, Voice of Palestine. She courageously highlighted, like a warrior, the issues of Palestinians that were sidelined by the mainstream media. One day, Annie went to Ashkelon and never returned. Her goal had been to interview the Palestinian engineer who had been kidnapped in Ukraine, and confined ever since in the Shikma Prison at Ashkelon. It was with great difficulty that Annie had managed to get the required permission. Nobody saw her again. Even after a police investigation, no trace was found of the missing young woman. The search was by the Jewish police, after all. Later, Annie's family shifted to Bethany.

At Tel Aviv, someone was waiting for Leah—Asher's friend, Joshua. At Levinsky Street's spice market, in a peaceful corner of Café Atlas, the trio sat silently. Then Joshua began to speak about Annie. She had called him before entering the Shikma Prison. 'Joshua, that engineer has some critical secrets to share, as yet unknown to the world.' But …

A photographer, who was a common acquaintance, had accompanied Annie. He was supposedly living in Tel Aviv at the time. From Café Atlas, they had gone in search of the man, based on the information Annie had shared. After a while, they discovered the padlocked flat. Nobody in the neighbourhood knew about such a person. It was quite natural, since it was a city.

That day, while returning from Tel Aviv, Leah opened her heart to Ruth. 'Did you notice Joshua? All stooped like an old man! He was super smart once upon a time. He has turned morose and moody after Annie went missing. I used to like that guy … I care for him still. But he fell in love with that Notzri girl, Annie. He would visit Nazareth just to meet her.'

True, there was a sea of anguish in Joshua's eyes.

'He does not know about my love, my ahavah, even now. I haven't told him yet.'

Ruth looked deep into Leah's eyes. A flock of seabirds, flitting above the Mediterranean waves, was taking flight inside her eyes too!

'Annie, rather a nice name. My Amma's name. She was also obsessed with birds.' Ruth did not divulge that her mother too had vanished one day. Annie was not like her mother. Surely, she would return one day.

'The Girls of the City' became Nazareth's first vlog. In that video full of Tel Aviv vignettes, Leah was the heroine. She spoke of the Palestinian journalist Annie, who had vanished from the city, and about her discoveries. 'Haifa works, Jerusalem prays, but Tel Aviv plays.' That was how the vlog ended. The main propagator of Ruth's vlog was Lilly who ran the 'Bird's Nest' vlog. There was an onrush of followers. Probably Leah's enchanting presence played a role in that occurrence.

A note appeared in the comment box of Nazareth, shocking Ruth. Written by someone with the sobriquet 'Akasha Mithai' or 'Sky Sweet'.

'*Paths of Fire Traversed by a Girl Called R.*'

Whoever the person was, whatever he or she scripted was the bare-bones truth. What the city of Riyadh had done to a young girl's life, a few decades back. Ruth saw in her mind the lonely girl, who was peering from the fourth-floor balcony, balancing on an upturned bucket. She observed the depths of her desolation. The sturdy Egyptian guard, standing next to the wrought iron gate came into view. A tremor of fear seized Ruth, as if she had sighted a wolf hiding in the darkness.

Haifa works, Jerusalem prays, Tel Aviv plays, but Riyadh shocks ...

I am Akasha Mithai, the Sky Sweet. I am going to write about an old story. It happened once upon a time.

The twenty-year-old woman had landed in Riyadh with four friends. We shall refer to her as 'R'. The agent had promised employment at a famous hospital, but had sent them to a fortress of mystery—a four-storeyed building. There were four rooms on the fourth floor. Five Malayali nurses were made to stay in a single room. In the other rooms there were Filipino nurses, technicians, Egyptian doctors ... It was a multi-speciality clinic which was to open soon. Nobody had any work to do, nor any salary. But the sweltering, insufferable heat was all-pervading. Fifty degrees Celsius temperature! There was just a single cooler in the room. The girls suffered terribly, as if caught in a furnace. They were terrified and disheartened by the ghost-like building. The Filipinos surprised them, with their never-flagging good cheer and loquacity, even amidst all those worries.

When two nations encountered each other in the common kitchen, tempers would flare up, and wars would break out at random ... Everybody was deeply frustrated. Consequently, they were very vulnerable and easily hurt. But they did not have to starve. There were lots of frozen chicken, eggplants, sauce and kuboos for their repast.

The world soon shrunk to the dimensions of the fourth-floor room. A sliver of sky could be sighted afar. Nobody knew what was happening below. The girls would climb on top of an upturned bucket and peep to see the world outside, since the balcony railing was at a great height. A giant of an Egyptian stood guard at the monstrous gate. He would periodically patrol the compound. Sometimes he rested on a rusted chair, smoked and dozed off.

The girl called R would have nightmares about cattle being readied to be slaughtered. She would wake up with a jolt hearing the desperate grunting of buffaloes. The snores of livestock would resound from the fourth floor then ...

The pages of the calendar kept turning, ignorant of the outside world. Riyadh swallowed them like a python, stealthily, soundlessly. As time passed, the girls spent most of the time sleeping. They became unaware of the hours passing by. The manager of the yet-to-be-opened clinic would visit intermittently. A dry, shrivelled-up man. He would offer them hope. The clinic would open next week. No, next month. Six months of disappointment crawled by in this manner. One day, they heard some sounds from the lower floors. Pickup vans trundled in and out of the campus, carrying furniture and instruments. Medicines and machines were being moved on trolleys. Uniforms were being distributed. There was delight and enthusiasm all around. India, the Philippines and Egypt embraced one another, laughing and teasing. Those days were filled with joy, as if someone one mourned for had suddenly resurrected. They had no clue that all their hopes would come crashing soon.

The clinic opened. Months passed, two, three, four ... No salary. The first clinic in the world with more staff than patients! Frustration and misery grew in leaps and bounds. The python had swallowed the girls entirely by now.

Finally one night R stood atop an inverted bucket and peered down. For a moment, she demurred, 'What if I don't die? What if I'm doomed to be bedridden with shattered bones? There will not be a single human being on earth to cry for me.' That was the truth. She spent the whole night in the burning hot balcony, alone and weeping. It was the day when an unctuous, middle-aged doctor had tried to molest her in the clinic room.

The next day, when the watchman went off for lunch, two girls, two embodiments of utter fear, slipped down quietly. Wearing burkhas, hiding their faces, somehow they sneaked out of the compound. It was Saudi Arabia. They were women without refuge. There was no guarantee that anyone would believe them. The girls called the police from a nearby telephone booth. A Malayali, who had come for treatment at the clinic, had advised them after listening to their woes. They went to the Labour Court, determined to face anything. But misfortune was trailing closely. They were stopped outside the court. Not understanding Arabic, the girls stood bewildered before the official donning an intimidating headgear, who started interrogating them. Though they were verbally abused and asked to clear out, the girls stood their ground. Two girls, two embodiments of utter fear …

Hours ticked by. The young women knew that they could not return to the clinic. Things would turn bad for them. The manager would have come to know about their rebellious trip to the Labour Court. He could easily foist any number of accusations on them; even allege prostitution. The court might punish them by ordering stoning till death. They stood sobbing in the scalding sun. Two girls, two embodiments of utter fear …

Luckily for them, a man approached them, noticing their weeping. He was tall and spoke to them in Hindi. 'Sisters, are you from India? I am your neighbour. An officer in the court. Why are you crying?'

Soon, the man prepared an application in Arabic. They signed the paper and received an acknowledgement slip. Consoling them that they were now safe, the good man from Pakistan hailed a taxi for the girls. He turned out to be a true neighbour! There was a sudden inspection at the clinic by the department of health. An order was issued to shut down the illegal clinic. The management was asked to pay four months' salary to the staff and purchase air tickets for their return. After almost a year and six months of staying in the Gulf, and interminable mental torture, they boarded the flight home. Five unfortunate girls … Except Molly, nobody spoke to R any more.

Never would have R imagined that after two decades, another memorable Gulf trip was awaiting her.

Ruth sat stunned. Who was Sky Sweet? Was it Molly, who had accompanied her to the court on that parched day in Riyadh? But why should Molly play hide-and-seek with her? This was someone else. A strange man or woman.

For days on end, Ruth was haunted by the fourth-floor balcony in Riyadh. She woke up from her sleep multiple times, dreaming of the inflexible, hard-hearted official at the Labour Court gate. And two girls, two embodiments of utter fear … Ruth also dreamt of Annie, whom she had never seen in her life, stepping inside Shikma Prison.

Jerusalem was on the verge of an explosion those days. The disturbing ripples reached Shalom too. Asher's comings and goings became erratic. Eema became very anguished because of him.

11
GOODBYE, BAGHDAD

Intermittently, the streets went up in flames. The smell of gunpowder would saturate the air. Darkness stalked the city walks. This was the Holy Land of three religions … the Temple Mount of the Jews, the Calvary of Christians, the Masjid Al-Aqsa of the Muslims.

On the Facebook page of 'Warrior of Light', there was a photograph of a fracas between a Palestinian woman and an orthodox Jew, at Sheikh Jarrah, in East Jerusalem. Behind the raging woman, a small, sad-looking boy was holding the Palestinian flag, the red triangle, next to his heart. His long robe was covered by the black, white and green colours …

Ruth read aloud the picture's caption for Abba: '*You made our children stone pelters and imprisoned their fathers. Yet unsatiated, trying to encroach on our homes, are you?*'

The picture of another city flashed inside Abba's mind then. Those were the days when cities were up in arms against the Jews … Abba began to tell Ruth his story.

The evening twilight at Baghdad had been silent and sombre. The streets seemed desolate like a graveyard. The army vehicles sped past frequently, the sirens of death echoing. When Job Menahem shut his showroom earlier than usual, and rushed to his apartment on the first floor, six-year-old David was standing by the window. Seeing his uncle Elijah running towards the house, on the road beneath, he was about to wave his hand in welcome. Suddenly a mob surrounded his uncle. They kicked Elijah Dod cruelly, assaulting him with many weapons. David stood dumbstruck watching the scene. Someone shut his mouth from behind. When he turned, his father Job Menahem was standing behind him, frozen. Little David hugged his father desperately. It was like embracing a tree struck by lightning.

In a matter of minutes, there was an insistent knock on the front door.

'Open up, devils!' the bloodthirsty marauders were bellowing.

Snuffing out all lights, they waited, clinging to each other in terror. Soon, they heard the sound of footsteps rushing away. Perhaps, they were after another victim who was sighted on the road. To chase another unfortunate man …

On that harrowing night, the Menahem family hastily gathered whatever they could and fled to a neighbouring village. They travelled in an acquaintance's truck, used for transporting cattle. All through his living days, within David Menahem's heart, a little boy would sit trembling in a dung-stinking cattle truck, expecting a murderous mob to attack any moment …

Baghdad had turned into a horrific scream.

The Second World War had just begun. Like a bolt from the skies, the news came that criminals were being released from the jails: those willing to fight against Israel. Murderers and robbers swaggered through the streets of the city. They were on the lookout for Jews. A left-wing Jew was sure to be killed in cold blood. The Menahem family survived that dreadful time due to sheer luck.

The conflicts did not abate as time passed. One day, clutching David's hand, Job Menahem returned to the city of afflictions. Though the raiders had retreated, the streets looked vulnerable, as if readying for another disaster. David had been eager to see Elijah Dod. He wished to play with the toys his uncle had gifted him. But the sights that awaited them were heart-rending. The building they lived in and its whereabouts were burnt to the ground. There were only a mountain of ashes, half-singed bricks and ghostly remains of metal. Job Menahem sat down heavily under the electric post where his brother had fallen victim to the murderous mob. The sun blazed more furiously than ever. Little David would never ever forget that day.

'We shall scorch Tel Aviv!' The exhortation from Iraqi Radio would haunt David Menahem's dreams even after many summers.

The Menahem family joined the great exodus to Israel, fleeing for their lives. But what they encountered at Haifa wasn't pleasant. Those who carried the sunlight and breeze of Baghdad in their hearts, ended up facing utter bleakness. There were rampant discriminations, blatant degradations. Among a thousand Jews, a thousand groups! The European Ashkenazi Jews were accorded prominence everywhere. The Arab Jews were treated as if they were primordial cave dwellers. The most primeval among the primitive. Despicable vermin, who had arrived to spread epidemics. They were rehabilitated into vast camps. Those who prided themselves as the heirs of the Promised Land, wilted with inferiority.

David remembered the insecure childhood and adolescence spent at Haifa … His father Job Menahem transformed into a shell of his former self, losing all vigour and purpose. A devastated man, bereft of his pride, who no longer smiled. He was like a transplanted tree that failed to take root in the new soil, and withered away fast. The proud car dealer of Baghdad was downgraded to a mechanic in a workshop, forced to snivel and cringe before the Ashkenazi owners. Their condescension and preening, the attitude of 'what you have, is what we give', bruised his pride and wounded his self-dignity. The birthrights, offered as alms, angered and saddened Job Menahem. David still remembered his father's face as he exploded with fury after returning from a government office one day. Job Menahem had been beseeching the authorities for his family's emigration certificates. Their home had become a veritable hill of suffering and silence. Miriam Menahem, David's Eema, was the lone spark of light in that darkness. On the verge of utter collapse, Job's succour was his indomitable wife.

Job Menahem eventually joined the Communist Party at Haifa. But he could not find solace there. Either the members were anti-Semites or they were Jews who hated Arabs. Unable to reconcile with the reality, Job left the party. Miriam's lone goal was to provide the best education to her children. The land dreamt and slept in Hebrew. It thought, smiled and wept in Hebrew. The land breathed Hebrew. Possessing that insight, Miriam ensured that her children were well versed in Hebrew right from childhood. David would wonder later about his Eema's perspicacity.

'Which is my land?' This was a question which troubled David Menahem in his youth. The smouldering city of Baghdad which left behind fire and smoke, violence and screams? The same Baghdad which cast him aside as a stranger overnight? Or Haifa, which had always considered him an outsider?

After overcoming the canto of agonies from his childhood, David Menahem plunged right into the Arab–Israel conflicts: The Six-Day War, the invasion of Lebanon, the Intifadas … He saw, heard, endured it all. The heart became hard-bitten by the relentless wars and exiles. Abba knew that all those forced to flee their homelands, anywhere in the world, were frozen-hearted too. He knew that all the world's victims spoke about the same sorrows. Abba knew that it was the consuming fire of anxieties that made fathers hang down their heads.

'Bat, the regime is akin to a gang of criminals.' Abba sighed heavily, his storytelling interrupted temporarily. A police vehicle, with its deafening siren, rattled through the narrow street outside the main gate.

While studying Arabic literature and psychology at the University of Haifa, David Menahem met a girl. In the words of Solomon, '*a rose of Sharon*'. '*Beautiful as Tir'zah, comely as Jerusalem, terrible as an army with banners'*... Esther, born in an Ashkenazi family. She awakened David's love.

David could have been anyone; even greater than Solomon himself. But he was a mere Iraqi in the eyes of Esther's family. Though '*His eyes were like doves beside springs of water*', and '*His posture was stately, like the noble cedars of Lebanon*', the youth was just an Arab. How could those, swelling with pride at their Ashkenazi lineage, send off their precious daughter with such a man? Impossible! For David, Esther fought a battle which was more formidable than the Six-Day War. She emerged from *'the lion's dens, the mountains of the leopards'* ... '*to see if the vines had budded, and their blossoms had opened*' in David's vineyard. To see, '*if the pomegranates have blossomed* ...'

Abba laughed heartily, narrating the story which began with an exodus and ended with falling in love. Ruth could see a burning city behind that smile. A small boy trembling inside a dung-stinking truck ... the petrified look in the child's eyes while embracing his father, a tree struck by lightning ...

'Bat, if you are hampered by the terrors from the past, you cannot move forward effortlessly. Throw away those old bundles!'

Imparting ineffable courage and hope to Ruth, when Abba finished reading his life's story, the swing on Mariam's fig tree started swaying gently in the zephyr. Beyond, the apple trees quivered in tandem. Ruth felt embarrassed about the time spent brooding on insignificant problems. Scolding her grievances, shooing them off, she affirmed steadfastly: 'Sobbing over a bruised finger in the land of bullets? Goodbye, my sorrows ...!'

That day, she would send a WhatsApp message to Nina.

'Some burning cities can often laugh heartily.'

In reply, a question mark would reach her inbox. Some lives are half-solved puzzles, filled with questions without answers.

12

'FOR YOUR LOVE IS BETTER THAN WINE'

As she sat listening to the love story in the University of Haifa, Ruth started thinking of *him*. He, who showed her the way to the green meadows from the dark forests. He, who rowed his boat to reach her side across the surging, roiling river. '*Many waters cannot quench love, neither can flood drown it.*'

When the girl who escaped from Riyadh returned to Padamala, there was no trace of her ever having lived there. There was a mound of sand where the house once stood. A childhood that was wiped clean … Her Appan was still wandering through unknown lands. When the Mother Superior invited her to Amala Bhawan yet again, Ruth contemplated joining their congregation, unable to tolerate the loneliness any more. She would gain friends, who would work and pray with her. Besides that, she would get employed in Amala Bhawan's own hospital. It would have been the most desirable decision under the circumstances. However, it was in between, '*that he made haste like a young stag upon the mountains of spices*'. Such an unexpected arrival! Apparently, the young man had fallen in love with the slim, lissom girl who stuck like a shadow to the Mother Superior. When he confessed it in the churchyard, Ruth had gazed at Albert unbelievingly.

'Dearest, withdraw that glance of yours … I am rendered weak with passion.' Only Ruth heard his lips whispering those words.

Thus, forgetting the childhood which was tossed away by rain and storm, forgetting the ghoulish building in Riyadh, forgetting the abyss of loneliness, Ruth became Alby's co-traveller. Manjottil Tharavadu, his family house, was on the verge of collapse. Alby's father Lonappan spent his days languishing in the memories of the past, shambling around the farms and yard, holding his ancient, crook-handled umbrella. His mother, Kunjanamma, spouted grievances while lumbering her way from the kitchen to the veranda, dragging her body that weighed almost a hundred kilos. Teresa and Catherine were born in such surroundings.

However, before the onset of a Lent, the tiny joys ceased abruptly. A monstrous, overspeeding lorry came hurtling through a turn as Alby was returning home on his motorbike. Life was tossed up like a ball of feathers flying with the wind—destination unknown … Alby never walked again. The horror of that day haunted Ruth even in Nazareth.

Slowly, the pepper vines started drying up. The areca palm grove turned yellow; the coffee plants forgot to bloom. A Dubai agency came with a job offer for Ruth. Teresa was sixteen and Kathu was fourteen at that time. It wasn't the greed for money or the ambition to build a palace that motivated Ruth. She wanted enough money to ensure Alby's treatment at Vellore, and the education of their children. Her Dubai journey was decided suddenly. Lord, how the four of them had wept while hugging one another! Those tears had been the precious repast that sustained Ruth in the journey forward.

On hearing about Ruth's travel plans to Dubai, Alby's mother protested vehemently, while his brothers were openly sceptical. The neighbours gossiped away scurrilously. The Gulf journey of Ruth, Albert's better half, became a conundrum debated by the entire village.

She hadn't forgotten anything.

Varkkichan: (Seated on the portico, shaking his legs, clearing his throat loudly, occasionally peering inside the house) 'Are we facing such desperate conditions that the women of Manjottil have to go away to foreign lands? Forgotten about the aunt who went away to do nursing in Germany and married a Sayyip over there? Albert, Ruth will go away for good and you will end up ditched.'

Albert: 'Manjottil family bought all the property in Malabar with the money sent by the aunt in Germany, right? Forgot all that? By the way, if Ruth abandons me, I have no issues. Don't worry about me.'

Chackochan: (Scratching his bald head sheepishly and sneaking closer to Alby's bed) 'That is not the problem. Aren't we there for you? But who will take care of our parents if Ruth leaves? My wife Mercy has terrible back pain, as you know! We all know our mother's nature … she simply cannot adjust with anyone. Ruth is the only person she gets along with.'

(Ah, how compassionate! 'Aren't we there for you,' he says so sweetly … This Chackochan calculates the money owed even for buying a strip of paracetamol pills!)

Tea-shop proprietor Kanarettan: (The unspeakable secret revealed to the tea drinkers) 'Pretty women going off abroad, are we dumb to believe that it is for nursing work? … It's for the other work of terrorists! And this girl's beauty can turn heads.'

Kanthari Chettathy aka Green Chilli Woman: (Hand on head, eyes rolling in disgust) 'Leaving behind a bedridden husband and go wandering about in the Gulf? Domineering woman! Didn't she go off to Gulf back in her youthful, glory days? What happened afterwards? How great this family was once! This accursed girl stepped right in, and everything crumbled!'

Eli Kutty Teacher: 'Albert, Ruth is a smart girl. Let her go and work. Nurses earn very well in Dubai. All these gossipmongers also educate their daughters, and send them for jobs, don't they? They are just green with envy.'

Two months before the Gulf offer came, Ruth had gone to Ernakulam, with her friend Bincy from Kottiyur, to attend the

Israeli interview. Her medical tests were over and the visa papers arrived too. But the employment agency demanded eight and a half lakh rupees. How could they ever manage such a humongous amount? The Israel contract was for four and a half years. One could not return very quickly either. Ruth had requested a few months' extension to decide on the offer when, luckily, the Dubai agency entered the scene. Having sold off half an acre of property at a very cheap rate to a neighbour, Ruth handed over three lakhs to the agent. The very recollection of those moments made her shudder now.

It was due to sheer grace that Alby's Ruth was still alive, breathing in a land where the blessed footprints of the Lord lay imprinted; where she could follow the Good Shepherd's path through the pastures. Before reaching the Promised Land, one had to neccssarily experience a wandering in the desert, and swim across the Red Sea …

13

YOM KIPPUR

The orange groves, shimmering green and yellow by the Mediterranean shore, and the vineyards of Magdala city, which awaits the harvesters, have many stories to tell. The Golan Hills also have stories to narrate—how in the east, the Syrian army was fighting to assert the right to water and the right to life. And the river, emerging from the Sea of Galilee and surging towards the Dead Sea, has more tales to reveal, as it races desperately through the region between Jordan and West Bank. About devastated villages … about orphaned cities …

They stole away
Our bike rides,
Hill-climbing trips,
Our joyous running sprees
Under the shades of the fig tree,
Never to be reclaimed …
Yet,
Dreaming of the land becoming an Eden,
Dreaming of the day when the dead shall return,
Even today,
The river flows
Through our lives …

I was very good at climbing trees in my childhood. I would clamber atop branches which others could never conquer, often at dangerous heights. 'Ummu Sahal, better be on guard, your son is very adventurous!' the neighbours would warn Mama. My mother would simply smile in reply. She was secretly proud of me. Mama never stopped her son's courageous steps. The dark past had taught her that a timid boy would never reach anywhere in life.

When I was five, Baba had purchased a bicycle for me, paying money in instalments. I would circle the streets on my new bike. Baba would often say that I would become a fine athlete or engineer one day. The little boy on the bike grew up. He graduated in electronics from Technion, Israel Institute of Technology, at Haifa. Also, he became an artist and poet. Friends referred to him as 'the one whose soul was filled with Marcel Khalife's music; the one who assuaged his hunger by consuming Mahmoud Darwish's poems ...' But neither Mama nor Baba waited around to listen, to see, to be proud of all that.

(*Howdy Death, Hello Freedom,* Sahal Al Fadi)

On the tenth day after the Jewish new year, when the evening light was waning, Asher came home. Along with him was a tall, lean youth. He evoked the charm of tender, morning sunshine. The eyes, seemingly on the verge of tears, met Ruth's. The strand of straight hair on his forehead lifted in the breeze. He was the one who dreamt of cycling without a care to the heights of Mount Zion.

It was Yom Kippur. The Day of Atonement. The Day of Repentance.

Eema started heckling Asher, as soon as he entered, for not fasting. 'Non-believer! Infidel! Ought to throw you into the sea!' On hearing Eema's mutterings, Ruth remembered the vibhuti, the holy ash, and her Valiyammachi, back at Padamala. After returning from the church with the holy ash smeared on the forehead, her grandmother would deny even a drop of water to her till afternoon.

Yom Kippur's fasting regime was tougher than that. It stretched for almost twenty-four hours, from one sunset to another.

Eema would intermittently touch the mezuzah reverently and kiss her finger—and read the Torah. She would read 'The Book of Jonah'. It commemorated the Prophet, who, while running away to Tarshish, was thrown overboard and spent three days inside a fish's belly. Leah would not partake of any rituals. Instead, totally engaged with her laptop and mobile phone, she took delight in rebelling against Eema's dictums.

Abba perked up when Sahal arrived. 'Ah, here comes our poet!' He embraced the young man warmly. The trio sat under the fig tree and started their conversation. When Leah peeped out, Asher threw a twig at her. She pulled a face before disappearing. 'The lad who purifies himself with poetry'—that was how Abba praised Sahal. Due to his insistence, Sahal recited poems in English. The lines were so simple and clear that Ruth could translate them into her mother tongue.

Sahal's posture, as he stared at the overcast skies above Mount Olive, touched Ruth's heart. His eyes were welling up with tears. The voice was anguished, as if a thorn had impaled his heart. Ruth would frequently reminisce about those moments. She would remember that the peacocks in the desolate house by the hillside were dancing then.

'An orphaned childhood is like a sky filled with deep, dark rain clouds that persist forever. It is the same experience across the world. Nina, our sufferings are insignificant compared to that.' Ruth would message her friend. 'Ruthie, I am going to compile a book of your messages,' Nina would reply, with a plethora of emojis.

Although Abba seemed happy, a heavy unease crept inside Shalom with Sahal's arrival. Eema's prayers were disturbed. The Torah recitals were interrupted. While watering the garden, mother and son squabbled; their voices shrill in pitch. Whenever she became incensed, Eema would spout English. From the random volley of exchanges that flew around, Ruth could gauge that Sahal was the cause of the conflict. The bickering must have troubled him. The one who had planned to stay for a week left before the next dawn, his grey old bag dangling from his shoulder. The pained chirping of a wounded bird was heard for long amongst the grape vines in the backyard after he left.

It turned out well that Sahal left early. An officer, in a uniform of pale blue, gun in tow, dropped in that afternoon. The visit whipped up a storm at Shalom. Once the officer left, after an intense bout of interrogation, without seeing the one he came to find, Eema's screams began in earnest. She created a scene, adamant that Asher should cut off all contact with Sahal and that he should never bring his friend home again. Abba, indifferent to Eema's inciteful speech, appeared to be deliberating over matters. Asher was clearly perturbed.

Asher and Sahal had met during an art exhibition at the Hebrew University. The similarity of their thoughts brought them together; and soon they became tight-knit friends. The anti-Zionism which blossomed out in Sahal's sketches and poems had made him the cynosure of the police's eyes. Whenever they came searching for Sahal, Asher would prepare a hideout. Abba would get in touch with his friends in the police circles and somehow get Sahal out of trouble. But Sahal would keep writing, drawing and leading processions. The shoter would come searching yet again. This circle of events kept repeating at frequent intervals.

Sahal had garnered the attention of Palestinian media when he was hardly eight years old with a remarkable drawing. It depicted a young woman getting crushed by a bulldozer. It was around the time when human rights activist Rachel Corrie was killed brutally at the Gaza border. The eyes of the gun had been focused on the boy right from that point of time.

The parched day died; its thirst unquenched.

When the policeman entered Shalom, many bitter memories about Dubai regurgitated in Ruth's memory. The bristly hair on the man's head reminded her of date palm leaves. A woman stood inside a cold apartment on the nineteenth floor of a glass building, looking down at the sea. In the city of sand, Ruth saw yet again, the gold souk and a path veering off to a narrow gully with a suffocating, vault-like room. The two date palms which sprang up out of nowhere. The stinking hideaway behind the dustbin. Ruth could not sleep that night. Just like another night at the seaside mansion of Deira, she lay awake, watching the sea till sunrise.

A woman in purdah was walking, all by herself, towards the ferry boats, the abra, moored at the shore. She approached the sea in that desolate midnight hour and quietly vanished from sight. Someone dressed in a kandura followed her furtively. He too disappeared mysteriously into the darkness. The boats heaved rhythmically, as if they were the abodes of ghosts. Ruth looked towards the sea, waiting for the woman to return.

The cries of the seagulls were sounding exactly as on that day. The Maktoum Bridge across the Dubai creek was shaking in an earthquake. Ruth hadn't forgotten anything.

14

THE CITY OF GOLD

Events which turn life upside-down mostly occur unexpectedly.

That day, until she landed at the Dubai airport, Ruth had been overwhelmed by a sea of anxiety. In the flood of lights and sounds, she flowed like a leaf. What sort of a world was this! Everything was happening so fast! Everything was awe-inspiring and wondrous. Finally, everything turned topsy-turvy at the emigration counter. Ruth could not answer the questions posed by the Arab dressed in white. The sponsor's name and address, the details of her destination, phone number … Since the agency had promised to take care of everything, Ruth was unprepared for the questioning. The Arab glared at her, and pointing towards his left, asked her to step out of the line. Those who were behind her in the queue moved ahead smoothly. Time passed by … ten minutes, twenty minutes … an hour. The Arab was not paying her the slightest attention. Possibly observing the wilting, hapless woman, someone approached her.

'What happened? Are you alone? Do you need any help?'

He was a tall man, with a grave demeanour. After listening to her, the man offered her his phone. 'Call the agent.' Ruth desperately dialled the lone number she knew. 'The number you are calling is not available.' A tremor seized hold of her at that moment.

'Someone will come to pick me up. I have to clear the emigration procedure somehow.' Her voice sounded like a whimper.

'Don't worry, you have a valid visa. Right now, all you need is an address and a phone number. I shall help you with that.'

Consoling her thus, the good man walked to the counter and spoke to the Arab. By the time the emigration officer stamped her passport and called out 'Next', Ruth had started trailing behind the stranger. After he picked up his luggage from Belt Number 4, the man offered her a business card. 'Call me if you need any help.' At that instant, Ruth felt that the most enchanting voice in the world belonged to him. As new luggage dropped on to the belt, passengers moved past, retrieving their bags. Ruth's red airbag was nowhere to be sighted. She stood stupefied in front of the conveyor belt which was circling ceaselessly. The wait extended interminably. Would the person, who had come to pick her up, have left already? Ruth became frantic with worry. An official who observed her state advised her to give a complaint in writing about her missing bag; it was likely that someone had taken it by mistake. He helped her to draft an application.

As she walked, bewildered and confused, towards the 'Exit' sign, her mind rebelled. 'Ruth, you have been robbed the very moment you landed in Dubai.' Her handbag, containing her passport and purse, was her only possession.

Just as the agent had informed, Ruth saw a man holding a placard, 'Ruth, Kerala', standing in the lounge. A rather rotund, clean-shaven young man. The exasperation of having waited for long was visible on his face. Somehow, she got inside the car. The stress from losing her bag was getting to her. Along with that, there was a strong sense of foreboding. Ruth was obsessively wondering where the man was taking her.

'Is the hospital nearby?' The driver pretended to be deaf. Could it be that he wasn't a Malayali? Ruth repeated the question in English. Ignoring her completely, the man started gabbling in Hindi with someone on the phone.

'What a crude, mannerless man!' Ruth thought.

Four-lane roads stretched endlessly ahead. Towers were racing past the vehicle. They frightened her like light-spitting monsters. Far beyond, an eternal darkness reigned. She was feeling the exhaustion of a long journey.

'*Erangaan* ... Get down.' When Ruth jerked awake at the driver's harsh command, the car was standing before a huge building. When had she slipped off to sleep? Ah, the driver was a Malayali. She would get the details soon enough. Gathering her scattered courage, Ruth got out of the car. The very next moment, pointing towards the reception, the man started the car and whizzed away. Ruth mindlessly chased the vehicle for a while. It was a futile exercise. She couldn't even read the name of the building since everything was clouded in darkness. A dim glow emanated from the reception.

'Good evening.' A dark-skinned man raised his head from his phone at her nervous greeting. His head was closely shaved. Ruth was reminded of a wrestler. The man grinned widely at her; his teeth were startlingly white.

'Shahjahan!' the man hailed loudly. A lad appeared in an unlit corner, wearing a navy-blue uniform. He gestured that she should accompany him. When they were inside a lift, the boy yawned. Ruth asked in a rush, 'Where is this place? Is the hospital close by?'

Apart from staring at her dumbly, the boy did not respond. The lift started moving upwards with a grunting sound. Deafening Western music blared from the lift's sound system. There were two rows of numbers glaring at her from its blinking panel, counting up till 40. The lift came to a noisy halt at the nineteenth floor. When the lift door creaked open, Ruth leapt out in relief. She followed the boy through the dark corridors, navigating many twists and turns. Now she could see the board imprinted with the number '1967'. Ruth had no idea then that she would repeat the number to many people, many times, later. After opening the door and handing her the room-card, Shahjahan disappeared. The phone rang out shrilly then.

'Hello Ruth, welcome to Dubai! I am Freddie. I'll come there tomorrow. Take rest, goodnight.' The voice sounded effeminate.

'Freddie, are you the one to take me to the hospital? Why have you left me alone in this gigantic building? How will I get my lost bag back?' There were many questions Ruth would have liked to ask Freddie. Luckily, there was nothing precious in the lost airbag, except a diary and a photograph with Alby and the children. Of course, the saris inside the missing bag were an issue. But she could easily purchase a few after getting her salary. In the meanwhile, she would make do with the sets of uniform she would receive at the hospital. The main thing was, a guardian was going to arrive to take her to her destination. Ruth tried to reaffirm her own courage. She even felt a rush of affection for the name 'Freddie'. As soon as Freddie would arrive the next day, she should call Alby. Maybe Freddie would give her a Dubai SIM card.

When Ruth turned the bathroom tap, scalding hot water gushed out from the shower. Taken aback, she heartily cursed the inventors of such contraptions. Turning the handle left, right, up and down, and finally surrendering herself to the exploits of the water, Ruth washed herself clean of all the day-long journey's exhaustion. The air-conditioned room was spacious; there were double-layered glistening curtains and wall almirahs. Ruth was experiencing such luxuries for the first time. Like an exclamation mark stuck oddly in a sentence, she observed a dusky girl's image in the mirror. 'Don't be afraid. Everything will turn out fine!' Ruth consoled herself. As she covered herself and lay down to rest in the air-conditioned room, Ruth felt like laughing at her silly worries ever since she had landed at the airport. 'Poor mind of mine, how quickly you panic!'

Ruth slept like a log and it was very late when she woke up. Beyond the glass wall, she could see the sea. Speedboats were racing on the waves, froth and foam rising. Flocks of birds were in flight, crossing the sea. Was she on another planet? There was no remnant of the previous day's darkness or terror. She could have caught sight of the sunrise, had she awoken earlier.

Ruth and Alby had once watched the sunrise at Kurumbalakotta. It had been a surreal experience—seeing the sun rise through the mist surrounding a hilltop. Would the morning of this city be as beautiful? As she stood gazing at the glittering, quavering waves, a knock sounded at the door. As soon as she opened the door, a heavily built man of middle age stepped in briskly. An unsettling smell of deodorant accompanied him.

'I am Freddie. Did you sleep well?' He smiled.

She responded with another smile. 'I lost my bag and have no change of dress.'

'That's not a big worry ... You do have the documents, don't you?' The tone was kind.

His wide eyes looked attractive, but there was a gap in his front teeth, which was jarring. Freddie's lips were like those of a woman and his voice was effete too.

'Ruth, you are much younger than I expected. I was expecting to meet a rather portly woman of forty!' The man shook with laughter.

Ruth did not laugh. This man was blatantly talking about bodies with a strange woman. A Lothario, undoubtedly.

Freddie the Lothario settled himself in a chair. From her previous day's experience, Ruth had become wise enough to gather information as quickly as possible.

'Where are the other sisters staying? Can I shift there today? In which hospital have I been posted?' she asked hurriedly.

'Haha ... don't worry about it. I am there to take care of all that. My agency carries out the recruitment for the famous hospitals in the Gulf.' Freddie laughed loudly.

Was he the owner of the agency? Ruth had expected him to be the public relations officer. Agent Niyas had told her that the PRO would get her visa ready. As she stood dithering, the man continued.

'You might have to write a few more tests. I will give you all the necessary support. For a few days, you will have to stay here. It will take almost a week before you get hospital accommodation.'

'Freddie, but …' Even before Ruth could complete her sentence, the man interrupted.

'Don't worry at all. The company will bear all the expenses, including room rent, until you earn your salary.' He was turning more compassionate by the minute.

Trying to escape from his open leering, Ruth gazed at the sea. He came closer, as if trying to share a secret. The deodorant smell wafted closer too.

'It will take time to begin your hospital duty since many formalities have to be completed first. I guess, at least a month. You can even visit home in that time. I have something to be sent to Kerala. Look, you are being provided with a golden chance, denied to many others. You know, thousands are waiting for such an opportunity.'

As she stood flabbergasted, Freddie went on yammering. 'Most candidates who have arrived from Calicut are more qualified than you. But getting to know about your husband's accident …'

This man, who stared at her shamelessly, had all her personal information at his fingertips! Was she dreaming? Was this man, standing in front of her, a reality or a fantasy? The enormous mansion, the sea, this inexplicable moment … were they all true or figments of her imagination? 'I have something to be sent to Kerala.' Wasn't that what he just said?

'What do you want to send home, Freddie?' Her booming voice which leapt out even before she realized, left Ruth stunned.

The man came close, closer than breath, and placing his hairy, heavy hands on both her shoulders, he whispered, with an owner's affection: 'Relax, Ruth, relax. Shall tell you everything … later.'

Without revealing anything more, the man with the disturbing scent, slipped out of the door. 'I don't want any favours from you,

Freddie! I shall not accept whatever you offer. I will not obey your commands.' Ruth's mind reiterated a hundred times. Had it been a movie or a story, an attempt at molestation, or a threat at the very least, would have ensued at this point of time. Freddie hadn't turned out to be that treacherous. But, didn't his wide eyes warn, 'You will have to obey me'? Ruth's tension mounted. She slipped out into the corridor, after Freddie. Ruth felt the need to study the surroundings.

The corridor was convoluted; twisting and turning umpteen times, to the left and right. The room numbers were not sequential. Ruth became scared that she would get lost in that labyrinth. That man's smell was still wafting around—along with that disgusting leer. If only she could speak with someone, even a stranger! She contemplated exploring the streets below. Her sari looked rumpled. Yet, Ruth decided that she had to get out of the building.

A few young men sitting around in the lobby on her floor looked at her. A thin, old man was snoozing away, seated in a chair near the lift. As she tried to press the arrow button pointing down, the man jolted awake.

'Hey, the lift is out of service.'

The stentorian voice was in stark contrast to his physique. Ruth remembered the dreary sounds that had frightened her the previous night. Lord, there was no end to the mysteries around! After a lot of exploration, Ruth discovered the entry to the staircase winding down. But the door refused to budge even after much effort. 'Ruth, you have been locked away on the nineteenth floor!' A shiver passed from her head to toes!

Having nothing else to do, Ruth spent the time in her room, staring at the sky changing colours. She was served no food or water. Neither did she feel any hunger pangs. It was twilight when she remembered the man at the airport. The business card said that his name was Aravind. Ruth tried to dial Aravind's number. But the phone in the room was locked! 'Lord, what sort of trial is this! Am I in a fortress with no escape route?' She was dazed. 'Ruth, you have fallen into a terrible trap.'

The terror started at that moment. Darkness covered the sea. Hunger started gnawing at her. Ruth dialled the reception; but there was no reply. Fear was throwing her into a turmoil, much more than hunger. She was in a forest where wild animals were waiting to pounce on her. The old clock that was stuck on the wall, looking oddly out of place, emitted an ugly grumble. 11 p.m. Ruth wondered about the timing, since the clock had been silent till then. She wished to take a shower and sleep. After washing her clothes and hanging them to dry in the bathroom, Ruth caught sight of herself in the mirror—a woman, clad in a towel, shivering in the cold. Somehow, she managed to switch off the air conditioning. Pushing away the curtain, half-naked, she stood gawking at the lights twinkling on the sea surface. A voice rang out in her mind. 'Ruth, a secret camera could be recording your every move!' She scrambled to switch off every light.

Ruth could not sleep that night. Freddie was such a weird man! After reassuring her of handling every issue, he hadn't even arranged for her food. Ruth had heard of mafias who controlled their victims by denying them food. That was the easiest way to weaken both body and mind. She had to ensure that she had all the details the next morning; and reach the hospital as soon as possible. If the building was a hotel, she would have sighted some name-board somewhere. Nothing was to be seen. Probably it was an apartment block. But things were definitely awry … the man's sound … the crooked grin and the gap in his front teeth … the grin that grew into a raucous laughter.

When Ruth fell into an uneasy slumber, the sounds of airports and their announcements reverberated in her memory. There were ten or twenty men, holding the placard with her name: 'Ruth, Kerala'.

Lord, who was the real host among them? Who were the abductors? Ruth sweated and trembled.

Later, on many cold mornings in Nazareth, she would wake up sweating after reliving the same nightmare. Ruth would be shaking in terror, just as she had during that cold night back in the mysterious mansion.

15

BEYOND THE SEA OF TIME

Some songs evoke the odour of deserts. A smell that penetrates the senses and seats itself deep within. Ruth did not have the words to elaborate further. Was it the odour of the camel or of the petrichor? Was it the smell of a slender snake which slithered away, having shed its skin? Or was it the scent, emanating from a herd of gazelles, that coursed past, trampling the moonlight? She alone knew how the most traumatizing memories about the desert, could hide in a song. Such a song was waiting for Ruth in the ancient city.

'Akhot, would you like to come? I'll introduce you to someone from your land.'

Asher invited Ruth when setting off to Jerusalem. Leah was travelling with him. Abba had been uncomfortable throughout the night. The surgical area was sensitive, stinging. Ruth sat awake the whole night, giving him company. She was thinking of a nap during the day but sleep fled, crossing the Jordan River, when she heard the word 'Jerusalem'.

'That's a great idea. We wish to be home alone today.' Abba encouraged her. He felt guilty that Ruth was undertaking so much trouble on his behalf. Abba would remind her not to miss out on chances to enjoy herself.

'Thirty-five years since Mount Hermon encountered Tirzah city! Today, let the lovebirds reminisce about how the pomegranates were in bloom,' Leah teased. 'Look, she is blushing! Yet Queen Sheba pretends to be grave.' Leah planted a kiss on Eema's cheek.

Asher Menahem's car sped through the Mediterranean coast. The vast blue sea was on one side. Tiny, matchbox-like buildings speckling the hills, were on the opposite side. 'Those are settlements which mushroomed on erstwhile barren hills,' Asher explained.

An impassive-looking young man was leading his herd of goats along the roadside.

'The hills, once where his goats grazed.'

'Whose goats?' Leah lifted her head from the mobile phone. A flock of birds took flight, parallel to the rail tracks running between the sea and the road. Leaving behind the dignified city, crossing three or four fishing ponds, they were moving past some orange groves. On the roadside, beneath a date palm, a man and woman were standing. A donkey was grazing nearby. Ruth imagined that they were going from Nazareth to Bethlehem, David's city, to participate in a census. Asher started humming a carol tune then. He was no longer the young man who silently drove all the way from Ein Karem to Nazareth. Now he was chattering nineteen to the dozen and was shaking with laughter, listening to Ruth's pidgin English and Hebrew.

'Akhot, it will be easier for our Messiah, whose advent we've been awaiting for two thousand years, to arrive, compared to your struggle to master Hebrew!'

'Aha! Could it be that you are the Messiah? Your Eema keeps bragging about your great lineage!' Ruth answered saucily.

'His age too is that of the Crucified One.'

Leah joined in the banter. When it came to Asher, she was always in the opposite team. Eema would quip that the sibling rivalry began when she was a toddler! The ceasefire agreement that brother and sister had settled on would be violated frequently, similar to regions with territorial strife.

In the ancient building within the Old City, some wonders were awaiting Ruth. As they entered the outer gate, a song came floating in:

Arabikadaloru manavalan …
Karayo nalloru manavatty …

The Arabian Sea, a veritable bridegroom
And the seashore, lo, a pretty bride …

Joshua came out, seemingly stepping over the waves of the Arabian Sea, evoking remembrances of an ancient port city. His saba, grandfather, welcomed them with an open smile. Seeing a Malayali girl, Saba rowed towards his memories of old Cochin.

'Even though many of my friends and relatives migrated to Israel, in the great homecoming "Aliyah", we took another decade to return, my dear. It was the sixties then. We were waiting for our great-grandfather to pass away peaceably. Joshua's father Opher was around seven or eight years old. We left behind a thriving shrimp business in Cochin.'

Saba was listening to the hustle and bustle of Cochin. He was enthralled by the exciting shouts reverberating from the boat jetty. Shrimps and prawns were piled up before his eyes. Those who had arrived in search of the Promised Land overflowing with honey and manna ended up in a barren land crawling with centipedes and snakes. Life became inexplicable, like a ghost story. Nights and days went in toiling on the infertile land apportioned out to them. First, they tried flower cultivation. Then, they branched into production of vegetables. Beersheba's Nevatim became the equivalent of their village in Cochin.

'We are not into agriculture any more. My six children are working. Life in Jerusalem is not like Nevatim, dear. How expensive! We are living here for Joshua's sake. After two generations, nobody in the family knows a word of Malayalam. Joshua is clueless about the language.'

Saba was talking in perfect Malayalam, in an unceasing flow. Joshua gestured to Ruth, wondering whether she was getting bored.

Ruth gently shook her head to indicate that she wasn't. In truth, she was relishing Saba's talk. Another post for her vlog was getting ready! She could visualize the title: 'A Jewish family in Cochin, beyond the sea of time.'

Sabta, Joshua's grandmother, was getting a Kerala sadya—the traditional feast—ready. When Ruth peeped inside the kitchen, she was wonderstruck by the cooking implements from Kerala: puttu kutti, the cylindrical apparatus used for steaming the rice and coconut mixture, and the arakallu, the grinding stone! Saba grinned seeing her astonished look.

'Those are Sabta's treasures, which she carried from Cochin. The old lady does not allow anyone to touch them!'

The song from the Malayalam film *Bhargavi Nilayam* was playing in the background. The same haunting song which had transgressed into Ruth's life back in the day at Deira. She felt the desert maliciously hurling a fistful of sand towards her.

'The old man listens to this song a hundred times a day! Even if he misses reading the *Torah*, he shall not miss playing the song! He had a Malayali sweetheart, before he married me.' Sabta spoke with a grave face while Saba enjoyed an infectious belly laugh.

'I watched *Bhargavi Nilayam* two days before we left the Kerala shores, my dear. I remember sitting cross-legged on the sand in that old theatre ... Yes, the last memory of the homeland.'

Beyond the old curtains of the window, they caught a glimpse of a young man talking to Joshua. It was Sahal. The one who had arrived at Shalom on Yom Kippur and vanished mysteriously thereafter.

'Is this place his new hideout?' Leah's eyebrows furrowed.

'Here for a day,' Asher whispered.

'He might put Joshua's family into danger. Do they know about him?' Leah's face was pale.

'Why are you so anxious about Joshua?' Asher grinned meaningfully.

Saba was singing all the while, his voice trembling.

Kalakadalinte akkareyakkare,
Maranathin mookamam thazhvarayil…
Kannuneer kondu nanachuvalarthiya,
Kalkanda mavinte kombathu …

Far beyond the sea of time,
In the desolate valley of death …
On the bough of the honey-sweet mango tree
Moistened and fostered by my tears …

Saba insisted that they visit him again while bidding them farewell. He gifted an exquisite embroidery of a China net to Ruth. 'The land which we leave behind is like an unrequited love. It shall be attached to the heart forever.' Leah gazed deeply into Joshua's eyes. He quickly averted his gaze and adjusted Saba's kippah. Even when he waved goodbye, Saba was humming.

Arabikadaloru manavalan, karayo …

The return journey was through West Bank. Asher needed to meet someone urgently at Jericho. He had some information about Annie's disappearance. The news was showing the fractious happenings at West Bank. Though Leah warned that driving through West Bank in the darkness, amidst the unrest, was not advisable, Asher ignored her. Hardly had they driven a few kilometres when a petrol bomb exploded right in front of them. The car ahead was engulfed in flames. They had escaped by sheer good luck. When Leah created a furore, Asher diverted from that route. She scolded Asher until they reached Nazareth.

Ruth felt herself inundated with the rhythm and smell of the desert all through the journey.

Deira, the street of gold souks. The old house inside a monstrous gate—Noor Jehan Manzil. Three dilapidated cots, soiled paraphernalia and the rank, musty smell of centuries past. Ruth had reached the place on the third day after arriving in Dubai. She, the most helpless woman in the world …

16

NOOR JEHAN MANZIL AND THE CONDOM THEORY

It was the second day in the Golden City. A still sea, and grey skies. The promenade was deserted like a gravesite, utterly forsaken. There were seven or eight date palm trees with their umbrella-like foliage. Yonder, a few skiffs were floating on the waves. A flock of birds took flight across the sea. Ruth was hanging on for dear life, floating on an ocean of mysteries.

She had been shocked when the phone rang unexpectedly.

'Ruth, how was your day?' The effeminate voice of a man.

Silence.

'Why are you not talking?' The voice turned hard in a moment.

'I need a SIM to call home. They did not give me food yesterday. And I need to buy some dresses …' As soon as she started to speak, the man interrupted.

'Oh, Shahjahan forgot to give you the SIM, you mean? Idiot! I will fire him today. My assistant Usha Das will meet you today. She will handle everything. You will be clear about the next steps. Good day.'

Without allowing any leeway to probe further, the man cut the call. 'Why is he always in such a hurry? Would the sky fall on his head, if he paused a bit?' Ruth could guess that Usha Das would not be a harbinger of good news. Yet, she prayed that her instinct was wrong. Shahjahan came to the room then, carrying a tray. There was a bottle of water and some snacks. The food was hardly enough for a small child. As he scurried away, Ruth forcibly stopped him.

'Where is the SIM card which Freddie told you to give me?'

The lad gave her a strange look, which reminded her of a wounded puppy. The boy disappeared after shutting the door. A puppy, injured by stone pelting, started moaning inside Ruth's heart. The ancient clock on the wall grunted again.

'Ruth, Freddie's men are keeping watch outside the shut door. The well-built man at the reception might stop you if you attempt to run away.' Her gathered courage was dissipating. The sea beyond the glass walls was approaching her, violent and raging. News snippets sizzled through her mind—about snares, betrayals, sufferings. Even then, like a summer drizzle, a hope persisted that everything would turn out all right. Ruth planned a million things in her mind, then revised them. Every step had to be undertaken with utmost caution. Much tact was required. Freddie should never feel that an ingenuous village girl could ever outwit him. Stealthily, she would escape the snare. It was evident that if she was caught, both the public and the systems of justice would not support her. 'Why didn't you escape, when you knew it was a trap?' They would question her sceptically. How could a woman, without any money or even a phone connection, flee from danger in a strange city? That too, making her way out of a net laid skilfully by a mafia! Nobody would mull over such facts. Ruth decided to wait for Usha Das's arrival.

The day crawled by slowly. Like a bird that relentlessly hit its head at the crossbars of a window, Ruth walked to and fro in the square room, for a hundredth time. Her mind clamoured to escape but she stifled the urge, sensing it would lead to more peril. The clock ticked away the hours: two, three, four. But Usha Das never made an appearance. There seemed to be no point in waiting for the lady anymore. All of Ruth's fortitude was slowly abating. Even her strength to walk out of the room was lost. If she was forced to spend another night in the room, hungry and forlorn, she would lose her mental balance.

'Lord, my Lord, do not forsake me!' Ruth stepped out of the room, ready for battle. The phone started ringing that instant. 'Should I pick up the receiver or not?' The ringing did not cease and she hesitated. Waves were engulfing the bizarre mansion. They could swallow her at any moment. Anxiously, Ruth re-entered the room. The same voice of that man … the sound of a woman.

'Where are you off to? Don't even dare to think of getting away! We will simply send you to jail on some trumped-up case, Ruth. You will never see the outside world again. You are under my observation. Be a good girl!'

'Oh God! What sort of a trial is this?' The man was observing every movement of hers from some remote corner! Death was preferable to this life. Ruth felt dizzy. Every object in the room seemed to be whirling around her. She was falling into a great colourless void, exhausted, shattered.

When Ruth opened her eyes, someone was sprinkling cold water on her face. Two arms helped her up. A mellow, soft voice spoke to her.

'I remembered my elder sister on seeing you. But I don't know how to help you.'

It was Shahjahan. He retrieved a few currency notes from the pocket of his uniform and squeezed them inside her handbag.

'Pack quickly and reach the back of the building. I will hire a taxi for you. See, I know the driver. Ask him to take you to Karama church. The idea struck me after seeing the crucifix that you wear. Someone will help you there. I am sure Allah will protect you!'

Shahjahan, who hurried out, turned to whisper cautiously, 'Don't accompany me. Move out after five minutes. Don't use the lift; the emergency exit is towards the left. If you cannot make it, please don't curse me! I am risking my life and job for you.'

His footsteps receded. Ruth's heartbeats grew louder. She felt the building shake as if caught in the throes of an earthquake. Every minute stretched like an hour. Finally, she made her way out of the cold, frozen walls … As the door shut, the ugly grunt of the clock resounded from inside. The phone was ringing again. Shrugging off both sounds, she moved forward. Fortunately, she encountered nobody in the corridor. The old man was not seated in front of the lift either. Turning left, Ruth ran past the closed doors. After racing down the winding staircase of the nineteen floors, panting and heaving, she met Shahjahan on the ground floor. His eyes were blinking in terror, like those of a fish gasping for air on the shore. Hiding behind pillars, she manoeuvred her way out through the narrow back door.

In the backyard parking, a taxi with a reddish top, was waiting for her. After Shahjahan whispered something into the driver's ears, the rescue-vehicle started whizzing past the gigantic buildings. 'Fast … fast …' Ruth's heart was pulsating crazily. The path to the church appeared interminable. After crossing a few traffic signals, the Pathan driver started panicking. Was a vehicle trailing them? Apparently, it had been following them from the hotel parking. It was changing course along with their vehicle. Would Freddie sit calmly as his victim fled from his armoured Ravana's fort? He had tracked the taxi's number, and was sure to catch her before she reached the church! Ruth gasped for air. Suddenly, the driver diverted the car to a side path. The car chasing them was not in sight any more.

'Ghabarana mat! Taqleef kuch bhi nahi hoga.' The man consoled her, observing her frantic state. Shahjahan must have informed him about her. 'Allahu Akbar …' The call of the muezzin was heard, undulating in the air. Some people were praying on the meadow to the right of the road. A woman in purdah stood at a bus stop. As the taxi paused due to traffic, Ruth caught strains of Malayalam. She saw the purdah-clad woman run towards a bus that stopped nearby.

'Muche idhar chhodo,' Ruth pleaded.

'Church jaana hai na?' The driver looked back doubtfully.

'Nahin, idhar hi chhodo.'

As she stretched the currency notes that Shahjahan had gifted her, the driver declined her offer. 'Maafi mushkil. Salamu alaikkum.'

Was he showering compassion on a desperate human being? Sometimes God appears in the form of a Pakistani. After alighting from the taxi impulsively, Ruth boarded the bus which had started moving. Some decisions, taken in a moment's whim, can determine the course of our lives.

She made her way to the side of the purdah-clad woman and seated herself. *Lord, where am I going?* Her heart was palpitating in panic.

'I am Noor Jehan.' The woman in purdah smiled at her.

'Ruth.'

'Ruth, where are you off to?'

A sob broke out from Ruth, stunning Noor Jehan. Twenty pairs of eyes turned to stare at her from the seats in front. Ruth abhorred being looked down upon as a pathetic, helpless woman. As the bus trundled through the city, she started narrating the events of the past few days to Noor Jehan.

'I don't know how I can help you ... See, I am struggling to make ends meet. I work in four houses. Count the rent, food expenses, cost of taxis, money to be sent home ... what is left?' Noor Jehan spoke dejectedly. 'Listen, one hears lots of horror stories in this city, much worse than yours. You are educated, aren't you? Still you end up trapped and now howl about it! You should know that in this city, thousands of nurses work with dignity, taking care of their families. Try to find some way to survive! I get annoyed at the sight of weeping and sobbing. Once I tried to help someone and was badly betrayed. She was a real fraudster! I have escaped like you from an Arab's home, where I went for my first job. I remember running through umpteen gullies that night. The barking of the dogs that were chasing me still gives me the jitters! I spent the night in a bus shed, frozen, terrified … In the first bus at dawn, I went to the embassy … Allah!'

Noor Jehan looked into Ruth's eyes deeply.

'Don't worry, come with me tonight. We will make a plan after reaching my room. Allah the Most Compassionate will show a way.'

The woman who was the personification of a scream followed Noor Jehan. After disembarking from the bus, they crossed the gold souk and entered a huge gate. It was an ancient villa. There was a small room in the back with three cots, a small washroom and a narrow kitchen.

'This is Noor Jehan Manzil,' the woman said and smiled.

Stepping inside Noor Jehan Manzil, Ruth felt joy and relief, as if finding a hole to hide in. She was famished, having been denied food for two days in a row. She took the lone cucumber in the fridge and ate it without even removing the skin. Then she gorged on three pieces of bread before gulping down two cups of black coffee.

'I am yet to be paid for my work from three places. One person paid my dues. By the time I settled the taxi's dues, my wallet became empty. You are still hungry, aren't you? Please be patient for a little longer. Kanya will bring something.' Noor Jehan sighed.

After some time, another woman, Kanya, entered Noor Jehan's palace. She was taciturn by nature, and did not even acknowledge Ruth's presence. When she did, she glared at Ruth with subtle hostility. In Ruth's memory of that day, Kanya's entry at the twilight hour, carrying two huge parcels, stood out with crystalline clarity.

'I was waiting for you. Couldn't bring myself to request for food from the opposite shop. I am two months behind in my payment. The bastard might ask for a different form of recompense!' Noor Jehan laughed.

'False pride will not fill an empty stomach, Noor ji.' Kanya sounded displeased.

After placing kubbus on a plate with flowery designs, and liberally pouring dal curry over it, Kanya proclaimed, 'Manna of the desert!

Eat well. Nobody will starve in this land where you get unlimited kubbus for two dirhams.' Ruth would often remember Kanya's pithy words later in life.

She felt fatigued after having food. The fire and brimstone of Sodom and Gomorrah submerged her memories. 'Hey Ruth, how many cameras of that gargantuan mansion must have recorded your escape! Lord, may Shahjahan be saved from Freddie's cruel retaliation ...' That was her solitary prayer then. Stinging and burning while recollecting the events, Ruth slipped into a deep sleep.

Dawn. She was all alone when her eyes opened. Both Noor Jehan and Kanya were gone. Ruth became flustered. A note had been left by her bedside. 'Good morning! Hope you slept well. I called the number on the business card which you got from the stranger at the airport. Want to hear something curious? He is Aravind of the radio channel! I have known him since a long time. He is a fine gentleman. He will take care of matters now. So, no worries, my dear. I shall return quickly after work. Please do not go outside, okay?'

Ruth felt a great relief wash over her. A way out was right in front! By the time she went to freshen up, there was a song on her lips. Suddenly, the sound of a key turning in the lock was heard. Kanya walked in like a storm. Following her, a short, flabby middle-aged man. Though the man looked shocked at sighting Ruth, Kanya pulled him inside.

'Come inside, now! Don't dilly-dally. She is my dost. Koi problem nahi.' As Ruth stood flabbergasted, the stranger's lascivious eyes started evaluating her.

'Listen, girl, I have no objections if you want to watch! It will be good if you get out for a bit. Just ten minutes would do. Even that time is too much for these sorts of men!'

Kanya had loosened the strings of her semi palazzo bottoms by then, shouting to the man, 'Get a condom, hurry up!' Ruth forced her frozen limbs to move, and almost leapt through the door. She stood gaping in the scorching sun. The sun, unaware of the happenings, blazed fiercely. Inside the house, she heard Kanya holler, 'The money first, you yokel!'

Ruth shut her ears. She could see two more doors nearby. One was open. Who was inside that room? Another Kanya? Yet another condom man? What if she were to run away somewhere? But where? How far would she run? She walked towards the porch of the villa and stood cowering beneath the yellowing leaves of the drumstick tree. She could swear that an owl hooted at that moment.

The Hindi-speaking fellow hurried outside, his lust satiated. His wrongly buttoned flaming yellow-coloured shirt and the lecherous look he threw at her, haunted Ruth often. And on each occasion, the owl's hoot would trouble her.

Certain humans are birds. And certain birds are humans.

Ruth was horrified about returning to Kanya's room. More customers might troop in. She would have to abandon the room and run every time. The gate opened by the condom man was still unlocked. Ruth stepped outside. The street was jam-packed with cars that were racing past. It wasn't safe to stay there any longer. As she walked further, Ruth noticed a by-lane to the right. There were two date palms offering welcoming shade and shelter. It seemed they had sprouted just for her. A huge waste-bin stood next to the trees. Away from the sight of the vehicles, Ruth crouched behind the bin. A few cats were scratching and clawing one another, creating a ruckus. The afternoon sun was scalding. The last drop of moisture in her body was evaporating. Her tongue was drying up fast. If only Noor Jehan returned fast! Ruth became feverish and a severe migraine set in. The smell of fried fish wafted from nearby. The yowling of the cats became intolerable.

A little boy, who had come to throw away the household waste, stared at her wonderingly. With great kindness, he extended a half-sucked chocolate towards Ruth. The child turned back thrice to look at her, before he disappeared from sight. Tears streamed from her eyes. 'Lord, I will die parched and thirsty in this unknown city

... The municipal workers will retrieve the unidentified corpse of a woman from the street ...'

Ruth opened her eyes with a start when Kanya shook her awake.

'Hey, why are you sitting beside a waste bin?'

Kanya pulled Ruth to her feet. She was fresh after a shower, and her hair was loose. She was no longer the fiery Bhadrakali of the recent past. Now she was dressed in a sleeveless top and jeans. Her cheeks were rouged and a pleasant perfume wafted from her.

'Here is the room key. Don't tell Noor about the escapade, okay?' Kanya bestowed a blazing smile on her.

'You are all very decent human beings, right? No god came to rescue Kanya when she lived as per dictates of decency. It was this body which saved me and my children. This rounded, curvy body of mine! This is a dirty game which ends in a condom, that's all!'

Whenever she remembered Kanya later, those scalding words would fall into Ruth's ears again and again. She would see the fiery smile. Just like the day before ...

A car came rushing into that scene of uncertainty.

'Do you see that young man in the car? Poor boy, what he actually needs is counselling. Someone who caresses him and showers him with affection! That's why he comes searching for me.' Swallowing most of what she yearned to say, Kanya moved hastily towards the vehicle while directing a word of caution towards Ruth.

'Get inside the house, away from the sun! You might die of dehydration. Dear, the desert heat can be treacherous.'

Sitting in the passenger's seat, counsellor Kanya started joking with the young man. They soon disappeared from Ruth's line of sight. A bird took flight above the sand-coloured buildings and perched on one of the date palm trees. The ripe, red clusters of dates moved in the breeze.

Even with the passage of time, in Nazareth, ensconced in Shalom's affection, Ruth would get singed, remembering that searing mid-afternoon sun. The date palm trees, bridging death and life, would spring up inadvertently in front of her eyes. Lives were not like ripe dates and the sweetness would not increase with the heat. She knew that truth.

The heat surged, and so did her exhaustion. Ruth staggered towards Noor Jehan Manzil. It was then that a four-wheeler negotiated a sudden curve and sidled up to her, slowing down.

17

THE PROPHET

Kanya's laughter echoed, as if emerging from the depths of a cave.

'Ruth, man does not live by bread alone, but because of the words that fall out of my mouth too.'

Kanya was pulling her by the right hand and ascending the mountain. 'Stop, Kanya, stop! What are you doing?' Ruth was panting with fatigue. Now they were on the terrace of a building which had one hundred and sixty storeys. All the grandeur of the star-city was spread ahead, on all sides.

'If you follow what I say, the whole of Dubai will be yours. All that you see belongs to me.' The wind besieged all the massive mansions.

In the next frame, Teresa appeared. She was running through the farm ridges. There was a furious mob chasing after her. 'Teesa, faster, faster ...!' Ruth's breathing became rapid.

'Amma!' Teesa's scream. Ruth woke up in utter shock.

Should she call Teesa? No, it would be midnight back home. She must be asleep. Nina would often remind her that teenage was a bizarre phase—unpredictable and slippery. The mind would slither inside an abyss at unexpected moments and depression could overwhelm the psyche. The wings might fold unexpectedly, while soaring high and all enthusiasm could be lost. Sometimes, a manic high could take over the reins. One should closely embrace teenagers.

Kathu was garrulous by nature. She would chatter about everything, always. How Daisy teacher encouraged her to be a doctor, how the moustachioed man on the roadside stared at her, how the kite seized the chick, all of it … Teesa was the quintessential listener. 'Amma, are you sleeping well? Is the migraine troubling you still? Which book did you read today?' She would persist. Ruth would not get a chance to intercede. Teesa was also a mistress par excellence at hiding things; shrewder than mother earth herself. She was a cloud that hesitated to rain, and floated on the ripples of the river instead. A cloud, which bore the entire weight of the skies. Who could ever behold the lightning and thunder within her? Ruth wiped her eyes.

Abba was coughing. He needed another round of nebulization. She went inside the room. Abba continued to be an olive bough tossed by the wind, until Asher arrived for Shabbat. That was the pattern. They heard about rocket attacks by Hamas on the farms at the border. The wheat fields near Nir Am had caught fire. Eema had gone berserk after watching the news. Abba was saddened too, and his face showed the stress.

'Bat, haven't you slept yet?' The sightless eyes were glittering. 'Go and sleep. I am perfectly okay.'

She poured some warm water into a glass. After taking a sip, Abba smiled.

'If you aren't sleepy, let us read.' His eyes were curious like those of a little child. He searched through the bedside table and pulled out *The Prophet*. How precisely Abba's hands reached their goal! He would keep thc regularly used items at specific places. Even in half sleep, he would be able to find those objects. Sometimes, he would even open pages of books with his favourite passages! It was true that when vision faded, the senses of hearing, smell and touch became sharper. Asher would reiterate that Abba had an ever-open third eye. Whenever he came after a trip, Abba, without much prelude, would ask him whether he had met such and such a person in his journey! Asher would stand stupefied at that prescience.

'Come now, read!'

The clock in the drawing room was knocking at time's door … tick, tock. Apart from Abba's serene breathing, there was no other sound. In a low voice, Ruth started reading.

'You can muffle the drum, and you can loosen the strings of the lyre; but who shall command the skylark not to sing?'

'Bat, I am afraid for him. The boy is led by the laws of his conscience. Not the laws of the land.' Abba was getting anxious. Age enervated a man, that was a fact.

'Those taken by the shoter never return, Bat.'

Not knowing how to console Abba, Ruth followed the Prophet.

'While you build your sand towers, the ocean brings more sand to the shore, and when you destroy them, the ocean laughs with you.'

The sea laughs along with the innocent always!

Abba completed the lines in the tone of a person without refuge.

'But what of those to whom life is not an ocean, and man-made laws are not sand towers?'

He started wheezing and coughing without respite. Ruth gave him warm water and gently stroked his back.

'His focus and consciousness are on the horizons unreachable to me … even in my dreams.' Abba struggled to breathe.

Leah, disturbed by the sounds, came to check on them.

'Ruth, I will stay with him.'

'Bat, you have to go to work tomorrow. Go and sleep.' Though Abba insisted, Leah did not budge. She held on to Abba's hand. Leah behaved like a child at times, especially when she was disturbed. Her American trip was getting delayed. She had not received admission calls from her dream universities. She wanted to try again next summer. In the interim she had managed to get a temporary assignment in the Haifa oil refinery. It entailed an hour's drive.

That night, sleep was elusive; Ruth spent many hours tossing and turning on the bed. The foxes were howling from the den near the hillside. The surroundings glistened in the moonlight. As usual, the

Lady of Bethany came walking towards her. Whenever Ruth's heart was bruised, Mariam would appear from nowhere. The graceful gait, with the head held up proudly and arms flowing loose, was indelibly imprinted in Ruth's mind. The same dress—pale yellow robe. Dusting the small stool, Mariam seated herself comfortably.

'*Restrain not your wings to squeeze through narrow windows*,' Mariam completed the Prophet's words, throwing a languid glance at the moonlit night outside. '*Your children are not your children. You may give them your love, but not your thoughts.*'

Mariam dropped a kiss on Ruth's forehead. Her lips burnt like smouldering embers. A dark light was ascending the hills then.

Inside Ruth's heart emerged the picture of a young man dressed in a navy-blue helper's uniform. The crumpled dirham currency notes with the motifs of the Arabian oryx and the falcon that he offered her ... Vultures seated in a row over the sand mounds. A wounded bird crossing a desert ... The Deira memory flapped its wings inside her mind. Dubai city must be remembering another Ruth. Her memory was traversing many kibbutzes and small towns, towards a city whose belly held many millions of expatriates. A very forlorn memory.

18

WOMEN WHO GO TO THE ENDS OF THE EARTH, CARRYING THEIR HOMES ALONG

'The cartwheeling of many inexplicable events' would be the best summary of Ruth's Dubai days. To understand what happened when Kanya left her alone by the date palms, one should be introduced to certain other characters. Some people who entered Ruth's life out of the blue.

Only later did Ruth become aware of the happenings in a radio station in Dubai on that day through the station director Aravind. Radio Jockey Shivakami was the anchor of a live programme. Quick repartees and a gentle demeanour had made Shivakami a favourite of many listeners.

When Shiva was responding to Lakshmi who had called about the inherent fairness in snipping off caste-indicating surnames, Rafeeq, at work on the switchboards, gestured to Shiva to play it down. The segment was called *Between Us*, and the topic that day was 'Women who go to the ends of the earth, carrying their homes along'; the listeners' experiences and perspectives were coming in waves.

Shivakami had given her introduction after deep research on women who had left the shores of Kerala to seek other lands, starting from the early 1920s. The migration of women, primarily medical workers and teachers, to Africa, Europe, America and Singapore started much before the exodus to the Gulf countries. Nurses, doctors, teachers, artists, engineers, gaddamas or domestic workers, beauticians, business managers, researchers, entrepreneurs … a variety of female universes! Those who pride themselves on the knowledge of male migration from the age of the old shipping vessels forget the phenomenon of female émigrés, who went to different places, at many different time periods. They wilfully overlook the patience and tears of those pioneering women, and the families who survived due to their hard work and dedication.

It was when Shivakami was flying high with the female astronauts from India that Kalyani Menon called in live from Deira.

'Shiva, I am in my office. My son called me to speak about a helpless woman. If only someone in the vicinity can help her …' Kalyani was pleading. 'My son saw her sitting by the waste-bin. She was dressed in a sari and was fatigued. My child is weeping, "Amma, she will die in the sun!"'

When Kalyani started elaborating on the location, Shivakami intervened.

'I will call you back. Don't reveal it in the live programme.'

Rafeeq quickly played a classic song, with lyrics that highlighted 'the poetic imagination which equated a woman to a teardrop'. Another call came then. Shivakami mockingly threatened that she was banning the unbearable 'tear drops' forever from her programme, before attending the new call.

'Can you share Kalyani's location? The woman she spoke about might be the gaddama missing from my Arbab's house.' It was a man's voice, grave and hassled.

'Tell me your name.'

The man cut the call without answering Shivakami.

'There was something eerie about that guy! Wasn't there something creepy about that call?' Detective Rafeeq, who always read between the lines, digging up more than the obvious, voiced his apprehension. Shivakami and Rafeeq rushed to Aravind's cabin with the number of the stranger who had called. It turned out to be a grocery store's number. The shop owner, Shaji, hadn't made the call. The radio was blaring in the background and there was a crowd in the shop. Shaji recollected someone requesting to make a local call. The grocery shop was situated at Karama. The shop owner could not provide any more information.

It was then that Aravind remembered Noor Jehan's call. She often joined the live programme and sang songs enthusiastically. That very morning she had requested him to help a woman whom she had met on the way home. Aravind had forgotten about the matter, caught in the melee of the studio. He had to record the interviews of two politicians who had recently arrived from Kerala. Since that assignment was unavoidable, he had decided to postpone the visit to Noor Jehan's place by a few hours.

How could Aravind ever imagine that by the time he reached the ancient villa at Deira, Ruth would have disappeared!

'She was fast asleep when I left for work. No trace of her when I returned! Her bag is still here. I am afraid she is in some grave danger. Sir, we have to find where she is!' Noor Jehan stood gloomily by the grimy gate.

Aravind was taken aback on seeing Ruth's passport. The same woman whom he had helped a few days earlier at the airport—the helpless lady who could not provide a contact address. If anything untoward happened to Ruth, the cops would come investigating him! It was Aravind's address that was given at the emigration counter. Aravind found himself trembling. It was inherent kindness which had propelled him to help the poor woman. But that had turned out to be a big blunder. How would they ever trace a woman, who did not even have a phone connection, among the millions of humans living in that great city? Who was the stranger who had called in during the dial-in programme? Aravind decided to get in touch with the Indian embassy promptly.

Ruth became aware of these incidents much later, when Aravind apprised her. The city of light had been weaving a snare for her when these events transpired.

19

ROCKEFELLER MUSEUM

The Rockefeller Museum is situated in the east of the city. The building stands north-east of Jerusalem's Old City walls, at Sheikh el-Karim.

Working at the Rockefeller Museum, that held many historic enigmas, was Asher's dream job. Dr Eilat Mazar, of the Hebrew University at Mount Scopus, was his beloved guide and mentor. She was the most famous archaeologist of Israel. He participated in conferences with Dr Mazar and they wrote many research papers together. Asher immersed himself in research work, disregarding the passing of days and nights. For him, his work was a source of immense joy.

It was during a trip to Jerusalem when Asher took Ruth to the Rockefeller Museum: the same journey, where she had posted about Mount Olive and Calvary in her vlog. Ruth was busy creating and deleting the vlog post in her imagination. 'There are certain things you alone can speak about. Your task is to discover those nuances.' Asher prompted her gently. Neither he nor Ruth had any inkling of the events lying in wait for them at the museum.

Ruth captured Asher's image in her mobile camera as he entered the main gateway. A few pigeons were pecking around the well-manicured yard. There were red flowers moistened by autumnal mists. As she started capturing the images, there was a sudden hullabaloo near the front gate. The security guard was pushing away an old man. The man showed his identity card and started arguing vociferously. In that skirmish, the aged man fell down. As if he had sprouted from out of the blue, Sahal appeared on the scene. He helped the old man to his feet and started pacifying the guard. Disregarding all pleas, the security guard dragged the old man down ten steps, hitting him remorselessly with the butt of his rifle all the while. Until he crossed the parking lot and gate, the guard continued assaulting him. Ruth's mobile was silently recording the events.

'Hello, no photography!' A sudden intercession by a museum worker.

'Keep your phone inside,' Asher whispered. He showed his identity card to the man, soothing his concerns.

Sahal sat dejectedly on a bench in the quadrangle inside.

'This is the ninth time they are kicking that poor man out! He is a brilliant artist, born and brought up in this land. But they deny him entry on the mere suspicion that he is connected with Hamas,' Sahal fumed.

'It is this benevolent attitude of yours which makes the police adore you! Just two days before, we got you out of a mess. Now you have started again!' Asher was irked.

Remembering Abba's narratives, Ruth posed her question.

'Is this the Palestine Archaeological Museum?'

'Yes, after the Six-Day War, Israeli military seized control,' Asher answered, stepping inside the garden.

'Can we see the Qumran Scrolls? Abba told me about the ancient Bible scrolls and testimonials of war retrieved from the Qumran Caves,' Ruth said eagerly.

Asher was impressed with Abba's tutelage.

'But those are stored underground in the National Museum now. You are seeking what is inscribed and that which ignores the unwritten truths!' Sahal's voice evinced his ire and annoyance.

As they surveyed the surroundings from the terrace, the bearded artist was sighted once again. A police vehicle was patrolling nearby. The old man's hand moved quick as lightning. The stone shattered the glass window of the vehicle. The officer, dressed in blue, sprang down from the vehicle and brutally hit the man's head with the butt of his gun. He collapsed on the ground. In an instant, the screaming man was dragged into the police car and it disappeared around the corner. It was sheer coincidence that these scenes were captured by the mobile of Ruth Albert, the video blogger.

Ruth boarded the bus to Nazareth from the Jerusalem Central Bus Station. Asher did not leave until the bus departed. It was when the bus rushed forward, crossing small towns, hills and valleys that Ruth noticed Mariam of Bethany seated by her side. She was chanting a psalm in her mellifluous voice.

'How beautiful are your tents, Jacob
Your dwelling places, Israel.'

The face of the old artist appeared in Ruth's mind. If life stretched ahead, what more would he dare to sketch? Definitely not the beautiful tents of Jacob. Neither would he draw the minarets of Jerusalem. Perhaps, the darkness and nakedness inside the prison. Ruth felt that the man's face resembled another Nazarene, who was dragged by the soldiers.

'I went to Bethany,' Mariam intoned, stopping her humming.

'To Bethany? Was the family of Annie, who disappeared from Nazareth, still in Bethany? Mariam, do you know them?' Restraining her questions, Ruth started ruminating. Leaving behind the turquoise hills, the bus moved through the 'lake of roses' in the valley of Sharon, between Mount Carmel and Tel Aviv.

Mariam looked hopeless and despondent.

'Ruth, if the Lord had taken the human guise now, they would have stopped him at all the eight gates of Temple Mount. He would never be able step on the stone ways of the Old City. He would not be sentenced to crucifixion. Instead, the punishment would be a drone attack.' Mariam sighed deeply.

'I have started a revolutionary movement at Bethany. Let the battle-hungry Goliaths beware! Not another blood drop of an innocent should be shed in Judaea again!' Stars sparkled in Mariam's eyes. Years later, when she left Nazareth, Ruth would recollect Mariam's words with a shudder. The week-long mourning ritual 'Shiva' was being observed in Shalom then.

The scenes at the Rockefeller Museum did not find a place in Nazareth. Asher had warned Ruth against posting such matters in her vlog. Instead, thousands watched Mount Olive which Ruth climbed as the sun was westering, the stone archway of the All Nations Church, the grave of King David and the Garden of Gethsemane. They would also catch a glimpse of the shut Golden Gate faraway, as Ruth stood on Mount Olive. Spectators saw the Kedron Valley and the by-lanes where olive and fig trees stood as sentinels. And the narrow alleys, forbidden even in dreams, to those dispossessed of their homeland.

After two days a 'man missing' news appeared in the Palestinian newspaper *Al-Hayat al-Jadida*.

Asher called Ruth frantically. 'I need the videos you recorded that day at the museum. It is very urgent.'

The scenes caught on her mobile would appear on the Facebook page of 'Warrior of Light', leaving Ruth astounded. Al Jazeera channel would further transmit the news. Social media became a tumultuous space with the case of the missing artist.

The police interrogated Asher based on the updates provided by the museum security: that a woman, accompanied by a researcher working in the museum, had captured the events in her camera. Since the closed-circuit television showed images of Asher and Ruth entering the museum when the old man was being assaulted outside the gate, they could not point fingers at the duo. The follow-up investigations of the police focused on the vehicles that arrived in the museum parking lot. A few passersby and some car owners were summoned to Mount Zion police station. The video posted in the 'Warrior of Light' Facebook page was edited very efficiently. Nobody realized that it was taken from an elevated place.

That was just the beginning. After that, many scenes which lay in wait for Ruth in the vicinity of Jerusalem started appearing on the page of 'Warrior of Light'. Sometimes, a procession through the Muslim Quarters. Else, an incident at Temple Mount, the football game between children of two rival—brother—nations, in the ground where two roads intersected, at the junction of the four quarters; and the dejected gait of a woman selling lucky charms and talismans.

A message reached the inbox of Nazareth vlog.

'*Write your sad times in sand; write your good times in stone.*'

—Bhargavi Kutty Bernard Shaw

A bird, wounded by sand, started fluttering inside Ruth. Wrapped in a blanket, listening to Abba's wracking cough, Ruth remembered an old version of herself, before she reached the city of stones. She was standing beyond the 'Bridge of Return', the King Hussein Bridge, which passes over the Jordan river, symbolizing the exile of the Palestinians. She remembered a group of kind-hearted human beings, who took along a helpless woman with them. The woman seemed to be staring ahead, at a burning island, indifference writ large on her face. The city of Dubai crouched alongside. Deira, perhaps, was remembering her.

20

HAKUNA MATATA

Valiyammachi used to tell Ruth that the Lord assigned our guardianship to unknown people, without our knowledge. In the excruciating days of trial she faced in Dubai, Ruth acknowledged this was true.

Ruth was drowsily lying on a bed, the saline drip's coldness having a soporific effect. She was clueless about the duration of her sleep. As she slowly opened her eyes, someone gently caressed her forehead. She felt it was her daughter Kathu forcing her mother's eyes open.

'Hello, dear! Are you okay?'

No, it wasn't Kathu's voice.

'Dead asleep? Frightened me a bit! I am Dr Shahana.'

The same voice again, as if reverberating from a deep well. Hospital smells around. Pitch darkness. Faraway, at the end of the earth, three hurricane lamps … sounds scattering across the world map …

'Nothing to worry. Just a matter of dehydration. You will be all right soon.'

Somebody was stroking her cheeks. Ruth struggled to keep her eyes open. Now, she could see everything. The drops of perspiration on the doctor's brow, the anxiety in her eyes and the green window curtains. On the stand nearby, drops of life were dripping into a transparent tube. There was an IV canula on her left hand and a hospital band around the wrist. 'My God, what happened to me?'

'Ah, she has opened her eyes at last! Nina, can I leave now? My husband and children would be waiting for me. They will not eat dinner until I serve it myself. As per the Indian Penal Code, it is a crime to make engineers wash dishes!' The doctor was laughing and bidding goodbye.

Now another young woman appeared at Ruth's side. She had an enchanting smile. In the following days, she would get acquainted with the curly headed woman. The dusky face had a smattering of pimples. Ruth listened in a daze as the young woman told her about Noor Jehan finding her lying unconscious outside her home and calling an ambulance urgently. 'You are lucky, because Noor Jehan ensured that you reached the hospital in time!' That sentence alone imprinted itself lucidly in her mind.

Ruth recollected Noor Jehan's tragic face, her sharp nose, and her callused hands. She was travelling with Noor Jehan in a crowded bus. Ruth saw Kanya and the condom man. The destitution she had endured beneath the two date palms and the four-wheeler which turned a corner, moving towards her … One by one, the memories became pellucid.

'Noor Jehan called Aravind after you were hospitalized. He entrusted you to my care. Ruthie, you are Aravind's responsibility now!' Nina told Ruth.

Like Dr Shahana predicted, Ruth recovered quickly. After getting discharged, she was welcomed into a house with just two inhabitants. It was Nina's villa in Silicon Oasis. Nina and her three-year-old daughter Riya were eager to keep their unexpected guest tranquil and happy. Ruth sat silently, despite a barrage of questions aimed at her. She resembled a tree denuded of leaves, lifeless and forlorn. In truth, Ruth wished to speak, but all the words seemed to have vanished somewhere.

'A manager who leads a big team at the office. The brilliant officer who manages different sorts of people with such consummate ease … How vain I was about my own abilities! Ruthie, all my arrogance lies shattered in front of you.' Nina conceded defeat. Noor Jehan had told her most of the stories, except that of one night. She wished to know about the night of Ruth's disappearance.

'The world's tallest building is in Dubai. More than one hundred and sixty storeys! Do you know the price of a two-bedroom flat in that structure? Ten million dirhams,' Nina informed her gently. 'There are people who live in such flats. And there are those who cannot afford three hundred dirhams for bed space. Now, that is Dubai. Ruthie, every city is a small replica of our world. You are lucky, usually those who get trapped hardly escape. The boy helped you due to the Lord's grace. Anyway, it is all over now. We will arrange a ticket for you to return home.'

Ruth was shocked. She felt her strength leaving her. Arrange a ticket? The three lakh which she got by selling off half an acre of prime property … The money handed over to the agent … The endless, insufferable mockery awaiting her from the relatives, the villagers …

'Nina, I need a job. Please, I don't want to return.'

Ruth looked as if she was staring at death, and Nina was taken aback by her look and tone.

'Look, this city is not safe for you. We will think of a solution. Ruthie, you should open up about what happened to you.'

'What happened to me? I don't know, Nina!' Ruth wished to yell. There was somebody who knew everything. A man who stood alone under the grey skies, in an isolated place. Where did he drive away to, from the gulley near the gold souk?

'Hakuna matata … That means no worries!'

Riya was chasing after Simba, still in the thrall of *Lion King*. She was scampering around, laughing at the petrified Simba. Ruth's heart wept. An inferno was consuming one end of the earth. 'Lord, to which end of the universe shall I run?'

Nina was pondering too. She had helped a lot of victims in the past with the help of Indian associations and other organizations. Women who were ensnared in sex rackets after being promised jobs as sales girls and domestic workers. When they tried to escape, the net closed in surreptitiously. There would be responsibilities and burdens, of Himalayan proportions, confronting them. Consequently, suffocating, wounded, they would endure the sufferings. Some would risk their lives and flee. These were the courageous ones who brought the kingpins of the rackets before the long arm of the law. But Ruth's recruitment had been for a hospital. How could it turn out this way? The whole matter was wrapped in mystery.

'Cities are akin to wild forests. There are ferocious animals. The deer should not visit the lion's den and naively hand over itself.' Nina looked enquiringly at Ruth, as if expecting her to respond. After a while, she offered her phone to Ruth to call her family. When Ruth heard Alby's voice, she struggled to hide her whimpering. Her husband and children were worried sick about her.

'Dearest, how are you? Is the hospital good?' Alby asked.

'The job is yet to begin. Some formalities are left.'

When Ruth answered, her voice trembling, Teresa grabbed the phone from her father's hands.

'Amma, how is the stay? Air-conditioned room, am I right?'

'Let your mother speak, please,' Alby intervened. Ruth felt as if someone was weighing her heart down with a heavy stone. All of earth's hurricane lamps were being snuffed out.

'Children, please don't create problems for your Chachan. Alby, I will call later.'

Ruth burst into tears after cutting the call. Riya, unaware of the happenings, curled up in her lap and hugged her. Ruth would replay all these scenes, countless times, during the silent nights at Nazareth. She would feel that she was Simba, running away into a deep wilderness.

'At least you could have told Alby everything. If you suppress everything, one day it will explode out of you.' Nina's voice echoed her dismay.

'No, Alby should not know about anything. He is very sensitive, like the touch-me-not plant. He won't be able to handle it.' Ruth sobbed. She would remember the sobs forever. Also, the strange life story that Nina narrated afterwards.

'Ruthie, be strong! You are a nurse. There are many enviable jobs in the world. But I adore nurses. They are the joy, the anchor, the very life of many families! Once upon a time, there was a nurse working in Alexandra Hospital at Redditch.' Nina became contemplative, cutting short what she was about to say.

'Take a look at this diary. Just a single page.'

Ruth leaned in and glanced at the diary that Nina held out. Ink stains had spread from the alphabet written on the almost tattered page. Like the wailing of a river, forcibly stopped at her origin itself …

I am Nina's mummy. That is the only description that would define me on this earth. In the eyes of society, my husband and I are a model couple. Salary in lakhs, owners of multiple houses. Nobody knows how the home is on fire, and how the body is caught up in flames. Getting a divorce is not possible since I cannot hurt my parents. Even when my mind weeps, I pretend to laugh in front of them and before my patients. Lord, I am tired of playing this drama.

The man who clung to my nursing job, to gain an entry into England, brought along a bundle with him. Inferiority complex. One day in the future, Nina might accuse me, 'Mummy, why didn't you escape from this dungeon?' Shall I be able to walk into a free life, all of my own, ever? Humming a song, as in the past? If Shiny dies, Nina will be a motherless child. The world will remain the same, nonetheless.

A woman is always an occupied territory. A forbidden land, where somebody else's flags flutter high. When she steps away from the home of her birth, she turns into a refugee.

'Ruthie, this was my mummy's last diary entry. I called the cops when I was ten, when the candlestick that Papa hurled hit mummy's forehead. See, I became an orphan on that Christmas night. When I was sent off to a boarding school in Mysore, I took with me only three things. A pale blue nurse's uniform, the red sari with white flowers, which Mummy had been wearing for the midnight mass, and this diary.'

A river lay dead within Nina's eyes.

Wiping her tears, Nina continued. 'I got my Riya from an orphanage. She asks me intermittently, "Where do I come from?" From Nina's mind … I reply. I am reminding you that there are many lives, unfathomable stories, around. The moment we assume that our sufferings are the most intolerable, we will surely get defeated in life.'

Nina held Ruth's hands close to her heart.

'Ruthie, everybody praises me. Wow, what an inspiring woman, charismatic leader, motivating manager, courageous lady, compassionate buddy …! Nobody knows about the old Nina.'

Nina laughed mirthlessly.

Ruth gazed unblinkingly at her. It was unbelievable that such a vivacious, cheerful young woman had had such a desolate childhood!

'If I speak about my life story, it will be alleged that I have cooked up something for my motivational classes. Tell me now, Ruthie, do you think your life is extremely complicated? Whatever that may be, running away from problems is never a solution. By the way, do you know anyone here?'

The roiling river was settling into serenity again.

'I have a cousin, Agnes Chacko, who worked here as a nurse. But I have not been in touch for a long time.'

'We'll find out,' Nina reassured her and started searching on Facebook. From across the wide world, twenty-four profiles of Agnes Chackos emerged on the screen. One of it had the face of the young girl who had traipsed by the farm ridge leading to the forests. The fragrance of wild champaka flowers enveloped Ruth. However,

Agnes Chacko was no longer in Dubai. Facebook informed them that she was residing in Switzerland now. Nina sent a message to her, adding her phone number.

'Hello, I am Nina. Do you remember Ruth, your cousin? She has reached Dubai. Can you call as soon as possible?'

Later, during the solitary times in Nazareth, Ruth would often hear the sobs of a young girl. She was calling out for her mother, inside a boarding school surrounded by enormous walls. Ruth would realize that her own sorrows paled in comparison to the sufferings endured by others.

While they were waiting for Agnes to respond, Dr Shahana dropped in to visit Ruth. Dressed in a light yellow kurti, she radiated energy. 'Wah, my patient looks very fresh!' Shahana embraced Ruth warmly. Nina felt relieved at her arrival. It was time that they planned Ruth's future course of action.

'You know what? I love watching horror movies. Thrilling, aren't they? You apparently acted in one. I want to listen to the story. That's why I gave up on sleep and came running to you after my night duty.' Shahana grinned.

'Ruthie, the doctor is a scaredy-cat in reality! Loves horror movies indeed! She has a nickname—Amygdala,' Nina chortled in glee. 'She turns nervous at the slightest turn of events. So her medical college classmates gave her that name.'

'Haven't changed much even now. Yesterday, I became dizzy in the accident care unit.' Shahana laughed embarrassedly. 'They brought in a young accident victim from Al Ain road. He passed away in front of my eyes …' Shahana's eyes expressed her inner turmoil. In a jiffy, she changed the topic and seized control of her emotions. Nestling close to Ruth, Shahana queried, 'Where did you disappear that night from Noor Jehan Manzil?'

Ruth sat impassively like a child staring at someone else's ruined artwork. That night … it was equivalent to a thousand days and nights. What should a woman, abandoned amidst sand dunes in the moonlight, speak about? About the bone-chilling terror? The soul numbing cold? The deathlike loneliness? The hands that pulled her back to life?

She played that memory, familiar like a constantly rewatched movie scene, yet again in her mind. How Kanya went away with a young man in his car, and how the four-wheeler decreed to decide Ruth's future, sped through the road towards her.

21

THE 'WARRIOR OF LIGHT'

The news that arrived from Jerusalem was disheartening. Sahal went searching for the old artist. He knocked at many doors in vain. There was no cooperation from either the military or the police. Instead, they started suspecting him, based on the visitor details of the museum on that day. They trapped Sahal when he went looking for the old man the third time.

Asher was waiting for him outside the police station. Hours went by. Even after the favourite songs stopped playing on 87.6 FM Hebrew Radio and Radio Mevasar Tov broadcast the *News Week* updates, there was no sign of Sahal. Asher smelled something fishy. A news anchor shouted herself hoarse that the 'Warrior of Light' Facebook page was suspended and that cyber police was tracking the administrators who aimed at instigating terrorism in the land. It was evident that Sahal was in danger!

Asher anxiously went searching for him. An unpleasant-looking officer hollered that nobody should be waiting around for Sahal since he was in custody and was undergoing questioning. Asher panicked and wondered about the way forward. A face rushed into his memory. Dr Mazar was on her regular evening walk when Asher called, requesting for help. Silence loomed for a while, and after that poignant pause, Dr Mazar consoled him, 'Don't worry, Asher. If Sahal is innocent, they will not harm him. They are already in a defensive mood after "Warrior of Light" transmitted those pictures. Guess they won't provoke human rights activists by undertaking harsher steps at this juncture. You should be cautious. Do keep an eye on Sahal too. He has a bright future. Sahal's talent shouldn't get gutted due to display of unnecessary audacity. Let me do what I can. Remember, I won't support any action against the law.'

The professor who excavated David's City and Solomon's Palace from amidst the ancient ruins also had good contacts in both academic and social circles. Once she took up an assignment, Dr Mazar would complete it assiduously. She kept her word. Since she convinced an officer, a kind-hearted one, that Sahal was a bright student waiting to go abroad for research and that his future should not be spoiled merely on suspicion, Sahal was allowed to go free. He was given strict instructions to respond to the summons at the police station whenever these were issued. However, before the professor's call came, they had shown much love to that slender body. The horrifying memory of the night in custody haunted Sahal for the rest of his life.

The next morning, Sahal did not utter a word to Asher in the courtyard of the police station. Neither did Asher ask him any questions. As he helped his wounded friend to the car, Asher was grief-stricken. He was remembering a gratuitous threat issued by a wicked army commander recently. The latter had warned that he would mutilate every youth at the Dheisheh refugee camp! Not a single person would be spared.

When his wounds started healing, in a meeting organized by HOPE, Sahal revealed more about the hours when he met death face to face. Asher sat shivering by his side when Sahal recollected the events, choking at the memories. The wounds in Sahal's heart hadn't ceased to sting. Later, Sahal would write about the agonies which scorched his soul. The Al Jazeera website would publish his memoir.

Prison

'Across the world, the perpetrators have the same face.
Their weapons stoke the same dread.
Their tongues spume, with the venom of serpents.
When their fangs sink, all the wounds of the world
Froth and foam with humiliation.
Death is far better.
Their vengeance, the Roman soldier's whipcord—
One flogging, the body is scourged and bloody.
The mind too.'

I went in search of a gifted artist. But those cruel men enjoyed sculpting my thin body. The guardians of the country had to fulfil the oaths they had sworn. Who are there to stand guard over those without a country? Beloved people, we are our own guardians.

I pray that nobody else endures what I have gone through. I would like to believe that our prayers shall be answered one day. It is one of the greatest wonders of the world that I am alive to speak to you.

'Where did you dump his body? The poor old man!' I could not control my fury. A burly policeman slapped my face heavily. Then he dragged me into some sort of grotto. I sat shivering on that freezing cold floor. It was pitch black. When my eyes got used to the darkness, I saw a ray of light streaming through a hole and observed my surroundings. Was I buried alive in a qabar? Did they lock me up in a vault? I panicked. My head hit the ceiling when I stood up. I curled up on the ground. Footsteps were heard soon enough. Someone pulled me up. The sharp shards embedded on the roof of the cave pierced my head. I shrieked in pain. 'Moaning, you filthy swine?' Someone kicked me brutally. They played a game of football with my body. They thrashed me, taking turns. It was as if they relished the torture. One hit me with a truncheon on the face. The second, battered my back with the butt of his gun … The third, tried to shatter my thigh bones with his baton.

They hung me upside down in some scales. My arms were tied to my body. Someone inserted a pin inside my penis. The agony cannot be described. Yet, I tried not to scream. The truth was, I no longer could whimper. Someone offered to stop the torture session if I confessed to being a spy for Hamas and that I ran the 'Warrior of Light' page. I did not concede. 'Then tell us a name. Who is behind it?' They kept interrogating me and I kept denying any involvement. I was sure that my end was near. My final moments …

They had all information related to me at their fingertips. The intelligence reports had every titbit about me: where I had grown up, the schools and colleges that I had attended … the courses I had studied. That was not what worried me. They knew about my sister and where she stayed. 'We will tear apart your sister and throw her remains to the dogs!' one of them bellowed. 'How is she? Is she pretty?' Another leered. I saw Sarah's teary eyes. I saw her trembling, like on the childhood day when everything burned down. I was shattered. Then I lost consciousness.

When I opened my eyes, a sad-looking nurse was tending to my wounds. She was wiping my body clean. I was out of the cavern reeking with the stench of faeces and urine. 'Are you in pain?' she whispered. 'May you get well soon.' Her eyes showed that she was sincere in her wishes. The woman's smile was that of an angel. I thought either I had died or was dreaming. In a few minutes, the stamping of boots resounded nearby. A tall, hawk-like man entered the room. 'You can go now. But make sure that you answer every summons. Do not leave the city. Remember, we are watching you.' A warning note. The sound which haunts me till this day. Finally, life's door opened for me.

I was remembering the days following the Intifada. West Bank and Gaza were equivalent to large concentration camps in those days. Terrifying days, when we were shut inside the houses in the sweltering heat. One could be riddled with bullets on stepping out to the yard or terrace. There were restricted hours to purchase food. The frenzy to make it back home in time! When we languished without a drop to drink, they enjoyed the newly constructed swimming pools. When old mothers huddled wretchedly, recollecting the days when they cooked kebab for breakfast, and now unable to find food for their children, they stuffed themselves! I remembered my baba who taught me to find happiness in small things. He used to say, 'Our sorrows are just pictures and news to outsiders. Our wounds too.' Even today, the situation has not changed.

(*Howdy Death, Hello Freedom*, Sahal Al Fadi)

After the HOPE meeting, as they bid salaam in front of the plaque 'I love Jerusalem', Sahal said, 'You should not have come to get me out, Habibi. How can a Jew befriend a so-called traitor? Have you forgotten what happened to Jacob?'

Jacob Daniel Cohen … how could anyone forget him? The drooping, faded olive bough in his right hand … The body like that of the Nazarene brought down from his Cross … Jacob, your memories evoke the scents of Nazareth's old market. The assorted smells of fruits and vegetables, also of blood.

Abba flailed about in agony all through the night, as if every battering which Sahal faced was penetrating his own bones and flesh. Ruth could not sleep for many nights. As she stood in front of St Peter's Church in Gallicantu, readying for the vlog on Maundy Thursday, Sahal's lock-up room and its darkness haunted Ruth. *The great love that never betrayed, that never denied, crying 'I know him not'; even after unbearable torture …*

The 'Warrior of Light' started functioning after a few days' suspension. It was essential for the cyber police to keep the Facebook page working. The *Times of Israel* reported that the administration was based in Malaysia. Even amidst the mayhem that was unleashed, 'Warrior of Light' continued to stream disturbing updates. As if trying to shout to the world whatever it could, before being shut down forever. Ruth had never dreamt that the pictures she collected for her vlog could usher in such chaos. How did those pictures reach Malaysia? Who was the 'Warrior of Light'? When she asked, Asher responded heartlessly.

'Akhot, there is no need to know everything! Sometimes, certain knowledge can be undesirable and unsafe.'

On that gloomy night, Sahal and his lock-up story reached Padamala too. Teesa, who was listening to her mother sobbing as she narrated, asked, 'How can soldiers be so cruel, Amma? Wouldn't they have sons like Sahal? Or a younger brother, perhaps?'

'They are helpless too. Obeying orders is part of their job,' Alby answered.

'Amma, I will be a nurse working in the war zone!' Teesa said, bubbling with enthusiasm.

'How will people live when the nation and the laws are against them?' Kathu asked. Ruth could see her lying on Teesa's lap.

'Kathu, the guardian angels are there for the destitute.'

'Big lie! If so, nobody would be grieving in this world.'

Kathu went away in a huff. The child who unquestioningly accepted everything that her mother told her, had grown up. As Ruth lay sleepless that night, she saw the fire in Kathu's eyes. 'Lord, when will I see my children again?' The long talons of anxiety started tormenting her again. Ruth leaned against the headboard of the bed. Mariam was sighted, seated on the low stool. Peering into Ruth's heart, Mariam read out the Psalm.

'By the rivers of Babylon we sat and wept
when we remembered Zion.
There on the poplars
we hung our harps,
for there our captors asked us for songs,
our tormentors demanded songs of joy;
they said, "Sing us one of the songs of Zion!"
How can we sing the songs of the Lord
while in a foreign land?'

Stopping her recital, Mariam aimed a fusillade of questions at Ruth. The enigma of the origin and existence of the universe, full of good and evil, was encircling her now.

'Tell me, Ruth … *Who cuts a channel for the torrents of rain, and a path for the thunderstorm, to water a land where no one lives, an uninhabited desert, to satisfy a desolate wasteland and make it sprout with grass?*'

'The rain on an uninhabited desert! Mariam, what do you know of that?' Ruth muttered. Mariam embraced her affectionately. Ruth felt that Mariam smelled like the camels. A suffocating aroma. She became a bird, scratching through the faraway reminiscences of someone else. A solitary bird, perched on a sand dune.

That day in the past … The silence in Nina's drawing room, at Silicon Oasis. Dr Shahana and Nina were all agog, waiting for Ruth's story. She could see their eagerness, impatience, as if it all happened yesterday.

'Have you ever encountered death face to face? Spent a night in a graveyard, all alone? Touched the acme of loneliness, as if you have landed on a strange planet? Any time in your life? Then, only then, will you understand what I am saying.'

Ruth was speaking, about the night that chilled her soul …

22

THE DESERT

As soon as Kanya got inside the car and it whooshed away, the four-wheeler negotiated the curve and came towards Ruth. A tall, sinewy young man stepped out of the vehicle, after stopping the car by the wayside. His gaze fell on the shadows cast by the date palm trees.

'Ruth?' He smiled.

'Lord, who is he?' A tremor seized hold of her from head to toe.

'No worries, I am here to help you. Someone called the radio station.'

Ah … how could anybody describe the relief Ruth felt then!

'Can't we wait for Noor Jehan to return?' Ruth asked, albeit with concern.

'Actually, we need to hurry. Climb in …' The man seemed to be in haste.

'Let me get my bag from the room,' Ruth replied and turned towards the house.

'Later! Just get inside!' The youth clutched her arm, stopping her.

In the blink of an eye, Ruth found herself seated on the front seat. He had shoved her inside the vehicle.

'It is very dangerous to dilly-dally here. Why don't you get that?' the young man muttered angrily.

He started the vehicle and accelerated at a dangerous speed. Despite the air conditioning, Ruth was perspiring heavily.

'Wear the seat belt. You know about the heavy penalty here.'

The car left behind the highway and whizzed through narrow by-lanes. The radio was blaring … S. Janaki's mellifluous voice …

> *Vasantha panchami nalil varumennoru kinavu kandu …*
> I dreamt that you would come, on the full moon
> night in spring …

'You have to stay away until things cool down. The place is in the city outskirts.'

Noor Jehan had praised Aravind as a kind-hearted man. Ruth did not know anything more except that he had come as a guardian at the emigration counter, when she stood defeated by the Arab's questions.

'May I speak with Aravind sir?' Ruth asked hesitantly.

'Oh, you know him, do you?' The man arched an eyebrow. Ruth panicked. Did that mean he wasn't Aravind sir's emissary?

He pointed at the radio.

'See, he is on air in the live show right now. Then there is a weekly update meeting. Must be super busy. By the time we reach, sir would be free. We will call him then.'

Ruth listened. 'You are listening to *Golden Melodies*. Today we will explore the songs of the movie *Bhargavi Nilayam*.' Sonorous voice. Was that the man at the airport? He spoke about cinema, about Vaikom Muhammad Basheer, about the lyricist P. Bhaskaran, the legendary music director M.S. Baburaj … Ruth found herself calming down as the words flowed through her. The young man offered her a bottle of cola in between. She was thirsty enough to drink up a well. Though she knew that it would instigate further thirst, Ruth gulped down the cola. Her tongue still felt dry.

Aravind was playing another song now.

> *Arabikadaloru manavalan, karayo nalloru manavatty …*
> The Arabian Sea, a veritable bridegroom, and
> the seashore, lo, a pretty bride …

The young man sang along, his fingers tapping rhythmically on the steering wheel. Then he bragged about his exquisite collection of old songs. Probably observing Ruth's impassiveness, he changed the topic and started prattling about personal matters.

'I'm still to get hitched though I have crossed thirty-three. All these unending responsibilities …! There is a girl waiting for me back home. Will bring her along in the next break.'

Ruth was not in a mood to listen. But she felt reassured about two facts. One, he was harmless. Two, he wasn't Freddie's henchman. There was a mesmerizing charm in the slightest of his gestures. Attractive eyes, thick moustache, well-trimmed beard … a very handsome young man.

The wind was blowing hard. Dust billowed around. A cloud, shaped like the African continent, hid the sun. The light became dimmer. They had long left the city behind. A desolate, isolated road. Just songs … only the songs.

> *Kattu chikkiya cherumanalil … kaladiyal nee kadhayezhuthi …*
> In the light sand swept by the breeze, you wrote stories with
> your footprints …

Ruth slipped into a sleep inadvertently. She was walking in the evening sunlight on an unknown seashore. The waves were speaking to her in flawless silence. The city of darkness was scribbling poems behind her.

She was oblivious of the vehicle leaving behind the main road, the gravel pathway, the sand dunes and unpaved lanes, and entering the heart of the desert. She was unaware of the instant when the young man halted the vehicle to reduce the tyre pressure, to drive over a sand dune. He filled a syringe with drugs to finish off the woman who had fled with lethal secrets. She was unconscious when the agent of death glared at her face and grabbed her right hand determinedly searching for a vein; and then, wavering at an inscrutable memory, hurled the syringe with the deadly liquid away at the final moment. She was inert then, caught in a deep slumber woven by the sleeping pills mixed in the cola. She remained comatose when he left her to her fate amidst the sand dunes, and ran away from his homicidal assignment, leaving a note behind.

Intense cold. Her limbs had frozen. The tip of her nose and cheeks were hard. Was the air conditioning in the car at the maximum level?

> *Vayikkan jnan anayum munpe … vanthira vannathu maychallo …*
> Even before I could read the words, the monstrous wave came in, washing it away …

Ruth's lips moved to repeat the missing lines of the song she had been immersed in.

As she struggled to open her eyes, the full moon appeared on the skies above. A roof embedded with stars. Silence. Great stillness. Where were those slender fingers tapping the tune on the steering wheel? The song? Was she dreaming? The whistle of the wind could be heard then. Ruth could hear her own heartbeats. They became rapid like a drumbeat. 'Lord, where am I?' Ruth made an effort to sit up, but her arms and legs seemed to be sinking. She spread her hands around, searching. Rough, bristling, cold sand! Grains of sand! 'Lord, who has dumped me in the sand?' She managed to raise her head. Pulling herself up, Ruth looked around from that half-huddled posture. Her teeth were chattering in the cold. Sand waves were shimmering in the moonlight. Glistening hills. Sand, only sand all around.

'Ruth, you have been cast into an abyss of sand!'

She shook in terror. 'Lord, my Lord, what sort of a nightmare am I caught in?' The solitariness of this hallucination was insufferable. The piercing chill was beyond endurance. The desolation, the moonbeams of the dream, stars, sand dunes, all were terrifying. If only she woke up! Ruth hit herself harshly on the cheeks and chest. But she could not lift herself out of the stupor. Neither did the reverie disappear. Like a feral animal's growl, the noisy wind blew intermittently. Wind, only wind all around.

'Ruth, you have been ruthlessly abandoned in some desert wilderness!' Freezing, she fell on the cold sand expanse. 'Lord, give strength to my children to survive without their mother! Help Alby walk again.' Ruth had nothing more to pray for. She felt her eyes overflowing with tears and the last remnants of her strength ebbing away.

Ruth lay on the sands, motionless.

23

BHARGAVI KUTTY

Hours must have passed by. Ruth did not recollect how long she had lain like that. From the sky above, a drop fell on her forehead. One, two, three, four … raindrops. Her dried lips were moistened. The water drops clung to her eyelids, caressed her cheeks and slithered to the hollow on her throat … winding their way down … to the life-giving cells. Greedily, Ruth opened her lips, and wet her tongue. The taste of cola … She forced her eyes open. 'Ruth, you are still alive!'

The drowsiness was not leaving her. She could hear the chirping of birds at a distance. Was it a delusion? She moved her limbs, and tried to sit up. The exhaustion was no longer intense. A hunchback was descending the slope of a high hill by her right.

'Little one, don't be afraid. I am here.' Valiyammachi!

'Is this a dream, Valiyammachi?' The rain was real. The drizzle had soaked her skin. There was a huge stone nearby and a paper was fluttering beneath it. Ruth stretched her hand. The heaviness of the Himalayas! In blue ink, the letters were in perfect alignment.

'The order was to kill, but I couldn't do it. Wait till sunrise. Then look at the sun and move east. Within a kilometre's distance, there is a motorable road. Just beyond a sand mountain. Climb it slowly. Surely, a car will come. Sincere apologies.'

Bereft of compassion, the wicked one had run away, leaving behind his apology in a few lines!

How long for the sun to rise? Ruth did not know. She stood up slowly. A snakeskin lay nearby. The serpent's sinuous path was imprinted on the sand. She shuddered. Ruth could see a few small animals prowling on the hill to her left—some sort of a pack. Wolves and foxes were a common sight in the deserts. 'Lord, would they harm me?' As she watched fearfully, the animals frolicked down the hillside. The horns glinted in the moonlight. As Ruth held her breath, the herd of deer leapt past gracefully. A few tall shadows could be seen moving afar on the mountains. Could those be camels?

'Have you forgotten the forests at Padamala? Little one, if you don't harm them, the animals shall never disturb you,' Valiyammachi's voice echoed. The camel-like shadows vanished from her sight.

The bitter cold increased with the passage of time and Ruth found herself shivering. She walked towards the sand mountain, her hands crossed across her chest. Since her body, combating the intense chill, was trembling, and her legs were being sucked in by the sand, Ruth's walk had been reduced to a crawl now.

Valiyammachi was walking ahead, holding on to her stick. Ruth's strength, solace, resilience. *'And even the very hairs of your head are all numbered.'* Valiyammachi's trembling lips were murmuring.

There were dried twigs on the path. Short, thorny shrubs. Ruth was startled at the sight of a thin snake slithering in front. Its smooth body glittered in the moonlight.

'Snakes are out to delight in the summer rain. Be careful.'

Valiyammachi used the tip of her walking stick to remove it from their path. It crawled away into a hole beyond the thorny plants.

As Ruth moved forward, the sand mountain seemed to grow taller. There were wet tyre marks on the way. The young man had driven this way. The marks were still fresh. Later, Nina would quip about those marks, and about the desert wind.

'The desert can remove all the marks with a single gust of wind. A few moments, that's all … to bury an unconscious woman forever in the sand. Lucky that there was no strong wind that night!'

'Higher, higher ...' Valiyammachi called out, as she made her way up the hill.

It was a very difficult climb. Ruth had to grit her teeth and inch her way forward. But the more she worked, the less cold she felt. After what seemed like ages, Ruth reached the summit. The desert spread all around in the moonlight. Desert, only the desert all around.

At a distance, Ruth saw a fire. Who would be kindling fire at this time? As she strained to see, she could discern a few tents. She remembered the young man gushing about how he stayed in night camps in the desert. Ruth felt both relief and dread. She was definitely not in a risk-prone area of the desert. There was a chance to escape. But then, who would be camping over there? The dread began, and as she vacillated, a grunting sound was heard. Was it the wind? An aeroplane? Two lit-up eyes started moving from the campsite. Headlights of a vehicle! It trundled towards her, as she stood numb with terror.

'Valiyammachi, will the vehicle help me?'

As Ruth looked around, Valiyammachi was no longer to be seen. The vehicle stopped suddenly. 'Ruth, they will help you reach the city.' The mind propelling her, Ruth hurriedly started descending the hill and her feet gathered speed. By the time she clambered down, the vehicle started grunting again. As she watched on, it climbed over a sand hill and disappeared from sight.

'Where are the fires? The camps? Was it all an illusion? Ruth, at this moment, are you yourself a fantasy? Perhaps I am dead or lying unconscious somewhere ...' Ruth whimpered.

Colours started spreading at the corner where the sky met the earth. That was the east! She started walking in that direction. A few solitary trees were scattered hither and thither. Chirpings of birds. The desert was awakening. She must have walked for almost an hour or more. But there was no trace of any motorable road. Now she was walking on the hill which the four-wheeler had traversed an hour before. Though the cold was abating, Ruth's body was still reeling from the frost. Colours were spilling over at the horizon now. The sun was rising reluctantly. Ruth was yet again seized with the feeling that she was dreaming.

There was a gravel path trailing away to the right, with some sort of a hut on its side. She dragged herself towards it with great hope. A shack? A room without a door, a wooden bench in front of it. The bridge between death and life …

'Ruth, you have reached a human habitation!' Her heart leapt in joy inside the fatigued body. She stooped down like a question mark on the bench. There was a prayer on her lips; Valiyammachi's psalm: *'Even though I walk through the darkest valley, I will fear no evil, for you are with me.'*

Ruth would often wonder how she had covered the long distance, surviving the bone-chilling cold and unspeakable terror. She would have died of fear, had Valiyammachi not been there. Dr Shahana later exposited that the 'flight or fight response' had kicked in within Ruth that night. A chemical formula that the body produced to survive stressful, emergency situations.

Ruth heard the rumble in the middle of a nap and she woke up, startled. The vehicle arrived like a flying saucer and halted in front of the shack. A young woman in a pickup van. She was dressed like a gypsy. A lengthy garment covered her from head to toe. Ruth remembered reading about Bedouin women who drove pickup vans. The girl was humming a tune as she disembarked from the van. Seeing the hunkered-down woman on the bench, she stood disconcerted. After evaluating the strange creature, the girl stepped inside the hut. She was carrying a container in her hand. Soon, water was boiling on the stove. She came out with a warm cup of Suleimani tea. An enchanting aroma of masala filled the air. She observed Ruth warily. When she gestured to Ruth to sip the beverage, Ruth obeyed. Ruth felt that it was the tastiest tea she had ever drunk in her life. The girl did not utter a single word. Yet, her kind, poignant look and the spice-scented, cold dawn would be imprinted indelibly in Ruth's memory.

The Bedouin girl placed her hand on Ruth's forehead and let out a shrill cry of alarm. Perhaps she was alerting her about a fever. Refilling Ruth's cup, she stood staring at the road, as if expecting someone to arrive soon.

Within minutes, another pickup was seen trudging up the path. Lord, who was it this time? For Ruth, it was another heart-in-the-mouth moment. An Arab stepped out of the vehicle and spoke to the girl. He looked at Ruth as he gabbled ceaselessly. Though she couldn't decipher the conversation, Ruth uttered two words: 'Dubai … Deira.'

After heaving four or five bundles of grass onto the girl's pickup, the man bid goodbye. 'Shukran, ma'a salama.'

The girl had petite feet. There was a silver anklet around her left ankle. She looked into Ruth's eyes and smiled occasionally. The smile was their language of communication. Ruth would remember the scene, with an overwhelmed heart, many times again. Soon, the girl handed over to Ruth an earthen cup filled with warm milk. Ruth would embarrassedly recall that she had morphed into a famished spectre, due to the combined attacks of fear and hunger. Ruth went on repeating, 'Dubai, Deira', as if she was crazy, seemingly afraid of forgetting those words. As she mulled over the incident after a passage of time, Ruth would surmise that though it was a horrifying day, there was a strange, surreal quality to it.

When the sun became brighter, Ruth caught sight of another vehicle on the gravel pathway. She was familiar with that particular four-wheeler. Her heart started palpitating fast. Stopping the vehicle before the shack, the young man stepped out with folded hands.

'Please get in,' he requested humbly.

Ruth and the girl gazed at each other.

In the same vehicle, on the same seat, a journey back to Dubai. Ruth cast a backward glance before the hut disappeared from her view. The girl was waving at her and Ruth responded likewise. Much later, during the Shalom nights of reading, Ruth would encounter a description of the Bedouins of the desert, who welcomed strangers with water, food and dates. She would gratefully remember the young woman again.

The man was silent.

'Why didn't you kill me?' Ruth glared at him.

'Your time to die hasn't arrived yet.'

'And you decide that, don't you?'

Ruth was surprised at how harsh she sounded. Had she been expecting the man to return? Was it that sole hope which helped her survive the night of horror? Sometimes, the mind trusts in the most incongruous occurrences. Then, even the impossible turns possible.

'No point in living after betraying certain people.'

'Who asked you to kill me? Freddie?'

'Freddie is a concept.'

'What's his name?'

'Don't ask.' The man looked at her pleadingly.

'A team had come to verify your death and they went back after scouring the desert. I was afraid that they will find you.'

'Did you come here for that? To verify my death?'

'To save you. Please don't ask me anything, not even my name!'

Vultures were perching on the sand dunes. Yonder, there was a lone tree with a single green leaf. A caravan of camels was moving at a distance. Sometimes, a nightmare would haunt her, of being buried alive in a frozen vault in a snow-filled desert.

The young man switched on the music system, presumably to avoid further conversation. Another song from the movie *Bhargavi Nilayam* filled the air...

Innee thandiya vazhi athi dooram
Munnil ajnaata marana kudeeram.
Aadima bheekara vanaveedhikalil
Nilaavil mayangiya marubhumikalil.

The distance that I crossed today was formidable
The spectre of death at my doorstep.
In the primordial wild forest trails,
In the deserts slumbering in moonlight.

An enraged Ruth switched off the song. The man gave her a beseeching glance and pressed the play button.

Mohaandhata theernethiyoridamo
Ekaanthathayude apaara theeram …
Where did I reach, crossing the darkness of desires?
The infinite shore of loneliness …

In deep frustration, Ruth turned off the song yet again. The man sighed deeply and drove at a devilish speed. The vehicle swayed heavily while hurtling through the unpaved roads riddled with potholes. After careering through a curved road, it stopped in the nick of time on the wrong track, next to a big truck.

'Set out to kill me?' Ruth became peevish.

'Life should not be thrown away lightly. I know that but she didn't.' He muttered in response.

Ruth had no idea who he was referring to. Hiding her feelings of gratitude, she looked daggers at him.

'How did you find out Noor Jehan's house?'

'Oh, some lady called a live programme on the radio. I was sent to check out the location she gave …'

Ruth was not aware of Kalyani Menon calling the radio station. Aravind would tell her about it much later.

'Tell me, what is your intention? There has to be some reason for a killer to come back to save the victim.'

Beholding the endless road, he answered softly, 'Once upon a time, there was a woman like you who came here in search of a job. She left her son behind back home. Her job was to take care of new mothers. She had been a talented theatre artist in her time. After spending the best years of her life in this city, struggling in a narrow little room, she returned as a sick, old woman. Maybe she would have been alive if provided with proper medical care. I could not even go see her for the last time … When the syringe was in my hand, her memory churned up inside. That's why you are alive now …'

The wind was blowing with the carcasses of a thousand leaves. An intense dust storm was lashing the air. Nothing was visible. The four-wheeler wheezed to a halt in front of the ancient villa. She tried to slip out as quickly as possible. The young man caught hold of Ruth's hands, as if he was begging for mercy.

'Forgive me for everything. We won't be seeing each other again. I told you about my girl yesterday, remember? She is no longer alive. The girl from my village had reached the finals of a "star singer" programme. When she won by singing a song from the movie *Bhargavi Nilayam*, I sent her a message. We fell in love after that. I told her that I was a big shot in Dubai. Last year, she got to know about my profession … She went away, once and for all. Once she had laughed and said, "Even after my death, I shall not leave you alone. Like Bhargavi Kutty, the lovelorn female spirit in *Bhargavi Nilayam*, I'll be haunting you!"'

Trying desperately to smile, the young man started his vehicle; and then leaning out of the car window, he said drily, 'Don't think that you are safe! They will find you one day. See, even this trip of mine, they will sniff it out! Nobody is allowed to reveal their secrets … Be careful.'

Ruth stood shell-shocked amidst the grey buildings. A thousand-year-old wind brushed past her that moment. A truck collecting waste huffed and puffed its way to the date palm trees and creaked to a halt. The sunlight became dazzling.

Crossing the main gate, Ruth hobbled her way to the back door of Noor Jehan Manzil. When she knocked on the door, her legs threatened to give away. Her body was scalding hot … she was sinking in the fiery depths of an unknown river.

Noor Jehan opened the door.

'Allah, where were you till now? We searched for you all night!'

Noor Jehan dialled 998 and waited anxiously for an ambulance, while Ruth lay exhaustedly on her lap.

That was how Ruth ended up in front of Dr Shahana in the hospital's emergency. Even today, the memory of that day would float to the skies of Galilee, like a kite that had escaped from the hands of a stranger.

When the bus journey starting from the Jordan border reached the Judaean mountains, culminating in the village where Zacharias the priest, belonging to the Abiyyah order, once lived, Ruth would recall the young man in the desert. At that point of time, she would be moving from Ein Karim to Nazareth with another young man. Silence would be her language then.

24

SUKKOT—THE SEVEN-DAY WAR

Forests of figs,
Build a bridge across Jordan.
A bridge without check posts,
A bridge without flags on either side.
Help these across the bridge:
Our childhood,
Our dreams,
And the everlasting waiting.

The pilgrimage festival of Sukkot arrived. The Feast of Tabernacles. Seven days and nights were spent in booths or tabernacles, remembering the fragile dwellings of Israelites during their travel in the desert, after the exodus from slavery in Mizraim or Egypt. It began on the fifteenth evening of Tishrei, the seventh month of the ecclesiastical year of the Hebrew calendar.

In Shalom, they would usually build a small booth near the house. Sukkot would arrive again, but who knew where the present inmates of the house would be at that point of time? Abba insisted that before Leah left for America, Sukkot should be celebrated in all splendour, honouring all the rituals.

The tent was raised on the serene hillside where the deodars reigned majestically. They cooked, ate and slept there too. The meadow glowed with a pristine moistness in the October dew. The naked trees stood bereft of leaves. A rivulet flowed quite nearby. Truly, it was a very tranquil ambience. Ruth remembered an old tent in the desert. The woman abandoned amidst the sea of sand was called neither Hagar nor Hajar. The name of the young man who had abandoned her remained unknown.

Abba slipped into sleep while fanning himself with a palm frond. Ruth's vocabulary became enriched with new words: etrog, citron and lulav, palm frond. Leah and Asher started fencing with each other using a myrtle and willow branch. It was then that Sahal arrived, holding a yellow Sukkot lemon. The one who transcended the night of death, enduring the torture. Though Eema frowned, Abba warned her with his eyes that she shouldn't utter a word of protest. Like always, songs and cheerfulness accompanied him. His laughter made it seem as if he had forgotten about all the suffering. His sound reverberated on the hill slope.

My olive boughs,
You decorated their turrets.
Then why, why do they spit fire
On our wind-shaken tents?
My blue sky,
You poured more blue—
Compared to the Nile and Euphrates, in their stars.
Then why, why do they crush
Our dreams of feasts?

The light-hearted ribbings in the booth soon turned into arguments. Asher and Leah started fighting over breakfast and salads. Asher wanted vegetable salad while Leah insisted on Caesar salad. Asher ordered hummus, while Leah insisted on mutabal. Eema was obdurate that she would prepare just one of these! As always, Asher ceded defeat and Leah won. Sahal watched on with a gentle smile.

Ruth remembered Teresa and Catherine then. It was always Teesa who accepted defeat. Abba and Eema would fight with each other relentlessly. 'The Seven-Day War of the Menahem family'! That was how Asher referred to that phenomenon.

Ruth had stoked the war, by reading aloud an article published in the 'Warrior of Light' site.

> *There is a truth forgotten by those who follow the customs by theatrically raising the booths. Those whom they had driven away are still in exile, fighting the sun, storm and snow ... How many women languishing in the dark hovels, choked by epidemics, without any smidgeon of privacy? Their children, unable to access education ... Leaders who don the role of saviours, growing fatter on the generous funds received from across the world. That is today's Palestine.*
>
> *The occupying forces tell those who cling on to the last strip of land, face to face with death: 'Look, how generous we are! We grant you electricity and we provide you with vaccines. We give you permission to walk through the paths that once were yours, to pluck olives from your olive groves. We do not impose taxes on your water or air. We endow you with our scientific achievements. Yet you continue to pelt stones at us.'*

Eema became enraged on hearing what Ruth read. Esther, the daughter of a Zionist leader, had been imbued with hatred for the Arabs right from childhood. In Eema's eyes, the Jews alone were the chosen people. And God meant Israel's God. All the heathens who lived in Israel since ages should leave the land. A trio of inmates of Shalom would launch their joint warfare against Eema, the lone warrior! Eema would recount each and every cruelty of Hamas. For the unfortunate woman who lost her mother due to the Hamas attack on Tel Aviv, there was no tally of missiles or stones in consideration. There was only truth, the truth called Israel.

On the seventh day of Sukkot, towards afternoon, two police men laboured up the hill. Leah was the first to catch sight of them. All celebrations ceased abruptly. As usual, they had come in search of Sahal. After a futile interrogation session, disappointed at not seeing Sahal, they descended the hill. Eema started lamenting and shrieking. She threw down the gauntlet, that the next time Sahal visited Shalom, she would be the one to inform the police! Abba was silent, and so was Asher.

'How efficiently he sneaked away! Ahkh, do you keep spies to inform you about the imminent arrival of shoter?' Leah muttered in Asher's ears. Her brother pinched her and Leah pushed him out of the tent. In truth, the booth on the hilltop had been a ploy to keep Sahal safe.

Later, the memories of Sukkot transformed into reminiscences of Sahal's poetry.

Which tabernacle can hold your waves, Tiberius?
The dolls scream,
Inside the partially ruined walls.
From the weed-infested gardens
The bleak cries of goats,
Stolen by rioters.
The bones in burnt Musakhan …

The church was on the shore of the Sea of Galilee: Mensa Christi, the Table of Christ. The waves of Galilee formed the beautiful background. As Ruth recited Sahal Al Fadi's poem standing at the doorway of the church, her heart was anguished. She knew that scooping up the embers burning inside another's heart was tougher than writing down the murmurings of one's own. Perhaps he was hiding amongst the pilgrims, or was one of the boat riders on the lake. Else, why would Asher start at dawn and travel all the way here, with a stuffed backpack? Why did he insist that Ruth shoot her vlog though it was not her assigned holiday?

The incident had occurred two thousand years before. The Apostles were fleeing the city with their lives, after the crucifixion. The Roman whiplash could land on their back out of the blue! The horses might trample them to death any moment! And so, they were running like the gazelles of the Judaean desert, without leaving any trace behind. Then they saw a young man, roasting fish over a fire, seated on the wayside.

'My friends, you seem to be anxious. Come and have some food. The devil will seize the minds which are hungry.' The youth invited them lovingly.

'They murdered our Teacher,' the Apostles wept.

'Fools, why don't you trust that truth never dies?' The young man upbraided them.

He served them roasted fish generously, and sat watching them eat to their fill. Then rising, he raised his hand in blessing and walked away quickly.

In a sudden awakening, John the Apostle leapt to his feet and started chasing after the young man. 'That was our Lord!'

And now at Mensa Christi, it was a friend, not the Rabbi, who was preparing food for the one fleeing the soldiers! Asher, how long would you play this game of hide-and-seek?

It was a blue-eyed passerby who recorded Ruth's poetry recital in her mobile. The man was an Arab by his appearance.

'What was the poem about?' he asked Ruth.

'About those who have to leave their homes behind.'

'You are Indian, aren't you? Any day, you can return to your country. You can sleep embracing your children in your homeland, safe inside a home from which nobody can force you out! You do not have unsurmountable bridges between your land of birth and yourself. Then why do you sing about those exiled from their homes? Do you understand the pain of those without a country?'

The traveller's words exuded fury, dissent and helplessness. He disappeared in the crowd. Ruth remembered Sahal and what he spoke about scalded lives that warm afternoon in the tabernacle. 'Sahal, which sea can ever cool the undying flames of your childhood?'

Asher, who had vanished amongst the boats at Tabgha, returned without meeting Sahal. They returned distressed and disappointed. However, it turned out to be a blessing in disguise. The duo figured out during the return trip that the police had been following them in mufti.

'Ahkh, why do you vex Eema by trailing behind Sahal? Aren't you wasting your future?' Asher was annoyed by Ruth's question. He had received many warnings from the office already. It was only due to Dr Mazar's affection for him that no disciplinary proceedings had been initiated yet. Abba was well aware of that fact.

'Akhot, who else does he have, apart from me? When he gets wounded, it is my heart which hurts. My job and career are irrelevant compared to his life,' Asher declared firmly.

Ruth remembered a woman running for her life from a seaside mansion, in a city of fortune seekers. And a taxi with a red roof.

The world remains so beautiful because of those willing to be wounded for others!

25

TO THE PROMISED LAND

'An eternal, infinite desert. A roof of stars overhead. The pervasive, penetrating whistle of the desert wind. The lonesome moment when one concludes that no other living being exists in the universe. The shock of having been discarded at some desolate spot. It is unbelievable what the poor woman overcame that night! I have heard of travellers losing their way in the desert. Stranded birds of passage! They were all invariably men. Stories of female travellers are rare, right? How many adventures of women remain unchronicled by history! Many women lead solitary lives in marooned isles of sand—like the Bedouin girl.

'Once my colleague informed me about a woman running a shop in the middle of the Rub' al Khali desert in Saudi Arabia. No trace of inhabitation anywhere in the surroundings. My colleague asked the woman, "Aren't you afraid?" "Are you afraid of living in your own home? The desert is my home," the woman replied. Those who reach the desert are open-hearted, not suffocated by borders. Perhaps, some were helpless too.'

Nina was speaking in an emergency meeting of the association that evening. Ruth was the reason behind that sudden meeting.

'We should gather more information about that recruitment agency. There are registered, authorized firms eligible to hire nurses abroad. The candidates pass the exams in their country. They update the biodata online on the hospital websites. Yet, so many get deceived and end up working in massage centres! There are plenty of fish, naive and vulnerable women, for the likes of Freddie to ensnare.

'I have worked in three continents; lived in many cities. Every sunrise would lead to a day of uncertainty. Would the rented room remain, when I returned from work? Would the employer dismiss me the next day? Would someone be prejudiced by the colour of my skin? What if the police stopped me on the way and found my documents insufficient? If a medical emergency arose, would the hospital deny me treatment, quoting the lack of a medical insurance? Nobody knew, nobody …

'Today, nursing is a profession filled with great hope. But there was a time when the situation was different. Nursing used to be the sole anchor of penurious families. Many women fought hard for success, crossing double the number of hurdles that men faced. Most women have existences similar to camels. They travel long distances in search of a small oasis; struggling in bitter cold, heat and dry winds. Sometimes, their journey takes them to the ends of the earth.

'I am saying that Ruth's case is not a standalone one. Her interview was conducted in a hotel at Calicut. It was a WhatsApp advertisement; the number no longer exists. Ruth was granted a visitor visa instead of a job visa. The maximum cost would have been around ten thousand rupees for the visa and ticket. They extracted three lakh from the poor woman.

'After great difficulty, when Aravind found the building, Room 1967 turned out to be a single room booked in the name of an Arab. Nobody had a clue about him. There were some workers from Malabar. The Ethiopian at the reception counter laughed mockingly when asked about the woman who had lived there for the past three days. "Mister, there are countless guests living in the rooms, spread across forty floors. How do you expect me to keep track of their movements?" The man was flabbergasted when asked about Freddie;

and swore that he did not know anyone by that name. When Aravind enquired about Shahjahan, he was regretfully informed that the lad had gone missing since the past few days.

'Aravind found out the details of the Arab who had rented Room 1967. He took Aravind to the room where Ruth had purportedly stayed. It was his courier company's office. There was no sea view. What about the sunrise she watched? The waves, the speedboats? Everything sounded mysterious. There was a Filipino girl working in the office. And there were indications of the room having been used for office purposes ... printer, scanner, racks. No bed or sofa. So, Ruth's room was not 1967! So why was that number boarded outside her room? That still remains incomprehensible.

'We got to hear about an accident soon enough. The body was found on Al Ain road; a case of hit and run. Unidentified, unknown Asian ... that was how the news anchor described him. When the chubby face of the young man, dressed in a navy-blue shirt, appeared on the TV screen, Ruth screamed in horror. It was Shahjahan.'

The audience turned gloomy at Nina's words.

The club singer started humming, '*Dukhame enikku ninte karutha chiraku tharika* ... Sorrow, please lend me your black-feathered wings.'

Much later, Ruth would write to Nina from Nazareth.

'Nina, how could I not think about Shahjahan when standing in Caiaphas's dungeon and in front of the Lord's statue, the One scourged by the Roman whip, in Via Dolorosa? You quoted once, "Greater love has no one than this: to lay down one's life for one's friends." Jesus, what should I call that love which lay down his life for a stranger? I railed at the Lord and, as usual, he silently gazed back at me. When I return to my land, I will visit Shahjahan's home, and meet his family. But where is his home? Who are his parents? I don't know, Nina ... Inadvertently, when selfishness raises its head within, I recollect Shahjahan's face. That instant, all my hubris disappears!'

When Agy Chechi's call came, with the apology that she had seen the message late, Ruth was already fast asleep. Nina and Agnes had a long chat before they woke up Ruth. When she rubbed her eyes and stared at the phone screen, Ruth was astounded to see a face with the 'Diana haircut' before her! Agy Chechi was in front, holding a forgotten childhood by the hand.

'Wow, a true copy of Annie Kunjamma! Ruthie, how long since I saw your face!' Chechi wiped her eyes. 'Padamala stood for Annie Kunjamma and you. That was such a pleasant time. I never checked on you all these years and I feel ashamed of myself. It took Nina and Facebook to reconnect with you once again.' Agnes's eyes displayed her deep regret.

'Valiyammachi?' she queried.

The toothless grin appeared in front of Ruth's eyes, earrings dangling from elongated earlobes ... Those words: '*Go, go and make something of your life.*'

'She passed away.'

'I saw her once when I came home. You were in the nursing school then. Valiyammachi was happy. She laughed saying, "My little girl will be smarter than you, Agy!"'

Agy Chechi sighed. Her eyelids fluttered in a distant memory.

Then she murmured softly, 'Just imagine it was a nightmare. You should learn to cherish the feeling of victory after overcoming all obstacles. What's the point of living otherwise? When I heard your story, I remembered the old Agnes. The girl who escaped from the third floor of an apartment in Connaught Place ... straight into darkness. That is a strange tale. Half frozen, I ended up in a Working Women's Hostel. There I met a woman called Shiny, from Kottayam. A very confident woman who would walk alone through the street even at midnight. She would have a pepper spray ready in her handbag always! She taught me to live in Delhi. Unfortunately, she is no longer alive ... I helped many girls to secure jobs in Delhi. They all did well. But I could never help you ...'

Pausing for a while, Agnes pondered over something, and then started laughing.

Ruth grinned to herself that Agy Chechi was still the vivacious, gregarious woman!

'In that Working Women's Hostel in Connaught Place, there would always be a mishmash of 'cousin brothers' out to visit the pretty women! None of them was cousin or uncle to anyone. No tomcat came prowling around to meet Agnes, the eternal spinster. And then, out of the blue, someone did: a real Devan, God!' Agnes started giggling. 'Instead of sitting all defeated and depressed, get on with your life dear. Let me do my bit too.'

Ruth remembered Valiyammachi when Agnes cut the call. She would lose her temper on seeing anyone miserable and hopeless. 'How ridiculous to mope around! Just get going, girlie. Everything will turn out all right then.' Sometimes, one did not need pity. A scolding, a recrimination was far better. Ruth slept peacefully that night. Her thinking brain sent a message to the 'department of emotions': 'Ruth, you are in a safe zone now.'

Nina was delighted that Ruth had found someone in the guardian's role. In Agnes's story, a name had cropped up, and that made Nina wonderstruck! Without revealing it to anyone, she hid it inside her heart.

It was Aravind who encouraged Ruth to step out, so that she could regain her enthusiasm. They had already lodged a police complaint. The indications were that the cops were investigating Freddie's gang. They wouldn't dare to mess around with Ruth any time soon.

When Shivakami arrived at the creek that evening, an army of four women were marching near the moored abras. Nina, Shahana, Noor Jehan and Ruth. Nina was holding forth on old sailing ships, merchants from various lands, Emirati women who were nannies to the English families and Arab pearl divers who tied Hajjar stones around their bodies as diving weights, to quickly drop down on the seabed while relying on their held breath. Shivakami embraced Ruth affectionately.

'The brave woman who survived a desert night all by herself! I was super thrilled on hearing about your story. See, it is my dream. One day, I'll accomplish it too.'

'Please warn us beforehand. I'll have an ambulance on standby,' Dr Shahana responded wryly.

The women burst into laughter. It was for the first time that Nina noticed Ruth laughing openly. The phone call from Father Aloysious came in the midst of that laughter with a surprise offer for Ruth. Nina had informed Father about Ruth's predicament. The pilgrimage had been planned much earlier. But even she had no clue that a door was opening for Ruth unexpectedly. Sister Matilda of the Franciscan convent at Jerusalem had called Father requesting the services of a caregiver. The fact that Ruth had already cleared the Israeli interview back home turned out to be a blessing in disguise.

Ruth became a Ghaf tree at that moment. The Ghaf tree's roots stayed green and alive beneath the earth, despite harsh desert summers that withered its trunk. It would spring back to life after a single rain.

She hugged Nina and wept. 'Who will handle the expenses, Nina?'

Shahana smiled, observing Ruth's confusion and turmoil.

'Ruthie, the Lord will not bestow never-ending sorrow to anyone. The world has good human beings too, not just villainous Freddies.'

Ruth would often recollect those moments of delight and wonder. She would see a bird flying close to the waves then.

The days went by quickly afterwards. The necessary documents were prepared in a jiffy. Ruth called home to update them about the events. It was Teresa who received the call.

'Amma, someone came searching for you two days before. He did not reveal any details about himself. When we told him that you were in Dubai, the man left quickly. His vehicle had a Maharashtra registration number. Chachan has been anxious after that man's visit,' Teresa whispered.

Vultures circling around again! When Ruth was rendered to a state of weeping, Nina grabbed the phone. Father Aloysoius's Jerusalem pilgrimage group had been waiting for them in the parking that moment.

Faraway, in Galilee, Shalom was waiting for the metapelet.

THE WINTER WANED. Spring and summer went by. The money from Abba's pension fund found its way to Ruth's Padamala. After his surgery in Vellore Medical College, Alby started walking again. Teresa joined nursing school, while Catherine joined a coaching centre to prepare for the medical entrance exams. Intermittently, clouds of despair gathered over Padamala. Alby would feel guilty about sending away Ruth to toil in a foreign land. 'Alby, let things settle down. Time is on our side,' Ruth would console him, giving him courage repeatedly.

Whatever Dubai had perpetrated on Ruth had now been whittled down to vague, inexplicable memories of a distant past. Time was the magician who healed wounds. Now, Ruth was like a newly liberated land, a free republic in Sharon valley. She was the keeper and guardian of her own happiness. She alone was the judge and the legal treatise. Travel, books, vlog … If someone wondered about the multiple possibilities blossoming from a metapelet's life, they were the blessings and gifts of Shalom. Also the encouragement of Lilly Jospeh, who acted as a catalyst in her growth.

'The humans of this land are great books replete with tears and a fighting spirit. Those who had to pick up their infants and flee from their homes at midnight. Childhoods, that were cast into an abyss of helplessness. Before their unparalleled life experiences, any desert wilderness seems like a pleasant meadow,' Ruth would write to Nina and Teesa.

26

THE BARBED WIRE FENCE AT THE BORDER

For Sahal, childhood had been a furnace. In his memoirs, he would write about the days of losses and sorrows spent in camps. About the dark days, where the laughter and joy of the olden days could never be retrieved. About the most mournful shrines in the world, unable to re-offer the most valued of possessions that had been taken away. Palestine embodied the words Sahal scripted in Al Jazeera …

A Hundred Stones

Listen, have you ever dwelled in the camps of those without a homeland? Have you experienced the relentless movement, from one tent to another? Have you ever felt terrified of the night lurking to swallow you alive? Have you ever loathed the days that roasted you as in burning ovens? If not, how will you know us, how will you understand us?

From Lydda and Ramle, we were driven out like cattle. We hobbled along, carrying the bundles of our childhood. The hearts of our mamas were at the earthen ovens where pita was cooked, in the kitchens which were gone forever. And the hearts of our babas were still under the vanishing olive trees, on the hill slopes that were inaccessible forever. Even when our parents stood for hours in that sweltering sun, waiting for a piece of bread, utterly fatigued and hungry, they narrated the stories of springs and golden harvests. They spoke of wheat fields which were lost forever.

For Sarah, Gazan and I, no baba or mama existed to tell us stories. Our days reeked with the smell of burning flesh. Our stories were tainted with smoke and dust. We were children who had forgotten to laugh and play; forgotten about washing up and bathing. They had ruthlessly shut away the pathways to the riverside. Beyond the walls, we could hear the churning waters. The roar of the tributaries of River Jordan, where we used to once dive and swim in utter abandonment.

The rivers were lamenting about us …

We—Sarah, Gazan, myself and many other children—grew up due to the compassion showered by kind souls. When the catastrophe struck, we were staying in the Jalazone camp and were enrolled in a school run by the United Nations Relief Agency. The school was faraway from the campsite and we had to walk quite a distance to reach it. The very location of the school was problematic, because it was by the side of a Jewish settlement that had cropped up in the occupied territory. It was under the control of the Israeli army. Intermittently, there would be clashes between Hamas and the Israeli occupation forces. We were equally afraid of both. Periodically, there would be search operations by the security forces. They would enter the school with excuses of suspected Hamas terrorists hiding inside, or illegal arms and ammunitions purportedly stored in the premises. The children would scatter and run for their lives when the tear-gas shells exploded. Whenever a child fell during that mad rush, disaster was imperative, ending in broken bones and wounds. One's life too was at risk. My Fatima died during such a stampede. She was waiting for me when the pandemonium broke out … The beautiful blue eyes that gazed at me from the front bench went away from my sight forever.

The tear gas played a villainous role in our daily lives. Inhaling it continuously, most of the children became sickly and prone to asthma attacks. Many could not study, or even play. The nights I spent soothing Gazan as he gasped for breath! Ah, those were some of the longest nights of my life. Those were the nights which made me lose hope in the possibility of a dawn. And the longest days were when I carried a dehydrated Sarah, infected by diarrhoea, and waited for the camp doctor who dropped in rarely. Those were the days which made me disbelieve in the possibility of a sunset.

We had the fables of the hare and tortoise too during our childhood days. Our hares would never dare to sleep. And neither would the tortoise ever win. We were the tortoises. By the time we crawled our desperate ways to the destination, the food baskets would always be empty. Hunger, hunger … We, the children were hunger incarnate. But we never cried for sweetmeats, toys or a piece of bread. When batons rained on our backs, that was when we cried.

How shall I forget the day when the army visited our school? Gazan did not return to the camp even after night fell. I tried to believe that he was in some camp with his friends. Or that his kind teacher must have taken him along. Sarah dropped off to sleep after a while; and so did I. I woke up seeing a terrible nightmare. My Gazan was weeping all alone in some dark room! It was not morning yet, but I crept out of the camp. The sky was devoid of stars, it was a very dark night. A bird fluttered from the fig tree and the leaves of the date palm tree swayed like ghosts. I was very scared. The school building could be seen at a distance, shrouded in darkness. I clambered up the hill and crossed the olive groves. Moving past the sleeping buildings, I walked towards the madrasa. The massive gate was closed. What could I do except try to scale it? I fell down and hurt my knees. I called, 'Gazan, where are you?' I called many, many times. Amidst the din of night-sounds, my faint voice shattered into smithereens. Utterly helpless, frantic with worry, I started weeping in front of the school gate.

A soldier appeared out of the blue. He glared at me fiercely and started shouting at me for wandering about at night. 'Scram, go back to the camp!' he bellowed. How could I return without Gazan? Ignoring that formidable man, I hobbled away. Ah, how can I ever forget that night?

The eastern horizon flickered with light. I had reached the barbed wire fence of the Jewish settlement by then. Allah, that horrid sight! Just beyond the fence, my Gazan lay dead. His white uniform was drenched in blood … the school bag was open … birds were pecking around a few breadcrumbs … I saw the open, staring eyes only once. Those eyes are still following me.

I crawled under the fence with great difficulty. My knees were terribly bruised. The sharp barbs of the fence pierced my back; but I did not notice the pain. I sat numb, with Gazan's motionless body on my lap, unable to even whimper. Never in my life shall I forget the fear, terror and agony. I can still see the pale, lifeless face of Gazan and the red mud even as I write. In that frozen posture, I became aware of a vehicle of death, with dust billowing behind, screeching to a halt nearby. A bullet could come flying my way any moment! A truncheon could bash me any second. Sarah would be bereft of any family. 'Gazan, I am leaving' … as I dropped a kiss on his little forehead, I felt he was warm. My lips still tingle with that last kiss. Somehow, I crawled through the same way I came, and ran helter-skelter for my life; through the blinding light, through brambles and thorns … For a long time afterwards, I continued to run even in my sleep. From death to life …

Someone saw me lying unconscious on the road and got me to the camp. I could not speak for days together. He was my sound, my happiness, my life.

The next day, The Palestine Telegraph *published the news: Gazan Al Fadi, age six, missing from Jalazone Camp.*

And the day after, in the same newspaper, his picture appeared. The orphan boy who died in a mine explosion while crossing the barbed wire fence near the settlement … He had been caught in the camera of some unknown photographer.

Afterwards, a hundred stones lay waiting for me by the wayside, whenever an army vehicle came in sight.

The Sahal who sat weeping for Gazan outside the school gate, while the frightening ghosts of the night stuck out their blood-red tongues at him, the same Sahal continues to cry inside me even today. Even today, a soldier hails abuses at me for wandering around at night. I clamber over the school gate, calling out to Gazan, even today. As if yesterday, I see the shattered piece of my heart, my very soul, lying broken beyond the barbed wire fence.

Gazan, I long to walk for you all the distances that you should have run and relished. I wish to sing for you Baba's melodious songs; I yearn to scramble up the trees which you should have climbed, frolicking on swings hanging on their boughs. But Gazan, our ways are not ours any more. Our trees aren't ours any more, Gazan. They stole our songs, Gazan. Gazan, can you hear me? There will come a time when my drones shall shower olive leaves on the hills of Jerusalem. Undoubtedly, the time will come. Listen, the robot I shall design then, shall be named after you. They took away our soil and our pathways. But Gazan, nobody can steal wisdom, knowledge or the soul.

Postscript: I got to know later that the photographer Basil Abu Assad, who took the photograph of the orphan boy, which made headlines globally, became a suspect in the eyes of the police. Apparently, they seized his camera and destroyed it as he was shooting the iron-fisted retaliations of the army during a protest rally in Gaza Strip. Though relentlessly assaulted, Basil Abu Assad endures every time, with new cameras purchased with the help of human rights activists.

(From one of the notes Sarah discovered in the apple-scented house, later published in Al Jazeera)

However, Sahal did not know that the same Basil Abu Assad would capture a moment of great criticality at the Jordan border, much later. A pickup van was burning due to a drone attack on the Allenby bridge, near the Israeli check post ... Next to it, a young man was aiming a gun at the police ... Abu Assad would also not know that the picture he caught had anything to do with Sahal Al Fadi.

Ruth was thinking about Sarah, only Sarah, after hearing Sahal's story. How did an innocent little girl survive those unbearable days? Her baba and mama were scorched lullabies; Gazan, a never-to-be healed wound, lying near the barbed wire fence, drenched in blood. Seated all alone in the cemetery of the holy city, she was screaming, staring at the moist grave—a ceaseless, uninterrupted scream. Her childhood was coloured deep red, and even the light in front was dark in hue. They were building more settlements and army barracks on her childhood's hills. Slowly, her villages were being saturated with buildings. They were establishing check posts in every nook and cranny. Bulldozers were thundering over her dreams.

Who gave you the right to do that? Who gave you the right?

27

THE HIDEOUT

Mount Zion loomed ahead. A familiar house, hidden by lush apple trees, stood on its slope. Would Sahal be there? Anxiety, unease, fear. The nightbirds were flapping their wings. The sound of a police siren was heard. They were probably patrolling the new road constructed in the Old City. The driveway of the solitary house on the hillside was slanted. While making his way up the roadside shaded by the cypress trees, Asher cast a glance on the narrow, winding path below. A vehicle could be seen, possibly that of the police. He hid behind the fig tree until it whizzed by. Ignoring the driveway, he climbed the steps to the house, from the eastern direction. Twenty-one steps in all. Flowerpots were placed at both ends. The apple trees were resplendent with fruits. A window unobtrusively opened above, then closed quietly. The sound of someone descending the stairs was heard.

An old woman, her head covered in a tichel, scarf, opened the door and stepped out. The illuminated picture of a young man on the wall inside threw light beams on her harried face.

'Quick, step inside,' she whispered, casting frantic looks around. 'Hope nobody saw you coming.' Her voice was tremulous with concern.

Asher shook his head to reassure her. Someone was leaping down the banister. Asher looked up hopefully. It was a black Pomeranian puppy. As if meeting an eternal favourite, it rubbed its nose against

Asher's feet. In the drawing room there was a full body portrait, the picture frame in coffee brown hue. The smile, that sparkle in his eyes ... Jacob Daniel Cohen.

The murderous roar of an armed mob racing through the street in front of Shalom ... The flies buzzing around, as Jacob lay near the wall of the Synagogue Church. As if it all happened yesterday ... When Asher raised his hands to squat at the flies, did Jacob's eyes wink at him?

The old woman became melancholic on seeing Asher gaze at the picture.

'Sahal?' Asher's eyes scanned the surroundings eagerly.

'He was here till evening.'

'And now?'

'I don't know,' the old lady whispered, while latching the bolt of the front door. 'Nobody knows when he comes and goes. Why are they following him? Once the Malaysian admission happens, he should just get across the border.'

Asher pitched in hurriedly, 'Eema, let the scholarship come through. I will help him reach Jordan through the Allenby bridge. That will be safe.'

The old woman called a number. 'Abram, Asher has arrived. Any news of Sahal?'

Even before she finished, the call was cut from the other side. Her face fell. Peering inside, the old lady called out, 'Sarah!'

A young woman, draped from head to toe, slowly emerged from a room.

'I came to take you along,' Asher spoke softly, so that only she could hear. Sarah felt that it was the most loving, poignant voice on earth. He stood tall and regal like Mount Carmel. The locks of his hair were fluttering in the breeze, captivating the onlooker.

'Fibber ... how did you know that I was here?' A faint, hesitant smile appeared on her lips.

As the aged woman shambled to the inner rooms, Asher wrote on WhatsApp.

'Girl who resides in the garden, I await your sweet voice.'

Gazing into Asher's eyes, with a naughty smile, Sarah messaged him back.

'You are my holy mountain. The one who eternally entrances me with its secrets.'

They stood motionless for a few moments, looking into each other's eyes … Like the mist embracing the mountain peak, they held each other.

'Dearest, please ask Sahal to be inactive for the time being,' Sarah pleaded, her voice fraught with sadness.

To ask the smouldering volcano to restrain itself? Asher was unaware that Sahal would soon join the El-Kurd siblings, Mohammed and Muna, in their protests against the forced evictions at Sheikh Jarrah, in East Jerusalem. He did not know that it would have unforeseen fallouts. Uprisings happened unexpectedly; and so did the upending of lives.

By the time the old woman returned with grape juice, Asher had vanished in the darkness, without even bidding goodbye. *He was an ocean of unspoken words.* Asher yearned to confess to Sarah … In front of an ancient temple of worship, in the valley where the sheep grazed amiably, he had been waiting for her arrival … How many nights of such beautiful dreams …

Sarah was a continent of unspoken words too … 'Asher, I was following the caravan of camels in the desert. In my dream, there was a slender youth swaying atop the camel. He was calling out to the stray ones, one by one. Once, he called out your name! Asher, though I searched high and wide for you, scouring the sand dunes, I could never discover you. Though the camels vanished, I kept waiting for you. In that scorching sun, all alone …' Sarah's heart became as heavy as the earth.

'On the cliff of Masada, two thousand years ago, a princess stood gazing at the Dead Sea, on the turret of the western palace tower. Do you know about her? The one who was waiting for you to sneak inside the palace, making your way through the secretive paths of the east ...' Sarah's message gleamed dark in Asher's phone.

Surely, he would return. She lay awake, sleepless.

The birds of the night screeched chillingly. As Asher clambered down the hill, unsure of his next move, he observed three birds roosting on a cypress bough. They seemed to have alighted from yesterday's smoke-covered camps; they were shrieking as if deeply wounded. The luminosity, radiating from Jacob Daniel Cohen's portrait, showed him the way forward.

Later, the same house—with Jacob smiling from the wall—would feature in Sahal's memoirs.

The Apple-Scented House

The house, whose terrace and roof were flooded with apple leaves, had the scent of apples. The days and nights had the same fragrance. But the first few days in the house had the sickening stench of high fever and perspiration. I felt it was the smell of death.

I was staying in a room with a double window, which opened to the view of the street outside. My world was limited to the four walls for almost three months. Whatever poured in through the slightly parted curtains—the sunlight, moonbeams, bird-chirpings and the sweet scent of apples—I cherished them all in my heart. I was afraid that I would never be able to relish these again.

I was burning with a 104-degree temperature when I entered that home. I am alive today only because of the kindness of two good human beings, Rebecca Eema and Dr Yehoshua. After surreptitiously parking his car by the slope of Mount Zion in the shadow of darkness, hiding himself in a black coat, and manoeuvring his way through narrow, winding paths, Dr Yehoshua would reach the backyard of the house, almost like a thief. At the sound of the shuffling shoes, alerted by the coded knocks (two knocks repeated thrice in a row), Rebecca Eema would tentatively open the door. The doctor would leap down the stairs and reach my side.

His stethoscope would record my heartbeats. I was aware of everything even in my comatose state. It is a miracle that I survived that tightrope walk between life and death, and made it safely across, albeit clinging to Rebecca Eema's fingertip. The day when I recovered from the dangerous fever and opened my eyes was redolent with the aroma of apples too.

Though I was out of danger, Rebecca Eema sat by my side, ever watchful. I saw her shudder in terror at every police siren. Eema was deeply afraid of the police discovering me. Perhaps, her fear was more than mine. The dark circles deepened under her eyes and the furrows increased on her cheeks and forehead. Her hand shrivelled up like tender leaves scalded by the sun. I was apprehensive that she was transmitting her own life force to me, and drying up in my stead.

I saw my mama's love in Eema's eyes. The love which was looted from me on that childhood day, which smelled of burning flesh. Rebecca Eema was the clever bird which hid her fledgling inside a nest amidst the leaves, far away from the sight of the eagles. While looking at her, I felt as if everything lost was being reclaimed. I started falling in love with life, as I continued to gaze at her. It is always like that. Whenever we get back what we considered lost forever, we would hold them closer to our hearts. They would appear utterly enchanting. We would pray that we don't lose them ever again. We would feel so grateful to those who returned them to us. Today, Rebecca Eema is everything to me. After decades, I hear melodies of the lullabies again. The lullabies, evocative of scorched flesh.

I want to live. Live undefeated.

28

EREZ CROSSING

Asher descended the hill, forgetting the birds on the cypress branch. Was he caught in a commotion triggered by tear gas? The same turmoil, when Sahal's little brother Gazan had lost his way. He could not even speak comfortably with Sarah. It was likely that she was upset with him. Regardless of that, Asher's thoughts were consumed by Sahal alone. The one, who loved the stories about children flying around like birds in a country without walls.

Sahal, I am now wandering through those distances you traversed in childhood, searching for you.

The call from Beit Hanoun changed the direction of Asher's journey. He aimed to catch the first bus from the Central Bus Station and reach Erez Crossing.

Habibi, what are you doing in Erez Crossing, in the northern end of Gaza Strip, in between the Israeli kibbutz Erez and the Palestinian town Beit Hanoun?

It was good that he wasn't in his car. What if Sahal accompanied him in the return journey? To evade the eagle eyes of the cameras, the bus was always better. Asher sat amidst the sleeping labourers who toiled to build the roads and bridges. He was enveloped in the aroma of olive oil emanating from the farmers of the kibbutz. The wind blowing across the wheat farms embraced him lovingly, cooling his body. Could he hear the rumbling of a forcibly stopped river? Or was it the resounding echoes of armed fighters, making their way through the network of underground tunnels?

Most of the travellers were in long robes worn while working in farmlands and groves. The dress served to evade the distrustful eyes of the machine-gun-totting Israeli guards straddling the border towers. The traditional attire showcased that the person was not an infiltrator. How many such undocumented lives were there!

Those who waited for the olive trees to bud and blossom. Those who stood guard until the grapevines flowered and ripened. Those who relished the ceaseless grinding of the olive presses as if they were lullabies. They went to the gardens at dawn, checking if life was budding afresh. Undoubtedly, these folk were not warmongers. Neither were they merchants of death. Those who made it past Erez Crossing and proceeded to Beit Hanoun were not enemies of the farmers at the Erez kibbutz. The wholesale dealers of hatred and enmity were the authorities, never the people.

Asher imagined Sahal crossing the border dressed as a farmer. An unbefitting smile flickered about his lips. He searched the internet for the time at which the crossing shut down.

When crossing out of Gaza into Israel, it is strongly recommended to arrive at the Hamsa-Hamsa checkpoint at least an hour before Erez Crossing closes.

These were instructions for those wanting to cross from Gaza to the Israeli side. Asher presumed that crossing over to Beit Hanoun should not be so difficult.

Near the check post, taxis and minibuses were waiting for the people, their burdens and their heavy bundles of sorrows. The morose, dense yellow sunshine silently streamed down on the animals and humans thronging the border. An eagle or a vulture was circling overhead. People were jostling, their arms laden with bags and packages. Some were resting, their faces drawn and anxious. The same bleak look was in all eyes: brimming over with helplessness, uncertainty, insecurity.

The wounded and the diseased were waiting for their turn to return to Gaza. They had probably visited the city for medical treatment. Pain growled amidst them, like a ravenous, untamed beast. What was seen at the border was a simulacrum of Gaza itself.

A little girl was crying relentlessly. There was a plaster cast on her right arm. Asher visualized her chasing after a few goats in a remote village. She was now reprimanding a frolicking black kid, which had slipped across a fence. It went on ignoring her blandishments. Now, she slipped her little arm across the fence and pulled it by the ears. Stomped on by the goat's hooves, a treacherous mine, hitherto buried, burst out unexpectedly. Now Asher was watching the little girl screaming in agony, her bloodied arm dangling, as she ran back home. He rubbed his eyes and drank deep from his water bottle. The sunlight was intensifying, and the monstrous bird was still circling the skies.

If Sahal had crossed the border amidst such tight police bandobast, it would have been to get urgent medical treatment for someone. Probably to help someone staggering towards the edge of death. Why would he risk such a danger otherwise and for whom? The same instant, the visage of the disappeared artist appeared in Asher's mind, the one who went missing from the Rockefeller Museum, his old eyes filled with pathos.

Asher's hunch was correct. Sahal had gone to visit the sick artist. As he reached his destination, in a few hours' time, Asher would come to know that Sahal had been carrying money for the old man's medical treatment.

Sahal held the reins of HOPE at Gaza Strip. There were children, hopeless due to unrelenting hunger and putative restrictions; little ones bereft of joy or refuge. HOPE was their sanctuary. A group of youth was always awake in Gaza. They were guardian angels who would bring food and medicines for the kids. They were messengers of knowledge, who taught the children various skills like carpentry, embroidery, handicraft, et al. What Sahal spoke about, during a trip to Jericho, still reverberated in Asher's ears. 'A time when not a single child would sleep hungry; a society full of educated, healthy citizens. That's our dream, Habibi. That alone is the weapon of resistance.'

Sahal was an English tutor in many West Bank camps. Once they had taken him away, while he was teaching in the Dheisheh refugee camp. As if yesterday, Asher could see a group of enraged children raining stones on the police that day. 'Shoter, nobody is indulging in terrorism here …' How much the elders had pleaded and begged that day! Yet, the police had not relented. They bundled up Sahal and took him away. Indeed, the fierce arrow they feared was education.

Asher saw in his mind Sahal making his way inside a refugee camp with a stack of twenty books. A crowd of children was surrounding him, attracted like iron nails to a magnet. The wind, awakening from a slumber of centuries, was growling from the date palm trees in front of the camp.

Children were not allowed to freely walk around their homes or schoolyards. The random arrests, raids and searches provoked them. A resource centre working for refugee rights and Palestinian residency had documented the covert goals of the army: to crush the resistance, exhaust the protesters psychologically, intimidate and debilitate them by all means.

An aged woman who was plodding towards the screening booths looked beseechingly at Asher. She was clueless about the line to join. Asher took her by the hand, guiding her to the Palestinian queue. She smelled of olive oil and bread roasted in open fire. The woman was muttering to herself.

'Four zatoun trees, Alhamdullillah, that was all we needed for our livelihood! Those kept away hunger, gave us food and fuel. The devils cut down those too!'

Asher did not know how to mollify the trembling woman.

'Mama, this is the Israeli police booth. There are more of these for people crossing into Gaza. Palestinian police booth, then another of Hamas …'

Asher wondered whether she understood what he said. He imagined her standing in the queue all day, being questioned repeatedly by the officials, and being able to cross into Beit Hanoun very late at night … until she hobbled through the dark pathways of the village. But Asher could not visualize the face of the person whom the aged woman would encounter, as she entered her dilapidated house, devoid of light, late at night. Neither did he realize that moments, far more critical than what could be imagined, were lying in wait for the old lady in the imminent future.

There were armed guards behind darkened glass enclosures, next to the passport control counter on the second floor. Was a dark shadow staring balefully at him? 'Sahal, how shall I bring you back through this route, Habibi?' Even that thought evoked the smell of gunpowder.

The grey-eyed tractor driver, with whom he became acquainted in the bus, heaved into Asher's memory. He remembered the man's slush-stained attire and the intoxicating scent of grapes wafting from him. The tractor driver had promised to help Asher. He tried to imagine Sahal in the driving seat of the tractor as they moved out of Gaza the next morning. As Asher crosschecked the driver's phone number in his mobile and turned for a backward glance, he saw the man waiting for his turn in the Palestinian queue.

The officer in the first booth smiled amiably at Asher after checking his passport. 'Be careful,' he wished and signalled him to move forward. There was a scent of Oudh about the young officer, and he possessed Jacob's eyes, the same profound look! For a moment Asher felt that a swarm of flies was buzzing around his head! He shook his head to clear them off.

The crowd was already jostling in the Palestinian queue. The young woman who stood just in front of the old woman caused a beep from the metal detector. The warning knell of danger! Six or seven soldiers surrounded her immediately. Asher observed that the old woman was aghast and utterly confused. The woman was trying to explain, in a rather loud voice, that she had a platinum bolt inside her leg that had been subjected to surgery. The army officers were ordering the rest of the people to clear the area. Those who had waited for such a long time to gain their places in the queues were not willing to listen. Even the old woman was rooted to the spot.

The same officer, who had wished him 'Be careful', the one with Jacob's eyes, was also rushing to the particular booth now. Observing Asher, he cautioned him. 'Haver, why are you loitering around? Go ahead.'

Asher looked into Jacob's eyes yet again. Then he walked away slowly, his long arms swinging.

29

HAYAL, THE SOLDIER

They were schoolmates, Asher and Jacob. They had done their military training together too. As per the laws of the land, every able-bodied person had to undergo mandatory military training. Jacob had been determined to be an army officer while Asher started his journey of searching for Jerusalem's legacy. As in the autumn night of the past, Jacob's teasing laughter, poking fun at Asher's craze for archaeology, still echoed in his ears.

'Haver, try doing something for the nation, instead of wasting time digging out useless relics!'

Asher hadn't forgotten anything. Jacob had taken up his eviction assignment of Jewish settlements at Amona, in central West Bank, for the sake of the nation. But then, did the nation protect him?

Jacob had been a fearless warrior. Personally, he preferred justice to law. He had never contemplated how his life would be affected while taking up the new duty—the forceful evictions of Jewish settlements on Palestinian lands at Amona. That mission had been extremely challenging; it was a declaration of war against one's own people. The Jews had been living there for decades but the land belonged to Palestine. Perhaps they were aware of the fact when they migrated to Amona. However, the settlers never believed that the authorities would turn against them. It was with the ostensible support of the government that the settlement had come up. And one morning, the national army was out there to oust them from their homes!

The sun never rose over Amona that dawn. Like hideous gargoyles, the clouds clung to the sky. The settlers were up in arms in the streets, all ready to fight it out with stones and weapons, assuming the roles of the ancient fighters combating the Roman siege. Jewish women and children crowded the alleys, the steps of houses, the entrances of synagogues. There were screams and shrieks everywhere. The army had arrived to set fire to their dreams, to destroy the brick structures constructed with their sweat and toil. 'Dig us out first!' Curses and wails rang out.

The mayhem that ensued witnessed much use of force—while evicting the protesters, demolishing the synagogues, razing the homes, filled with dreams and hymns, to the ground. Gut-wrenching screams filled the air, incantations and prayers spiralled to the skies. The mothers cursed and thundered with flowing tears. Amona transformed into a terrifying, thundering echo.

Flaming curses fell into Jacob's ears. 'You devil, didn't you forget your own people, your own brethren? May the vultures tear apart your corpse ... May the wild animals mangle your corpse!'

That night ... may such a night never occur again!

Jacob had returned home shattered, unable to even whimper, after participating in the army operations. The village was distressingly silent. Even the birds had forgotten to chirp, as if something loathsome, brutal and inhuman had been wrought. The neighbours started hurling abuses as soon they sighted him at the crossroads. Jacob stood a criminal, with his head bowed, in the front yard where the fig tree cast its monstrous shadow.

His abba turned his face away, not uttering a single word. 'Get lost ... go away!' Jacob's Eema, Rebecca, screamed before shutting the door on his face. The young men peering in from all sides, those who were of his age, his childhood friends, showered malicious accusations on him. Everybody knew that Jacob had had no option but to undertake the task assigned by the government. If so, why had they treated him like a despicable felon? Why had they driven him away?

Asher was remembering …

How many times had Jacob reappeared in Asher's dreams, a repetition of the night when he crossed the street defeatedly, and entered Shalom's doorway? His face was flushed, eyes overflowing … At that moment, Jacob's body language was not that of a vanquished warrior, but of a friend, whose heart was deeply wounded. As Asher raced towards him, an unexpected windstorm had started blowing. The wind unleashed a demonic dance among the fig leaves. The branches broke, leaves and fruits started falling on the ground. Asher's heart yearned to hug Jacob, and offer him refuge at Shalom. But Eema was on the warpath already.

'Who shall hack off the hands of the scoundrel who turned against God's own people?'

By the time Abba stumbled into that scene, shouting, 'No, Esther … Stop that …', Jacob had already disappeared into the darkness. Asher remembered how he hadn't dared to run after Jacob. Instead, he had behaved like a coward, and felt excoriated by pangs of guilt inside. A murderous mob was on the rampage in the streets; armed with batons and petrol cans. Shouts, howls, filthy abuses … The fierce storm battered the by-lanes of the village all through that night.

It was after two days that Jacob was discovered, in the heart of the Old Market of Nazareth. Near the left wall of the Synagogue Church … Asher was the one to identify him. Jacob Daniel Cohen lay, more decrepit and decayed, than any other relic Asher had ever excavated from archaeological sites. He was curled like a foetus in the mother's womb … The white kippah which had fallen on the side, slipping from the head that was bashed in, had been soaked in blood. There was a drooping olive bough in Jacob's right fist, as if somebody had planted it in his hand … The lifeless eyes were half closed ... The face resembled the Nazarene who was brought down from the Cross ... There were flies swarming around the corpse.

The image, of how the body lay, was nailed forever into Asher's memory.

'Haver, in which museum, in which excavation site, in which archives shall I store that memory which has annihilated me?'

Abba spoke only a line on hearing about Jacob's unbearable death.

'*Those killed by the sword are better off than those who die of famine; racked with hunger ...*'

MOVING PAST THE soldier with Jacob's eyes, Asher entered the ash-coloured corridor made of concrete. Next to the arrow pointing right, printed in English, Hebrew and Arabic was the word 'Gaza'... A word as heavy as the earth.

An interminable corridor, looking like a desolate warehouse, sprang into view. There were many intricate doorways within. Turnstile gates where only a single person could pass at a time. These were elaborately planned doors designed to ensnare any infiltrator. 'Asher, you are under the observation of security cameras now,' his mind warned ominously. The formidable path ended in front of a steel doorway. The intimidating entrance opened into a fenced walkway. Asher crossed the border. From the land of plenty he had now stepped into the precipice of misery, into a shore of horror, of abject ruthlessness ... Asher was seized with a tremor, as if his feet were steeped in blood and tears.

He observed the watchtower at the border of Gaza Strip. The fortress of a dead land! Huge machine guns were arrayed; many spectres watched over the borders. 'The remote-controlled machine guns can riddle with bullets anyone who encroaches into the forbidden zone, which stretches a few kilometres from the boundary walls.' A uniformed official was explaining to a volunteer. Presumably, the man had arrived to help in the camp. A military vehicle hurtled past.

Pandemonium broke out suddenly. An ear-splitting explosion! Asher stood shell-shocked. The blast had occurred in the check post which he left behind moments ago. Soldiers sprang out from the vehicle which halted to a side and rushed forward. Utter chaos reigned for a while. It was a suicide attack! The young woman had pressed the button of death when the officers surrounded her. A few soldiers and some members of the queue had been killed instantaneously; their bodies shattered into smithereens. Body parts, limbs strewn in all directions ... blood, screams ... The poor old woman ... the soldier with Jacob's eyes ... Asher felt as if his soul was departing from his body. For a moment, it felt as if he was dead too.

That day, wracked with grief and anxiety, Asher ended up by the side of an extremely sick patient, lying in the portico of a crumbling building. After seizing the old artist from the Rockefeller Museum, the police had heartlessly dumped him at some remote place. His life was saved because a few brave young men had found him on time and rushed him to Dr Yehoshua's house. The doctor was a friend of Professor Menahem and was a member of Denying to Be Foes. The night Sahal—who was searching for the old man—ended up in police lock-up, Dr Yehoshua was guiding the artist back to life from the steep slopes of death. They had sent the man to Beit Hanoun when he recovered and had started walking by himself. But his condition worsened when he returned to his village. Sahal had arrived to see him, risking his own life. The old artist had to be admitted in Gaza's Indonesian Hospital urgently. That was why he had sought Asher's help.

Asher called Dr Fahid Hakim, a friend of Dr Yehoshua. The Arab doctor, a citizen of Israel, was working in a border hospital. The doctor asked them to get the artist to his hospital. The whole road was chock-a-block with police vehicles. Fear and terror were palpable in the air. When they reached the hospital, the sights were devastating. The doctor was attending to those injured in the bomb blast. Most were fighting for their lives. Corpses were piled up in heaps, and the allotment to the mortuary was awaited. The caregivers were running in all directions. There was a long queue even in front of the Operation Theatre.

'Asher, I have patients with intestines spilling out of their stomachs! We do our best to save as many as possible. But we don't have much facilities. Though I am an Israeli citizen, I do not have many rights either. Forget it, most people do not enter our towns. We survive somehow … Even our lives have no guarantee over here. It was a missile which took my Rashida! What was her mistake? She had treated so many Jews, sutured the wounds of so many soldiers … And then what?' Dr Fahid choked with emotion.

'This is our watan. But not all possess your heart, doctor!' Sahal responded impassively.

After entrusting the old artist to Dr Fahid's care, two young men would dare to attempt a border-crossing fraught with great risk, the next morning. One was in the guise of a farmer, dressed in soiled clothes, emanating the intoxicating scent of grape juice. The other was a part of his heart. The hidden light of the dark ages guided them. The check post would still be reeling under the onslaught of the previous day's bomb blast. The bloodied kippah which fell by the side, from the head of a wounded soldier, would flutter in Asher's heart. Like the flag at the border.

Shalom was waiting for them.

30

MEZUZAH

Abba was struggling for breath. Ruth helped him use the inhaler thrice and followed it up with thirty minutes of nebulization. Yet, the life-giving breath hesitated in filling his lungs. Abba's lanky body shook with the effort to breathe; a hide-and-seek game between the respiratory system and the essence of life. Ruth gently stroked his chest, after fitting the home oxygen mask on Abba's face. She was anguished by his suffering. Eema could not stand what Abba was going through. She had even collapsed once at the sight. Typically, when asthmatic attacks struck, Eema would assign Abba to Ruth's care and slink away. Laments would emerge from the prayer room soon after.

Asher was not at home. He had far heavier problems of his own. After Ruth raised the knob of the oxygen to three litres, Abba's breathing regained its normal rhythm. He slipped into a drowsy sleep. The pulse oximeter on his forefinger showed the oxygen of his blood rising from ninety and reaching a steady ninety-five. Following the doctor's advice, Ruth reduced the oxygen level of the knob to one litre.

Ruth recollected how Valiyammachi used to struggle with asthma similarly during the December nights of intense mists, and sometimes in the monsoon days of July. Had she heard the bird-like squeaks emanating from Valiyammachi's fragile chest all the way down the hill? Was it not her Valiyammachi who was lying in front of her eyes now? The pathos in the furrowed face and the delicate body, all curved like a question mark … as she lay on the screw-pine mat draped on the narrow coir cot … 'Little girl!' Valiyammachi was hailing her from the olden days.

Abba opened his eyes and gently touched Ruth's forehead. 'Did you get scared? I am perfectly fine! This is a hide-and-seek game that happens regularly. Someone drags me to paradise; but the journey stops near a pond filled with cackling geese! How shall I go leaving Esther behind? Ha … ha …'

Abba smiled weakly.

'Call that coward!'

Eema came running as if she had been waiting for the summons. Her eyes were like ponds after a spate of intense rain. Leah arrived, light-heartedly teasing as usual.

'Abba, the Sea of Galilee never dries up because of the tears shed by the women at Nazareth!'

Abba's face brightened, the clouds dissipating. Once Leah went away to America, Shalom would always be clouded and gloomy. Leah was Nazareth's radiance. Her presence mollified Eema's worries while Abba thrived on her liveliness and cheerfulness.

'Esther, I am longing for your special falafel.'

That was all what Eema was yearning for: to hear that Abba adored her cooking, to know that Leah liked the dress she made for her … These were the sheer joys of Eema's life. When Eema went away to the kitchen, surreptitiously wiping her eyes, Abba picked up a book with a bookmarked page, and handed it over to Ruth for reading aloud. The book was *I Saw Ramallah*, by Mourid Al-Barghouti.

'And who listens to the stories of those men, women and children who are taken by their displacement to that other shore from which no one ever returns? Our dead are scattered in every land. Sometimes we did not know where to go with their corpses; the capitals of the world refuse

to receive us as corpses as they refuse to receive us alive. And if the dead by displacement and the dead by weapons and the dead by longing and the dead by simple death are martyrs, and if poems are true and each martyr is a rose, we can claim to have made a garden of the world.'

Ruth was reading those lines when Eema returned with the falafel. The conversation rambled, and reached Sahal. Poets were dreamers and did nothing for those who were alive. That was Eema's opinion. 'What do you see in his writing anyway?' Eema was incensed. Leah provoked her further: 'The prophecy of disaster to befall the holy mountain!'

Eema's retaliation was fast and furious.

'*On the mountains of Israel you will fall, you and all your troops and the nations with you. I will give you as food to all kinds of carrion birds and to the wild animals … Then those who live in the towns of Israel will go out and use the weapons for fuel and burn them up—the small and large shields, the bows and arrows, the war clubs and spears. For seven years they will use them for fuel … For seven months the Israelites will be burying them in order to cleanse the land.*'

Hearing Eema quote the Old Testament with full gusto, Abba laughed quietly.

'Esther, people seek a God who looks after them, not one who leads a war.'

Eema's eyes darkened with displeasure. Casting a withering glance at Abba, she picked up the *Torah*, turned on her heels, and walked away. Leah clapped her hands in glee at that little drama. On her way out, Eema kissed the Mezuzah—the parchment inscribed with religious texts and attached in a case—at the doorpost. 'Eema is an exact replica of Valiyammachi—who at every opportunity would drop a kiss on the family Bible with the tattered old cover!' Ruth reflected, a smile playing on her lips.

'There is a prayer in the Mezuzah. *The Lord is our God, the Lord is one.* The people whom the Zionists abhor, believe the same. The same river, the same sea … And yet the brother fights with the brother! They kill each other … After every battle, our boundaries expand more and more. We had strong leaders but they didn't. Even Arafat failed in uniting a hundred different factions. How could they withstand the power of our weapons?'

Even before Abba completed his speech, there was an outburst from the kitchen.

'David, I won't forgive you for joining hands with those who murdered my mother!'

Eema's lips were trembling with emotion. Her eyes were ablaze with some inner fire. Ruth became petrified. Though she was used to mild skirmishes between Abba and Eema, this sort of fulmination was rare. The cackling of geese could be heard by the window.

Luckily, the one whom Shalom was waiting for entered the battlefront at the opportune moment. As soon as they sighted Asher, all the rain and thunderstorm ceased suddenly. A pleasant sunshine spread all around. Eema laid out her bundle of gripes before her son. She was insensitive to the fact that he had returned after a gruelling journey. Eema even forgot that Asher had not been reachable by cell phone for many days. He embraced her affectionately.

'Eema, Abba will never accept the cruelty of Hamas. Always, on both sides, the innocent people end up getting killed. Maybe we will both die too, one day. The authorities are the ones causing all these troubles.'

Eema covered Asher's mouth with her hand.

'Inauspicious nonsense! Wicked boy, you always side with your Abba, as if I don't know!'

Abba winked as Eema trounced away in a temper. Asher secretly shared the sweets he had brought with his father. In a very low voice, Abba queried: 'Ben, why did you risk the Erez Crossing?'

Asher's eyes twinkled.

'How did you know, Abba?'

'My third eye! Is he safe?' Abba smiled.

'Yes, he is with the farmers at the kibbutz.'

'Be careful at every step. Every word should be weighed before uttering. Remember: "*The mind of fools is in their mouths, but the mouth of the wise is in their mind. For our own mind sometimes keeps us better informed than seven sentinels sitting high on a watchtower.*"' Baba cautioned Asher.

Abba did not ask for any more details. That night Asher slept in Abba's room. The breeze climbed down the Golan hills and embraced Shalom with its coolness.

As Ruth lay sleepless, she started ruminating. 'Abba is a wonder! Because human beings like him exist, the fig trees are lush with fruits; the migratory birds remember the ways they have flown ...'

In her nightmare, Ruth was ushered to a pond where the geese lay cold and dead.

31

HANUKKAH

Aviv, Ka-itz, Stav, Horef: Spring, Summer, Autumn, Winter … Different seasons passed by in Ruth's life. Celebrations, without Alby and the children.

That December, there was heavy snowfall on Mount Hermon, whose summit straddles the border between Lebanon and Syria. It was colder than normal. The streets lay waiting for a ray of light. When Ruth, wrapped in protective woollen clothes, disembarked before the Damascus Gate to participate in the peace march starting from Temple Mount and ending at Bethlehem, both Lilly and Binu were waiting for her. Rubbing their hands together to combat the intense chill, they walked briskly. The Hebron road and the by-lanes had transformed into red rivers. There was a mélange of flags belonging to different nations, many bands, carols … happiness filled the air.

The police force was alert on the roads through which the peace procession would move; a distance of almost fifteen kilometres. 'Police guard for a peace march! Very interesting indeed. Freedom was lost when the British mandate ended up creating a country within another, that too a religious nation.' Binu's sagacious quip was interrupted by a Santa Claus who shook hands with them and sang a song to match his sprightly dance.

They robbed us, our mama's lullaby
Our baba's laughter and light ...

As if emerging from a rivulet's tender breast, the mellifluous song evoked pain and coolness. Ruth was familiar with that voice. As the Christmas Father disappeared, leaving ripples of wonder in his wake, Ruth called Asher.

'It was Sahal, I swear!'

A hearty burst of laughter was heard at the other end.

'Akhot, let him be! A lost opportunity is like the kite which has snapped free from your grip!'

There was a meeting of HOPE that day, at a refugee camp in Bethany. Maybe the Santa Claus mask was Sahal's disguise to cross the border. But how did he join the carol group? Asher was left wondering.

The next day, in the *Times of Israel*, there was a news article about the protest march in Al-Asaria city. There were young men holding placards: 'Stop Annexation', 'End the Occupation', 'To stand up for Palestine, you just need to be human'. The news elaborated that the protest turned violent at a check post, and ten or twenty participants were arrested. Abba expressed his concern that Hamas must have infiltrated the peaceful march and that the arrested were most likely innocent.

And soon, Hanukkah arrived. The eight days in the Kislev month converted the land to a lake of light. There were lighted menorah lamps everywhere and the calls of shofar, the ram's horn trumpet. The neighbourhood children were singing and floating about everywhere. Sofia, Ruth's little friend of the afternoons, was part of the children's ring. She danced before the camera. Defying her relatively short right leg, Sofia danced energetically, keeping up with the rhythm.

Hanukkah, oh Hanukkah, come light the menorah
Let's have a party, we will all dance the horah

'What is the relation between the Maccabean Revolt and the Festival of Lights?' Ruth did a vlog using that hard-hitting, historic title, featuring the scenes from Hanukkah. Sofia and Leah were the stars of her show. Leah exposited before Ruth's camera that the 'burning bush' which Prophet Moshe saw at Mount Horeb was symbolized by the seven branched candelabrum, the menorah lamp, which stood for wisdom. When Ruth referred to Prophet Moses, pronouncing the name in her native tongue as 'Mosa', Leah started giggling helplessly.

'What's in a name? The idea is what matters. Names are for mere convenience. Like calling God Yahweh or Lord or Allah or Eswaran.' Abba scolded Leah. Suffice it to say that the missile of 'protecting one's legacy' ensued from Eema's eyes. 'Making heathen gods equivalent to Yahweh? David, what's the difference between you and those who worshipped Baal?' Abba gently smiled as usual. 'Seven syllables turn the world into a paradise of music. Seven colours make the world marvellous. Shall the world's darkness be removed if seven lamps are lit up?' Ruth finished the vlog episode with Abba's question.

Nobody knew about an imminent event, lying in ambush, soon to sink the village in melancholy. Someone hurled a petrol bomb into the procession of singing children. Two kids were severely burned, one was little Sofia. She had been struggling to keep pace with her group when the explosion occurred. The river of light plummeted into a tunnel of darkness … Ruth was heartbroken. Lilly did not respond to her frantic calls. When Binu picked up the midnight call, he was very miffed. When Ruth wept over Sofia and voiced her apprehension that Sahal might have been arrested at Al-Asria, Binu criticized her vehemently.

'Listen, Ruth, what you sow, so you reap. You are justifying revolutionaries! Don't forget little Sofia. Guys like Sahal threw the bomb at her, right? Israel gives us our daily bread. Aren't they taking care of our needs? Just do your job. Now, get back to bed.'

Ruth was furious with Binu. A message came in the comment box of the Hanukkah vlog. It was Bhargavi Kutty again.

'Ruthless woman, instead of highlighting the Zionist celebrations, try to depict what the children of Gaza are enduring! These people are enjoying their great lights after firing missiles at them. Read the Book of Exodus! *"You must not mistreat or oppress foreigners in any way. Remember, you yourselves were once foreigners in the land of Egypt."* Is that why they are killing off the natives?'

Did he know the Bible so well? Then the unknown man was a Christian for sure! Or a Muslim. The next moment, Ruth shrugged away the uncharacteristic conclusion. Let Bhargavi Kutty not get stereotyped with a religion.

'The smart aleck's philosophy! Not all Jews are Zionists, Mister Bhargavi Kutty!' Ruth typed her reply.

Nina's message popped up in her mobile; she had seen the Hanukkah vlog.

'Ruthie, that lamp reminded me of Redditch town.'

Ruth could not sleep that night. A diary, with ink spreading over the pages, appeared in her memory again. And a small girl weeping over her mother, inside the solitariness of a school campus with massive walls in Mysore. Ruth started sobbing over Sofia again. The aroma of aloe wood and frankincense was spreading around her. 'Ruth, you are sitting next to a tomb,' her mind warned. Sofia's voice was still humming around her.

Gather round the table, we'll give you a treat
Sevinon to play with, and latkes to eat.

'*Your house shall be not an anchor but a mast. It shall not be a glistening film that covers a wound, but an eyelid that guards the eye.*' Ruth heard the voice of Mariam of Bethany. She was contemplating deeply, her hand cupping her chin. As usual, she was seated on the low stool.

'You who wander about Galilee with your unfinished gospel, arc you deprived of sleep too?'

'Sofia died.'

Ruth sat stunned.

'Better that she died. Life would have been a living death.'

Mariam sighed deeply and started scribbling down something, with her quill dipped in ink.

'Havera, I have no idea about the revolutionaries arrested in Bethany.'

Moonbeams fell on Mariam's book. She raised her head and stared at Ruth. 'Listen, two thousand years before, a courageous mother dwelled in this same place. "*Son, it is time to start your journey, for the sake of man.*" She imparted strength to a revolutionary. Somewhere nearby, she sat sleepless, waiting for him. Somewhere nearby, she heard that he had been captured by the enemies.'

Thousands of lamenting mothers thronged Ruth's heart. Mothers, waiting for the children taken away by the shoter.

'But a sword pierced her heart, Mariam!' Ruth whispered.

'Do you know that the word "amma" has a synonym, "wound"?'

Mariam was observing her. Ruth aimed at Mariam all the arrows of ruminations that had been lacerating her.

'Mariam, where is your Lord? How can he forgive all the hatred, injustice and horrible infractions?'

Gently pulling the curtains of the window to a side, and looking out at the moonlight outside, Mariam began to speak. 'Ruth, are you not aware of the story of Prophet Jonah? We Jews read about him on Yom Kippur. Though we read with our eyes, we often forget to see. And we fail to understand in our minds. God commands Jonah to go to Nineveh and prophesy against the city, notorious for its wickedness. But Jonah, terrified of the king, runs away and sets sail for Tarshish instead. A huge storm arises and the ship starts sinking. Blaming Jonah for the disaster, the sailors throw him overboard. Jonah is swallowed by a large fish and remains in its belly for three days and nights after which the fish vomits him out. A repentant Jonah reaches Nineveh and prophesies its destruction. He stays in a tent in the eastern part of the city, waiting for the fulfilment of his prophecy. The king and the citizens are humbled and broken, and willingly withdraw from the wickedness. God sees their repentant hearts and spares the city of Nineveh. Jonah is enraged at God's decision. God creates a plant to provide Jonah with shade in the scorching sun. Later, it withers due to a worm bite. An incensed Jonah, exposed to the full force of the sun, questions God.

'But God said to Jonah: "Do you have a right to be angry about the vine?" And he said: "I do. I am angry enough to die."

'But the Lord said: "You have been concerned about this vine, though you did not tend it or make it grow. It sprang up overnight, and died overnight. But Nineveh has more than a hundred and twenty thousand people who cannot tell their right hand from their left, and many cattle as well. Should I not be concerned about that great city?"'

Mariam looked into Ruth's eyes. 'The existential secret of the universe is in two syllables: *mer-cy.* He who has ears, let him hear!'

Mariam stepped into the moonlight languidly. Ruth watched her climbing the hill. The night smelled of the sea and a large shark-like fish, and it had the rhythm of sea waves. A hundred and twenty thousand people and their cattle were floating in a huge ship.

Screams arose from Sofia's house the next morning.

32

JOSEPHUS PERMUTATION

The police arrested us during the protests at Bethany and beat us black and blue. We were incarcerated in different cells. Nobody knew where his friends were. A lanky policeman dragged me to the office of the Mudir, the boss, in the morning. The Mudir was a rotund man with a harsh visage. He donned a cap embedded with stars of authority. The man was writing something with his left hand when we entered. There was a book on his table entitled The Atlas of Akeldama. *The author's name was hidden by the paperweight. In another language, having curvy, round letters, the title was repeated, beneath the English.*

After a few minutes, the Mudir raised his head. His eyes gleamed greedily like those of a lion seeing a prey after a long wait. The irony was that the man was squint-eyed. His glance fell somewhere else. 'Did you write this novel?' he bellowed. 'This is a translation by an Indian woman. Are you the author of the original book?' I swore that I wasn't. He grinned, and his face turned ugly. He gesticulated to the policeman who had brought me in.

I was blindfolded and taken away to someplace. About fifteen minutes must have passed. I must have climbed up and down many staircases by then. In between, we also crossed a tunnel. I could hear the vehicles rush above my head. When they removed the blindfold, I saw that we were on the summit of a dark hill. Rocks and boulders were abundant in the location. I was forcibly seated on top of a rock and tied up with a belt soon after. 'Allah, am I going to be killed?' Fear swallowed my tongue. I remembered Sarah.

I presumed that it was an isolated cliff like Masada. It appeared like a peak, surrounded by craggy rocks. There were spears and cannons nearby. I started trembling in terror. Soon, I discerned that there were twelve or more seated in a circle near me. Men and women, elders and children. Below us, there was a deep ravine! The squint-eyed man, holding a gun in his left hand, entered the circle of the captives. We sat shell-shocked, goggling dumbly at him.

'Listen, as far as we are concerned, Gaza, West Bank and this mountain are mere laboratories for new weapons. Who is there to question us? You are idiots! The world is not going to take umbrage at anything. Because, the world always stands with power and weapons. Hamas is busy creating tunnels for their own safety, rather than build shelter for you people. Now see what happens to overeager folk!'

Even when death was staring at me, I felt my blood boil. I was angry enough to kill him. His contemptuous preening! I shall never forget that. They destroy our towns, and raze our hills to hand over new projects to their capitalist conglomerates. And now, we have been brought here, as guinea pigs for their weapon testing!

Stopping his sermon, the Mudir yelled to a woman opposite me to start counting. In a trembling tone, she said, 'One.' In clockwise direction, the counting escalated. After skipping three, he chose the fourth. The man was blindfolded and taken away to the edge of the cliff. A gunshot rang out, making all earth quaver for a few moments … A scream was heard plummeting into the ravines! The echoes never ceased … The man stared at us impassively. Now he started the count from the one seated to the right of the murdered man. One, two, three, four. A chilling, shivering four.

The number four was a little child, a boy of eight or ten. Tears were streaming down his eyes as he stood up. Ah, Allah, how shall I ever forget that helpless stance? The shivering number four was looking at each of us, one by one. We were old enough to be his father, mother, sister or brother.

The poor child must have longed for someone to take over his sentence. I wished to yell, asking them to kill me instead of him. But my tongue remained numb. When the boy saw that nobody was moving, he followed the killer with sturdy footsteps. From the cliff edge, he turned to cast a backward glance at us. His eyes were shining with hope even at that moment. One more gunshot. One, two, three, four ... the selection of the unlucky men and women continued. Finally, in the circle of death, only three of us remained. I was in the middle.

A wind slashed the cliffs viciously, raising dust. The boulders swayed, as if entrapped in an earthquake. I had deduced by then that this game was based on the 'Josephus Permutation'. I would be the last one left. That was my lone hope.

What happened next was totally unforeseen. The young man and woman, seated on either side of me, held hands and leapt off the cliff, without waiting for the murderer's bullets. The Mudir vanished from the scene. The sinewy policeman untied me from the rock and led me away, seemingly from a game show for spectators. He blindfolded me before the journey. More tunnels, more corridors; many, many steps. 'Do you know the meaning of the word Akeldama?' he asked me as I stumbled forward. 'Field of blood,' I answered, unsteadily.

When I opened my eyes, I was in a desolate spot. I was pushed inside a bus waiting there. I saw a boy, startlingly similar to the one murdered just a while before, in the front seat. There were a few more passengers in the bus. I disembarked at the Damascus Gate. I could not sleep for weeks together. Whenever my eyes shut, I heard gunshots. I saw corpses plunging down the cliff. I would panic that my turn had arrived. Then, I would see the little boy's teary eyes.

I am still searching for the author of The Atlas of Akeldama. *(*Hello Death, Howdy Freedom: *Sahal Al Fadi)*

33

MASADA

'David stayed in the wilderness strongholds and in the hills of the Desert of Ziph. Day after day Saul searched for him, but God did not give David into his hands'.

Hello, I am so near you. Find me!

Ruth gaped at the memo on the Facebook messenger. A man standing all alone on a huge boulder. The sun was setting on the horizon afar. Who was that dark shadow with the obscure face? There were two pictures in the timeline. A lonesome tent in the desert. The next, a slender tree, swept by the wind.

Ruth remembered having seen the tree. As she sat sipping kahwa with the Bedouin girl, the tree had slowly emerged from the fog. The Arab's pickup van had trundled past the tree. The young man, the sweetheart of Bhargavi Kutty, had crossed the same tree in his four-wheeler. She felt a lightning streak through her innards. Was he stalking her, as Saul did David? What was the connection between the Desert of Ziph and the youth otherwise?

Abba and Agy Chechi had spent lakhs of rupees for Alby's medical treatment and her children's education. Ruth had a mountain of responsibilities to shoulder. She had absolutely no intention of getting trapped in someone's snare. The present visa, sponsored by Abba, was for four and a half years. Perhaps it could be extended—but it all depended on Abba's state of health. 'Dear Lord, may Abba remain healthy and safe forever!' The status of the visa was immaterial when it came to Abba's well-being. Ruth made the sign of the cross and drove away the despondent thought that had butted in.

Losing courage, Ruth gently turned the pages of the Bible. She explored the prophecies of Samuel, and read the psalms. '... *Be my rock of refuge, a strong fortress to save me.*'

'Abba, on which mountain did David hide?' Ruth asked hesitantly, scared that it would sound silly. Abba, who was resting in the armchair, listening to the calls of the shofar from afar, laughed quietly.

'These are all assumptions, Bat. Some say it is Masada.'

His eyes were locked on the army van which was skidding through the gravelly road, raising a cloud of dust. Was Abba seeing the vehicle?

'Anticipating a siege of Jerusalem, King Herod created a secret escape route to Moab, today's Jordan. And a few forts too. One is Masada.'

A flock of bright-coloured birds was circling the synagogue. The shofar calls were coming nearer. Was the army marching to the tunes of the trumpet, across the hills? Ruth remembered the tragic events that transpired at Masada during the first century, as recorded by the Roman Jewish historian and military leader Flavius Josephus. She had started reading historical treatises inspired by Abba, for adding more gravity to her vlogs. Josephus the ancient historian, with his impressive headgear and snow-white beard, fascinated her.

Abba started coughing ceaselessly.

'Professor, please take a nap instead of telling tales at noon,' Leah teased affectionately, having rushed in, worried by the bout of coughing.

'Isn't your test tomorrow? How is your preparation, Bat?'

'Nothing much ... but Leah Menahem shall return victorious.'

'How can you be so sure of that?' Abba laughed.

'Well, I am Professor David's daughter!'

Leah hugged her father and planted a sound kiss on his cheek. Then she started fretting that Abba was feverish. It was Shabbat. And the one person who was supposed to arrive, hadn't made it home yet. Abba had seated himself in the portico, in anticipation of Asher's arrival. Leah knew that Abba was extremely worried about him. As she coaxed him inside, blaming the dry December wind as being bad for his health, Leah pouted.

'Ruth, you spoil him too much! See, how obstinate Abba has become?'

Some unvoiced words hovered around Abba's lips. As it is, he got to see Leah rarely enough. Laughter and playful banter would fill the air. Ruth would remember her father then.

Did he ever think about her? At least in certain moments when the mist of forgetfulness moved away? Now Ruth's father was in a care home run by nuns. Sister Violet had divulged that he no longer remembered anything. Ruth remembered his eyes overflowing with tears as she set out for Riyadh; and the taste of the fish that he had caught and cooked for her that day. Such fond memories were rare. Somehow, Ruth's appan had been a transient, hazy presence in her life. Occasionally, she would feel guilty about not being there to take care of him. What other choice did she have? She had to find a way to earn a livelihood.

All through the day, Ruth wondered about the relationship of the nameless young man with Masada. Wasn't there something symbolic in him reaching the hideout of David and Herod? The Jewish revolutionaries had sought refuge in Masada when the Romans burnt down Jerusalem. After setting fire to logs to burn down the fortress gate, when the Romans entered the palace, what met them was a formidable sight. The warriors had killed themselves, unwilling to become victims of Roman swords. Just a few children and women had been left behind alive. 'Freddie's henchman, why did you come to that fortress of death?'

Caught in her reverie, Ruth watched Mariam of Bethany descending the hills, disentangling her robe from the briars it was caught in.

'I was one of the Jewesses who escaped death in Masada.' Mariam smiled soberly.

'And what is your proof of that?' Ruth countered.

Mariam clambered up a fig branch.

'Hasn't the historian of the first century written about a Rabbi who worked miracles? A truth seeker, who won debates with innumerable scholars? What about Pontius Pilate sentencing him to death by crucifixion?' Mariam started swinging, after aiming the salvo of questions at Ruth.

Ruth had only vague notions about Mariam's queries. She decided to read more from Josephus's writings.

'Well, he would not have inscribed about a woman from Bethany amongst the living!' Ruth mocked.

'Ah, you believe only what's written. Those who are scribes for their emperors, they are bound to write a multitude of untruths!'

Mariam was annoyed, and she entered the home through the western door. Seated at Eema's tailoring machine, she started stitching an emerald green dress. Eema had been embroidering white designs on it. It was then that Asher's call came.

'Akhot, can you please come to Masada tomorrow? There is something important.'

'Ahkh, what are you doing there?'

'I am caught up in some work at the site. Shall wait for you in the cafe, beyond the restrooms, okay? Call me when you arrive.'

It was a bizarre coincidence. Asher was at Masada, the same place mentioned by the young man in his message. Two sentinels of secrets were waiting for her. Abba was greatly relieved, having waited for Asher's call all day. Happiness started encircling Shalom like a bird set free from the cage.

Binu and Lilly accompanied Ruth as she climbed the Masada cliff the next day. Ruth told them about the excruciating, inexplicable events that had transpired after Sahal was arrested at Bethany. Lilly was sceptical about such a hideous punishment being carried out in a place like Masada. In her opinion, it was some sort of a 'show', enacted to terrify the rebellious young men. But Binu refuted that argument. The place was rife with many mysterious tunnels, caves and hills. He affirmed that there was a high probability of such a cliff, as Sahal described, being somewhere in close proximity.

They were climbing a winding 'snake trail' then. Ruth felt as if someone was dragging her through the boulders. She clutched at Lilly desperately. She saw a group of slaves moving uphill, carrying huge leather bags full of water. They were panting and heaving, holding onto stone ledges, as they ascended the hill, with water for the palace. Among them were workers toiling at the fortifications meant for the emperor's protection. Some slaves were being crushed under the rocks that rolled down during accidents. Ruth shuddered in horror.

The Dead Sea lay lifeless in the west, oblivious to everything around. The sea breeze tightened its hold on Ruth's kurti and tried to dislodge her footing. The wind gathered strength. Was the fort on the hilltop quivering?

'Lilly, better hold her tight! Either the wind will take her along or the squint-eyed cop!' Binu guffawed.

The young man from the desert was not seen anywhere. Neither on the flatland at the summit, nor at the museum or even inside the cable car. Ruth was grossly disappointed. Without a clear, specified spot, how was one supposed to find another in the vast space of the Masada National Park? They loitered for some more time and then moved to the cafe to wait for Asher. A waiter, with an unusually long nose, was observing them with alacrity. Perhaps he was the cafe owner himself. 'Namaskaram!' Hearing him wish them in Malayalam, the trio was taken aback. A Malayali shop atop Masada? The man roared with laughter at their befuddled looks.

'We open shops even on the moon, let alone Masada!'

When he served them steamed maize and grape juice, a tall man wearing calipers stepped inside the cafe. After hailing the new entrant with a 'Salam', the long-nosed man hugged him. The man, who was addressed as Suleiman, whispered something into the cafe owner's ear and went out the same way, with a peculiar gait, leaning towards the right.

'What about a shawarma? A special from Safa Marwah?' the long-nosed man suggested. They were not interested.

'Did you see the synagogue? Where they discovered the Ezekiel scrolls?'

'What scrolls?"

'The highlight of the scrolls dug out at Masada by those Akri fellows!'

'Akri fellows?' Lilly started giggling at his bizarre reference to archaeologists.

'Don't laugh! It is written that the bones will be put back together again and that the Jewish people shall return to their land from all over the world. If you had come yesterday, you might have watched the army's march and oath taking ceremony.'

The long-nosed man was getting more eloquent when three people stepped inside the cafe, clad in military uniforms. His attention was diverted and he became busy in welcoming them. After waiting for some more time in vain, as the breeze from the Dead Sea wafted around, the trio descended the hills, frustrated at not meeting anyone they had come for. Ruth tried Asher's number again. It was ringing but the call was not being answered. Before she reached Shalom, his message would arrive: 'Sorry, I couldn't meet you since the circumstances were adverse.'

That night, as Ruth googled for more of Masada's history, she sat dazed at a piece of information. 'The ones who remember Josephus today, are mathematicians and computer scientists. It is due to the Josephus Permutation.'

The algorithm, which selected the murder victims, on Sahal's black day of custody …!

34

COVID-19

Out of the blue, the earth darkened. A heavy sense of despair spread everywhere due to the Covid-19 pandemic. Like the rest of the world, the wind of horror raged around Nazareth too. Israel toughened its control and restrictions. The effort to create vaccines started in earnest.

The hospitals and nursing homes in Europe were overwhelmed with Covid patients. The nurses and doctors risked their lives while combating the virus. Agnes hardly slept in those days. How could she, when all around her were lifeless bodies? They were shifted to cemeteries in hearse vans. How could she call them corpses? They never had an opportunity to see or even bid farewell to their loved ones. They lay stacked like luggage waiting for airplanes. Many who expected to return from the hospitals, had left behind half-sipped teacups, meals cooked partially in kitchens … and went straight to stretchers, ventilators, gurneys, electric crematoriums … Who could have ever imagined that the world would face such dismal days? Those who went away believing it was temporary, never returned again.

Like in Kerala, Nazareth was better off compared to many regions of the world.

Now the world was another Palestine—running for refuge at the sight of a missile, without even shutting the door of one's home …

When Ruth and Leah were exchanging complaints about Asher's inexplicable vanishing acts, seated on a hill slope as twilight set in, Agy Chechi's video call arrived with sad news. A medieval church appeared on the screen. The stonewalls were ashen in hue. The Gothic church tower seemed to reach the skies. There were silent pine trees around. The huge gateway of the cathedral, constructed of dark wood, opened slowly, making a grating noise. Four or five human figures covered from head to toe stepped out. They were carrying a coffin on their shoulders. Who was the priest? Who were the good folk? Who was the corpse? Ruth and Leah were at a loss to understand what was happening on screen. Everyone was in PPE kits. Agy Chechi was videographing the scene from a distance.

The funeral dirge stirred waves of sorrow. The ripples reached Nazareth too.

Agy Chechi came in front of the camera.

'Father Aloysious is no more.'

Ruth sat frozen in shock. Someone was hitting her head hard with an iron cudgel. Due to the tears, she couldn't see anything at all.

'He could have lived. You know, he got a ventilator yesterday as per rules. But he gave it up.'

Agy Chechi's voice broke. The camera turned to cover the funeral procession again. The requiem was moving to the cemetery now. She was probably standing enervated, beneath the pine trees. Later that night, when Agy Chechi elaborated on the events, Ruth had been shocked.

Father Aloysious had been on a European tour. When the flights got cancelled unexpectedly, he could not return. His health deteriorated rapidly. Back at home, a village waited with bated breath for his updated medical report. Ventilators were scarce, and there were thousands in queue.

'Agnes, I am not one to succumb so easily! I don't want that contraption. The plight of lying like this, without even seeing a human face is intolerable. I have always lived amidst human beings.

Now I feel that I haven't seen anyone smile for centuries! The nurses and doctors are covered from head to toe, and I hardly know their attitudes or expressions. But I know one truth—they are angels, carrying the gift of life!'

Father Aloysious's words resounded in Agnes's ears.

A depressed young man and Father Aloysious were on adjacent beds. Though he knew nothing about the utterly silent, immobile youth, Father was greatly concerned about him. His condition was extremely critical.

'Father, I am going to die. I wish to confess to you before that. I have never believed in any religion, but I have committed some sins, which God, if He exists, will find hard to forgive.' The young man atoned in a feeble voice.

'My job was very strange. You will be shocked on hearing about it. It included looting and murder. I ended up in the blacklist of my boss and had to hide from him and his gang in multiple countries. Finally, I landed up here, this land of death. Father, if you have the authority to condone my sins, please do so. Let me die in peace.'

Father Aloysious felt a great grief.

'My child, the moment you decided to move away from the sins, you have been forgiven! Right now, I, who might brag about being holy, would be more sinful than you.'

Father Aloysious embraced the young man as if he was hugging the whole world. Afterwards, Father told himself, like the Crucified One: '*It is finished.*' He took the decision with unflinching determination. It was the moment when a human being realized that his life had been fruitful.

Before offering his ventilator to the young man, Father Aloysious had called Agnes. The duty nurse had helped him. 'In my seventieth year of living, there is nothing holier to undertake, than bringing back a young man from the edge of death, my dear!' When Agnes heard that frail, yet steady voice, she felt swamped by sadness.

Certain human beings depart after leaving behind a lighted lamp on the pathway. They do not know how many find their way to the opposite shore, guided by that radiant beacon.

That night Ruth dreamt that she was lost in a deep forest. There was pitch darkness everywhere. A strange moonlight illuminated a graveyard decorated with beautiful roses. A flambeau, made of coconut leaves, was burning nearby. Ruth was kneeling on the spot. After some time, she took up the flambeau, and walked through the forest. She reached a village at dawn.

Some day, Ruth would journey to the resting place of the one who had pulled her out of the abyss of distress. Through the snow, in a ski pulled by reindeers … It was that strange fantasy which jolted her awake from sleep the next morning. The cathedral, with its sky-high stone tower, situated amidst the snow-drenched pines, continued to call out to Ruth …

On many nights that followed, Ruth would wake up hearing the dark wooden doors of the gigantic church creak open.

35

PESACH, THE PASSOVER

1 April 2021

The *Bordeaux Itinerary*, also known as the *Jerusalem Itinerary*, written by an anonymous Roman pilgrim in the fourth century, mentions that Caiaphas's residence is visible during the ascent from the Pool of Siloam to Mount Zion. The writer hailed from the then Roman province of Gallia Aquitania, now a part of Bordeaux, France. On the location, where the Jewish High Priest's house stood as per the writer, one sees the Church of Saint Peter in Gallicantu. On the opposite side of the courtyard of the church, one can view the Garden of Gethsemane and the All Nations Church.

The live vlog which Ruth conducted at the church, dedicated to the episode of 'Denial of Peter', was watched by nearly one thousand two hundred viewers.

It was Pesaha, or Pesach, the Passover. The doorposts of the Jewish homes were smeared with the sacrificial lamb's blood. The night, when the Angel of Death 'passed over' Egypt, without smiting the firstborn of the Israeli households. Ages hence, the night when Jesus the Nazarene was betrayed with a kiss. Ruth was enduring the night of Christ's passion and sufferings, just like Him. It was a miraculous, narrow escape.

When vaccination rates increased, the Covid restrictions became less severe. The pilgrims started arriving in Jerusalem. Asher had dropped Ruth at the churchyard and gone off towards the Old City's Western Wall. He wished to visit Jacob's Eema. Rebecca, who had forsaken her son, for merely carrying out his assigned governmental task, was yet to forgive herself. Jacob's Eema had come to the Wailing Wall for prayers that day. Asher had promised to return by the time Ruth completed shooting her vlog. Eema was staying in an apartment with a view of the Golden Gate. A house hidden by apple trees. It was a place so familiar that Asher could reach there even in his sleep.

Though Ruth was unaware of what was about to transpire on her fourth visit to the church, rather uncharacteristically, she got emotional while shooting her live vlog. Things spiralled out of control all at once. On hearing the harsh command, 'Catch her', Ruth stopped breathing. 'Are those men coming after you, Ruth?' She had no idea. She ran up the steps and hid among the crowd. It all happened in the blink of an eye; even before she could reconcile herself to what was happening.

Mariam of Bethany was standing dejectedly near the wall embedded with the picture of the Last Supper. In the iridescent brilliance of the light streaming in through the glass mosaic of the cross-shaped window, her sapphire eyes were glittering. Ruth clutched Mariam's hand, and found herself rushing furiously forward. 'Woman, I know him not!' A headlong haste, past the Maccabi steps. 'The flight or fight' mechanism under stress, which Dr Shahana once mentioned, had taken hold of Ruth. She was oblivious of the devotees, who were kissing the stone steps, look askance at her mad flight. Crossing the parking, the cafes and restrooms, the shops selling rosaries and crucifixes, she ended up in Akeldama: the field of blood. It had been purchased with the thirty pieces of silver, which Judas Iscariot had thrown away. 'Ruth, Akeldama shall betray you,'

Mariam was muttering into her ears. Ruth's only goal was to reach the Wailing Wall.

Ruth knew that the Western Wall was in the Jewish Quarters. The Old City had eight entrances. Which gate shall she choose? What was the direction? She sought help from passers-by but they could not guide her. Most were pilgrims who were not acquainted with the layout of the city. Ruth joined a group of pilgrims who were moving in a line, singing hymns. She must have trailed along for almost thirty minutes. Ruth never comprehended that the group had moved past the Dung Gate as well as the Damascus Gate near the Dome of the Rock, and moved out of the city walls.

They were now at Kedron Valley, in front of a Byzantine church. 'This is the place where Stephen was stoned to death,' a Benedictine monk was explaining to the onlookers. The group trooped inside the church. 'Ruth, where are you going now?' She gazed in bewilderment in all four directions, standing next to Saint Stephen's statue. Was someone following her? Ruth was sweating heavily.

To her surprise, a bald head gleamed amongst the crowd. Binu! Ruth started crying on seeing him. She ran to him and caught hold of his hand.

'Binu, quick, help me reach the Wailing Wall.'

'What are you doing here? What's the matter?'

On hearing Ruth's story, Binu started laughing.

'Why should the Israeli police follow a water snake? Are you a notorious spy by any chance? They mistook you for someone else! You shot off like a rocket on seeing them. Ruth, your head is in the clouds most of the time! You crossed the Western Wall on the way here. Fool, how long did you wander?' Binu chortled with glee.

'They would have stoned me to death!'

Seeing Ruth's bafflement, Binu shook with laughter.

'Oh sure, they would have crucified you! You are so dim-witted at times. Listen dear, this is not the first century any more. If you had only activated the GPS while you ran … Idiot!'

'Mariam was my GPS,' Ruth murmured.

Binu looked at her as if she had turned crazy. They moved towards his vehicle, and started off. Since there was no parking nearby, he agreed to wait at the Christian Quarters. He sketched the route to Wailing Wall on a piece of paper for Ruth. He also marked the return path, in case Ruth could not meet Asher.

'Be careful. Don't go chasing after Mariam to Bethany. In case you miss the directions, you will end up at the Muslim Quarters or the Armenian Quarters, remember!' Binu cautioned her.

Ruth crossed the arched façade of the Damascus Gate, and re-entered the Old City. Many narrow alleys, thronging with shops. Kiosks selling figurines of saints, Menorah lamps, textiles and wine. Junctions cropped up in between. Ruth cast furtive glances behind, and quickened her pace. Fear, carrying a cross, trailed by her side. She felt as if Temple Mount was a gargantuan tree and that she was a delicate leaf dangling at the tip of its bough; on the verge of dropping.

Ruth reached the intersection of four roads; the Seventh Station on the Way of the Cross, the Via Dolorosa. The spot where Jesus fell with the cross, for the second time. Ruth stared at Binu's rough map. Where should she turn? Left, or right? She saw that the chapel, towards the right of the pathway, was open. Suddenly, she sighted a policeman in uniform. She panicked and ran towards the chapel. It was as if someone had pulled her inside. She fell, like a freshly hewn fig branch, amidst the crowd of devotees prostrating themselves. Ruth lay prostrate, her head bent low. She was alert to the sound of boots approaching her, even amongst the prayerful chants around. After a few minutes, she felt as if someone was nudging her. The cop had vanished. Ruth hurried out of the chapel. An old man, wearing a mask, stared at her. She asked him the way to the Jewish Quarters. He pointed left. 'Jewish Quarters to the left, Christian Quarters to the right.'

A vast courtyard loomed ahead. On one side, there were offices of the Jewish organizations, shops selling *Torah* and *Talmud*. People were praying, their heads leaning reverently against the wall. Some were chattering happily. Mothers were pushing babies in prams. Men wearing kippah caps wandered about. Women, with their heads covered, were walking about too. When a blue-eyed woman glared at her, Ruth hastily covered her head. How was she supposed to discover Asher in this crowd? His cell phone was switched off. 'Ruth, did he discard you in Caiaphas's dungeon?' Maybe his phone battery got discharged. What if he had returned to Saint Peter's Church? She metamorphosed into an elegy amidst all the lamentations …

Finally, Ruth called Binu.

'Binu, please come over. I don't see Asher anywhere and I'm scared to go to the parking lot. I will stand in front of the place where they distribute food for free.'

Ruth captured the scenes at Jewish Quarters until Binu reached her side. A dignified old man, with snow-white beard, was raising his hand and speaking loudly. It was the same man who had showed her the way. There was a group of curious kids surrounding him. His voice was rising over all the laments reverberating around.

'Dear folk, here is our Holy Wall. The massive wall that was constructed in the time of King Herod by stacking huge stone blocks one above another. Our Western Wall, which triumphantly stood undestroyed, though the Romans wrecked the city and the temple. Beloved people of Jerusalem, for whom are you lamenting? For the destroyed temple? Or for the ancestors, hounded and tortured all over the world? Or for the innocent Rabbi, whom our forebears crucified, tricked by the wily Romans? If we continue to torment the 'son of man' on our streets, what's the use of our lamentations? Shall the stains of our sins disappear if we hit our heads against the wall? Dear people, are you not afraid that the tears of the mothers of the murdered young men shall shatter this wall?'

A police officer in blue appeared at that juncture. He gesticulated that the old man should shut up.

'Listen, Jerusalem means the City of Peace. This city on Mount Moriah …' The old man's enthusiasm did not abate. Two people caught hold of him and dragged him away. They disappeared inside the two-storeyed limestone building nearby.

As soon as she entered Binu's vehicle, a flustered Ruth pleaded, 'Binu, drop me at the Central Bus Station.' She wished to reach the sanctuary of Shalom as quickly as possible.

'Tonight? No way.'

Binu drove to Lilly's apartment. The city was shrouded with despair and the streets were desolate. Police checking was happening at regular intervals.

'Where are you? Come quickly, there is something afoot in the city.' Binu's friend called him. It was then that they became aware of the happenings that day. Near the Al-Aqsa Mosque, there had been an incident of gunfire; and many were hurt, including a policeman. Since it was presumed to be a Hamas attack, the police were diligently checking all suspicious vehicles.

When Lilly opened the door, she saw Binu's grin and Ruth's anxiety.

'Please ensure that this woman spy, chased assiduously by the Israeli police, is dropped at the bus station tomorrow morning. It is Shabbat the day after and there will be no buses then. She will have to hire a sherut, service taxi, instead.'

Binu left quickly, wanting to reach home before the problems on the street got aggravated. Ruth called Shalom. Eema was miserable because she had not heard from Asher. He had never missed the Passover ceremony at home, despite a million tasks. Something was surely amiss. Eema was waiting for him with his favourite traditional Pesach dish of Gefilte fish. The sumptuous Sedar meal of Passover, lay cold on the dining table at Shalom. Ruth reminisced about Eema's recipes. Especially, the wondrous paste she made with fruits, nuts, honey, wine and spices. It was so delicious … spread on unleavened pita bread. Asher would grab Leah's portion too. Thus the Pesach fight would begin! Where on earth was Asher?

Al Jazeera featured the picture of the young man shot dead near Al-Aqsa Mosque. One television channel was showcasing the Passover custom of hitting each other on the back, with leeks or scallions. The ritual symbolized the Egyptian slave driver's whips in the time of Pharaoh. Had they flogged the bloodied young man with scallions too? On the night, flailing about in a swamp of turmoil, Ruth lay sleepless on Lilly's bed, watching the news. She was expecting the doorbell to ring any moment and armed cops to march inside. The fear was oddly persistent.

Ruth thought that she heard the grunts of swines. It was the fourth or the fifth time that she was hearing the ugly sound! Every time before, it had been a bad omen. Once, Ruth had hit her head on the glass door at Shalom and got bruised very badly. The second time, Abba had collapsed suddenly and they had to call an ambulance. Ruth shut her ears and closed her eyes. After a while, she shook awake Lilly, since the niggling fear was overwhelming.

Though vexed, Lilly took pity on her. 'Just a second, let us drive away all fears!' She opened a bottle of wine. Before long, the 'Jezreel Valley' was emptied! As intoxication seized them, the grunting of swines vanished slowly. The streets of Jerusalem disappeared from sight too. Ruth saw Valiyammachi, and Maluvettathy's cinema hall. She skipped through the village pathways in a gentle drizzle. She sat watching by the farm ridge as her father ploughed the land with oxen.

Lilly started giggling.

'Do you know something that my father said? Bring me bottles of Lueria Rosso or Masada when you come home! How did my appan discover these names?'

'Maybe the parish priest told him. Could be Father Google too!' Ruth laughed. 'His daughter is in a land where wine was brewed ten thousand years before. And he gets to drink local arrack!'

They laughed so much that tears streamed down their eyes. Lilly hummed a sardonic ditty her appan sang, while relishing Lueria Rosso and Indian mackerel, prepared with kokum.

Padikkale Mariye, Pentecosil cherane …

Maria dear, join the Pentecose …

In the middle of many joyrides with Maria, Lilly slipped into deep sleep. Watching her sleep, Ruth posted the scenes caught at the Wailing Wall in her vlogging site.

The viewers of Nazareth had different responses to the post.

Bhargavi Kutty: 'Whew, good to know you are safe! They are praying for the reconstruction of Solomon's ancient Temple at Temple Mount! The Dome of the Rock stands there now.'

Jesus: Aren't you ashamed to post the video of the old man preaching for the Palestinians?

Nazareth: (With a smiling emoji) A New Age Jesus!

Bhargavi Kutty: If Jesus comes back, he will first drive away such pathetic Christians!

Nazareth: Please desist from dragging in religion and caste in the comment box!

Ruth would not return to Nazareth the next morning. The message would come searching for her by then, from the seclusion of the Old City …

36

THE CITY OF PEACE

They were planning to have an Easter vigil at the Church of the Holy Sepulchre, aka the Church of Resurrection, in the Old City of Jerusalem. Lilly was firm that Ruth should return to Nazareth only after exuberantly celebrating Easter, relishing the exquisite combination of appam and mutton stew! But why was Ruth suddenly adamant on returning on Good Friday? Lilly was displeased with her.

The Malayalis working in Israel usually arrived in Jerusalem for the Easter week. They would move towards Calvary, from Beersheba and Tel Aviv and other places, a motley crowd of men and women, from towns and kibbutzes.

Lilly watched Ruth's Pesaha vlog post. There were restrictions on video shooting in the city. Maybe the cops had come for someone else, who had broken the rules. They must have realized their mistake. Nobody had followed Ruth afterwards, had they? Lilly consoled Ruth.

Ruth's plan was upended by a message that unexpectedly arrived in her Facebook Messenger that night.

'Erev tov. Akhot, where are you?'

The message was from an ID called 'Jericho'. New profile. The profile picture was of a lush tree, with a broad, domed crown. 'Who does it belong to?' Ruth shook awake Lilly. Though irritated at her sleep getting broken, Lilly said, stifling a yawn, that it was the sycamore tree at Jericho. The short-statured Zacchaeus had climbed a sycamore to see Jesus as he passed by, at Jericho.

There was a news item about Jericho in the timeline. An underlined sentence ... *These events happened in the oldest cities known to the world, where the itinerant human beings settled down for the first time.* 'Wasn't that what Asher spoke about Jericho city once?' Ruth wondered.

'Where are you? What happened to your phone? I am with Lilly.' Ruth's fingers flew on the keyboard.

'Neruda's message came, as they started following me, when Peter was crying. Somehow, I got here. Tell Abba that I am busy. But I have something for you. Come to see Veronica tomorrow around 10 a.m. She will be standing next to the sixth Greek, after the Arabic school and the Franciscan chapel. Then go and meet Neruda's sis. I guess, Akhot, you haven't met her yet. She is like a rosary with olives, in the house of bread, in the cave where the cattle were tied. Enter through the door of modesty.

'Look for Eusebius Sophronius Hieronymus. She will be there with him, where he sits and writes. She is actually waiting for me. Tell her to be safe. Give her a kiss on the forehead, for me.'

'I don't understand a word,' Ruth replied.

'Ask your friend. You won't see this profile again.'

The 'Hello' which Ruth typed afterwards, remained undelivered. What was happening? Was Asher at Jericho? Ruth was caught in the whirlpools of anxiety. She understood one hint ... 'when Peter was crying', surely meant the Saint Peter's church! 'Did someone follow Asher? Did they come searching for her, after he slipped away?' He had not written anything clearly. However, it was evident that he was afraid of the message getting leaked. Lilly got up and with the gusto of playing a game of treasure hunt, organized all the clues on a piece of paper.

1. Neruda 2. Veronica 3. Rosary of olives 4. Arabic school and the Franciscan chapel 5. Sixth Greek 6. House of bread 7. The

cave where the cattle were tied 8. Door of modesty 9. Eusebius Sophronius Hieronymus.

Ruth scoured her memory for a girl named Veronica. Did Asher have a friend called Veronica?

The television channels were showing the conflicts in the city. The afternoon skirmishes at Temple Mount were being played repeatedly for the fourth or fifth time. The police were strolling the Way of the Cross, the Via Dolorosa, the route through which a procession was to be undertaken the next day. The security forces were vigilant after the day's events. Suddenly a Franciscan chapel appeared on the screen. It was the church situated on the Way of Sorrows.

Lilly shouted enthusiastically, 'Got it! The place where Asher will be waiting!'

'The Sixth Greek. The sixth station in the Via Dolorosa … the place where Veronica wiped Christ's face with her veil!' Lilly was exuberant at her deductions. 'There is a Greek catholic church on that spot. Asher will be there.'

But how would Asher reach that place with all the police check posts around? Ruth couldn't bring herself to accept the finding. Though they searched the internet for a place connecting Veronica and the Greeks, they found nothing.

'Neruda is nobody else but Sahal. That's his nickname,' Ruth observed. She guessed that the clue to find Sarah, Neruda's sister, might be a bakery. Lilly laughed out at her innocence.

'You idiot, do you know the meaning of "Bethlehem"? House of bread! Sarah is at Bethlehem. Clue number seven. The cave where the cattle was tied. Maybe it is "Shepherd's Field"? The place where the angels proclaimed about Jesus's birth to the shepherds. But I am bewildered by the last clue. Eusebius Sophronius Whatever!'

Ruth felt that she was seated in the bus rushing to Jerusalem from the Jordanian border. She remembered Nina. She had written a travelogue, based on her pilgrimage. Nina was fast asleep when

Ruth's call reached her. She kindly forgave Ruth for interrupting her slumber and replied after a bit of contemplation.

'True, Sarah is at Bethlehem. But not in the "Shepherd's Field". In the "cave of the cattle", where Jesus was born. That means, in the Church of Nativity. The Shepherd's Field is very far from there. Clue number eight: Door of Modesty, happens to be a door which has to be crossed with a bowed head. That is the entrance of the Church of Nativity. I still remember what Father Aloysious spoke about that day ... "Nobody can access God without walking through the Door of Modesty!" Undoubtedly, Sarah will be there. Now, for the last clue ... Eusebius Sophronius Hieronymus. Try googling. It is the name of Saint Jerome. Someone called Jerome will be around. Find out.'

How easily Nina had unknotted the riddle!

'Ruthie, stay safe. Jerusalem is all over the news. Be loyal to the country. They will not tolerate any violation of laws.'

Nina was apprehensive that the one who had survived the desert would be entrapped in a demolished vessel mid-sea.

But how could Ruth stay away from helping Asher? She was sure that he was in deep trouble.

Lilly called Binu and requested him to accompany them to the Via Dolorosa at Temple Mount, sharp at nine in the morning.

'Is that why you woke me up at midnight? Wicked woman! I thought the cops had come searching for our water snake!' He laughed.

When Ruth informed him that they might have to travel to Bethlehem, Binu teased her, 'Visit Bethlehem on Good Friday? After yesterday's running race, have you gone crazy?'

'Ah, I have always been like that. I celebrate Vishu during Onam and vice versa.' Ruth laughed along, hiding her trepidation.

'By the time we finish walking the Way of the Cross, it will be near afternoon. Bethlehem is ten kilometres further. We have to cross the border. The checking will be tough due to yesterday's conflicts. Bethlehem is in Palestine, remember!' Binu tried to dissuade Ruth.

That night Ruth did not sleep. She saw Asher hiding among the branches of a sycamore tree. Standing at the foot of the tree, she hailed him, 'Asher, come down.' At that moment, the army was advancing through the Carmel Valley, from the city of Haifa, along the shore of Tiberius. The beat of the march was medieval.

37

VIA DOLOROSA

The next morning dawned. The Via Dolorosa, the Way of Sorrows, began. Narrow, stone-paved pathway. Ancient fortresses on either side, and medieval façades. Sadness and fear were palpable in the darkness permeating the corridors.

9 a.m.

They stood at the beginning of the path that ended at Golgotha. 'Out of the fourteen stations of the Cross, nine are by the wayside. One is outside the Church of the Holy Sepulchre. Four are inside it,' Binu informed, as they started the journey. Only the sixth station was etched in Ruth's mind. The rest of the thirteen were irrelevant. They joined a Malayali group of pilgrims who were singing mournful gospel songs.

'And I was sentenced to be crucified ... tell me what sin had I committed?'

An old nun, dressed in sky-blue attire, was singing mournfully. A group of armed police men marched past them.

9.10 a.m.

At the place purportedly to be the Praetorium or headquarters of the Roman Governor Pilate, there was a board: 'Al Omaria'. Lilly quipped, 'That's an Arab school. Look, there is a Franciscan church to the right.'

'Asher's first clue … Arab school and a Franciscan chapel.'

'The first station where Jesus was sentenced to death by crucifixion,' the old nun was crying in a sing-song voice. On the wall of the chapel was a glass painting of the bleeding Lord, scourged by the Roman whips …

'Saying "Here is the man!" Pilate handed over Jesus to the Jews here …' the nun said, repeating it twice or thrice for those who came behind. The group knelt down together on the gravel path. They all were wearing sky-blue headdresses. A blue rivulet seemed to be flowing out of the stone path. The prayers reached a crescendo.

'Crucify Him! Crucify Him!' The high priests and officials shouted … Asher was standing in their midst, wearing chains. Pilate was proclaiming the punishment … 'Here is the man!' An innocent was being accused as a criminal. Ruth was searching the crowd for Asher. She looked at the shops on either side. If only she saw a board titled 'Veronica'.

9.20 a.m.

Moving past a colossal statue—a fallen Jesus with Cross—the mourning procession edged forward. The third station was behind them. Elegies in all the languages of the world rose in the air. Were there so many languages in the world? Ruth felt that everything incomprehensible had the same language. She moved closer to the walls intermittently.

'What's up, Ruth? Do you want to visit the washroom?' Binu asked with concern, seeing her distress. She shook her head. The olive trees swayed in the breeze. The yellow leaves were kissing the stones … Pigeons roosted silently in the oak trees. The almond trees bowed, participating in the sorrowful journey.

'Now we are walking through the heart of the city. Imagine how the roads must have looked two thousand years before! Maybe the ancient road is somewhere underneath, right?'

Binu was in a garrulous mood.

9.30 a.m.

The fourth station. A statue that embodied anguish in every inch. *The mother, meeting her son, carrying the cross.* Ruth remembered countless mothers. A thousand mothers chasing after the police who came to take their sons away ... '*That's my son, my son ... let him go!*' One human having innumerable mothers!

9.40 a.m.

The fifth station. Franciscan church. In front of the church, where Simon of Cyrene was made to bear Jesus's Cross, seven policemen were doing the rounds.

'Asher, I am too feeble to bear this cross ...' Ruth's fatigue increased greatly; so did her anxiety. Many faces waltzed in front of her ... Asher, Sahal and Jacob, the young boy who stood next to Asher in the school photograph ... Shahjahan of the nineteenth floor, who never betrayed Ruth even for thirty gold coins ... the young man in the desert ... Ruth's heart ached. She felt dizzy.

'What's the matter?' Lilly clutched Ruth's hand. 'Not too far now. Asher is somewhere close.'

Ruth felt that a policeman in mufti was following her. Soon, he would catch Asher and beat him up in front of her. She started trembling.

9.50 a.m.

The sixth station. Cafes, tea shops, fast food joints ... Inside a white-coloured tent, a girl was busy selling veils. The Veils of Veronica!

Ruth rushed inside the tent. There were five people there. Three Indian missionaries and two white men. 'Where is Asher?' Ruth gazed at Lilly, bereft of all hope. Lilly pointed towards another direction. There it stood, a Greek catholic chapel. The fifth clue! They briskly walked towards the church. A little boy was standing in front of the main doorway.

'Why are you stopping? We should climb Calvary before afternoon. Come on, walk fast!' Binu was impatient with their dithering.

Lilly mollified him that Veronica's Chapel was worth a quick visit. The sky-blue-clad nun and her group left them behind. Three cops were standing nearby, talking amongst themselves. Ruth felt fear gnaw at her bones. The little boy was holding a packet, half-hidden from their sight. 'To Neruda's Sis' was inscribed on the cover. Ruth's heart started palpitating faster and her body trembled. Casting a wary look around, she moved closer to the boy and whispered, 'Where is Asher?' The little boy stared at her for a moment, handed over the package and vanished in the path of Via Dolorosa. His running reminded Ruth of the frolicking of a sweet lamb. She tried to follow him but it was a futile exercise. He had long disappeared amongst the throng of pilgrims. There was something else written on the package. Binu started laughing, reading it aloud.

'ATA KOL KAKH KHASHUV LI'

'Who is your acquaintance in this place? You are getting gifts too! No wonder you were tense!' Binu teased. 'Do you know what this means?'

'Must be some coded language. *Ata kol kakh khashuv li.*'

Lilly and Binu started laughing at Ruth's pronunciation.

'Silly woman! This is what the Sea of Galilee tells River Jordan.'

Ruth looked askance at Lilly.

'*You mean so much to me* … Got it? Dunce!' Binu laughed uproariously. A priest walking ahead of them turned to cast a furious look at him. Embarrassedly, Ruth hid the package in her bag.

'Shall we go to Bethlehem straight? I need to entrust this packet to somebody.'

Binu was piqued at that request.

'On Good Friday, you expect me not to climb Calvary?'

Binu instinctively sensed that the women were hiding something from him.

'Sure, we will climb Calvary first. But please help me. This is terribly important for me. And please desist from asking what it is all about,' Ruth pleaded.

10.10 a.m.

The chapel where, on catching sight of the cops, Ruth had hidden the day before, smiled at her. Mariam of Bethany was standing on the spot where Ruth had collapsed the day before—at the seventh station. She was wearing a blood-red-coloured mask. They crossed the chapel and moved towards Calvary. Mariam walked next to Ruth and whispered, 'I was always jealous of that Veronica. The image of the Lord's face was impressed upon her veil, wasn't it?

'*Daughters of Jerusalem, do not weep for me, but weep for yourselves and for your children.* He said that to the women of Jerusalem … He was predicting the imminent attack on Jerusalem.' The nun, donning sky-blue, was announcing as they reached the eighth station.

'*Weep for yourselves and for your children …*' She repeated the same phrase multiple times. Her gait became slower but she continued to sing loudly.

'I have seen the Rabbi walk in the courtyard, unable to sleep, whenever He stayed with us in Bethany. There was a conflict going on in His mind. How many nights I kept awake to give Him company! What if someone were to capture Him? I was always tormented by that thought. Do you know why He cried near the grave of my brother Lazarus? Because, I had needled him with my words. "When we needed you, where were you? Is this how friends behave?" I railed at Him …' Mariam of Bethany's voice became fainter with every word she uttered. At a distance, the turret of the massive church at Golgotha gleamed in the sunlight.

10.25 a.m.

They reached Calvary, climbing the twenty steps. Outside the church, the Chapel of the Franks, where the Lord was stripped of his garments, there were many policemen. Ruth started quivering as if carrying a time bomb inside her handbag. Her face blanched. She was wondering about the little boy then.

'There was no clue about such a boy. What if Asher, who stood waiting at the sixth station, has been caught by the cops? Suppose this package is a ploy to snare Sarah? Asher, did your message leak? Ruth, you are under observation currently,' her mind shouted.

'This is a church which, ever since it was built up in the fourth century, has been destroyed many times. The Church of Resurrection, which keeps coming back to life!' the nun, who was ascending the steps, was announcing to the group.

Her mournful voice reached the churchyard first. *The sound of horsemen came rushing in; the sound of weapons clashing with one another … Screams, the spire of the church falling …* Maddening thoughts were crowding Ruth's mind. She held Lilly's hand tightly.

'My Lord, when they pulled down your blood-spattered robe, the great humiliation you endured … when they crucified you, the unbearable pain you suffered …' The nun's prayer turned into a lamentation. 'This nun emerges as a scream from my own heart,' Ruth contemplated.

Beneath the statue of the Disrobed One, at His feet, Mariam of Bethany was seated pensively.

'How many times I must have washed the Lord's tunic, the seamless robe stitched by His mother! Even His perspiration emanated the fragrance of His love for humanity. They cast lots for the divided pieces of His clothes,' Mariam mourned.

Ruth was immersed only in one prayer: 'Oh God, let me hand over this packet safely to Sarah. Please protect me from the police.' In truth, she was commanding the Lord, with full authority. The Lord of Calvary gazed silently at Ruth.

'Shouldn't you be doing your live programme now, Ruth? From Calvary, your very own Ruth Albert?' Binu mimicked Ruth's voice. 'All my dears back home, in Japan and Mogadishu, listen ...'

'Where on earth did that Mogadishu spring from?' Lilly giggled.

'Is Golgotha some sort of skull-shaped quarry carved out by the Romans? They used to crucify revolutionaries here. This place was outside the city gates then,' Binu elaborated and then, bored by standing in the queue, looked at Ruth.

'I don't know about that. But for someone accused of blaspheming against the nation and God, they would have sentenced Him to nothing less than crucifixion. Even after two thousand years, the world is roused by His name. Though some still sell Him for a few pieces of silver.' It was Lilly who responded.

11.00 a.m.

They stepped inside the Church of the Holy Sepulchre. The crowd was unbelievable. The grieving Mother of Christ—Our Lady of Sorrows—with her right hand on her heart, was contemplating the Cross. Those eyes held the sorrow of all mothers of this world. The stone fragments of the Holy Sepulchre, encased in glass cases, lay frozen, holding within the great earthquake which had happened two thousand years ago. Ruth's mind was quavering too. Under the altar, there was a silver plate with a hole, which showed the spot where once the Lord's Cross stood. There was a long queue waiting to kiss the silver star marking the holy place.

'Binu, let us go now. The queue will not end even if night falls. The hole where the Cross stood is inside our hearts.' Ruth became impatient.

'Oh, you have transformed into a preacher, have you?' Binu scowled.

Ruth stood faint under the picture of the Pieta.

'Here is the Stone of Anointing! Joseph of Arimathea lay the Lord's body down on this stone. Then he prepared the Lord's body for entombment; anointing it with myrrh and aloes.' The sound of the sky-blue-clad nun again.

'Binu, please, let us leave.'

Ruth grabbed Binu's hand. He was praying with the rosary touching the Stone of Anointing. As he moved out with great reluctance, Binu spoke: 'I should have been born as the aide of Queen Helena. She was the one who discovered all these sites and built a church here. How many shall remember us when we die?'

'Even today the world is awash with people who are tormented by sorrows. There are those staggering with their burdens and many victims of discrimination. Carry the cross for all of them, Binu. At least one generation shall remember you,' Lilly replied curtly.

'Lord, I am fine with my own cross.' Binu's hands were folded in prayer. 'See, I prattle mindlessly to forget my troubles. My son has to undergo a surgery and I climbed Calvary today, seeking the Lord's grace for him. It has been two years since I have seen him.' They fell into silence.

Later, in pilot Binu's aeroplane, the trio set off to David's city. The sun was hovering, burning hot, over their heads then.

38

THE DOOR OF MODESTY

They entered the 'City of David'. It had taken fifty minutes to reach Bethlehem. At the border check post, the officers took away Ruth's handbag for checking. She stood frozen in terror.

'What's inside the packet?' When the security officer with laughing eyes asked the question, Lilly immediately answered, 'It's a book!' He wished them 'Salam', and returned the package. He browsed through their identity cards. Seeing that they were metapelets, he did not ask any more questions. Ruth was still trembling.

'If you start showing your fear so openly, they will get suspicious.' Lilly was annoyed. She pinched Ruth's arm warningly.

The white-coloured town was passive and quiescent. Stopping the car in the parking lot, they stepped through the buildings made of limestone. The Palestine police was keeping guard at the church premises. There was not much rush since it was Good Friday. Everybody was at Calvary. The fair-skinned, flabby policeman who approached them raised an eyebrow. Binu wished him warmly. He replied, 'Wa Alaikum Assalam,' and walked away with a smile.

The Basilica's walls evoked the airs of a fortress. Bearing the burden of history that spanned many centuries, those walls stretched endlessly, impassively.

'Just imagine! Mary of Nazareth travelled almost one hundred and fifty kilometres to Bethlehem to give birth to Jesus. Ruthie, how long would Joseph and Mary have taken, travelling on a donkey's back, to cover the same distance we did in two hours?' Lilly wondered aloud.

'Maybe they stopped at Zacharias's house at Ein Karem,' Ruth suggested, imagining such a scenario.

She saw Jospeh's donkey tied to a fig tree near the fortress. There was a profusion of caves in the vicinity. Caves that cropped up as if from aeons past. Caves, where cattle were kept. Caves, where humans lived. Caves, where Jesus and his apostles slept at nights. In some such cave, Sarah was waiting.

'Where is the Door of Modesty? The rosary made of olives? Where is the elegy from Ramallah's Jalazone camp? I am going to meet her for the first time!' Ruth's heart was palpitating fast.

Lilly pointed at a door, at a low height, in the middle of the fortress wall. 'Look, the Door of Modesty! Clue number 8.' Ruth was feeling frantic as she neared her goal.

'They built it at such a low height presumably to deter the riders on horsebacks from entering and wreaking disaster,' Binu deduced.

'No, to let go of all arrogance and pride, before seeing the Blessed One, born in the manger,' Ruth corrected him.

'You should have been a poet.' Binu laughed.

'In the land where Christ was born, Christians are less than one per cent in number. But they are present all over the world. Why is it so?' Lilly's question echoed, bending low through the Door of Modesty. Ruth quoted Father Aloysious in reply.

'One of the most enchanting histories is that of Jesus's birth in a manger. And his crucifixion, one of the greatest tragedies which shook the world.'

Two Palestinians, wearing keffiyeh, passed them by. A police officer was standing in front of the fortress. Even before he asked, Lilly opened her bag and showed it to him. The man inclined his head to indicate that they could go through. The crown-shaped badge on his cap moved as he did so.

They reached near the place, where once the manger was supposed to have been. There was a profusion of mosaic patterns on the ceiling. Many chandeliers shimmered beautifully. Twenty-four massive pillars. The steps descended to a cave. A silver star sparkled on the marble floor. There was a Latin inscription beneath.

Hic De Virgine Maria Jesus Christus Natus (Est-1717)

Ruth read it aloud: *'Here, Jesus Christ was born to the Virgin Mary.'*

'Ruthie can read not just Aramaic, but Latin too.' Lilly laughed.

'Oh, is it necessary to master Latin for knowing that?' Binu mocked.

Ruth was looking around. Where was Sarah? She asked a smiling priest, 'Are you Jerome?'

The priest shook his head to indicate that he wasn't. Was the clue defective? There was no Jerome or Sarah in the Grotto of the Nativity! After contemplating for a while, the priest pointed at the opposite direction. They stepped into another cavern nearby. There were three or four small chapels, where Qurbana was being conducted. The man standing near the fourth chapel hailed them.

'Welcome to the chapel of Saint Jerome. This the spot where Jerome spent sixteen years translating the Bible ...'

The man's pronunciation was like Abba's. There were only four people inside the chapel. One woman, dressed in flaming yellow, was seated on a bench at the back. She was counting rosary beads made of olives ... 'Sarah!' Lilly and Ruth called out in unison.

Sarah raised her head and looked up in amazement.

In seconds, Ruth rushed towards Sarah and embraced her warmly. Binu stood gaping, not understanding the story unfolding in front of him.

'Asher could not come. He asked me to hand this over to you.'

After giving Sarah the packet, Ruth stood panting. A heavy burden had been lifted off her back. The trio watched as Sarah cast a wary look around and hid the package quickly inside her bag.

'Stay safe. Go to some place which you consider the safest.' Ruth planted a kiss on her forehead. 'Asher asked me to give you that …'

Two teardrops flowed from Sarah's eyes. As they watched, pushing back the people in the queue, Sarah quickly climbed up the steps. Though they tried to follow her, nowhere in the churchyard was the chrysanthemum-coloured dress sighted again. Ruth felt miserable. It was as if finding someone very dear after much hardship, only to lose her at the next moment. Her mind felt a great sense of loss. Suddenly it struck her: Sarah had the same face as Mariam of Bethany!

'Don't chase after her, that would put her at risk,' Lilly murmured.

Binu had started walking to the Chapel of the Milk Grotto. 'This is the place where Mary and Joseph hid Jesus before they fled to Egypt, when King Herod of Judaea unleashed the infamous "Massacre of the Innocents". Look at the rocks that turned white, because a drop of Mother Mary's milk fell on them!' Binu was narrating the stories associated with the place. Ruth was oblivious of everything. Her mind was focused only on Sarah. The girl child who had to run relentlessly, from one refugee camp to another, from the tender age of six; the one who stayed in a burning town; the girl who watched the incinerated bodies of her baba and mama; the girl who lay frozen in dark, narrow rooms. 'In which cave shall she hide now?' Ruth wondered, sitting next to the statue of Mother Mary breastfeeding Infant Jesus.

Palestinian soldiers were seen everywhere, seemingly scattered on the streets. Sporadic gunshots could be heard. Binu reassured that it was part of the protocol; a few political leaders might be on the road. Ruth was worrying only about Sarah's impending paths. 'Lord, guard that innocent girl,' she prayed silently.

Feeling famished, they purchased some falafel for six shekels. 'At Jerusalem, the same food costs twelve shekels. The low prices showcase the state of Palestinian economy. Didn't you observe the roads and buildings?' The economist inside Lilly started her analysis. A little girl, busy selling sweets near the board proclaiming 'I Love

Bethlehem', started pestering them. A few hungry stomachs were awaiting her return in some shack ... Ruth bought shimon from the child, setting aside fifty shekels for her return bus trip. It was shaped like a zero, ironically symbolizing the girl's life. After sharing some with Binu and Lilly, Ruth kept the remaining shimon for Abba.

Ruth fell into a deep sleep on her way to Nazareth. She was not aware of Lilly's missed calls. When she deboarded the bus and called Lilly back, she faced Lilly's wrath.

'I was sick with worry, Ruth! Must have called you a hundred times! There is a curfew in Jerusalem, so I returned to Ashkelon,' Lilly said.

'Sarah, where are you?' Ruth fretted.

That night, Ruth had a bizarre dream. Josephus had arrived to meet Ruth. There were three other people with him. They were all standing in front of the Damascus Gate. His impressive headgear was studded with emeralds and fitted with a feather, the white beard fluttering in the breeze, all of which added immense regal grace to Josephus. His mother had descended from the Hasmonean dynasty as per records.

Except for a few snippets of their conversation, Ruth forgot most of the dream when she woke up. But the faces of the visitors were indelibly imprinted in her mind. Folding his black coat sleeves, stroking his thick black moustache and casting a fiery glance around, stood Theodore Herschel, the father of Zionism. Scratching absent-mindedly at his bald head was David Ben-Gurion. Sultan Salahuddin seemed to be in a trance. The bald head of Ben-Gurion gleamed like the never-dying light in front of the chapel.

Josephus raised a question, gazing at Mount Olive, which stood on the opposite side.

'If an animal is grazing in a field or vineyard and the owner lets it stray into someone else's field to graze, then the animal's owner must pay compensation from the best of his own grain or grapes. The Book of Exodus says that. The people who are supposed to follow that

dictum, are driving away the owners from the vineyards, from the olive mountains … in the same way we were driven away from these lands, in the olden days.'

Josephus glared at everyone and descended the mountain. By that time missiles appeared in the Jerusalem sky, which were rendered ineffective by the Iron Dome, that scattered fire-flowers all around. There were flames of fire beyond the Jafa Gate … Sultan Salahuddin, astride on his horse, called out: 'The revolutionaries have surrounded the city. You may defeat them with your weapons and military strength. But history shall not forgive you for a thousand crucifixions and exiles.'

The fire was spreading across the Old City walls.

Ruth woke up in the heat and smoke of the dream. The next day, when Abba heard the story, he heaved with laughter. 'How did you understand Josephus's Aramaic language? Dreams have meanings, Bat.' He told her about the Biblical character Joseph, who interpreted dreams in Egypt, and about his jealous brothers, who threw him into an empty well.

'Today, the world is full of empty wells, Bat.' Abba sighed deeply.

39

THE PSALM OF THE DISPOSSESSED

Asher returned after a fortnight, when the tensions had subsided to a large extent. He looked exhausted. Asher had been in hiding in Jericho, Tiberias and Capernaum. For ten days he had sought refuge in a fishing village at Capernaum. He lived in a house belonging to acquaintances of Joshua, in the archaeological site where the ruins of an ancient synagogue had been excavated; where a whole farming village had been unearthed.

Joshua had found the house when he was unrelentingly searching for Annie. An ancient house with narrow rooms linked by corridors and a courtyard in the middle. The family home of the photographer—probably the last man to see her alive—who had accompanied Annie, when she went for the interview of the inmate at Shikma Prison. He convinced the household that Asher was there for research purposes. The nights were spent with fisherfolk, by the shores of Galilee. The days, rummaging amidst the ancient olive presses and grain mills, almost resembling an ancient relic himself … so many inexplicable adventures!

Asher was clueless about the little boy who waited for Ruth at Via Dolorosa. It was all Joshua's doing. Sahal was still in Jerusalem. The police had laid their snares so wide that he could not escape from the city. But he was very safe somewhere; where nobody would ever suspect him to be! Interestingly, it was right under the nose of the police. Asher's sole goal was to ensure that Sahal crossed the border, as soon as the Malaysian scholarship came through. The path ahead was very dangerous.

Asher was of the opinion that Ruth should not trouble herself over the incident at Caiaphas's dungeon. She was worried that the cops were chasing after the source of the video, shot at Rockefeller Museum. However, Abba's anxiety was about something else.

Mossad's meticulously conducted assassinations and the undivulged conspiracies surrounding those clandestine operations were known worldwide. They had trapped the Nazi leader who was leading an anonymous life in Argentina, transported him to Jerusalem, and executed him. How they had managed to hoodwink the security arrangements, sedate the Nazi officer who was disguised as an airline employee, and stealthily take him out of Argentina was the stuff of legends, making even the Americans gape! How many such brilliant operations, ruthless exterminations! Mossad was one of the world's most reputed secret services. Sahal was merely a blade of grass before such an agency. How long would he evade them?

A deep sense of melancholy infused Shalom in those days. Nobody laughed, or bantered. Abba would complain about the cackling of geese that irritated him intermittently. Only Abba, and occasionally Ruth, heard the sounds which were inaudible to others. Sometimes Abba spoke of the old Baghdad. The city where dust and smoke billowed, the robbers who stalked the streets, the murderers; the little boy who fearfully stared out of the window in the first storey, the workshop days of Saba at Haifa … Nobody knew why Abba kept on recounting all these experiences.

The police came searching for Asher twice. Eema had been messing around amongst her rose bushes when they came for the first time. Asher was plucking olives in the western grove at that time. As the vehicle approached, Asher rushed inside the house, shouting, 'Police!' Eema had melted with trepidation. They were three in number. The tallest one had screamed, as he stepped inside the gate, 'Where is Asher?'

'He went to Jerusalem,' Eema replied exhaustedly, dropping the rose stalk and knife from her hand.

They had returned without any arguments. Eema had held her breath until they disappeared from sight.

Abba was serene.

'We are Jews and Israeli citizens. What's the need to hide? Asher, you are protected by the laws of the country. Next time they come, you should speak with them. They are searching for Sahal. You should not betray him, that is all.'

'You will put my son's life at risk for that Arab boy!' Eema was incensed.

Abba was seated on the veranda when the cops arrived the second time. Ruth was reading aloud from a book. They were young, close to Asher's age. One was dressed in navy-blue while the other donned a light-blue shirt. Abba warmly invited them inside the house.

'What are you reading?'

The police officer in the light-blue shirt was peering into the book.

'Not just reading, actually, reading aloud. These are stories.'

They gazed at Ruth.

'How long has she been here?'

'More than three years now. She is my daughter. My own Bat.'

Abba spoke, stroking his beard.

'Do you visit Jerusalem?' The question was aimed at Ruth.

'She visits the church occasionally,' Abba replied.

'Heard that she is into videography. What's the purpose behind it?'

Ruth felt a tremor start at the tip of her toe and slowly creep upwards.

'I have a vlog … it is for that,' she answered.

The police officer in navy-blue asked her to show him a few vlog episodes. His questions were in crystal-clear English.

'What are you explaining in your language?'

Ruth was flabbergasted for a moment at the unexpected question; but she quickly recovered and answered tactfully.

'The history of the Holy Land, the paths walked by Jesus Christ, the prosperity of the Jewish state, its beauty and courtesy to guests … about all of these.'

The officer seemed placated.

'What's the book all about?' He turned to Abba now.

'These are stories by an Arab writer, Mahmoud Shukair. About cities turned desolate, a town square bereft of people, about a half-empty cup of coffee left behind in a cafe, about the scent of perfume wafting from a house where the owners have been killed or driven away, about lovers who decide to commit suicide since they cannot live together, about a house which was standing in the morning but had vanished by evening, about a woman with ash-brown eyes and wax-like face, who came to advertise her own imminent death, about a people caught in throes of psychosis, about girls who adore libraries, flowers and plants, about the miserly mistress who refuses payment to a helpless Arab maidservant quoting a bizarre tale of the vanished balustrade, about a girl from the hills who wonders, looking at the peaceful village in the valley and utterly peaceful police men there, whether it was the same people who had taken away her sweetheart, about the three pieces of bread lying orphaned in a narrow jail cell and the pool of blood …'

'Enough!' The cop in light-blue raised his hand.

'Why are you reading books written by Arabs?' His voice reverberated with displeasure, annoyance, cruelty.

'To understand what they think of us,' Abba replied serenely.

'And what did you find?' the navy-blue-clad officer queried, darting a glance inside the house.

'We are ordinary human beings like them. But we have hung their lives at the tip of a tree branch that can collapse any moment!'

Abba's voice was firm and fiery.

'What's the significance of the stories Arabs scribble, seated comfortably in Europe or America, except to instigate the youth who live here? What do they lack in this place? What has our government denied them? The scoundrels forget that their lives are at our mercy.' The police officer became aggressive.

'You are loyal to the employer.' Abba smiled as he spoke. Discretion is the better part of valour. Abba was well aware of that dictum.

'Call your son. He is here, we know,' the police officer ordered.

Asher stepped into the porch as if he was waiting for such summons. His face was calm. The cops looked taken aback. Perhaps they never expected him to surface so fast!

'Shalom!' Asher wished them.

'Where is Sahal?' The question was fired quickly.

Without wavering, looking straight into the man's eyes, Asher replied, 'I am searching for him too. He has been missing for weeks now.'

They interrogated him thoroughly: Why was Asher searching for Sahal? Which were the places that he had visited? What was Sahal into?

Asher answered nonchalantly.

'Sahal is a puppet in the hands of the nation's enemies. He has a major role in the protests that broke out in Temple Mount and in launching hate campaigns through social media.' The cop in navy-blue was implacable. The arrogance of power radiated from his tone.

'The Sahal I know, is nothing of that sort. A brilliant scholar, that's what he is. All these are wrong presumptions,' Asher objected mildly.

'We never asked for your opinion. Mossad is never wrong, mister!'

The police officer sat up, enraged. After warning Asher that he should share any information received about Sahal's whereabouts with them, or else he would face the long arm of law, the navy-blue-clad cop made his exit, his footsteps sounding harsh and unrelenting. His colleague in light-blue followed suit.

Eema started lamenting again. Leah struggled to soothe her. Her eyes too were glaring accusingly at Asher. A dreadful silence loomed over Shalom, like the calm before a storm. The grunting of swines haunted Ruth yet again that day. The hordes were moving into a swamp beyond the apple trees.

40

Diplomacy

'I am the bullets, the oranges and the memory.'
—Mahmoud Darwish

10 May 2021, Monday

Asher left for Jerusalem the very next day after the police came to enquire about Sahal. Many Shabbats passed, but Asher did not return. He would speak about being too preoccupied with work whenever the family phoned. Abba was disturbed by the periodic conflicts in Jerusalem. Ramadan was coming to an end. On Eid-ul-Fitr, there was a great thronging of devotees at the Al-Aqsa Mosque. Meanwhile, the police had surrounded the mosque. The Zionist march on Jerusalem Day usually provoked strong reactions. But on 10 May, everything spiralled out of control.

Amidst all those skirmishes, in a viral video, Asher was seen standing near Lion's Gate at Temple Mount. Nobody saw him thereafter. Leah had called him before his phone was switched off and had pleaded with him to get away from the place. Asher was treading perilous paths. To avoid further anxiety, Leah and Ruth gave only the barest hint of the turn of events to Abba. Leah hid the *Times of Israel*, so that the news escaped Ruth's vigilant eyes too.

Leah would grumble that Asher was too impulsive for his own good. He would go to any extent to help loved ones. Leah, on the other hand, was practical by nature. Perhaps, once David won in the fight with Goliath. But the times have changed. It was wiser to retreat after assessing the enemy's strength.

Once Leah had reminded Asher of the Aesop's fable: 'The Oak and the Reed'. The mighty oak had fallen in a ferocious storm and was washed away into the marshes. There it saw the reeds singing merrily. 'It is unbelievable! When strong trees like me have been uprooted, how have you managed to survive the onslaught of the storm?' the oak tree asked the reeds. The latter replied, 'We bent our heads when the wind blew, but you chose to fight instead, in your pride.' Asher had laughed on hearing the story. Then he had retorted calmly, 'Better to fight with your head held high, even if you get defeated! Those who tread in your footsteps shall one day emerge victorious.'

Leah was scanning the TV channels, after lowering the volume. They were repeatedly showing the scenes of conflict. 'Asher, where are you?'

***Newsreader:** Following the police raids at Jerusalem's Masjid Al-Aqsa, protests were triggered, resulting in the injury of hundreds of Palestinians and many law enforcement officers. By seven in the morning on Monday, the police had entered the mosque compound and fired rubber-tipped bullets and stun grenades on the stone pelters. We are taking you to the reactions from various quarters.*

***Benjamin Netanyahu:** We shall not tolerate the attacks against the nation, the capital, the citizens or soldiers. Those who instigate assaults against our people at Sheikh Jarrah shall face retaliation. Whoever attacks us shall pay a heavy price!'*

***Military Commander of Hamas, Mohammed Deif:** Israel shall pay dearly for Netanyahu's statement.*

***The Arab Legal Experts:** This is a struggle by the dispossessed, wishing to free their homeland, houses and souls from the invaders.*

***Saleh al-Arouri, Senior Leader of Hamas:** We will torch the heads of those occupiers who destroy Jerusalem!*

***Diplomats:** Hamas is attempting to balance the equation by preventing Israel from launching provocative steps. If Israel does not take the hint, Hamas reacts.*

***Mark Regev, Senior Adviser to Israeli Prime Minister Benjamin Netanyahu:** We wished that the day passed unobtrusively, silently. Unfortunately, the Palestinian terrorists had their hidden agendas.*

***American Representative:** Israel shall exercise the right to defend itself. We appreciate the efforts of Israel to alleviate the tensions.*

***Political Observers:** The internecine factions within Palestinians are deepening the conflict. Mahmoud Abbas, the President of the Palestinian Authority, has announced that the impending elections have been postponed.*

***International Relations Thinks Tanks:** Donald Trump, the ex-President of the USA, the select Arab countries negotiating diplomacy with Israel, and the right-wing governments that ruled Israel for more than a decade continued to deny the fundamental problem of Palestine.*

***Newsreader:** Latest update for our viewers. The Biden administration is under pressure to censure the actions of the Israeli government.*

Shalom was reeling under melancholy that night. Abba was struggling to breathe. 'A disaster is about to strike!' In his abject distress, Abba behaved like a child. Sleep could claim him only after many hours' wait.

Tragic news came from Ashkelon the next morning. Ruth had switched off her cell phone so that Abba could have an undisturbed slumber. There were almost twenty missed calls from Binu. When Ruth called, Binu exploded.

'Where the hell were you, Ruth? We have lost Lilly!'

Ruth stood shell-shocked. Nothing that Binu said entered her ears or her consciousness.

'A Hamas missile … Both Naomi and Lilly died. They could not reach the shelter in time. Our channels are raging against Hamas. I was there with her the whole night. Now the body is in the mortuary. Israel's Foreign Minister has assured that he will do everything for transporting the dead body back to Kerala. An officer from the embassy shall accompany the coffin.'

The world had turned pitch-black at dawn. Ruth felt faint. Somehow, she managed to sit down. Darkness, darkness everywhere. Binu was continuing to speak.

'Our churches, back home, are holding prayer sessions for Israel's victory. They are reciting Qurbana for us all.'

Ruth stifled the sob that erupted from deep inside. 'I don't want to hear anything more, Binu, you are lying! That smile of Lilly's! The posture, with her glasses raised to her forehead … I can see it all right in front of my eyes.' The two-hour distance between Nazareth and Jerusalem, the serpentine paths descending the hills, the fig tree clusters, wheat fields, the boisterous drinking sessions, the shared moments of sorrow … all were inundating Ruth's memory.

Lilly was preparing to leave for London. While attempting the examination for the fourth or fifth time, she said, 'Will I score high enough to reach London, Ruth? With certain exams, even after we die, we shall keep on writing them.'

'Ah, Lilly, now you have gone to a place which never demands an entrance score.'

Lilly's final vlog post: 'The Iron Dome is at work, stopping the dreadful Hamas missiles right in the air! The skies are full of fire flowers … reminds me of the firecrackers of our famed Thrissur

Pooram. I have to rush to the shelter quickly. Naomi amma has difficulty in walking. Take care and God Bless.'

A fiery sphere was approaching, penetrating the Iron Dome ...

'If you want to see her, come to Jerusalem by evening. There are restrictions in place due to Covid protocol. I will wait at the bus station.'

Binu cut the call without waiting for Ruth's response.

'Binu, I don't want to see the Lilly destroyed by the missile. I want my old Lilly, the one who laughed and teased me ...' The dam of tears broke.

Teresa's phone call came when she was reeling from the devastation caused by Lilly's death.

'Amma, please return. There is a war going on there.'

'Not at all. The war is far away. Don't worry, dear.'

Teresa was not satisfied by that reply.

'Chachan has started walking slowly. My nursing studies will be over in a couple of years. I shall look after both of you then. Kathu is working very hard and I have no doubt that she will get a merit-seat. Why are you still struggling then? Am longing to see you.'

She was whimpering like a child now.

'Yes, but there is another operation which your Chachan has to undergo. Lots of money to be repaid even now, to Agy Chechi and others. After a year, Amma will come running to you. Okay?'

Ruth's eyes were streaming ceaselessly. Every teardrop held Lilly within.

Teresa seemed to hesitate about something.

'What's the matter? Don't you want to see Chachan healthy and well?'

'You know, some people here make fun of your work ... Chachan is depressed.'

Ruth felt enraged even in her grief.

'What's wrong with my work? Aren't you a nursing student? Give the phone to your Chachan.'

Alby came on the call.

'Ruth, come back immediately. We can do farming and manage somehow.'

Alby's voice was grave and sad.

'The ignorant lot will blabber about many things. Alby, why are you so bothered? I am treated like a daughter in this home.'

Ruth's voice grew sharp and Alby cut the call. She felt as if someone was impaling her heart with an iron nail. She started perspiring. The Iron Dome's humming resounded in her ears.

Teresa called back in a few minutes as Ruth expected.

'Amma, don't worry. There is a weird preacher hereabouts. He inveigles money from Chachan often, in the name of prayers. Today he had come home. Apparently, he watched your vlog. He went on and on about your wandering around with Arabs! The rest of the family, especially the uncles, pitched in, mocking that you shall now emerge in Afghanistan. Kathu lost her temper. The preacher shouted at her that Gog's army shall fall upon the mountains of Israel and the birds of prey shall devour them. Kathu shot back, "Uncle, do you know King Gog personally?" He went away in a huff!'

Teresa laughed, trying to appease her aggrieved mother.

'Are you ashamed of the nursing profession? Then do not study further, just for looking after your parents.' Ruth was vehement.

'Not at all ...' Teresa's voice cracked.

Ruth wept for a long time afterwards. She knew that Teresa must be crying too. There had been no need to lose her temper with the child. It was not her fault anyway. Why was she behaving so strangely? 'Lord, why did I endure all these sufferings? Is Alby disparaging me?' Ruth felt as if some shrapnel had penetrated her heart. 'Ruth, you are in Caiaphas's dungeon ...'

'Your house shall not be an anchor but a mast.' When did Mariam of Bethany arrive to sit by her side? Mariam embraced Ruth warmly. It was like caressing an erupting volcano. After she regained her

composure, Ruth remembered Lilly again. She was lying frozen and dead, a hundred and fifty kilometres away.

'Ruthie, I am ticking off my bucket list one by one. The next item is rather challenging. But I will accomplish it before I die.' Lilly had laughed.

'Oh, as if you are going to conk off tomorrow,' Ruth had teased her that day.

'Lilly, what was your desire?' Ruth wept.

The newspapers were filled with war news the next day. The front page screamed that a Hamas missile had killed the brave Naomi Bergman, the apostle of Denying to Be Foes, whom even Auschwitz could not crush.

Undoubtedly, every innocent's murder is a crucifixion.

Later, every night, Ruth dreamed about Lilly wandering lost and helpless in the desert wilderness.

41

'THE PASTURES OF THE SHEPHERDS MOURN'

The police sirens were wailing not too far away. Asher walked faster. The abaya shop and the white bearded old man faded into the distance. He reached the junction where the Muslim Quarters ended and the paths turned to the Jewish and Christian Quarters. The seventh station of the Via Dolorosa, the chapel, lay in the dark. Asher glanced at the narrow gully which travelled to the Wailing Wall. Darkness everywhere. The street lights were asleep too.

He remembered the light radiating from the hurricane lamp in the abaya shop. Once again, he recollected the old man's words. 'Sometimes, it is our light that betrays us.'

The street vendors had left, taking along their folded tents. Lights were gleaming at far distances. Perhaps, the offices of the Jewish organizations were still open. Undecided for a moment, Asher took the left path which reached the Damascus Gate. His mind urged him to hurry, 'Go faster, go faster.' There was a shop selling crosses at the right. There was nobody inside. But a table lamp, resembling a crown of thorns, glowed from the counter. As he watched, the thorns extended further and further towards all directions. Fences of thorns everywhere!

'What do you want?'

Asher stood stunned at the question.

A lanky man appeared from behind a huge, wooden cross. A middle-aged man, dressed in a priest's robe.

'I need a cross.'

'At this odd hour? How big?'

Asher pointed at the one-metre long, mahogany cross. The lights went off suddenly and the shop was drenched in darkness.

'Father!' Asher called out anxiously. No reply.

'Father …'

Someone clutched at his arm and Asher screamed. The man covered his mouth. 'Don't make a sound.' The light came back again. It was stark and scintillatingly bright.

'No, I don't need the cross. How will I carry the cross tonight?' Asher started to move away.

'Stop, who are you?' the slightly built man queried, his voice not raised in pitch but assertive in tone.

A police announcement was booming at a distance. A warning was being issued: that people should stay at home and desist from wandering around, since more attacks were expected. The rattling of vehicles could be heard a few streets away.

'Stay here tonight. It is dangerous to be outside now.'

The man spoke softly. Inside the narrow room, the words echoed loudly.

'I need to go … someone is waiting for me.' Asher was unyielding.

'Then, keep this with you.'

The man wrapped a cross, half-a-metre long, in a paper bag and gave it to Asher. Asher noticed the callus on his forehead, the mark of regular prayers.

'Just a moment.'

The man removed his robe and the rosary around his neck.

Asher was now moving towards the Damascus Gate, wearing the coffee brown robe of Franciscan missionaries. A gold-hued rosary gleamed around his neck and he carried a bag with the large cross.

The man was watching him, when Asher took a backward look. He waved. Then the light was snuffed out.

Asher walked briskly, and soon, almost broke into a sprint. The cross was in the bag hanging from his right shoulder and was heavier than expected. His footsteps resounded on the cobbled street. There was no other sound. Many twists and turns had to be negotiated before Damascus Gate came into sight. There was a police vehicle parked nearby. An armed officer in dark-coloured uniform stood next to it.

'Father, what are you doing at this hour? Didn't you hear the announcement?'

The police officer stared at Asher.

'What's in your bag?'

Asher opened the bag and showed the cross. Then he shifted the heavy bag to the left shoulder.

'Where is your monastery? I shall give you a lift.'

'Very near,' Asher replied. He wondered why he had said so.

'Please step inside.' The officer opened the front door of the vehicle for Asher.

Asher stepped in hesitantly. 'The man will probably take me to a police station. They would ask for documents. They will discover that I am an imposter ... Why did I have to go in for this fancy dress? Imprudence at critical times!' he rued to himself.

'Can you tell me the way?' The officer asked.

Asher caught sight of a church spire.

'Near that church.'

He sat in the front seat with the cross on his lap. It was as if he was holding the wounded body of Jesus the Nazarene himself. Asher hastily drew the sign of the cross on his forehead.

'Are you afraid?' The officer smiled at him.

Asher shook his head. What was the man hinting at?

'We respect all religions and faiths.' The police officer said with pride. His face radiated the contentment of a Good Samaritan, helping a Christian missionary, out on the road during a treacherous night.

The Hebrew Radio was chattering away inside the vehicle.

The Islamic terrorist group Hamas, which controls Gaza, attacked Jerusalem with missiles for the first time in seven years. Following the retaliatory air strikes by Israel, many Palestinians, including children, have been killed. The Israeli Army informs that a minimum of 150 missiles were fired by Hamas during the assault. Many houses were devastated in the village situated on the western hills of Jerusalem. Some lives were lost too. In the Israeli aerial offensives that followed, several Hamas activists were killed. Two of Hamas's military centres and an underground tunnel used by terrorists have also been destroyed.

The vehicle moved through the main road. Asher noticed his car, which he had left behind in the evening, near the Lion's Gate parking. The key was in his pocket. Should he ask to be dropped here? A voice shouted from inside, 'No.' That 'No' grew in tempo to become a big 'No, No.'

That was the place where Stephen was killed by the stone pelters. Asher's heart palpitated faster. At a short distance, in the Kedron valley, there was a church of Saint Stephen.

'Drop me at the Stephen's Church.' The cop did not heed what Asher said. His focus was on the news. The vehicle careened into a side path.

'They are begging for it, actually. How many will be alive in Gaza tomorrow morning? What were you saying, Father?'

Lowering the volume of the radio, the officer turned to Asher.

'There, drop me at that place.' Asher pointed at a grotto, shimmering with blue light, towards the left.

After dropping Asher at the monastery front yard, the police officer warned him, 'The situation is growing worse. Father, please don't wander around tonight!'

Probably hearing the sound of the vehicle and the conversations that ensued, a light was turned on in the balcony. Someone stepped on to the terrace.

'Come inside, Father,' someone in a mask called out from above. His face remained vague. 'I am affected by Covid and cannot meet you. I was intuitively feeling that a guest would arrive tonight. Please rest in the guest room downstairs. My helper will take care of everything. Please consider yourself at home.' The man's voice had a strong Asian accent.

A young man dressed in a strange-looking cap and wearing a mask around his neck, came forth to meet Asher.

'Praise the Lord!' He removed his cap and bowed. A small, bald patch could be seen on the crown of his head.

'Let me take your bag, Father.' The young man grabbed the paper bag; but at the unforeseen heaviness, his arms flailed a bit.

'Though small, the cross is heavy!' The youth grinned with embarrassment. There was a noticeable gap between his prominent front teeth.

Asher moved inside the monastery. The machine recording temperature beeped suddenly. The room was small but very tidy.

'Father, please freshen up. I will get your food ready.'

The young helper scurried away through the door on the left. On the table, there was a Bible with a thick cover and an identity card, which marked the pages. There was a photograph of a priest. Antonio Giovanni Vivaldi. Priest, Violinist.

Asher opened the marked page and read the first few lines. The prophecy of Amos of Tekoa. The first chapter.

He said: The Lord roars from Zion and makes his voice heard from Jerusalem; the pastures of the shepherds mourn, and the summit of Carmel withers.

'The pastures of the shepherds mourn ...' Asher repeated to himself. He listened with alacrity to the night sounds. There was a rattling of vessels in the kitchen and the cries of the cicadas outside the building.

As if he had made up his mind, Asher moved towards the door with the cross in his hand. 'Why am I carrying this load? Should I leave it behind? The cross has already showered its compassion on me.' Asher mused.

'No!' The same voice, as earlier. The same resonating tone. It glued itself to the cross and the coffee-brown robe. 'Do not leave any traces behind,' the cross forewarned. Closing the door gently behind, shoving his slippers inside the paper bag, Asher moved like a cat. There was no flicker of light anywhere in the balcony or front yard. Crossing the blue light at the grotto, Asher started his descent to the Kedron valley. Through the Maccabi steps, stealthily moving under the shadows of the olive trees, across the field of Judas Iscariot, sneaking under the shades of the towering walls, Asher's pace became brisker.

Asher stumbled amidst the relics of an ancient structure. Somehow, he managed to get a foothold at the edge of the steeply winding steps, descending all the way down. Weeds thrived lushly among the stone steps. A huge pit awaited at the bottom. Asher was familiar with the location. A well, almost four metres deep. The Pool of Bethesda. Asher remembered Ruth then. He had come with her for a video shooting just a month before.

Ruth's words brought forth the image of an ancient water reservoir, with five covered colonnades.

When the Angel of the Lord went down and stirred the water, there was a rush to jump inside. Whoever that first stepped in, would be healed of the disease which afflicted him. Who would have leapt inside the Pool of Bethesda? The Jews? The ailing, the sinners, the heathens?

Asher did not climb down the steps to Bethesda, instead, he hurried along, with the cross inside the bag. It was the same path, where in the ancient times, a Nazarene had walked with his own cross. Asher felt that a paralysed man, waiting for thirty-eight years to be healed by the Nazarene, was crawling after him. He threw a quick glance behind and saw the grotto of St Anne's Church. A light was flickering inside.

42

AS THE WIND DOES WITH THE MOUNTAIN

Asher's journey ended in a very familiar home, hidden by the apple trees, situated on the slope of Mount Zion. The Apple-Scented House. The police were doing their rounds. The siren was blaring continuously. He walked, keeping to the edge of the drive way. His coffee-brown robe hid him in the dark. Asher remembered the old man watching the news in the abaya shop. How the aged man had welcomed him, when he had peeped in. His voice came reverberating, as if from a hollow.

'My child, why are you wandering around at this time? Are you searching for someone? If you are not in a hurry, sit down for a while.'

Asher recollected the merged emotions, fear and anxiety, displayed on the old face. He could see those blinking eyes again.

'They caught my boy! That scoundrel was pelting stones.'

His voice, filled with pathos, was pounding Asher's ears. A hunch, that the old man might be in some deep danger, rocked him at that moment. Should he return to the old man's side? Going back was never easy. The distance wasn't too far, but the obstacles were many. The police were keeping watch at every nook and cranny.

The window on the top floor opened and then shut gently. The sound of someone coming down the staircase could be heard. The same old woman opened the door as in a past night. Asher's gaze fell on the portrait on the front wall. The same worried face was lit up by the glow of the lamp that never died.

'Come inside quickly,' Jacob's Eema muttered, looking frantically at the street below. 'Hope nobody saw you?'

As always, Asher reassured her with the tilt of his head. As he moved inside, the Pomeranian puppy came to nuzzle against his feet. The full body portrait of Jacob welcomed him in the drawing room. His smile, the look in his eyes, the posture—as if he was standing in front of Asher's home at Nazareth.

'Where is he?' Asher's eyes searched in all directions.

'Was here until some time ago.'

'And now?'

'At Masada,' the woman murmured, checking if the door was properly latched.

'He went away, crouching in the dicky of my brother Abraham's car. The Malaysian scholarship came through. Please help him get across the border somehow! There are many tourist buses that visit Masada. Many trucks too ... He might find some way or another to escape from here.'

Eema's voice was replete with eagerness and trepidation. Asher's premonition had been right. The details in the small diary that Suleiman had hurled away were significant. 'The old man seemed to have kept his shop open only for me!' Asher brooded.

'Tomorrow morning, there will be a pickup van crossing the border. Will try to smuggle him across the Allenby Bridge. The van is stuffed with textiles to be transported to Amman. I will follow in my car till the border.' Asher's voice was fraught with nervousness.

Eema dialled a number immediately.

'Abraham, the friend has come. Get ready tomorrow morning. Pickup is ready.' Eema cut the call quickly. 'Maybe they are tapping the phones!' she muttered worriedly.

Then she looked inside and called, 'Sarah.'

Asher's heart started drumming.

Like a night of old, Sarah came out, swathed in a blanket, covered from head to toe. As if repeating his actions of that night, Asher gazed at her. She lowered her face.

'Sarah,' Asher called softly. The sound was that of the river flowing through his heart.

'You can stay here tonight. Ask the pickup driver to come by in the morning,' Eema suggested. 'The moonlight is very bright. You cannot hide yourself this night.'

Eema's eyes were fixed at some distant object.

'There is a car beyond the driveway. Who could it be at this odd hour?' In a jiffy, she pulled the curtains to hide the sight.

'Sarah arrived when Sahal was about to leave. The tears that were shed! I don't know how, but she managed to reach here despite the furore at Temple Mount. It was sheer luck that they could meet each other. In another minute, Sahal would have gone. The spate of tears after he left …! Now, after seeing you, there is a smile on her face!'

After a poignant pause, Jacob's Eema wiped her eyes and continued. 'It has been three months since I have been hiding Sahal. He was suffering from high fever when he first arrived. I was dreadfully afraid that the Covid would take him from me. Every police siren made me frantic with worry. I sent my own son to his death. I know that unless I save Sahal, I would never be at peace. My brother Abraham was up in arms at first. Though Sahal is innocent, he has been condemned as an anti-national. To provide a sanctuary to such a person incurs stringent punishment. It is something which a Jew should never do. Where was the administration when my innocent son, a soldier and a Jew himself, was being murdered in cold blood by other Jews? Finally, Abraham accepted my decision. How many sleepless nights I must have watched over Sahal! If we had taken him to a hospital, the police would have found him. Sahal would have become yet another name in the list of missing young men. He is extraordinarily courageous and has a clear goal. Until he achieves it, no police officer or Covid can take him away.'

Her eyes sparkled with resoluteness. As she fed Asher with a sumptuous dinner, Eema must have felt that it was Jacob, who was seated next to her. Perhaps in her mind, the dinner prepared for Jacob on that horrendous night, was being served to this son. Asher graciously appreciated the food prepared by Jacob's Eema.

Before she went to sleep, Eema warned Asher.

'Do not open the door if anyone rings the bell. Just don't! Jacob's room is ready for your use.'

When Eema disappeared inside her room, Sarah embraced Asher warmly, as the wind does the mountain … as it does the trees, the flowers, the fragrances … She took him to Jacob's room.

'Sarah, please sleep now. I will leave early morning tomorrow.'

Asher pulled away from her unwillingly.

'Asher, please take me along with you. Jordan is where I am supposed to continue my studies. I have received my admission letter. Both Sahal and I have received our Jordan passes too. I want to see him one more time. Once he leaves for Malaysia, when shall I meet him? I could not even take a proper look at him today.'

Sarah's eyes overflowed with tears. The embodiment of desolation was standing in front of Asher. He felt an overwhelming love for her. A love, which made him want to pluck out his heart, and offer it to her. His people were drinking, eating and making merry in the settlements built over her devastated olive hills. Asher felt penitent.

Drawing the curtains back, he stood staring outside.

On the opposite hill, the white-stoned structures gleamed in the moonlight. In every slope, in layers, the buildings stood erect. 'Look at us,' the houses seemed to scream arrogantly. The common name was 'settlement'. In the blink of an eye, many had cropped up on the adjoining hills. White houses, moulded in the same pattern. Coffins, filled with the dreams of many … 'Move out from the way,' they commanded the hills, the trees, and the human beings who lived there.

Outside the monstrous gates where the flag—with the blue star and the white background—fluttered, a few fatigued men and women, their children and cattle huddled around, touching the stones and the earth that were once theirs. They caressed the wild creepers that were once theirs. They were inhaling the aroma of olives that were once theirs, exclusively.

An impressive road suddenly opened up before them. The latest cars, unattainable even in their dreams, sped through the streets.

'What are you thinking about? Take a shower and change your robe. Where on earth did you get it from?'

Sarah gently took the cross from Asher.

'Is this the gift you promised me once?'

She laughed and cried; then cried and laughed.

'Asher, I got a pen drive from this table. Do you want to check it out? It has some shocking information! I sent it to "Warrior of Light" ... Few notes, which Sahal hid from everybody. We should ask him to get those published after he reaches Malaysia. Maybe in some media with good reach amongst the masses.' Sarah wiped her tears.

> *After decades, I can hear melodies of the lullabies again. The lullaby, evocative of scorched flesh.*
>
> *I want to live. Live undefeated.*

Sarah wept, 'Asher, he wrote those lines.'

Jordan River was churning and heaving. The Sea of Galilee was waiting patiently. Until the night waned, they sat gazing into each other's eyes. He kissed her beautiful feet, pristine like a young child's, exhausted from running ceaselessly. She, in turn, cooled the manly chest, aflame with fiery passion, with her sweet kisses. Later, in their solitary moments, both would remember that the night had been as intoxicating as death.

Jacob's Eema came with a cup of coffee to awaken Asher at dawn. A cross gazed at Eema sadly. It was half-a-metre long, and rather heavy.

'Where are they ? Did they leave already?' the woman wondered aloud.

'Sarah,' she called out softly.

'They left.' The cross fell at her feet.

Jacob's Eema kissed the mezuzah and the cross.

The love of humanity flooded the soldier's room. As in a distant dusk, a lonely, lost bird started chirping, hidden in the green leaves of the fig tree.

43

HEROD'S PALACE

The wind which crossed the Dead Sea lashed against the Masada National Park. It caught hold of Sarah's yellow dress that flapped about loosely. Shamir, the driver of the pickup van, had driven them to the foot of the hill before dawn broke. He was now waiting in his pickup van, nearly a hundred metres away from the entrance, for them to return. They had travelled almost ninety kilometres from Jerusalem. There wasn't much traffic since they had started early; luckily, no police checking either. Before more visitors trooped in to watch the beautiful sunrise, Sarah and Asher had already begun their ascent.

Asher was a frequent visitor at the Masada Archaeological Site. The visitors' centre, museum and the ticket counter for the cable car were yet to open. The familiar security personnel grinned meaningfully at Asher. They had scaled the hill vigorously, challenging the strong wind. It was a formidable climb of almost four hundred metres. They took the serpentine path which traversed from the Dead Sea highway through the Snake Trail running east of the fortress.

'According to Josephus the historian, this place witnessed the mass suicide of 960 Sicarii rebels. But the evidence is not very conclusive. The remains of a few bodies were found—the skeletons of those who presumably were murdered or committed suicide before the enemy's siege.'

Sarah looked into Asher's eyes. He was holding her right hand tightly in his own, as if he was afraid to let go.

'I know all about it. Why are you speaking about death now?' Sarah asked sadly. 'From the Roman bathhouse they found remains of a male and female. Her hair had been shaved, probably in punishment for sinning. Asher, will they do the same to me?'

Without answering, he hugged her close and continued to climb. Asher was wondering how many security cameras were capturing their intimate moments. After an hour's arduous hike, they reached the summit.

It was six o'clock. The azure of the Dead Sea loomed at a distance. The scintillating colours of the morning bloomed over the Moab Mountain ranges of Jordan and the Dead Sea. There were only two human beings in the whole universe to watch that splendour! They crossed the relics of the storehouses and the Byzantine monastery, and stood close to each other.

'Those who cannot live together should die together.' Sarah's voice was brimming with emotion. Asher could not gauge the language of her eyes.

'No, Sarah! Even if we exist in two corners of the world, far away from each other, it is important to live. You should be there to remember me, and I should be there to remember you. Wherever we are, we'll meet in the realm of our thoughts.'

He gazed into her eyes. 'I feared putting you at risk by calling. How many days went by like that, without any contact! Yet, we were together, weren't we? To inhale your sweet scent, I planted a jasmine creeper next to my window.'

Sarah was silent.

'In a valley where lambs graze contentedly, I was waiting for you, in the yard of a dilapidated house. I saw that dream four times.'

Asher's voice became poignant. He dropped a kiss on her forehead and caressed her long tresses.

'It is fortunate that I could tell you about it at least now.'

They were in front of Herod's palace. The edifice stood regally, at the northern end of the cliff, at two levels.

The Roman army was laying siege to the fortress. The furore of the horse riders could be heard, approaching the palace. The lovers were hiding from the attackers. An ancient revolutionary … and his sweetheart.

'Asher, in my dreams there are no lambs or valleys, only the desert and blinding sunlight. And I am always waiting for you, the one who never comes.'

'But I have come, Sarah!' Asher kissed Sarah's fingers lovingly. Then he cast a wary glance around.

'Where is he? Not yet seen us?'

They walked around the ramparts of the fortress once more. The medieval granaries, bathhouses, deep grey caverns, they explored, yet again.

Sahal, where are you?

'Abba's acquaintance, a top military officer, had promised to help Sahal. I had gone to see him. But he called back the next day. Apparently, they have some evidence against Sahal. What evidence? They will hoist accusations that Sahal helped the missile technology of Hamas. Just because he has mastered drone technology! I first thought that they were terrified of poetry. No, they are afraid of education. Cowards!'

The wind circled around the stone embankments. A cold wind.

'If we separate … and are unable to speak to each other again?'

Sarah's eyes overflowed with tears. Neither knew who reached out first. Like the Sea of Galilee embracing River Jordan, they clung to each other.

'After a thousand years, another archaeologist like you would come here. He shall dig out the skeletons of two lovebirds from under these stones. We would be embracing each other even then.

He would write … *Even in the midst of the deepest terror, an emotion that transcended everything else existed in the world, a thousand years before* …' Sarah murmured.

There was a sudden movement near the bathhouse. They hastily moved apart.

44

NO MAN'S LAND

Something moved in the darkness. The grating sound of stones was heard. Then it died down.

'Sarah, please wait here!'

Asher dived into the shadows with his bag. A faint glow was visible. Sahal appeared from behind a dark pillar, as if emerging from a different era. Their eyes met for a moment and Asher noticed that Sahal had lost much weight.

In a matter of minutes, Father Antonio Vivaldi appeared in front of Sarah. Clad in the same coffee-brown monk's robe, he was wearing the golden rosary and mask. And dangling from his neck was the congregation's identity card: with Father Vivaldi's photograph, along with the address and phone number of the monastery.

Sahal gazed at Sarah for long. He was once again the shell-shocked eight-year-old who had hugged his sister close, on a blazing day that smelled of scorched flesh. A spring of water, originating from Masada, dashed against the boulders, eventually rushing towards the Dead Sea.

The trio began descending the hill, their hands tightly clasped. They chose to travel through the Roman ramp. The tourists had started climbing the hill through the western path. Cars were moving in tandem. The men walked with big strides and Sarah struggled to keep pace.

'The mornings are crowded in Masada. Everyone wants to finish the trip before the sunlight intensifies. We have to leave before the rush begins. Be quick!' Asher encouraged Sarah.

A car which manoeuvred a turn stopped near them. Jacob's Dod, Uncle Abraham, stepped out of the vehicle. He handed over the car keys to Asher.

'Hurry up. Go as fast as you can!' Uncle Abraham sounded harried. When their car moved into the uncertainties ahead, Uncle Abraham stood on the hill slope and watched, without ever averting his eyes.

Shamir was waiting impatiently inside the pickup van, parked near the Dead Sea highway. Asher gesticulated to him to follow his car. Both the vehicles turned to the highway and sped towards the border, often violating the speed limit.

'Ahkh, where are you?' The phone rang with Leah's querulous enquiry.

'I am going somewhere urgently. Emergency.'

'You should return today. Abba is not very …'

Even before Leah could complete her sentence, Abba grabbed the phone from her.

'I am absolutely fine. This girl gets anxious unnecessarily. Your Eema is another bundle of worries! I am fed up with these fussy women. By the way, the one with eyes in the front and back, he is fortunate. Be careful.' After a pause, Abba reminded him, 'I shall be waiting.'

Asher's heart skipped a beat. Abba had understood everything, without any words being spoken.

There were three rounds of police checking from Masada to the border. The police officer in the first booth curiously appraised the photograph of the clean-shaven Father Antonio Vivaldi and Sahal's bearded face. 'Covid lockdown effect, right Father?' He laughed. Father Antonio smiled genially in reply.

The officers manning the other two booths merely asked where they were headed to. It was a day which was unusually hot. What was the need for a policeman standing in sweltering heat to interrogate a Christian priest further? It was a path through which hundreds of priests and pilgrims traversed daily. Pilgrimage tourism was a great source of income for the nation. The Covid restrictions had put a severe dampener on it. But the border crossing would not be so simple. The real documents would be verified there. One could not confess that the passport of Father Antonio Vivaldi was at St Stephen's Monastery!

On the western shore of River Jordan, the check post of the King Hussein Bridge lay waiting for the passengers. The long arm of law were eager to pounce on the infiltrators and the runaways. The barrels of the guns were ready too.

'I undertook this risk only because of the old man who was murdered yesterday. Abu Murad Baba ... the one who gave me a livelihood.' Shamir started to narrate his story but was overcome by his emotions.

One kilometre before the first check post, the car took a detour to a side path. The pickup van followed suit. Both the vehicles screeched to a stop near the huge fig tree whose foliage almost touched the ground. Father Antonio got out of the car.

'Habibi, no matter what, I will cross the bridge. Drop Sarah at the western check post and wait for me.'

Sahal's eyes flamed with determination. There was no semblance of any perturbance. He hugged both of them affectionately and then placed Sarah's hand in Asher's. He felt that his sister's hands were frozen like ice. Meanwhile, Sarah noticed that Sahal's eyes reminded her of the dead. Just like the evening in childhood when smoke, dust and gunshots filled the air, a tremor seized her. She wept silently.

'You know that those with Israeli passports cannot step across this crossing. Otherwise I would have come with you. I shall stand in the western shore until you reach Amman safely.' Asher's voice was gruff with emotion.

'Habibi, we started the journey to finish it.' The reverberation of Sahal's words seemed to extend till eternity ... Asher kissed Sahal's cheeks lovingly.

Shamir, who was furtively glancing in all directions, became frantic with worry.

'Hurry up, children! We cannot lose a moment. An acquaintance has reassured me that he will help me with the checking formalities. The freight pass and documents are ready. I cross the bridge multiple times in a week. Do not worry, I shall ensure that you reach the other side safely. See, I have to take my son to the doctor afterwards. He has been diagnosed as Covid positive. Let Allah save him and us.'

Shamir opened an empty carton amidst the containers of clothes. When Sahal crouched like an animal inside one box, perforated with a few holes for his breathing, Sarah started sobbing. The vehicles moved from the side path to the main road, carrying bundles of woes and an ark tossing between life and death. Sarah felt that a huge sea was rising in front of her treacherously and that gargantuan sharks were on the prowl, with their jaws wide open.

The crucifix in the golden rosary around Father Antonio's neck gleamed. It was crafted from metal, and would not melt in any flame.

One kilometre ... crossing that distance entailed merely five minutes...

Black alphabet were inscribed on a white board. In Hebrew, English and Arabic ... *King Hussein Bridge Border Crossing (Allenby Bridge)*

They reached the Israeli terminal. There were standard formalities: cargo checking, payment of customs duty, immigration procedures and verifications.

Asher's car moved to the parking lot. He was afraid that they would interrogate Sarah while verifying the documents. His apprehensions did not materialize. After checking the call letter from Jordan University and the Jordan visa, the young officer asked her to proceed onwards.

Shamir's pickup van was still in queue.

Sarah waited for a shuttle bus at the Israeli terminal. There was a distance of five kilometres to Jordan's exit terminal and a small bridge en route. How long would that take? The first bus, packed with tourists, moved towards the bridge. Their hymns became faint as the bus moved over the No Man's Land. Another bus, exclusively filled with residents of Jerusalem, moved from the parking lot. Sarah's name was not called for that either. After an hour, Sarah called Asher.

'Asher, I am still in the waiting room. I'm yet to board a bus to the Jordan terminal. There is a special bus meant for Palestinians living in West Bank, they don't allow us to travel with the tourists. The bus will start only after it is full. Have they passed the bridge?'

'Not yet. There is not much rush at the check post, just a few vehicles. The pickup was at the very front, and the checking was over too. But when it started moving, they stopped it. Maybe there are some new formalities. The rules change almost every day. Do not worry, call me when you reach the other side.'

Asher loitered around. With the passage of time, his anxiety grew in leaps and bounds.

Among those bundles of clothes, beyond their eagle eyes, Sahal, are you burning in the searing heat inside the container?

After half an hour, Sarah called again. She had crossed the bridge and the Jordan terminal. Now she was in the land of freedom. Asher asked her to wait in the resting room.

He was desperate, his mind tangled in worries. A wooden bridge existed between Sarah and him now. Then, a No Man's Land of around five kilometres. It was a daunting distance indeed. The distance between two countries. The distance which some people could never cross. The distance of the earth which was pitted with deadly mines. A deep pain cleaved through his heart as if Sarah was moving to another end of the earth, to a faraway world that he could never reach … The River Jordan, dry and shrivelled, its waters scarce in summer, continued to flow between them.

Shamir was a frequent traveller through the border. He was very familiar with all the rules and regulations. Never had he faced any delay like today's. Asher's worries were growing by the moment. 'If they are caught … Yahweh! Sahal will never see the world again. Poor Shamir will be in deep trouble too. The man set out to help us when he should have taken his child to the hospital …' Beads of sweat trickled down Asher's face.

Sarah waited with Sahal's documents inside the resting room at the Jordan exit. Vehicles passed by every minute; but the pickup van did not come. The hours ticked by and she started panicking. When the anxiety became too much to bear, she moved to the Jordan counter in the east. The police officer was very busy at work and hardly gave her a glance. After a few minutes, he raised his head.

'How may I help you?'

'My friend's vehicle has been stopped for a long time now. Why are they not allowing him to cross?'

The Jordan cop looked at her with disinterest.

'How will we know that? You will have to ask the Israeli police about that. Maybe they asked him to wait. Ordered to stop, perhaps?'

Sarah's heart quaked in terror.

'Would I be allowed to go back, and see?' she pleaded.

'Sorry, sister. You have already crossed over, haven't you? Please wait.'

The man shrugged, and returned to his work.

Yet again, Sarah could discern the tide of desolation approaching her, roaring furiously. Her steps were leaden as she moved back to the resting room. At the western check post of the bridge, the flag bearing David's Blue Star in its heart, fluttered in the wind.

45

HARK, THE WATERS OF MY RIVER ...

Asher was impatiently walking to and fro. He observed that there were no automobiles near the pickup van now. It was solitary, like a vehicle abandoned in an uninhabited island. They had sealed Sahal off, leaving him stranded in the frontier of two ideologies, two worldviews. 'Habibi, they have confined me, my youth, my life!' Asher felt a terrible sense of debilitation seize hold of him.

At the edge of the open ground where the pickup van was parked, amongst the thorny bushes where his eyes reached, Asher thought he caught a glimpse of a coffee-brown monk's robe! Did Sahal, suffocated beyond tolerance,. break open the carton, and escape from the van? Or was he hallucinating? After a while, Asher walked resolutely to the armed officer guarding the western check post.

'Why is the pickup parked near the shrubs, so far away?'

The question was posed hesitantly. The man was nonchalant and ignored it.

'Hey, I am an Israeli citizen like you! You who are paid to be in uniform, to protect me, why are you not answering my question?' Asher yearned to shout those words, but the reality was different.

'The vehicle over there has been stopped for such a long time! You are allowing others to pass, without sticking to any order at all.'

'Why are you getting so riled up? Is it your vehicle? Everything happens as per the orders. An order from above.'

'Order from above!' The man's voice had been very grave. Asher felt the weight of those words, as heavy as Mount Hermon. Shell-shocked, he realized that those words had the firepower to scorch a nation, the annihilating power of a thousand missiles!

One second passed. An ear-splitting explosion! Tongues of fire leapt to the skies. Dust and smoke billowed up like a huge mountain. All sights were vanishing, yet Asher saw everything … Shamir and his pickup van … and … Asher stood frozen to the spot. Then he screamed like a mad man, 'Nooooo!'

The Roman army reached the pinnacle of Masada. They set fire to the double walls of the fortress. The valorous warriors were burning inside … Darkness spread all over the earth. The boulders split apart. Graves opened up in the valley of Temple Mount. The ancestors were waking up from their centuries' old slumber.

The siren boomed relentlessly. Three army vehicles full of soldiers reached the terminal in a matter of minutes. They spread out, controlling the crowd, diverting the incoming vehicles, taking over control of the situation …

In front of Asher's eyes, the pickup van was burning into cinders. The shrubs were in flames too. Asher, who started rushing forward towards the vehicle, breaking the cordon, had to be forcibly stopped.

'Do you want to burn to death? Stop!' the officer at the check post shouted at him.

Losing all his strength, like the most helpless man on earth, drained of every drop of courage, Asher collapsed on the ground. Many men in uniforms were running around him … light-blue, deep-blue, black … Darkness, only darkness prevailed. He heard someone say, 'Drone attack!'

Asher watched Sahal cycle down Sultan Suleiman Road, with his eyes blinking rapidly.

'This is not a city of peace, Habibi. It is a city of explosions, made of splinters! The hearts of the residents are also splintered into a hundred fragments.' Sahal's voice!

'Before my eyes, a nation is burning. It is a life, that I guarded so close to my heart, which is melting in those flames! My own heart … Oh, Habibi! Beloved of my soul … Are you leaving the house forever? Near the pyre of our dreams, here I am, utterly helpless, unarmed … Sahal, I could not prevent this misfortune. I am a Jew, the one who merits all the benedictions and rights granted by the nation. But I could not be a fair sentinel guarding your path! How pathetic …! My life is an unpaid debt now. They shall cast your bones and ashes in some wilderness. Dearest, I shall never allow that to happen! I shall run into the waters of Jordan, scooping you in my arms …' Asher cried wordlessly.

After a spate of silent sobbing, an inexplicable urge prodded Asher awake. He could hear Sahal's whistle from the rivulet near the Sukkot tent. The echo of his poetry …

Waters of River Jordan, you
Assuaged their thirst, that wasn't thirst.
Then why, why do they drink
The blood of my beloved children?

Asher lifted his head. The man in the light-blue uniform was next to him, with his rifle slung behind his back. The soldier's ramrod posture reminded Asher of an unshakeable rock. A very challenging stance. He had an impassive face. There were three stars on his uniform. Asher felt his muscles tightening in stress. His eyes blazed with fury. In a flash, he grabbed the rifle of the soldier. The next instant, the weapon was in Asher's hands. Aiming it at the soldier, maniacally, wrathfully, Asher yelled, 'You killed him … You killed him!'

The man in blue shivered for a moment, losing his composure. In that frozen look and stance, Asher saw Jacob, and his eyes. He saw the body lying next to the wall of the Synagogue Church … the flies buzzing around him … Asher's hands trembled. He sat down slowly, shorn of life. When Asher sat with his eyes shut, head buried in his knees, the security forces came rushing to handcuff him.

Sarah waited in the resting room across the bridge. 'Sahal should not miss the flight. It was the lone way of escape.' Her worries grew as the hours passed. Then she heard the new arrivals hysterically shouting that an explosion had occurred five kilometres away, near the western terminal. She could not reach Asher through the phone. He had forbidden her from moving out until Sahal arrived.

Sarah waited …

The international media extensively covered the incident.

A pickup van with Israeli registration caught fire at the border, near the King Hussein Bridge. The police confirmed that it was a drone attack. The driver died instantaneously. The official circles informed that Mossad had evidence of Hamas militants using the attacked vehicle. The police have found that the van was registered in the name of the merchant Abu Murad, who was killed at Temple Mount yesterday. There are unconfirmed reports that a priest had accompanied the driver in the pickup van. But the reports say that only the remains of a single body has been recovered from the site of the explosion. The traders of Muslim Quarters are preparing to protest against the incident. A young archaeologist, who tried to manhandle a security officer at the check post, was arrested. He was overpowered while trying to shoot a soldier with a rifle snatched from him. However, many prominent academicians of the nation are demanding his release.

Social media was overflowing with photos displaying the tricolour flag of Palestine. The 'Warrior of Light' showed only the photograph of the burning van at Allenby Bridge. The tagline read, 'This fire shall never die down.'

Much later, from an aged woman called Rebecca, the inmates of Shalom would hear about the strange paths taken by the pickup van. It would be the seventh day of departure of someone most beloved to Ruth. They would have no information about Asher's whereabouts even then.

46

CRUCIFIXION

Abba's asthma got aggravated. His temperature soared to 104-degree Fahrenheit and remained so. The cough was frightening in intensity. They were planning to shift him to a hospital as soon as Asher arrived. It was then that the headlines caught everybody's attention. The burning pickup van and Asher in police custody ... The television channels were showing the scenes repeatedly.

Eema went berserk. Leah begged her to calm herself. If Abba got to know about it, his sickness would get worse. Why did Asher go to the border? And why did he turn violent? What was his link with the pickup van? They had many acquaintances and relatives with influence in the power circles of the government. Eema was already on the phone, pleading with many, trying to get Asher freed.

'Did he lose his wits on seeing the explosion? Why did he commit that atrocity?' Leah wasn't sorrowful but incandescent with rage. 'Ahkh pokes his nose in other people's business! He is always asking for trouble.'

Leah remembered Dr Mazar of Hebrew University. Maybe she could help Asher. She found Dr Mazar's number from the University directory and tried to reach out. Though the phone rang ceaselessly, no one picked up the call. It was important to shift Abba to a hospital immediately. Eema seemed to have forgotten about Abba after seeing the news about Asher.

'Leah, get inside the car. Whether Abba agrees or not, we should take him to a hospital,' Ruth insisted. A suffocating and overwhelming doubt, with hazy shadows of masks and gloves, had been looming in her mind since the last few days. The hunch turned to be right. Abba was Covid positive. 'Esther, you are highly susceptible to diseases. Do not come near me!' Abba would warn Eema. In hindsight, it turned out for the better. Leah, due to her work pressures, had kept away from Abba too.

Abba lay delirious with fever in the fourth-floor ICU of the Scottish hospital called Nazareth Hospital. Though nobody was allowed to be with a Covid patient, due to Abba's obduracy, the doctor, who was his acquaintance, gave Ruth permission to sit by his side. The hours when she sat wrapped head to toe in a protective kit … The moments when she sat heartbroken, watching Abba's frail chest rising and falling rapidly … Some unspoken words were left on Abba's lips. The eyes, frequently glancing at the door, were inexorably searching for someone. His ears were expecting the sound of familiar footsteps. He was yearning for a voice calling out to him lovingly.

Abba was reclining on the bed which had been adjusted to a comfortable elevation. His arms were stretched on either side—his posture resembled that of a crucified person.

'When Asher comes, tell him that Abba is always with him.'

Though feeble, all the love in the world overflowed in those words … Ruth moistened Abba's lips, dried and cracked due to the fever. The sour wine, offered on the hyssop branch, fell drop by drop on Calvary. Abba passed away in utter tranquillity … Like a bird taking flight from its nest at dawn.

The sun was setting on the western shore of Tiberius.

The *Times of Israel* had a headline the next day: 'Another Hebrew University Professor snatched away by Covid.'

The funeral was over. Many visitors thronged Shalom till the seventh day of the rites. Everybody had the most loving, warmest words for Abba. 'What a wonderful man David was! How kind and generous!'

Most members of Denying to Be Foes arrived to pay their respects. Except Naomi Bergman, who had been killed by the Hamas missile. Dr Yehoshua was utterly devastated. He was Abba's closest friend.

'We should show our compassion when a man is alive. Whatever we speak in eulogy, after he departs, is akin to flowers on a funeral bouquet, liable to fade in a single day. Caught in multiple tasks, I could never find time to be with David … enjoying our usual bantering and soaking in the lighter moments,' Dr Yehoshua said, sighing regretfully.

Nobody asked Ruth anything, neither did she speak to anyone. Though Leah made an effort to find Asher's location, and inform him about Abba's demise, the police did not offer any assistance. Whether informed or not, Asher would have known about Abba's passing away, surely. They were one soul in two bodies.

On the seventh day after Abba's death, on Shiva, Jacob's Eema Rebecca arrived with the heaviness of a great secret. She was sobbing while revealing the events that had transpired. The dangerous, difficult and long paths traversed by the pickup van which caught fire. Mossad had surreptitiously tracked their course during the journey. Ruth's heart wept silently. She felt that Sahal's voice was resonating around them then.

My blue sky,
You poured more blue
Compared to the Nile and Euphrates, in their stars.
Then why, why do they crush
Our little lights?

Ruth's life at Shalom was a song, which had to be abruptly ended, while at the crescendo. Eema and Leah started preparing to leave for America. They planned to join Eema's brother Joel there. While Ruth was dusting Abba's books, Eema approached her.

'Why don't you take these along? They will be eaten by termites if left here.'

Abba's books would be termite-ridden … and much later, his memories too …

'Humans are the most ingenuous among all living creatures. How easily they forget and get forgotten!' Ruth ruminated. Two teardrops fell on *I Saw Ramallah*. She turned away to hide her tears from Eema. 'Bat,' she heard Abba's affectionate voice call out to her.

The Lady of Bethany peeped in through the window then. After reassuring herself that nobody was around, Mariam sat on a low stool. Ruth recollected that every visitor had seated themselves on similar low seats during Shiva.

Mariam spoke despondently.

'The inhabitants of a house of death, dwell in the incomplete dreams of the one they have lost. They are the guardians of a graveyard. Those who depart from the realm of memories, leave their loved ones grieving behind. Both are equally sorrowful. Listen Ruth, someone is awaiting you far away, amidst the snow.'

The truth of what Mariam spoke struck Ruth when Agy Chechi called. 'Ruthie, please come. I really need you …'

Agy Chechi had suffered from a bad fall. She had been advised bed rest for a few weeks. Of course, she could easily engage the services of a home nurse at Interlaken. However, Agy Chechi knew that Ruth too needed a change. She had been deeply affected by Abba's demise, just like her Valiyammachi's. In Agy's assessment, Alby might not be as empathetic as the situation demanded.

A pell-mell rush for a Schengen visa began after that call. Pilot Binu's Mitsubishi raced around day and night, conveying Ruth to offices and embassies. Since Israel was in the Green List, matters became easy.

As Ruth moved out, carrying Shalom in her heart, she thought she saw Asher gazing at the skies, seated on the stone steps! She closed her eyes for a moment. The cave in the hill slope, her companion of many languid evenings, was sighing about missing her forever. The ibis disappeared from Mariam's fig tree.

In front of the camera, Ruth spoke dispassionately: 'Hello friends, it is time for me to leave Nazareth, and the vlog Nazareth too …' The comment box would be overwhelmed with requests from viewers, asking her not to stop vlogging, even after reaching Kerala. There were a multitude of prayers for Abba too. The pebbles of the Mount of Olives kissed Ruth's feet once more.

As Ruth collected her Pikadon deposit—the monthly deposit from the caregiver's salary, which accumulates in a fund and is returned when she departs—she was told that all of Professor David Menahem's legal obligations were hereby over. She listened impassively. *How would the man know about riches that could not be confined within a bank!*

Nina called Ruth while she was at the airport. Noor Jehan had returned home. Her son, an engineering graduate, had secured a job. 'Poor woman, how she had struggled! Let her live in peace from now. Where is Kanya nowadays?' Ruth wondered.

As Ruth soared above Tel Aviv, she looked at the land, which she was unlikely to see again. The mountains, caves, limestone buildings, Byzantine churches, olive groves, fig trees, vineyards, and the Cypress valley merged into a lamentation. *'How beautiful are your tents, Jacob, your dwelling places, Israel …'* Ruth whispered.

'For me, this land was like an inn, a temporary home. But what about the humans who are born and brought up here, the earth's fragrance wafting from their eyes, chests, hearts and feet …! Which sea can hold the tears and anguish of the ones fleeing for their lives, leaving behind their homes forever? Like the coralline red algae blooming in the Red Sea, the crimson of misery, agony and uncertainty are covering their lives relentlessly,' Ruth mused.

In Ruth's imagination, a psalm was fleeing in terror through the mountain folds. Mariam was returning on a donkey's back to Bethany, to the hamlet of the penurious, to Al Azariya in West

Bank. Asher was driving through the Sharon Valley and his car was overtaking Mariam now. Mariam crossed through a date palm grove. Her donkey stopped in front of Bethphage.

'Mariam, I know that you shall tie your donkey there for the Lord's triumphal entry to Jerusalem on Palm Sunday. Then you will catch bus number 263 and disembark at Bethany Municipality Stop. Which check post can question your passport, stamped with the rights of land, spanning thousands of years? I can see, I alone can see, the pool of light ensuing from your beautiful eyes. I alone can see, the tributary of Jordan, originating from your lips. Mariam, I shall tread the boundless and infinite galleries of your memories, just to remember you again.'

Ruth had many questions for Mariam.

'Mariam, did you see Father Antonio Giovanni Vivaldi escape from the pickup van parked away from the main road, into the thorn bushes? Is he doing well?'

'Yes, he is hearty and well,' Mariam called out from miles below.

The aeroplane faced a sudden turbulence. The living and the dead were jostling in front of the closed Golden Gate.

Ruth recollected a few lines from *The Prophet*, which Abba had made her read out for the last time.

Yea, I shall return with the tide,

And though death may hide me, and the greater silence enfold me, yet again will I seek your understanding…

… For life and death are one, even as the river and the sea are one …

47

THE NIGHT IN THE STREET

It was the season when snowfall abated in Zurich. Regardless, the Eiger, Mönch and Jungfrau mountains continued to unleash snow squalls. Ruth wasn't a regular tourist, fascinated with mountains. Rather, she was forced to move under duress. It was her fourth or fifth exile.

Agy Chechi had sent her a long list of dos and don'ts: where to go from the arrival lounge, which currency to have at hand, the train she had to board … The Bahnhof Zurich Flughafen, the Zurich Airport Railway Station, was located underneath the airport. Ruth obtained a Swiss pass and boarded the Panoramic Express going to Interlaken. Passing through glades of meditating pines, and towns encircling blue lakes, she landed at Interlaken East. Darkness had fallen by then. The station was desolate. Ruth's teeth chattered due to the bone-chilling cold. She was supposed to catch another train to Interlaken West. Somebody would be waiting at the station to receive her. It was sixteen hours since she had boarded the flight from Tel Aviv. Ruth felt exhausted. The cold seemed to increase in a matter of moments. She desperately yearned to reach Agy Chechi's place.

There was a train at platform number five, possibly going to Interlaken West. The train bogie was empty and Ruth entered diffidently. Fortunately, the inside of the bogie was warm. She had forgotten to purchase a SIM card for local use. There was no way to call Agy Chechi at all. Out of the blue, a man wrapped in layers of clothes, and dressed in a red monkey-cap, jumped inside. He sat opposite to her. A very tall man. Only his eyes, hidden by spectacles, peered through the mask. He gazed unblinkingly at Ruth. She averted her eyes and wished that someone else would enter the bogie.

The stranger's phone rang liltingly at that instant.

Thamasamenthe varuvan …?

What causes you to delay?

Another song from the movie, *Bhargavi Nilayam*! What a relief, he was a Malayali!

'Will this train go to the West?' Ruth asked with an effort. The man ignored her, pretending not to hear, and tapped his fingers in accompaniment to the tune. She felt offended.

When the train stopped at Interlaken West, the man grabbed her luggage and moved forward.

'Hey, that's my bag!' Ruth shouted. He gave her a withering glance and stepped onto the platform. It was then that wisdom dawned. This might be the person sent by Agy Chechi to help her! Ruth felt acutely embarrassed.

The station was some sort of a dead end. All the rail tracks stopped there.

'Hey, please slow down a bit!' Ruth called out, unable to keep pace with the young man. 'Ruth, either this trip is the dead end of all your exiles. Or he will take you to Agy Chechi!' she told herself.

'Are you the man Agy Chechi sent to meet me?' she took her chance, and hollered. Still, there was no response. 'Is he deaf by any chance?' Ruth muttered, loud enough for him to hear.

In the brightness of the street light, she noticed the wooden facades of buildings, glowing and darkening alternately … An enigmatic darkness curled up like some unknown creature amidst the shadows. Ruth felt that she was entangled in an inexplicable dream …

The trolley bag made a tuck-tuck sound, while being dragged through the footpath, much like her own heartbeats. A solitary man stood near a cycle stand in the freezing cold. Was he observing her? Ruth had a déjà vu moment: this whimsical journey through the sleepy town, had she experienced it earlier?

The shop selling cuckoo clocks, adjoining a Thai Massage Centre, was closed. They approached a junction. Towards her right, the glass windows of a wine shop scintillated. On the patio, a few people were seated around a round table. Ruth stared wonderstruck at Valiyammachi, seated languorously on a bear-shaped seat. Suddenly, a man twittered like a bird from a side alley. Ruth was taken aback. 'Little girl, do not be afraid!' Ruth heard Valiyammachi's reassuring voice from across the years. The man who chirped, asked Ruth's companion a question, in a strange language. It was either in German or French. The young man disregarded him and continued with his long strides. She felt that she heard the thrumming of a river which flowed nearby. 'Ruth, you are a hollow log carried away by the floods!'

The man's phone rang again. *Thamasamenthe varuvan…?*

The lyrics resonated twice or thrice on the streets of Interlaken. Yet he did not heed that phone call. Now they were walking through a lake side. Circles of light shimmered on the waters. He paused for a moment.

'Please slow down. I have travelled almost twenty hours,' Ruth panted.

'Unless you walk briskly, the cold will get you!' he responded in Malayalam.

'Ah, finally, he has spoken!' His was a rasping voice. Ruth thought it sounded familiar. As she ran behind him in that moonless night, through the silent city, she felt it was a scene straight out of a fairy tale. She was seated, trembling in fear, in a vehicle dragged by a monster!

As soon as they reached a house situated on a hill slope, the weird creature, with only eyes exposed, deposited Ruth's bag and went away hastily, without bidding farewell.

'Welcome, my dear!'

An old woman opened the door. Her hair was snowy white. The woman stared intently at Ruth. Had she ever seen her before? In a dream, perhaps? Ruth crept inside timidly, like a kitten drenched in a heavy shower. Agy Chechi was lying on her back, with weights attached to her limbs. Her expressions and attitude were exactly as Ruth had imagined during her long journey from Tel Aviv.

'Remove that mask! Let me see you properly … The last time I saw you, you were a child. Ruthie, this meeting is so miraculous! I have to take rest for another fortnight. The Lord commanded, "Agy, stop running around for a while. Time to take some rest."'

Agy Chechi laughed loudly. It was a laugh straight from her heart. The same laughter, that used to arrive sporadically at Nazareth.

'By the way, this is Rachel aunty. She has come from Germany to keep me company. Devan is in Kerala, busy with building our house.'

Rachel aunty started gabbling even before Agy Chechi stopped.

'I belong to the first batch of nurses sent to Germany by Chackalakkal Achan. We were six in number. Basel is near the German border; you just have to catch the intercity train. My Benjamin is there, you see. He is not letting me go back home to Kerala. Someone should light a candle at the cemetery, right? The children are all super busy.'

'Aunty, let her take a bath. We will chat later.'

Rachel aunty looked chagrined at being gently snubbed.

After a shower, what Ruth did first was to hug Agy Chechi. The embrace soon turned into a flood of tears.

'We six girls used to hug one another and weep too,' Rachel aunty reminisced.

Ruth slept like a log for two days and nights. Agnes did not interrupt that serene, sweet slumber. She just ensured that Ruth took her meals in between the long stretches of sleep. It was as if Ruth had reached her home, where her mother was waiting for her. On the third day, she woke up, vigorous and fresh.

'Somebody is waiting for you at Lausanne. It is not too far. Visit the place, dear,' Agy Chechi said, while they were exchanging stories.

'Who is waiting for me in the land of snow?'

Agnes smiled, not deigning to answer.

'I will ask the young man who assisted you at the station, to accompany you. He is Devan's Man Friday.'

'Not him, please! Such a cantankerous fellow! I will go alone.' Ruth jumped in, unable to imagine another trip with the man.

'Climb to the summit of Alps on your way. Stand alone in that surreal silence. That's an ineffable experience ... Getting to know how insignificant we are.' Agy Chechi smiled.

Ruling aside Ruth's objections, Agnes ensured that the young man travelled with her.

'Have you ever wished to kill someone?'

The youth, his face covered with mask and cap, asked Ruth suddenly. She shuddered. They were disembarking from the cogwheel train, at the peak of Mount Pilatus. Ruth shivered as snowflakes, reminding her of star-shaped flowers, covered her.

'Look above, the St Beatus Caves! Named after the saint who killed the dragon haunting the land.' He sounded enthusiastic.

'Are we travelling to see the holy one?' Ruth interjected.

The man turned silent.

There was an infinite, majestic expanse of snow all around. Far off, a cross situated amidst a sea of pristine white! A stunning sight, five hundred metres down.

'Can we reach that place?' Ruth speculated aloud.

'As if your crosses are not enough!' the man retorted. She wondered how he knew about her life struggles.

'Close your eyes. You will hear the song of the mountains, audible only in utter silence.' He stood facing the cross, his arms stretched. Ruth kept her eyes open.

'You did not answer my question. Have you ever wished to kill someone? I have attempted once.'

Ruth stood rooted to the ground in shock. They were alone at the pinnacle then. 'Ruth, if he pushes you over, you will plummet into the unseen depths of the snow sea.' She felt suffocated. The next moment, the young man's cell phone started singing …

Arabi kadaloru manavalan …

The Arabian Sea, a veritable bridegroom …

'You? How come you are here?' Ruth was flabbergasted. The whole earth was suddenly covered with snow …

'Don't stand in the cold for too long. The pressure difference at the mountaintop is not healthy. You will fall sick.'

He walked ahead. As they descended the heights in the cable car, the melancholy Reuss river could be seen below. They walked into a cemetery near the riverside. A medieval church with Gothic architecture … Ruth found the sight familiar. She also knew the hill slopes where the lambs grazed. There was a brand-new tomb in the cemetery.

The epitaph read:

Father Aloysious Francis, Indian, Died on 7 May 2021.

'Whoever does not love does not know God, because God is love.' (1 John 4:8)

Ruth dropped to her knees on the gravel. She regretted not bringing a candle with her. The realization, about the futility of pleasures and sorrows, washed over her at that moment. An infinite peace embraced her.

'Inside the train that night, you could not recognize me from the ringtone, could you?' the young man asked, as they returned.

'Tell me, were you at Masada?'

'Yes.'

'Why?'

'Professional reasons. I have a textile business, back home at Kannur. I deliver uniforms for the Israeli police.'

'Is that true?'

'Why not?'

'*He's a thief indeed who robs a thief!* Now, I have seen one.'

'Who?'

'The thief who stitches uniforms for the police!'

They laughed together.

'What else do you do?'

'Like the Beypore Sultan, our own Vaikom Muhammad Basheer, once said—so many trades . . . pickpocketing, Sufism, washing vessels, office cleaning, driving taxis, smuggling gold, politics ... then ...'

'Enough!' Ruth covered his mouth with her hand.

'If you betray Agy Chechi, I shall hand you over to Mossad, remember that!'

'Ah, you spy for Mossad, do you?'

The train was tunnelling through rocky gorges then. The rivulets streaming from the mountain folds scattered beneath them. There was a bridge across the river—The Bridge of Return... 'When the Covid restrictions are over, I shall leave in the very first flight,' Ruth noted in her mind.

'See, the luggage you lost at Dubai airport,' the young man began to speak.

Frowning at him, Ruth interrupted his monologue, 'Tell me your name.'

'Call me anything. Even Aletsch Glacier will do!' He laughed in delight.

'Is it Asher's laugh?' Ruth wondered. 'Tell me, boy, what's your name?'

'Sky Sweet. Akasha Mithai!' He laughed yet again.

Ruth smiled through her shock. How did Akasha Mithai get to know of what Riyadh had done to her, two decades before? The inquisitive wind lashed against the mountain. Ruth pulled down the cap to cover her ears. The snow was continuing to fall on Mount Pilatus. The song of the mountain was awaiting new visitors.

The sun's unyielding heat lingered, unabated, over the refugee tents.

HOWDY DEATH, HELLO FREEDOM

The famous anthropologist Sarah Al Fadi arrived at the Sharjah International Book Festival as a guest for the release of the book *Howdy Death, Hello Freedom*, written by her brother Sahal Al Fadi.

'This world is full of human beings who live with stories. Nobody is alone. Two people who were supposed to be with us, are not here today. The first, Sahal, who gave life to these words. I would like to believe that he is watching this programme live, from some part of the world. Second, the friend, who guarded him like his own life. He is getting freed today, after five years in prison. It was he who suggested that we should release the book today; and that it should be received by Teresa Albert, who works as a nurse in Dubai's Rashid Hospital. This memoir has already been translated into a regional language in India. We are releasing both the original and the translation in the same stage. I would like to express my heartfelt gratitude to the translator who prefers to remain anonymous.' Sarah's eyes filled with tears.

After receiving the book from a renowned Arab poet, Teresa read out a few lines.

The house, whose terrace and roof were flooded with apple leaves, had the scent of apples. The days and nights had the same fragrance. Whatever poured in through the slightly parted curtains—the sunlight, moonbeams, bird-chirpings, and the sweet scent of apples—I cherished them all in my heart. I was afraid that I would never be able to relish these again.

The dolls scream,
Inside the partially ruined walls.
From the weed infested gardens
The bleak cries of goats,
Stolen by rioters …
The bones in burnt Musakhan …

There was a thunderous applause. Someone, who had been delayed by the late arrival of his flight, seated unobtrusively at the back, stood up and clapped without ceasing. Sarah stood speechless, gazing at him. Four eyes brimmed over and flowed as a single river.

Single river …

Do not ask her the name …

The Tree of Life sprouted in the north and south. The east and west arrived with snow and sunlight. They stood marvelling as the leaves sprung anew, branches grew lush, and the birds flew home to roost.

A CONVERSATION BETWEEN THE AUTHOR AND THE TRANSLATOR

A Conversation Between the Author and the Translator

Q. *Sheela, what inspired you to write this prescient book?*

At this moment, I feel that destiny played a role in the creation of this novel. In the Arab city where I worked, a lady colleague, a Palestinian, exposed the wounds of exodus to me. I would say that the novel sprang from within her heart. At that point of time, I was busy working on a script based on Malayali women, their job searches across the globe, and their exile from the native land. I wanted to speak about 'the women who carry their homes to the ends of the world', having seen many such lives during my two-decade stint abroad.

The story of female emigrants started early and many Malayali teachers and medical workers had reached the shores of Singapore, America, Africa and Europe prior to the Gulf. Kerala has many families that survived only due to the hard work of the women expatriates. Those who eulogize the male journeys across the sea, from the time of ancient wooden barges, often forget about these pioneering women and their dedication. It was this thought which triggered my writing about 'Ruth' the Malayali nurse, the paths she traversed while searching for gainful employment, and the canto of sufferings awaiting her. But unexpectedly, the narrative stepped into a different realm, the endless sorrows of another people.

During this time, my workplace came out with the list of 'to-be-terminated-employees'. The lack of job security is a clear feature of employment in the Gulf. At times, circumstances lead to dismissal of workers belonging to a specific nationality. Out of the blue, someone will not be able to login to her computer system. One's capability as a professional has nothing to do with that phenomenon. Muna Hasan's name featured in the list. (For protecting her privacy, I am changing the name.) Most colleagues disliked her, sniggering about her harshness and arrogance. Yet, it was on that dismal day I first realized that Muna was a different woman, while she wept and opened her heart.

Muna told me about the ravages of war and countless exiles. For those of us unfamiliar with wars, her story, fraught with intense grief and anguish, was unimaginable. She spoke about her birth city destroyed by missiles, the dark days spent in refugee camps, and the utterly helpless moments as her little sister died due to fever, unable to get medical aid. They were humans who embodied losses. The imprisoned, the dead, the maimed and mutilated, not knowing the fates of their loved ones, those who lost their near and dear in matter of seconds, those who were forced to flee, abandoning everything they owned ... The paths of fire that her people face cannot be captured by a thousand novels.

'Where will I go with my children? All of you have countries of your own ... Somewhere to return even after losing a job. There are loved ones waiting for you. We have no bit of earth to call our own, no country ... Even the world is against us!'

I saw a Red Sea in her tears. A sea, which can never be crossed. The roiling 'river' started flowing ... from Muna's village.

Following Muna's tears, it did not take me long to reach West Bank, Gaza and Sarah's burning city. Muna is just one among millions. Sahal and Sarah in the novel, are symbols. They are the representatives of every man, woman and child hunted down and relentlessly hounded by the powers that be, in every corner of the earth. Those who are driven away from their homes, shorn of any semblance of human dignity. As I wrote in the preface of the original novel, 'The human rights violations across the world have the same face. The face of the powerful regimes that silence human beings with the weapon of fear, also remains the same. The names of the countries are interchangeable. Even when the nations and languages are different, the vehicles of territorialization have the same shapes.'

The novel explores the deeply intricate religious, national, regional identities of West Asia through the experiences of two close friends: Sahal, who is pursued by Israeli agencies who allege that he has terrorist connections, and his bosom friend Asher, an Israeli citizen, who recognizes the truth and political philosophy of Sahal's life.

History has witnessed that at various junctures, the powerful and influential among the nations tend to assume silence, equip the besiegers, and denounce the sagacious voices of human rights activists as cries in the wilderness. In the middle of it all, we see the fight for survival and unceasing hopes of those who have lost everything.

We have never been driven away from our homes or lands. We have not lived in tents meant for refugees. We haven't been fated to live next to fire-spitting cannons or fighter planes. We have not stood in queues for endless hours, to receive a scrap of bread. We haven't struggled in hospitals for the next life-breath. We have never been crushed underfoot by army boots. We have not been deprived of human dignity. We have never seen our children dying in front of our eyes.

The excruciating sufferings endured by Palestinians are beyond our imagination. This novel is an attempt to open a small window into that experience. A river of human love, gently flowing amidst the ravaging flood of blood.

Q. *The recent political developments, especially after 7 October 2023, seem to be surreal considering the theme of the novel. How do you view the strange magic of writing and the truth of the storytelling process?*

I am speechless at the turn of events. Did the words turn prophetic, as one struggled to depict the reality? The UN refugee camp at Khan Yunis caters to those who fled from the northern parts of Gaza. There are thousands of men, women and children there, struggling for a drop of water or a piece of bread. There are many wounded and mutilated among them and those who have lost all their family members. There have been missile strikes on their camp. There is not a single hospital left to be demolished in Gaza today.

When I wrote the novel, I never imagined that a 7 October would be marked in black letters, triggering a war leading to the exodus of more than two million refugees and the deaths of thousands of human beings. In February 2021, a week after I started writing the book, beloved Palestinian poet Mourid Barghouti passed away. In May 2021, after a hiatus of many years, Israel was caught up in another major turmoil. It was Jerusalem Day: the anniversary of Israel's conquest of East Jerusalem. If it is a day of celebration for the victors, it is a day of bitter remembrance for the vanquished, when they were dispossessed of their homes and birth soil. Nobody knew that the seeds of a war were being sown; except the ones involved. Today, helpless mothers are writing the names on the tender hands and legs of their children, to recognize their remains beneath the debris and rubble!

This novel too, is the scripting of pain. We know that the Holy Land, which humankind has divided into three, based on three religions, reeks of burnt human flesh today.

Q. *This novel has so many layers to it. For example, the life of a nurse/caregiver, the human trafficking rackets around the world, the story of the Arab–Israel conflict, the Holy Land beloved to all religions, the Bible, poetry , songs, et al. Tell us about your research efforts.*

In the two decades of the diaspora experience, I came to hear about stories of the rampant human trafficking rackets, betrayal and exploitation. Today, we have the latest technological tools available to gather information about potential employers. Consequently, the number of victims has reduced compared to earlier periods. Some dear women friends of mine shared their staggering experiences of emigration, which helped me to craft Ruth's story. I was determined that the chronicle of human trafficking should not be focused on any particular country or religion, and should point out the hidden snares in the global job market. It is an international issue, and not just a regional concern.

The constraints of depicting an unknown nation and her culture were predominant. To overcome those restrictions, I did intense research work for six months. A lot of reading and explorations were entailed in understanding the history, politics, geography, culture and traditions of Palestine and Israel. I went through the works of many writers and thinkers: Edward Said, Ilan Pappé, Mourid Barghouti, Mahmoud Darwish, Larry Collins, Dominique Lapierre, Mahmoud Shukair, Najwan Darwish … I watched and rewatched many travel vlogs and films, becoming familiar with every nook and corner of the Old City. Slowly, Jerusalem, Bethlehem and Nazareth became my own cities. I had long conversations with caregiver friends, who worked with the Jewish families of Israel. Their descriptions of the work environments helped to ensure authenticity of the script.

I made a humble effort to study Hebrew in the meanwhile. My father, a very good storyteller, had once described his visit to Israel in detail. I watched the videos of that trip many times. I tried to see Palestine through the eyes of a Christian woman living in a Jewish household. Maybe it was the realization that all wars and transgressions are the result of a fundamental lack of love, which made me create the background in that manner.

Q. *What were the major challenges while writing this book?*

The most formidable challenge was to study the history and politics of Palestine and Israel. I endeavoured to overcome that by research. Even as I read about the history of Palestine, from a period of eleven centuries before the birth of Christ, travelling through time to the Nakba and Intifada episodes, I made a conscious effort to not let history take over the story. Though there are not too many stories about Palestine in Malayalam, there are lots of famous works available in world literature. Innumerable books—both fiction and non-fiction—have been written by Palestinians: straight from the soul, the quill dipped in the blood of their own experiences.

The ethical dilemma which I faced was about the significance of a book narrated from the perspective of an onlooker. Finally, it was a joining of forces, so to say. A proclamation of union with all the diverse people, who are facing genocide by authoritarian regimes, across the world. A mark of recognition of all the vulnerable humans tottering at the cliff of extermination. A union with every ethnic group hunted down and made destitute by the powerful, all over the globe. Even if I were to be reborn a hundred times, I shall not be able to fully capture their anguish, their loss of identity and the unimaginable horrors they face. Those are human experiences belonging to them and I am a mere observer. I accepted that limitation in order to tell the story more honestly. And that's how the river started flowing from the life paths of Ruth, the nurse, to all those who do not have any portion of the earth to call their own.

Even when highlighting the victim's perspective, I made the Jewish family the main fulcrum of narration, wishing to point out that not everyone is an extreme Zionist. The main characters are embodiments of humanism. We need amicable, peaceful co-existence today. My attempt has been to highlight the stories of those from either side, who work together in a non-violent manner, against aggression and territorialization.

Geetanjali Shree said that stories emerge wherever women and borders exist. And it is undoubtedly women, who have to make their way across the scorching paths, while encountering wars and exiles. I was extremely cautious about not portraying the sufferings in a romantic light anywhere in the script. Their stories are not meant to provoke pity or dole out entertainment to us. Their girls should not be violated again through letters. Their resistances should not be derided. Their emotions and passions should not be marketed to add spice to the story. That was a challenge every moment.

When I read certain books on the refugees, the marginalized and those who are no longer alive, I find myself sadly wondering why the dead are being murdered again and why those who have endured mortifications are again subjected to further degradations. 'But unless you describe, how will the reader experience those intolerable agonies?' The writer inside me rebelled and flailed about. It was then that a remarkable book came into my hands.

Mourid Barghouti had been a student in Cairo during the Six-Day War in 1967. He gained permission to visit his homeland after thirty years. Denied access to his home and native land, Barghouti wandered across the world, shuttling between cities. He wrote his much-loved book, *I Saw Ramallah*, describing the plight of his people and the sufferings they have borne. The genuineness and brevity of expression is remarkable, to say the least. I found the style of his narration deeply appealing, and it became the light in my path.

Q. *The Holy Bible and many characters from it appear in your book. Tell us about Mariam of Bethany, the third eye of Ruth.*

True, Mariam is the third eye of Ruth. The history of Israel and Palestine shall be incomplete without the Bible. The story evolves in the Holy Land of the people of three religions—Christians, Muslims and Jews. The Bible joined my journey, evoking the memories of a land of thousands of years ago. Though the Christian community in these lands is less than 1 per cent, for every believer, this is the Holy Land where the footprints of Jesus Christ are imprinted indelibly.

I introduced Mariam of Bethany as a conjoining factor of the story, who connects two epochs, without the differentiation of ancient and modern. Though she is the voice of Ruth's conscience, I often felt that her residence was within me. The silent disciple of Jesus seemed to be walking along my side, with words which she never expressed aloud. And thus, a divine equation between two eras took form inexplicably, and I remained unaware. The son of the carpenter in ancient Nazareth and the son of the professor in modern Nazareth were always found amidst the sufferers. The same brethren, the marginalized and the denounced, with whom Christ once walked, exist in Palestine today, seeking refuge. Every day thousands of young men undergo Christ's crucifixion. It was intriguing how Mariam of Bethany, ever eager to listen to the words of Jesus sitting by my side, transformed into being part of the Palestinian struggle in the manuscript.

Sometimes a story turns into a riddle. Mariam stepped in, to bridge two time periods, beautifully solving the disconnect of ages. She shall be walking about with her incomplete gospel, until the end of time. Mariam has unearthed many facets forgotten by the gospels written by the men. Jesus Christ stepping into the kitchen happens to be one such aspect. It is Mariam who transforms a detour of a few minutes into something infinite. Inside the writer's mind, Mariam was dictating about the inconsequence of time.

Q. *References to Arab Literature are profuse in your book. Tell us more about it.*

The world became aware of the Palestinian predicament and the depths of their woes through Arab literature. Many talented writers of Palestine are forced to be silent in our time. War has taken away the lives of a few of them. Just like Sahal was stopped at the border, today, poets are facing interrogations, and are being stopped from creating. Though I had read many translated works from Arab literature, I reread some books before embarking on my novel. The essence of the writings about exiles and departures, by Darwish, Gibran as well as Barghouti, is reflected in the flow of the book.

Sahal, the main protagonist, is a poet. He is described as someone who sustains himself on Darwish's words. The name of the book has been inspired by a line from Darwish's poetry. In the last chapter, Sahal Al Fadi's autobiography gets released. My attempt has been to segue the dual worlds of writing and imagination.

Mahmoud Shukair's stories play an important part in my book. Though they appear as part of a chapter, through them, the desolate Palestinian cities, the abandoned streets and squares, are brought to the reader. There is a mention of his story, where a house which was existing in the morning strangely disappears by twilight. I should say that these are my tributes to the great Arab writers.

Q. *Sheela, how do you view the process of translation of the book?*

Mini, I am fortunate to have you as my translator. You are aware of the Palestinian issue and have a balanced, humanistic worldview about it. It was strangely coincidental that the book reached you near the outbreak of the war. As the saying goes, 'The name of the person who eats the grain of rice is written on it.' Similarly, the name of the person who shall accompany the words is also written beforehand! I found myself astounded at your sincerity. I know that you completed the first draft in just two months, toiling through the night, while holding the busy day job of a civil servant. Sometimes, I had to struggle to keep pace with you.

I consider it a blessing to have a translator who understood the story, its background and theme seamlessly. I believe that our free interactions, via multiple phone conversations and WhatsApp chats, helped us to burnish the novel better. Nobody could have translated this novel as fast as you did! I think that for you, translation is not merely a hobby but a genuine act of self-expression. Mini, thank you for translating even the scent of my ruminations!

Q. *Mini, let me ask you a few questions now. Can you explain the coincidences which brought this book to you, the way we worked together within a tight deadline so that the world could hear the story of love, in a land of conflict …*

Sheela, I would first like to thank Sonia Rafeek and V.J. James, famous Malayalam authors whom I work with, for mentioning your book and asking whether I was interested in working with you. Then, of course, I got your mail.

I was reading two books at the time. The journey of a great river, and the history and unknown stories of all the lands it flows through. Meanwhile, I was fascinated by the bestseller *Mossad: The Greatest Missions of the Israeli Secret Service* written by Michael Bar-Zohar and Nissim Mishal.

So, when you asked whether I would like to translate a book called *Do Not Ask the River Her Name*, based on the Palestine–Israel conflict, I was astounded at the serendipitous events. When I got your novel, I was impressed by the depth, the simplicity and the fact that it is an ambitious, erudite work. I really liked the beautiful, spirited Mariam of Bethany.

One of those days, I went to have lunch with my favourite Malayali missionary sisters at their convent. Unexpectedly, my eyes fell on a picture I had never noticed before … *An unknown, beautiful woman follower of Jesus, seated by his side, eagerly listening to him.* 'Sheela's Mariam,' my mind shouted. What an astounding revelation! Here was divinity, beckoning me on my journey, with signs strewn all around! After that moment, I had no doubt about the assignment.

I think I threw myself into the translation, using every minute I could spare from my work and household responsibilities. Your generous encouragement and feedback made it a joy to work together. I tend to get stifled with too many dos and don'ts. But Sheela, you allowed me full liberty to play around with the words. I loved reading up more on Israel and Palestine, because one cannot afford to make a single mistake in such a sensitive work. It is a love story in a land of conflicts.

Fortunately, I was very familiar with all the cultural references, including Malayalam films and songs. And translating a book based on a woman's intrepid journey across the world, her resilience, her sufferings, her triumphs and her friendships ... it was such a beautiful experience for me too.

On 7 October, I remember looking in horror at the news and the book in my hand! Here was fiction turning into reality. My determination to finish the translation became fortified because the world badly needs to know the story of the human beings involved in this mindless suffering. It is so easy to judge and so difficult to listen. And yes, we did complete the first draft in two months' time.

Q. Mini, did you enjoy the translation process? How could you do it with such perfection in a short time period?

I tend to do a free-flowing translation for the first draft and return to polish the sentences afterwards. When a reader, who has no idea of Malayalam, seated in her comfortable chair somewhere, smiles and cries with the pages, well, then the translator has done her job. The beauty of the original script, the words and emotions, along with the essence, should be transmitted skilfully. Sometimes, one has to edit ruthlessly too. I truly believe that translation is like praying. You are under the influence of a greater power and being the medium, you surrender completely. The moment the ego raises the head, the obstructions begin!

But let me reiterate that without your encouragement and full support, I would not have been able to do it. The mutual trust between the author and translator is so very important and the slightest negativity can have ramifications on the final work.

Q. *As an officer of the Indian Administrative Service, did you have any previous exposure to the Palestine–Israel conflict, or the theme of the book?*

The diplomatic services, my colleagues in the Indian Foreign Service, have direct exposure to such issues. Though in this closely intertwined world, any repercussion in a corner of the earth has administrative implications elsewhere. I knew about the Palestinian conflict and also about the unimaginable sufferings the Jews underwent during the Nazi regime. Movies, newspapers and books have always played a vital role in informing me about world events. However, the minutiae which your novel presented demanded rigorous exploration. I cross-checked every name, every fact, every little reference before translating. I had the Holy Bible, both Malayalam and English versions, open before me all the time. The quirky character, Mariam of Bethany, would be giving Biblical references at the drop of a hat! The theme of your novel, about love and friendship, about humanity and kindness, is something which resonates strongly within me. And I love translating books that have strong women characters. Thank you for the opportunity.

ABOUT THE AUTHOR

Sheela Tomy is a novelist and short-story writer hailing from Wayanad, Kerala.

Valli, her debut novel, was awarded the renowned Cherukad Award for Malayalam Literature in 2021. The English translation of *Valli* by Dr Jayasree Kalathil bagged the V. Abdulla Memorial Translation Award (2023). *Valli* was also shortlisted for the 2023 National Translation Award from the American Literary Translators Association (ALTA), the JCB Prize for Literature (2022), the Atta Galatta-BLF Book Prize (2022) and the GreenLitFest Honour Books Award (2023). *Valli* also bagged the Book of the Year Award for translation from the Federation of Indian Chambers of Commerce and Industry (FICCI) in 2023.

Sheela is also the author of a short-story collection *Melquiadesnte Pralayapusthakam* (Melquiades's Book of Floods) published in 2012. She has won several awards for her short stories, including the Abu Dhabi Arangu Award (2007), the Puzha.com Short Story Award (2008), the Doha Sanskriti Award (2012), the Doha Samanwayam Award (2012), and the Kamala Surayya 'Neermathalam' Award UAE (2014). The other honours she has received include the Madhyamam She Q Excellence Award (2022), the KCBC Media Award for Literature (2023) and the 'Ashayam' Basheer Award (2023).

Sheela has been residing in the Middle East for more than two decades. She has a postgraduate degree in journalism and mass communication and has contributed as a lyricist, scriptwriter for radio, and is a presenter of literary reviews. Sheela's articles on contemporary issues have been published in various media forums.

Aa Nadiyodu Peru Chodikkaruth (Do Not Ask the River Her Name), her newest work, was awarded the Muthukulam Parvathy Amma Literature Prize and the Maniyoor Balan Novel Award in 2024.

ABOUT THE TRANSLATOR

Ministhy S. is an IAS officer working in the Uttar Pradesh cadre. In her civil services career, she has received various awards for excellence in governance including the *Hindustan Times* Woman of the Year Award, 2014, and *The Sunday Standard* Devi Award, 2016. XLRI Jamshedpur gave her the distinguished alumnus award in 2014.

She translates between three languages: Malayalam, English and Hindi. Her translation of the *The Poison of Love*, by Malayalam novelist K.R. Meera, was longlisted for the DSC Prize for South Asian Literature, 2017. *The Unseeing Idol of Light*, by the same author, was shortlisted for the Crossword Book Jury Award, 2018. She has translated three novels by V.J. James—*Anti-Clock*, *Nireeswaran* and *Dattapaharam*. *Anti-Clock* was shortlisted for the JCB Prize for Literature, 2021. She has transliterated four cantos—*Sundar Kanda*, *Kishkindha Kanda*, *Aranya Kanda* and *Lanka Kanda*—from Goswami Tulsidas's *Sriramacharitmanas* into English.

HarperCollins *Publishers* India

At HarperCollins India, we believe in telling the best stories and finding the widest readership for our books in every format possible. We started publishing in 1992; a great deal has changed since then, but what has remained constant is the passion with which our authors write their books, the love with which readers receive them, and the sheer joy and excitement that we as publishers feel in being a part of the publishing process.

Over the years, we've had the pleasure of publishing some of the finest writing from the subcontinent and around the world, including several award-winning titles and some of the biggest bestsellers in India's publishing history. But nothing has meant more to us than the fact that millions of people have read the books we published, and that somewhere, a book of ours might have made a difference.

As we look to the future, we go back to that one word—a word which has been a driving force for us all these years.

Read.

HarperCollins Publishers India

[illegible]

[illegible]

[illegible]